COAL BONES

Karen Rose Cercone

BERKLEY PRIME CRIME, NEW YORK

COAL BONES

A Berkley Prime Crime Book / published by arrangement with
the author

PRINTING HISTORY
Berkley Prime Crime edition / January 1999

The Penguin Putnam Inc. World Wide Web site address is
http://www.penguinputnam.com

ISBN: 0-425-16698-8

Berkley Prime Crime Books are published
by The Berkley Publishing Group,
a member of Penguin Putnam Inc.,
375 Hudson Street, New York, New York 10014.
The name BERKLEY PRIME CRIME and the BERKLEY PRIME CRIME
design are trademarks belonging to Berkley Publishing Corporation.

PRINTED IN THE UNITED STATES OF AMERICA

10 9 8 7 6 5 4 3 2 1

For Jackson and Kirby,
and all their friends.

And for Julia.

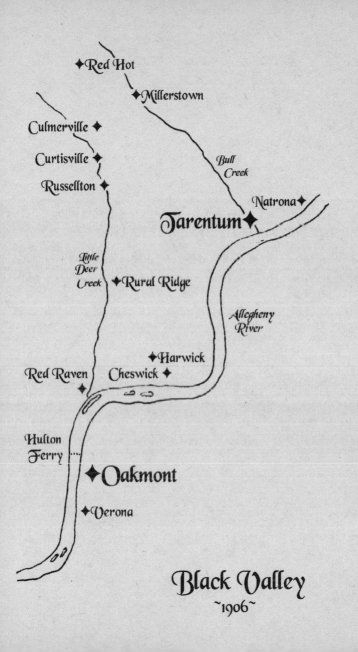

✦ Red Hot

✦ Millerstown

Culmerville ✦

Curtisville ✦

Russellton ✦

Bull Creek

Natrona ✦

Tarentum ✦

Little Deer Creek ✦ Rural Ridge

Allegheny River

✦ Harwick

Cheswick ✦

Red Raven ✦

Hulton Ferry

✦ **Oakmont**

✦ Verona

Black Valley

~1906~

COAL BONES

ONE

The telegram was from the Sedgwick Coal & Coke Company and it was blunt: "Trouble at Bull Creek Mine." Ten minutes later, the entire staff of the local county detectives office was clattering up the west slope of the Allegheny River, in a weather-beaten trolley Milo Kachigan had commandeered from the Tarentum Traction Company. There had been no other warning, no cloud of smoke or muffled explosion from the hillside mine, but as soon as they passed under the spidery shadow of the coal tipple, Kachigan knew something was wrong. Beyond the rattle of the trolley on the uneven tracks, he should have been able to hear the cataract roar of coal falling down the long metal chute. But Bull Creek's narrow valley held only silence and the rising mist of a late March twilight.

"Tell you what, Milo." Art Taggart glanced up from the newspaper that accompanied him everywhere, even to police emergencies. "This has got to be about the quietest miners' riot I've ever heard. Good thing we all brought shotguns."

Kachigan grimaced, hefting the weapon he'd insisted the detectives carry with them. "Well, what did *you* think 'trouble at the mine' meant?'' he asked his partner. ''That they couldn't get their telephone to work?''

''Maybe they couldn't get their coal tipple to work.''

''You don't call in county detectives for that.''

The trolley crossed a bridge and was engulfed by the barren landscape of coal mining: acid-yellow iron stains in the creek, rusty red-dog cinders on the road beside it, dark bony coal dumped outside the mine because it was too impure to burn. Kachigan couldn't see Bull Creek's portal behind that spoil pile, but the numerous narrow-gauge tracks threaded through the mine yard were as utterly silent as the tipple had been. It made no sense—in a boom year like 1906, there was no time of the day or week when a profitable mine like Bull Creek wasn't running. Even industrial accidents couldn't stop the extraction of wealth from western Pennsylvania's coal-rich hills. During the three months since he'd been transferred to Tarentum, Kachigan had heard about miners being crushed, suffocated, drowned, and just plain lost in the labyrinth of coal seams that underlay this region, but he'd never heard a lull in the productive thunder of the mines.

Until tonight.

Their trolley clattered past a string of squat coal cars waiting at the head of the tipple, and Kachigan scrubbed dust from the window to squint at them. No heaps of black rock showed above the edges of the coal cars, and he wondered if loading had been interrupted. There were no mine workers anywhere in sight.

''Those cars don't look full,'' he said. ''Aren't miners here paid by the ton?''

''Sure. Just like county detectives are paid by the arrest.''

Kachigan knew without looking that the caustic comment had come from J.P. Frick, a county detective who'd been exiled to Tarentum for shaking down Allegheny City brothels a little too hard. Frick was an older man with a balding head and what seemed like a good-natured smile. Most people liked him on sight, but then most people didn't have to put up with his constant griping over what he saw as an unwarranted demotion. His complaints were usually veiled in jokes or even in self-mockery, but after two months of working together, Kachigan had noticed none of the other detectives were laughing anymore.

"I guess that's why you never made enough money to live on, Jape." Art Taggart, who'd been transferred to Tarentum merely for the crime of being Kachigan's partner when they'd run afoul of the Pennsylvania Railroad, didn't have much patience for Frick's grumbling. Or for his insistence on being called just by his initials, which Taggart always slurred together as insultingly as possible.

Frick took a deep, angry breath, but the lingering pall of coal dust inside the trolley sent him into a coughing fit before he could reply. Owen Riley, a newly hired detective whose pleasant face was marred by a large wine-colored birthmark across the forehead and left cheek, took advantage of the pause to clear his throat and answer Kachigan.

"The reason the cars aren't loaded higher, sir, is because the Upper Freeport seam's only about four and a half feet thick along this part of the river. The miners don't take out any more rock than they need to from the mine passages, so the roof stops them from putting in any more coal."

"Thanks, Owen." Kachigan started for the front door while the trolley was still rolling to a stop, mostly to get away from Frick before he finished coughing. A lucky stroke of nepotism had given them the Tarentum-born Riley, mustered directly into their detective office from his army police unit. Kachigan only wished he could break the ex-soldier of the ingrained "sirs" he used in nearly every sentence. It wouldn't have been so bad if he'd applied them equally to all three of the older detectives, but through some unclear chain of deduction, Riley had decided to reserve the title just for Kachigan. Needless to say, that drove J.P. Frick to even sourer fits of sarcasm than usual.

Kachigan stepped down from the trolley and looked around at what he could see of the mine yard. The afternoon's cold rain had left the hillside dappled with scarves of fog, obscuring the sheds and weighing platforms that surrounded the portal of Bull Creek Mine. Now that the trolley's clatter had ceased, the hushed quiet of the mine workings seemed even more eerie than before. He could hear the distant hoot of a coal barge from the Allegheny River and the echo of a dog barking from almost as far away, but no gunshots, no running footsteps, not even the sound of cursing voices.

"Maybe they're all dead," Frick said. It was hard to tell if he was joking, since his face was still wearing the scowl Taggart's wisecrack had put there. And the silence around the mine did sound almost funereal. "Maybe some kind of gas came out from the mine and suffocated them all."

"Including the men who work outside?" Taggart asked.

"Sure, why not?"

Kachigan glanced at Owen Riley, who was already shaking his head. "Black damp doesn't kill when there's a breeze like this to stir it around, and if it was the white damp we'd already be sick from it." He bent over to scratch a match across his shoe sole, then showed them its pale blue flicker. "And if it was coal gas, that would be a whole lot brighter."

"Or we'd be a whole lot deader!" Frick sounded aggrieved. "For Christ's sake, Riley, do you have the brains you were born with or did you give them away to the gypsies?"

"Hey, I can smell. I knew there wasn't enough—"

"Detectives." The unexpected sound of their trolley operator's voice broke through the argument. "I think there's a light on up at the company office."

Kachigan swung around to squint at the straggling sheds, wondering which was Bull Creek's official headquarters. Before he could embarrass himself by asking, however, the distant glint of electric light through bare-branched trees told him where the mine's office was located: as far upslope from the mine's spoil piles as it could get and still be within easy reach. Apparently coal barons didn't like staring at their own waste any more than Pittsburgh's steel barons liked breathing in their own smoke. A set of ramshackle wooden stairs led past the mine portal to that secluded glimmer.

"Thanks, buddy," he said, and meant it. "Can you stay

here while we go see what the problem is? We'll pay you double time if we go past the end of your shift.''

The elderly trolley driver gave him a tobacco-stained smile. "You did that halfway up Bull Creek," he told Kachigan. "Don't worry, I got no wife waiting for me at home. Take as long as you need.''

Kachigan grunted and hefted his shotgun onto his shoulder, taking the stairs two at a time despite the ominous way the rotting boards creaked beneath his feet. He could hear Riley pounding right behind him, while Taggart and Frick took the climb at a more leisurely pace. Kachigan wasn't sure why Frick's laziness irritated him so much more than Taggart's equally slothful approach to life, but he suspected it was because his partner never made excuses or lied about what he was willing to expend energy on. The older detective, on the other hand, was always talking about what he could do, might do, really should get around to doing one of these days. . . .

"Sir, I hear voices ahead," Riley warned in an army policeman's hiss.

Kachigan paused to silence his own footsteps, but it wasn't until the cold March breeze swung in their direction that he heard what the younger man's sharp ears had already caught. The deep bass rumble of words was punctuated occasionally by an odd flat crack. Something about it seemed familiar to Kachigan, but he couldn't pin the trace of memory down. He craned his head to peer through the gathering darkness, and was rewarded with the sight of what looked like a stone-walled hunting cabin in the trees.

"Let's go scout the place out," he said to Riley in an equally quiet voice. "It'll take Taggart and Frick another five minutes to get up here. We may as well see what's going on in the meantime.''

The younger man looked as if he wanted to salute, but he caught himself and nodded instead, then followed Kachigan up the last few steps at a more cautious and quiet pace. A graveled walk led up to the mine headquarters, but Kachigan stepped off that betraying crunch and walked through the dead scruff of weeds instead. The closer they got to that muffled rumbling voice, the more convinced he became he should know it. He dredged through his memories of the coal operators and foremen he'd met in Tarentum, but no one seemed to match. A moment later, a pistol shot exploded through the silence and chased away the nagging sense of familiarity.

Kachigan paused and swung his shotgun down from his shoulder, pleased to see Riley had done the same thing. There were always a few gangs of thieves and gunmen roving the hills around Pittsburgh, and although he'd never known them to rob a coal mine's front office, the amount of money carried on such a large payroll might make it a worthwhile venture. Of course, the robbers would have to be very well-organized and heavily armed to overcome the contingent of Iron and Coal Police that patrolled every mine property. Kachigan wasn't sure four county detectives with shotguns could be more effective than a dozen pistol-packing company guards, but judging from that shot, he wasn't going to have time to send for reinforcements. Instead, he led the way quietly toward the nearest window, where a newly shattered pane let out a drift of cigar smoke and the clearer sound of voices.

"Keeping your mouth shut's not going to do you a damned bit of good, you know." That rumbling threat was all the more effective for its matter-of-fact tone. Kachigan's sense of familiarity returned, along with a vague shiver of remembered fear, but it still didn't jog his memory into spitting out a name. That was the problem with patrolling a beat for several years, you just couldn't keep track of every thief and brawler you ever arrested. He took a chance and leaned a little closer to the window, but all he saw was the rigid backs of a few men in blue uniforms.

"Listen to me, you stupid dago." The words were punctuated with another flat crack, which Kachigan now recognized as the sound of a backhanded slap. "Your best bet is to stop pretending you don't know English and cooperate. Otherwise I'm sending you back to the old country in a six-foot stateroom!"

It wasn't the racist slur that sent a jab of recognition

through Kachigan, or the final angry roar, or even the burly, broad-shouldered silhouette that passed just beyond the shattered window. It was the frightening speed and silence of the big man's whirl toward his own shadowy presence and the ruthless way he aimed his gun. Kachigan cursed and hurled himself backward.

"Flinn, don't—" The explosion of another pistol shot and the sound of shattering glass drowned out the rest of his protest. Kachigan slammed into the weeds hard enough to wind up with a mouthful of mud, but the only pain he felt was the needle-sharp stitch of thorns through his coat. He rolled over and spat out the dirt he hadn't already swallowed, then looked around for Riley. The younger man was splayed belly-down in the shadows, his shotgun cradled against his cheek and aimed straight at the electric glow of the window.

Kachigan cursed again. "Riley, put that gun down, *now*. Flinn, stop shooting! It's the county police!"

A brawny arm elbowed out the last clinging shards of glass, and the big man inside leaned out through the broken window. His gaze settled on Kachigan in mingled disgust and resignation. "Christ, it *is* you. I thought I recognized your voice. What the hell are you doing here, Kachigan?"

"Responding to your telegram!" Kachigan didn't believe for a moment Bernard Flinn could be as surprised as he was by this encounter. Despite the badge that gleamed on his fancy tweed coat, the burly Irishman wasn't just another coal company police chief. He was an infamous troubleshooter who went from one coal and steel company to another, hired to subdue their restive labor forces and break up their unsettled strikes. Kachigan had tangled with him on his very first murder case, back when Flinn was the police chief at Black Point Steel and Kachigan was a Pittsburgh city detective. If Flinn was now working for Sedgwick Coal & Coke, he would have found out who the local county detectives were long before he'd ever telegraphed them for help. "What the hell did you shoot at me for?"

"Maybe I like my county police to knock on the front door, not listen at the window."

"Then next time, try giving us a little more information than just 'trouble at the mine.' " Kachigan bent to pick up his dropped shotgun, then waved over the shadowy figures of Taggart and Frick, who had prudently taken shelter behind a few scraggly pines. Riley was already on his feet and waiting for orders. "And don't tell me you have to pay by the word—you've got a company telegraph line up here."

"Which goes right through the West Tarentum telegraph operator," Flinn growled. "Come on in, and you'll see what I didn't want the Little Europe side of town to know about."

He pulled back from the shattered window, leaving Kachigan the focus of three sharply critical glares. He scowled back at his fellow detectives.

"What's the matter?"

"We should arrest that man for shooting at us!" Riley protested. "He didn't even stop to ask who we were. If that's not reckless endangerment—"

"No," said Taggart firmly. "Reckless endangerment would be us walking into that mine office right now. Milo, for Christ's sake use your head! Bernard K. Flinn doesn't work for dinky little companies like Sedgwick Coal & Coke. If he's here, it's because Pittsburgh Coal sent him to keep an eye on the whole Allegheny River Valley. He doesn't need our help, no matter what the problem is. What he needs is a nice convenient scapegoat to blame something on."

"No doubt," Kachigan agreed. "But if we *don't* go in, he can get us all fired for dereliction of duty."

"It would just be his word against ours—"

"No, it wouldn't." Kachigan fished the crumpled telegram paper out of his coat pocket and showed it to his partner, who winced in understanding. "The West Tarentum telegraph operator can verify the date, time, and reason we were called in. We'd be out of our jobs before she even stopped talking to Big Roge McGara."

Taggart heaved a resigned sigh. "Well, now we know

why the damned yellow dog didn't just ring us up on the telephone.''

"Yeah. And if you're smart, you won't call any coal policeman a 'yellow dog' in front of him.'' With Taggart and Riley both silenced, Kachigan swung a questioning look at Frick. The older detective was still frowning at him. "What's your gripe?''

"Aside from working with idiots who go rushing into a mess before they've even consulted with the rest of the office?'' Frick's good-natured laugh assured him the words weren't serious, although Kachigan knew they were. "I guess I don't like seeing the Detectives' Bureau represented by grubby-faced Turks who look like they just got done digging a ditch.''

Kachigan grimaced and felt the clinging dampness of mud crumble off his chin and forehead. He reached up to scrub the rest off too, then cursed himself for giving in to Frick's petty needling. "Let's go,'' he said and led the way around the corner of the mining office. He knew better than to begin an argument about his real nationality. To most Americans, all the myriad nations in between Europe and Asia belonged to the Ottoman Empire. The fact that Armenia was now a subjugated province of the Turks didn't make Kachigan any happier about being called one, but he'd long ago resigned himself to it.

The stone-walled mining office *had* once been a hunting cabin, he saw as he came through the open front door. Deer antlers adorned the walls, and the moth-eaten head of a black bear snarled over the cold fireplace. Against that backdrop, the furniture looked as if it had been kidnapped from a downtown skyscraper: black iron typewriters on brand-new metal desks, a polished wooden telephone box on the wall, and a big iron safe for the mine's payroll flanked by filing cabinets. A half dozen men in the dark blue uniforms of the Iron and Coal Police were ranged around the room, truncheons gleaming in their hands and pistol holsters unstrapped.

What they guarded barely looked worthy of that vigilance, or of the heavy iron handcuffs that bound him securely to his chair. The wiry young captive peered up at Kachigan from under a mop of curly dark hair that couldn't hide the stubborn hostility in his eyes. The skin on his neck and hands was a dusky shade of olive, the kind Kachigan knew came from the southernmost parts of Italy. On most of his face, however, that tint had been replaced by the shiny reddish-purple of brand-new bruises. Fresh blood stained one shoulder of the woolen shirt beneath his denim miner's overalls, dripping down from what looked like a bullet-graze across the top of his ear.

Kachigan paused just inside the room's chilly threshold, the other detectives flanking him in a solid wedge that probably looked more coordinated than it really was. He threw a disgusted glance at Flinn, who now sprawled with lazy grace in the nearest leather-padded chair. Kachigan had known the industrial policeman could be both arrogant and brutal in his treatment of an adversary, but outright torture was the one thing he wouldn't have expected.

"What did you shoot at *him* for?" he asked before he could stop the disgusted question. "Resisting arrest with his hands cuffed?"

"I didn't shoot *at* him," Bernard Flinn said. "Do you think I normally miss what I shoot at?"

"Only when you're trying to intimidate someone. What's the matter, did he jump and get in the way of your bullet?"

Flinn sighed and reached into his open desk drawer. "I'm starting to remember why I don't like you, Kachigan. You may have the common sense of a gnat, but you're almost as smart as you think you are." He hefted something briefly in his hand, then tossed the jangling metal across the room. Kachigan caught it more by reflex than intention, then frowned down at the set of keys he held.

"What's this for?"

"To unlock those handcuffs, so you can haul the damned dago off to jail." Flinn rubbed one hand across the other, wincing. "He won't answer my questions, and I'm getting tired of hitting him. I really have to remember to take this signet ring off before I start interrogating someone as bony as that."

Kachigan gritted his teeth on another intemperate remark. Before he could erupt, his partner cleared his throat and saved him. "I assume we're arresting the boy for a reason, Mr. Flinn. Other than assaulting your fist with his face, I mean." Taggart's voice was so bland that the insult buried in it barely seemed to register with his victim. It was a technique he had honed to perfection on their corrupt detective captain. "Or are you calling in a favor from Big Roge McGara?"

Flinn gave him a baleful look. "I'd rather call in a glass of water from a cesspool. And you can save your wisecracks for your stinking boss, Fat Art." The use of that nickname confirmed Kachigan's suspicion that Flinn had known exactly who he was summoning tonight. "I'm dealing with a crime up here, and all I'm asking you boys to do is your job. You do remember how to do that, don't you?"

Kachigan reached into his coat. Several of the coal policemen straightened abruptly, hands dropping to their pistol butts. With a deep breath, he pulled out his battered leather-bound evidence book, then flipped it open to a blank page. He didn't bother consulting with his coworkers first—neither Taggart nor Frick ever bothered to take notes when they investigated, and Riley hadn't had enough experience yet to know which questions to ask.

"What's the prisoner's name?" The question was nominally addressed to Bernard Flinn, but Kachigan kept an eye on the handcuffed boy to see if he got a reaction. The mop of curly hair didn't quiver, nor did the dark eyes dart in his direction. He was starting to suspect the young coal miner's only crime was not understanding English.

"I have no idea," said his captor.

Kachigan wrote that down, with his usual slow penmanship. "Then he's not employed by Sedgwick Coal?"

"I don't know whether he is or not." Flinn saw his puzzled look and snorted. "We've got a couple hundred men digging coal in this mine, Kachigan, not counting the ones

who work loading it outside. Any of you boys recognize
him?'' he asked his guards.

Shaken heads and muttered negatives circled the room,
coming back at length to the burly man in its center.
''There, you happy?''

Kachigan didn't bother to answer. He wrote, *Not recognized by any company guards. New worker?* in his evidence book, then glanced back up at Bernard Flinn. ''And
what exactly was this crime you couldn't let the telegraph
operator know about?''

He'd expected the answer to be stealing, or spying, or
maybe even the most heinous crime in western Pennsylvania—labor organizing. But Flinn's unhappy grimace surprised him.

''Murder,'' said the coal police chief.

Kachigan paused with his stubby pencil lifted above the
page, eyeing not Bernard Flinn but his handcuffed prisoner.
Had the boy's face looked just a shade too utterly blank
during that last exchange? Or was the shock of his gunshot
wound wearing off at last, opening the door for pain to
leach the hostility from his eyes?

''Where's the body?'' Taggart asked in the hushed silence. ''Do we get to see it, or do we just have to take your
word about how dead it is?''

''It's down in the mine, right where we found it,'' Flinn
said. Kachigan lifted his eyebrows, startled by this evidence
of good faith until the coal policeman added, ''It was stuck
under one of the big coal cutting machines, and we didn't
feel like turning it on and getting ourselves plastered with
blood and guts. We'll take a winch down later tonight to
get him out.''

''If he was stuck—'' Riley's voice came out pitched a
little too high, a young man's nervous trait that made him
sound even more inexperienced than he was. Kachigan
heard J.P. Frick snicker under his breath, but Riley gamely
cleared his throat and went on. ''If he was stuck under a
cutting machine, Mr. Flinn, how do you know it was murder and not an accident? Those are the most dangerous
machines in the mines.''

"Sure are," Flinn said with deceptive cordiality. "But I've never seen one that used a stiletto for a cutting blade."

Kachigan frowned. "You found a stiletto at the murder site? Bloody?"

"I expect so, since it's sticking out from between the dead man's ribs." The brief gleam of teeth on Flinn's face was not a smile. "Don't worry, I'm not planting evidence, Kachigan. All you need to do is take one look at where that corpse is stuffed, and you'll know that stiletto went in there with him."

"Does that mean you're going to let us examine the scene of the crime?"

"Sure. Just as soon as you arrest my suspect here."

Kachigan scrubbed a hand across his face, feeling the rough shadow of evening stubble everywhere but on the aching crescent-shaped scar where a shard of metal had gouged his cheekbone years ago. He should have known Bernard Flinn wouldn't make it easy to conduct an honest investigation of this murder. The company police chief was probably counting on the unwritten policy of the County Detectives' Bureau to arrest men first and discover the "evidence" of their guilt later. But the same corruption and laziness that made Kachigan's stomach churn when he was stationed in Pittsburgh also allowed him to be a defiantly clean detective at this distant regional office. He wasn't going to let his first independent murder case start with the kind of unjustified arrest Big Roge McGara would make.

"What makes you so sure this Italian boy is your murderer?" he asked. "Did anyone see him do it?"

"No one had to," Flinn said impatiently. "We found him down there with the body, after all of the day shift had left."

He spoke as if that simple fact was as damning as a bloodstain. Kachigan glanced back at Owen Riley, but this time the young Tarentum native was no help. He looked just as puzzled as Kachigan felt.

"So?" Kachigan asked. "Wasn't there a night shift coming into the mine at the same time?"

That question got him a cascade of laughter from Flinn's

guards, and a quizzical look from the coal police chief himself. "Don't you read the newspapers, Kachigan? Or do you just not know what day it is?"

"March thirty-first," he said. "So what?"

Flinn grunted and then rummaged in his desk again, this time throwing a folded newspaper at him. Kachigan shook it out and saw it was that morning's *Valley Daily News*. On the front page, in letters as thick and dismal as those normally used to announce the death of presidents, the headline read, "Bituminous and anthracite contracts expire at midnight. No settlement in sight."

"Coal strike," Flinn said curtly. "Read all about it."

Kachigan didn't have to. He'd heard about the brewing coal miners' strike from his favorite socialist reporter Helen Sorby, who was currently assigned to the story for the *New York Herald*. But it had never occurred to him there could be any connection between that event and any company which employed Bernard K. Flinn as their police chief.

"Don't tell me you're working for a *unionized* mine?" Kachigan asked incredulously.

"All of Sedgwick's holdings let the unions in years ago," Flinn said. Surprisingly enough, the renowned strikebreaker and bane of labor organizers sounded amused rather than annoyed about that. "So the shift of men who just left was the last one we'll have on-site until the strike's over. And this dago sure as hell wasn't on it."

Kachigan didn't have to ask how the police chief knew that—the young Italian suspect had clean hands, a clean neck, and only a scattering of coal dust across his faded, too-large overalls. The badly fitted coal miner's clothes and utter lack of English made his next question an obvious one. "Did he come up here to work as a strikebreaker?"

Flinn lifted an eyebrow. "If he did, it was his own idea. Sedgwick refuses to bring in scabs while he's still negotiating with the miners' union. He does business the old-fashioned way."

"With integrity, you mean," Kachigan said before he could stop himself. Flinn vaulted out of his chair with snake-strike quickness, but Kachigan's reflexive backward step wasn't necessary. It was the Italian boy that the burly policeman was heading for. The handcuffed prisoner gasped and jerked back from his approach, skittering his chair sideways with his convulsive movement, but all Flinn did was lift a hand and let it hover in the air beside his bruised cheek.

"Well, dago? Did you hear about the strike and decide to come scrape up some work as a scab? Maybe even get a head start on the other scabs by filling a few cars all by yourself tonight?" Flinn gave the chair a push with one foot, spinning the young Italian around to meet his gaze. "The trouble was, you snuck in a little too early and got yourself caught by a union man, didn't you? And when he threatened to drag you down to the mine-workers' rally, you killed him. *Isn't that right?*"

The dark-haired boy flinched, but even from several feet away Kachigan could see he hadn't responded to the question, just to the threatening outward swing of Flinn's hand. "Stop that," he said sharply. "That's my prisoner you're abusing."

"Is it?" Flinn smiled and patted the boy on his bruised cheek instead of hitting him. "So you're convinced he's the murderer?"

"Not quite," Kachigan said dryly. He'd been subjected before to the flights of Irish fancy Bernard K. Flinn could conjure up when he wanted to disguise some industrial mayhem. "I'm sure Big Roge McGara would buy your story in a minute, but there's one little detail I'd like to pin down before I take this boy to jail. Do you know for sure the murder victim *was* a union man?"

"He must have been," said Flinn, just a little too quickly. "Hell, almost all our workers are."

"Can't you tell from your payroll records? I thought union men all donated part of their earnings to pay for an independent check-weighman."

"Yeah, they do." Flinn rolled his massive shoulders in a shrug, his mouth tightening with an expression that came close to real embarrassment. "Trouble is, we don't have the dead guy's name. None of my guards could recognize him.''

Kachigan threw a consulting glance back at his fellow detectives. Taggart wore the mulishly stupid expression that meant he was thinking hard but hadn't quite managed to figure out what was going on. Frick's mouth had twisted with cynical disbelief, and Riley just looked downright confused.

''Let me get this straight.'' Kachigan slid his pencil into his evidence book and folded it shut. ''Based on purely circumstantial evidence, you want me to arrest a boy whose name you don't know and who may or may not be one of your miners, for the murder of a man whose name you don't know and who may or may not have been one of your miners.''

''That's right,'' said Flinn. ''Are you going to do it?''

Kachigan weighed his options for a moment, then took a deep breath and made a decision he knew he'd probably regret. ''Yes.'' He deliberately waited for the flash of triumph to light the big Irishman's face, then added, ''But what I'm going to arrest him for is trespassing on company property after work hours. I can hold him in jail on that indefinitely, as long as he's a material witness in this murder case.''

''*What?*''

Kachigan made himself meet Flinn's slitted gaze with all the self-command he could muster. ''You asked me to do my job, didn't you? Well, this is how I do it. If you don't like it, you can keep the boy in custody yourself.''

Flinn heaved an aggravated sigh, but he made no move to take back the keys he'd given Kachigan. ''Arrest the stupid dago for loitering in that chair if you want to,'' he said in disgust. ''Just get him the hell out of my office!''

His voice had risen to a roar, but Kachigan still heard the ominous sound of self-satisfaction beneath the surface bluster. He felt his jaw clench with the feeling he'd been had, but there was no way to back down now. With a muttered Armenian curse, Kachigan went to release the silent prisoner.

It didn't take long to see what Bernard Flinn had to feel smug about. The dark-haired boy tensed when Kachigan unlocked the cuffs around his hands, eyeing the cordon of company police around the office as if weighing his chances of escape. Apparently he wasn't stupid, though— when Kachigan dropped a warning hand on his shoulder, he relaxed again and began rubbing at his raw, chafed wrists. As he did, one tattered woolen sleeve fell back to reveal a crude charcoal tattoo on his forearm, in the shape of a clenched fist holding an upraised stiletto.

It was an emblem Kachigan had seen several times before, and to anyone familiar with the many strands of ethnic crime that ran through Pittsburgh's immigrant neighborhoods, there could be no doubt about what it meant. Young and innocent and uncomprehending as he looked, his young Italian prisoner was a full member of the secret criminal society known as the Black Hand.

TWO

"Female reporter goes mad at coal miners' district union meeting, slaughters thousands by stabbing them with her fountain pen. 'The world would be a better place if we burnt union leaders and let lumps of coal decide whether to go on strike,' she proclaims before vanishing into the night—"

Helen Sorby paused to gauge the effect this had on her audience. The scratch of a fine-point drafting pen, barely audible over the whisper of gas in the drawing room lamps, was the only response she got.

"So," she said conversationally. "Do you think I should send it to the *Herald* just like that, Thomas, or should I reword it a little first?"

"I think you should send it down the street to Police Patrol Station Seven," said her brother without looking up from the fire insurance map he was drawing. He lifted his ruler and wiped off the excess ink on his gartered shirt-sleeve, adding another line to the spiderweb of blue and black that already feathered the cloth. "This is the second time in two months this same female reporter has run amuck. Granted, the first bunch of people she slaughtered were all running for mayor, and nobody could be expected to miss them. But if she's going to disrupt the entire coal industry, somebody really ought to arrest her.''

Helen sighed and threw her scribbled-over telegraph forms onto the big oak table she and Thomas had long ago converted into a shared desk. "The ones who really need to be arrested are the United Mine Workers district leadership!" she said fiercely. "Do you know what their mutton-headed ex-president said at the convention today?"

"Obviously nothing worth quoting, or you'd already have a news story for your deadline tomorrow."

She crumpled the topmost telegraph form into a ball and threw it at her twin's oblivious head. As usual, it wasn't Thomas's lack of social conscience that annoyed her as much as his astute powers of observation. "Dolan said coal miners ought to go out on strike and stay on strike until every mine in the country has raised the pay scale back to what it was before the depression of 1904."

"That's not exactly breaking news, is it?" Thomas added an ink spider to his web-covered sleeve by wiping off his drafting pen as well as his ruler. He slid the delicate steel tip out from its steel stem, then added one with a wider flare and dipped it back into his bottle of ink. "All the papers have been wringing their hands about the possibility of a nationwide coal strike for the last week and a half. The steel mills down in the Strip have stockpiled so much coal you can't even see the Allegheny River through the coal barges."

"It's news when Patrick Dolan says it!" Helen stood up and began pacing the dining room, so exasperated that she didn't even bother lifting her skirt to keep it from sweeping the day's accumulation of steel-mill soot off the floor. "If you'd listened to even half of what I've told you lately, Thomas, you'd know that. Dolan is the one who's been trying for months to get the union to ratify a new coal-mining contract with *no* pay scale increase in it whatsoever!"

"So?"

"So now that Pittsburgh Coal and the other unionized coal operators have finally agreed to give their miners a five-percent pay scale increase, why is Patrick Dolan telling the union it should go out on strike instead of ratifying *that* contract?"

Thomas raised his head, looking interested for the first time since they'd come in from supper. "I don't know. Why?"

Helen took a deep, angry breath. The furious comprehension that had ignited while she'd listened to Pat Dolan give his astonishing turnabout speech that morning was still red-hot inside her, like an underground mine fire smoldering in silence. "Isn't it *obvious*? Dolan's selling out his own union. Since he couldn't get them to accept a contract with no pay raise, the next best thing he can do is wreck the agreement that calls for a five-percent pay raise, and drag the strike out so long that they'll end up settling for less. And you know who must have bribed him to do that!"

"The big coal companies?"

"No, of course not." Helen started pacing again, retracing the steps that had brought her to this frustrating standstill in the first place. First, the drawing room's front window with its view of Pittsburgh's firelit skies, shrouded with smoke and peppered with blasts of rising sparks wherever a Bessemer furnace was blowing. "The big unionized companies like Pittsburgh Coal all have ironclad contracts with steel mills this year. That's why they agreed to the five-percent increase in the first place."

"Then who?"

"*That's* who." Helen strode around the table to point out their narrow back window. Beyond their yard and alley, an empty lot opened the view across Pittsburgh's South Side to the gaslit hulk of the Cunningham Glass Factory. A big locomotive sat steaming there, on the spur that served the bottle-packing department. The railroad line itself curved back toward the distant glow of the Pennsylvania Railroad freight station, whose tracks had arrogantly appropriated the entire twenty-third block of Mary Street.

"The glass factories?" Thomas asked blankly. "I thought they all used natural gas now for their furnaces—"

"No, idiot, the railroads! They never want to pay a

penny more for a ton of coal than they can get away with, because their profits ride directly on their fuel costs. And who else would have the gall to interfere with a union settlement in an industry they don't own? An industry they're specifically *prohibited* by law from investing in or interfering with?'' Helen strode back to the oak table and smacked her fist down on her pile of telegraph forms, hard enough to make Thomas's loose scatter of pen points leap and jitter. ''And who can I not even *begin* to investigate?''

Her twin was accustomed enough to her outbursts of socialist indignation not to joggle his ruler and smear the line he was drawing, but he did give her a warning look. ''Catch that tip,'' he advised, as one of his hollow silver points rolled toward the edge of the table. ''If it breaks, you're buying me a new one. Why can't you investigate the railroads? If you can prove that they paid Pat Dolan to sabotage his own union—''

Helen obeyed him, careful not to close her fist around the fragile metal as tightly as she wanted to. ''But that's exactly what I can't prove. Do you think I'd be standing here yelling at you if I could be writing this up for the *New York Herald*?''

''Can't you just leave out the names and call the railroads a 'transportation concern' the way you did in the Westinghouse story you wrote for the *Herald* last December?''

''Not after the way the Pennsylvania Railroad's lawyers threatened to close down deliveries of paper stock if the *Herald* ever published another unproven statement about a 'transportation concern' in this state. Max Fortune says if I want to write another railroad exposé, I'd better have enough proof to start a congressional investigation.''

''Is that so impossible? Ida Tarbell's articles started a congressional investigation of Standard Oil, didn't they?''

''Yes, but I'm not exactly Ida Tarbell.'' Helen scowled down at the stack of scribbled and scratched-out telegraph forms, the botched remains of her effort to write a coal news story that did not keep veering into forbidden railroad territory. ''I can't even think of a good way to expose Patrick Dolan for a traitor. The only facts I can report are that he changed his mind so drastically on the strike vote that the rank-and-file coal miners threw him out of the hall. That makes it sound like—''

''—union politics as usual,'' her twin finished for her.

''Yes.'' She crumpled the half-written drafts into a solid mass, taking her frustration out on the pulpy soft paper. ''And that's not the kind of news the *Herald* expects from a special correspondent.''

''Well, what *do* they expect? You can't exactly go undercover as a coal miner, the way you posed as a secretary at Westinghouse to catch that industrial spy.''

''No, I can't.'' Helen slid her brother a speculative look. ''I don't suppose you'd consider—''

Thomas was already shaking his head, vehemently. ''Dressing up like a woman for a two-hour lark is one thing—but I will not spend twelve hours shoveling coal in an underground shaft only four feet high, Helen, not even for you. Between the floods and the rockfalls and the natural gas explosions, it's even more dangerous than working in a steel mill.''

''I know. And the mine owners still send in young boys and men straight off the boat from the old country, who barely know what they're supposed to be doing.'' Helen tapped her fountain pen against the tabletop, heedless of the ink spatters she knew she was putting on the cuffs of her white shirtwaist. ''I wonder if I could talk Julia Regitz Brown into assigning me to an immigrant settlement house closer to the coalfields, so I could document the high rate of industrial accidents—''

Thomas slid her a mischievous look. ''There's always Tarentum, isn't there? It's smack in the middle of the Allegheny River coalfields. And there's a particular Allegheny County detective working there . . .''

Helen gave her twin an exasperated look. ''Thomas, I can't waste time going back and forth to Tarentum in the middle of this coal strike.''

''Why not? You certainly wasted plenty of it going back and forth during the mayor's election last month,'' Thomas retorted. ''You said the long trolley ride gave you time to gather your thoughts. Maybe another trip up there would help you write up this coal strike story of yours.''

"No," Helen said flatly. "It wouldn't."

That made her twin brother look up from his map again, this time in concern. "Helen, have you been fighting with Milo again? I thought you two were getting along lately."

"We were—I mean we are." Helen heard her voice rise with impatience despite herself. "And I am *not* fighting with him. I talked to him on the telephone twice this weekend, remember? Once for so long that the operator at the Tarentum exchange had to break in because she needed the line."

"That's true," Thomas admitted. "And I didn't hear you yell at him either time. But I *did* hear you say you couldn't come up to Tarentum for dinner again this week."

"That's only because I've been covering the coal strike—"

The buzzer on the front door rang through their argument, so long and loud and insistently that even Helen's voice was drowned out. She swung around to answer it, then paused on the threshold as she remembered what day it was.

"You weren't expecting another Sanborn Company surveyor to drop in, were you?" she asked her brother. His fellow fire insurance mappers had a distinct tendency toward boyish high spirits and peculiar senses of humor. "Tomorrow is Fools' Day, you know."

Thomas shook his head. "None of the traveling men is even up in this neck of the woods. There's a big push going to get Georgia and the Carolinas done before the summer heat sets in." The buzzer rang again, stopping and starting with such ferocious urgency that he lifted both eyebrows. "That sounds more like a crisis down at the settlement house. Just make sure you see who it is before you open the door."

"I always do," Helen said, but went out through the drawing room door without quite meeting his gaze. Years ago, she had gotten into the habit of stepping up onto the mahogany telephone seat in the hall, to satisfy her curiosity by peering at visitors through the stained-glass transom before she opened the front door to them. It had only been for the past week and a half, however, that she'd done it with such an odd mixture of apprehension and wistfulness bubbling inside her. It was true she wasn't fighting with Milo Kachigan, but she also knew her unexplained absence from Tarentum wasn't going to be tolerated in puzzled patience forever. Sooner or later, the person on her doorstep was going to be a county detective demanding to know why he hadn't seen her in weeks. Helen just hadn't quite decided what she was going to say in reply.

This time, she saw in relief, wasn't going to be that time. Not unless the Allegheny County Detectives' Bureau had suddenly permitted its men to wear large-brimmed hats trimmed with floppy silk magnolia blossoms and velveteen bluebirds. Helen dropped back down onto the floor with a sigh and opened the door to her only surviving aunt.

"There you are at *last*." Pat McGregor flung herself at Helen as if the Iron and Coal Police were chasing her, heedless of the umbrella she was clutching. Helen evaded the damp canvas folds with the ease of long practice and gave her aunt back a welcoming hug. Soot puffed out from her thick mink coat along with the expensive smell of lilies of the valley.

"What's the matter?" Helen asked, but the spike of alarm the doorbell had generated was already fading. She loved Aunt Pittypat dearly, but she also knew her well enough not to assume her frantic demeanor meant a crisis was afoot. "Have you lost a cat?"

"No, dearest." Pat McGregor stepped back to blink up at her. "Why, have you found one? I have room for a few more up at the new Oakmont house, you know."

Helen shook her head and stepped back, drawing her aunt in far enough to close the door. "You just seemed upset about something. Thomas, Aunt Pat's here!"

Her aunt winced and clapped both hands to her ears, heedless of her delicate silver curls. "Helen, you *can't* have been born in a barn, I'm sure I would have remembered if you had. Must you shout as if your brother was a mile away?''

"He is a mile away, in his mind," Helen retorted, unabashed. There were times when having a loud Italian voice came in handy, no matter what the more genteel Irish side of her family might think. "I doubt if he even heard me now.''

"Well, there's no need to yodel for him again. You're the one I came to get." Pat McGregor resisted Helen's attempt to take the mink coat that was slipping off her shoulders. "Do hurry up, dear, we were supposed to have been at the Hotel Grand fifteen minutes ago.''

"We were?" This time it was Helen's turn to look blank. "For a temperance meeting, Aunt Pat?''

"For our appointment with the Murchisons." Pittypat swept over to the coatrack that hung against the far wall and tugged down the hand-me-down sable coat Helen seldom wore, because it reminded her too much of its late owner. "You'll look presentable enough in this, as long as you don't offer to shake hands. Honestly, Helen, you're getting as bad as Thomas with ink.''

She glanced down guiltily at the blue-stained cuffs of her shirtwaist, then took a step back, shaking her head when the sable coat was thrust at her. "Aunt Pat, wait. I don't remember an appointment with anyone named Murchison.''

"That's because I haven't told you about it yet, dear. Put your coat on, and I'll explain along the way." Pat McGregor glanced across the hall when the drawing room door swung open. "Good evening, Thomas. I see you heard your sister call you.''

"No, Aunt Pat," Thomas said, with an innocence too perfect to be real. "All I heard was you yelling at her to hurry up.''

Pat McGregor snorted, an earthy Irish sound that betrayed the impoverished childhood she'd had before she married into money. "Don't you talk to me about yelling, young man, you're almost as bad as Helen. I could hear both of you before I even took a step onto the stoop. What on earth were you arguing about?''

"We weren't arguing," Helen said. "We were—we were just discussing my work schedule."

"I was trying to talk Helen into taking enough time off to visit Tarentum," Thomas said helpfully.

That got him an annoyed look from his sister and an unsympathetic one from his aunt. "So you can sneak another keg of beer into the kitchen and play poker with your friends while she's gone?"

"No, no." Thomas looked so deeply shocked by the accusation that Helen knew it was probably true. "It's just that she hasn't seen Milo for a while. Not to mention all of our relatives up in Tarentum, on our mother's side—"

"Most of whom are either dead or in jail," Helen retorted. "I stopped in to see Cousin Lena just a week and a half ago."

"Which is also the last time you saw Milo," her brother pointed out. "If you aren't fighting with him, Helen, why haven't you gone up since then?"

Helen opened her mouth, momentarily goaded, but explaining to her family exactly what had happened ten days ago in Tarentum seemed no more helpful now than it had then. She snapped her teeth closed on a curse that would have scandalized her aunt if she had understood the Italian, and reached out to grab her sable coat. "Come on, Aunt Pat. The Murchisons are waiting for us."

"Do try to be polite, dearest," Aunt Pat said. "The Murchisons are quite in despair over the situation, you know."

"No, I *don't* know," Helen said in exasperation, while their hired carriage pulled up outside the gaslit brilliance of the Hotel Grand's main entrance. The lights were functional rather than ostentatious—visitors who weren't used to navigating the smoke-filled streets of Pittsburgh usually needed a beacon to find their way back to their lodgings. But today's drizzle had watered the smoke down to a pale mist, almost the same color as the fog rising off the rivers. As a result, they had been able to see their destination from the moment they turned off Smithfield Street onto the financial blocks of Fourth Avenue.

The approaching glow had galvanized Helen into trying to drag her aunt's erratic attention to the subject of the people they were going to meet, but the savings banks, real estate trusts, and stock exchanges that jostled each other for space along this street always sent Pittypat back to the days when she had been married to an influential city banker. By the time Helen had managed to cut through a meandering story of security-theft and scandal, they had reached the gritty shoulders of the Diamond Market district.

"What do you mean, you don't know?" Pat peered at her across the darkened carriage interior, looking more worried than repentant. "Dearest girl, I've just been telling you all about them. Weren't you listening?"

Helen bit her lip against a rush of remorse. "I'm sorry, Aunt Pittypat, I assumed you meant someone else."

"Really, dearest? Who?"

"Never mind." Helen gathered up her aunt's mink muff and handed it to her, then followed her out into the Hotel Grand's welcoming glow. She waited patiently while Aunt Pat handed the driver far more money than the ride had been worth. The gaunt young man touched two fingers to his threadbare cap, then pulled out a thick woolen blanket to shield his old but carefully groomed gelding from the evening drizzle while his employer watched approvingly. Pat McGregor always chose her cabbies for the care they gave their horses rather than for the efficiency of their service, which was why she was always late.

"Now, then, Helen." Pittypat took her arm and turned her toward the hotel's luxuriously polished brass entrance doors. "Do you remember *anything* I said to you?"

Her niece strenuously dredged her memory. "Coal mines. Missing securities. And some sort of scandal about a second wife and a stepdaughter, but I don't remember their names."

"That's because I don't either," her aunt admitted. "Although I should, because I've heard about them ever since I bought the summer house up in Oakmont. They're the

richest family in town, you know, quite probably millionaires.''

"You've only *heard* about them?'' Helen pulled the
nearest brass door open for her aunt, ignoring the uniformed doorman's reproving look. She didn't believe in the
widely held view that women should never touch door han-
dles when males were anywhere in sight. ''Does that mean
you've never actually met them?''

"No, but it doesn't matter, dearest. I spoke to Charles
Murchison for a long time when he rang up to ask us here.
He seems like a very nice sort of man, for a coal baron.''

Helen sighed and brought her feckless aunt to a halt on
the threshold of the hotel's lobby, scanning the wine velvet
sofas around the fireplace and the mahogany stationery desk
that took up an entire side of the room. Most of the
distinguished-looking businessmen she saw were alone,
whether they were sitting with their newspapers or writing
notes on hotel letterhead. Only a few were being held at
arm's length by the stiffly embroidered silk evening gowns
of their wives, and most of those wore tuxedos, which
meant they were probably on their way to the opera. "I'm
not worried about his manners, Aunt Pat. I just wanted to
know what he looks like.''

"Oh.'' Pat McGregor followed her gaze in dismay, as if
it had never occurred to her the hotel might contain more
than one Pittsburgh millionaire. "Oh, dear. I don't really
know, although I have had Mrs. Murchison pointed out to
me at a distance. I remember thinking she looked just like
a Gibson Girl.''

"Oh, good,'' said Helen dryly. "All we need to find is
a female who's gasping for breath and wearing far more
hair than one scalp could possibly support.''

Her aunt gave her a distraught look. "Helen! You said
you'd be polite!''

She opened her mouth to deny making any such promise,
but a cleared throat from behind caught her attention first.
Helen turned to see the hotel doorman following them into
the room, still with a look of strong reproof on his mus-
tached face. For a disconcerting moment, she thought he

was going to chime in with her aunt about her inappropriate manners, but instead he bowed and held out a folded sheet of hotel stationery. "Mrs. McGregor, Miss Sorby," he said. "I believe this is for you."

Aunt Pat lifted her veil to peer at the note in some amazement. "How on earth did you know—"

The doorman bowed again. "I have sent your carriage around to the back alley, ma'am. Please let me know when you require it again."

He handed over the note and returned to his post without another word. "I don't think the Hotel Grand likes your taste in cabs, Aunt Pat," Helen said in amusement. "What does the note say?"

"Nothing." Pittypat sounded bewildered.

"That's because it was just a ruse," confessed a voice from behind them. Helen swung around again, startled not so much by the easy confidence of wealth that rang in those words as by the fact that it was a woman speaking. "I didn't want to embarrass you with a hotel page shouting out your names. I thought telling the doorman to deliver a note would point you out to me just as well." A smile curved her generous lips. "Until Miss Sorby sailed right past him, that is."

Aunt Pat gurgled with laughter, and held out a gloved hand. "It's a pleasure to meet you, Mrs. Murchison."

"And you, Mrs. McGregor." The millionaire's wife offered her hand to Helen next, and surprised her with a clasp as firm and straightforward as her smile. Aunt Pittypat was right, she did look like a Gibson Girl, but it wasn't a resemblance of coiffure or silhouette. The occasional silver strands that glittered in her modestly upswept brown hair proved she hadn't used a fall to augment it, and her elegant watered-silk evening gown managed to suggest the svelte curves of a fashion model without actually pinching hourglass tight. The distinctive look came more from her graceful movements, Helen decided, and from the hint of laughter that lurked at the corners of her lips. "If you'll come with me, ladies, my husband is anxious to meet you both."

Helen's eyebrows lifted when Mrs. Murchison led them, not back into the lobby but across to the twin elevators that faced the hotel's front desk. Her opinion of the millionaire's wife rose yet again, as she realized that she'd come down to greet them without benefit of male escort. Helen wondered briefly if perhaps the unseen Mr. Murchison had some disability that prevented his attendance on his wife, but when they reached the top floor of the hotel and were ushered into an elaborate sitting room suite, the sound of energetic strides and an even more energetic voice dismissed that possibility.

"—no reason to panic," Charles Murchison told the telephone's mouthpiece impatiently. He saw his wife halt the visitors on the threshold in deference to the conversation and shook his head vehemently, gesturing with the detached receiver for them to come closer while he paced. When they did, Helen could see the ultramodern black metal telephone stand was attached to a long, movable wire to allow it to be taken anywhere in the room for convenience. How the other half lived, she thought wryly.

"It's the front office, fretting about reserves," the millionaire told them in the booming voice of a man who'd made his fortune in industrial work. Helen noticed he didn't bother covering the mouthpiece. "Just give me a minute—no, no!" he snapped at the telephone. "It'd be a waste of money to ship more coal from Illinois. Our stocks are full, and the strike won't last long. Pittsburgh's ready to settle now, and the Allegheny Valley never holds out more than a week past the city. Just keep new orders to a minimum and we'll be fine. Got it?"

Whether they had it or not, the conversation was over. Murchison clapped the receiver back on its cradle to cut the connection, then set the telephone stand back on its table hard enough to make its bell jangle from the impact. He was a large, raw-boned man who seemed to do everything with just a little more effort than required, as if the thumps and thuds and slams assured him things were really getting accomplished. Despite that vigor, his sharp peak of thin gray hair and the loose folds of skin that draped his jaw told Helen he was considerably older than his second wife.

"Miss Sorby, Mrs. McGregor." Murchison didn't come forward to shake their hands, gesturing them toward a brocade sofa instead. He barely waited until his wife had joined them to take his own seat. "Sorry I had to send Lillian down alone to meet you, but I had that telephone call scheduled for eight."

"I'm the one who should apologize, Mr. Murchison, for being so very late—" Aunt Pat began.

"All the more reason not to waste time on chitchat now." Did all millionaires think their money allowed them to dispense with the bother of being polite, Helen wondered, or was it only the brusque Pittsburgh variety who made their fortunes in uncouth industries like steel, lumber, and coal? "You've told your niece the whole story already?"

"I tried to, but I'm not sure I remembered all the details," Pat McGregor said without the slightest hesitation. Helen threw her good-natured aunt a speaking look of gratitude. "Perhaps you could relate it to her again, Mr. Murchison."

The millionaire grunted, as if his opinion of Aunt Pat had been confirmed rather than disappointed by this development. Instead of launching into his story, however, he scrutinized Helen for a long, silent moment.

"I gather from the newspaper stories you wrote on the mayor's election that you're a socialist reporter, Miss Sorby," he said at last, almost pugnaciously. "That right?"

"That's right." She met his intent gaze without wavering. "Is that why you asked us here tonight?"

"Unfortunately, yes." Murchison levered himself up from his chair and began to pace the sitting room again. Helen wasn't sure if he even realized he was doing it. "At your socialist meetings and rallies, I don't suppose you've ever met a young woman named Emily Murchison?"

"No."

He paused beside his wife's end of the sofa, looking grim. "There, you see? I told you she wouldn't know her."

Lillian Murchison sighed and turned to face Helen, leaning out to talk around Aunt Pittypat's wide-brimmed hat. She looked more than ever like a Gibson Girl in that graceful pose. "Miss Sorby, we're worried that our daughter—"

"My daughter," Murchison said, clearly laying the blame on his own parental shoulders. "Your stepdaughter."

"—that our Emmy has joined a group of either anarchists or socialists recently. We hoped you might have seen her with them, and could tell us who they were." There was no hint of laughter lurking now in Lillian Murchison's face. "Do you think it might be possible to find out by asking among the socialist circles you travel in?"

Helen frowned up at Charles Murchison, whose pacing had taken him over to the brocade-draped windows with their glittering view of Pittsburgh's skyscrapers. "Have you tried just asking your daughter who her new friends are?"

"That's the problem," Murchison said curtly. "Emmy's gone. She left while we were out at a dinner party the other night, didn't even leave a note." He sounded more disgruntled than distraught, as if having a daughter disappear was just one of the problems a coal baron had to face every day. "We haven't heard from her since."

"And you think she's run away with some of her socialist friends?" Helen tried to keep her voice as neutral as possible, despite an urge to ask this self-centered millionaire if he had considered any other possibilities. Kidnapping, for instance. "Why is that?"

"Because she wouldn't have been tempted to run away with any of her other well-bred friends!" Anger tightened the sagging skin around Murchison's out-thrust jaw, giving Helen a glimpse of the ruthless autocrat he must have been in his younger days. "Emmy was always a good girl, at least until she started reading Jack London and those other misbegotten socialists. Since then, she's been slipping out of the house and never telling us where she's going."

Aunt Pittypat cleared her throat delicately. "I don't mean to cast aspersions, Mr. Murchison—but is it possible she might have been going out to see a young man?"

The millionaire grunted again. "Not Emmy," he said flatly. "Not with her face."

Helen frowned at that comment, but Murchison left it to his wife to explain. "Emmy suffered a fever in childhood, the same one that took her mother," Lillian said. "She has a slightly crooked left side and her face is—well, I suppose you could say a little mismatched in appearance. It's a very slight defect, and takes away nothing from her charm, but she does seem to feel it. I have never seen her look truly comfortable around a young man." She cast a hesitant look up at her husband. "And then there is the matter of the securities . . ."

"The missing securities," Helen remembered her aunt saying something about that. "What sort are they?"

Charles Murchison had gone back to the window again, staring down at the electric lights of John Dimling's lunchrooms through the gathering haze of smoke and river mist. He didn't answer her, although Helen doubted that he could have missed hearing the question. She didn't exactly have a die-away voice.

"The sort that could be worth a lot of money, if they got into the wrong hands," his wife said after a moment. "And although we have no real evidence to prove it, we're concerned that Emmy might be the one who took them. They turned up missing on the same day she disappeared."

"Which was how many days ago?" Helen could hear the crisp sound of a newspaper reporter's questions creeping into her voice despite herself.

"Three," said Lillian Murchison promptly. "Emmy left on Saturday night, sometime after nine." She cocked her head at Helen in an inquisitive gesture. "Does this mean you'll look into Emmy's whereabouts for us, Miss Sorby? We are truly terribly worried about her."

Helen took a deep, considering breath. Did she really have time, in the midst of a national coal strike, to go chasing after a missing heiress? Even one who, as a brand-new socialist, had possibly dared to deprive her millionaire father of his ill-gotten capitalist gains?

"You can use my summer house in Oakmont as your

base of operations," Pat McGregor suggested helpfully.
"That will put you right in the area where Miss Murchison
must have met with her new friends. And it's quite a bit
closer to Tarentum—"

"But a lot further away from Pittsburgh," Helen said,
frowning. "Which means it's too far away from the coal
strike negotiations, the miners' union meetings, and all the
other things I'm supposed to be reporting on for the *New
York Herald*." She stood up, shaking her head reluctantly.
"I'm sorry, Mr. Murchison, right now I just don't have the
time—"

Charles Murchison grunted, the same irritating sound of
confirmation rather than disappointment that he'd previ-
ously condemned Pittypat with. "Just what we need, more
reporters writing about the coalfields from the streets of
downtown Pittsburgh," he said brusquely. "If you people
would bother to actually investigate half the things you
write about—"

Helen swung around to glare at him. "If *you* people
would let us into your coal towns to report on the actual
conditions—"

Two voices intervened, one soothing and one alarmed.

"Charles, these are your guests—"

"Helen, *dearest*, no shouting please—"

"It's a deal," Murchison said.

Helen's teeth snapped shut on the rest of her protest.
"What's a deal?" she asked warily.

The raw-boned old man came to stand directly facing her
for the first time since she'd entered the room, and Helen
felt the force of his personality full blast. "You find out
who the socialists are who sweet-talked my daughter into
joining them. And I'll let you have free run of any Murchison Brothers coal patch you care to write about."

Her breath caught in her throat. The predatory glint in
Murchison's eyes warned her he'd deliberately baited her
to this offer, but it was still too enticing to resist. "Your
word of honor as a businessman?" she demanded.

"My word of honor."

Articles on the effects of the coal strike. Articles on the

economics of the company store. Articles on worker injuries and unfair labor practices and all the social injustices that hit hardest in the isolated towns owned lock, stock, and barrel by the coal companies. Articles almost as satisfying as the one she couldn't write about the railroad corrupting the coal miners union.

"All right." Helen thrust a handshake onto Charles Murchison before he could pull away, using enough unnecessary force in her grip to wring an approving grunt from him. "It's a deal, Mr. Murchison. I'll start looking for your daughter first thing tomorrow."

THREE

Since he'd been transferred to Tarentum back in January, Milo Kachigan had dodged trolleys full of coal miners on his way to work in the morning and watched shadowy coal barges float down the Allegheny River on his way home again at night. He'd warmed his leftover supper on the coal stove in his boardinghouse kitchen and then lain awake listening to the late-night thunder of coal tipples up and down the valley. He'd paid for deliveries of coal to the Detectives' Bureau, and filled their dusty scuttle with big lumps of bituminous more times than he could remember. But he'd never been inside a coal mine until now.

"We found the body about an hour after the last shift left." Bernard Flinn's booming voice threw hollow echoes back from each dark mine heading they passed. The mantrip they were riding in, a squat open-sided railcar with seats only six inches higher than its cold metal floor, was picking up speed as it rumbled down the sloping main drift of the Bull Creek Mine. Already, Kachigan could no longer hear the whine of its electric traction motor over the rattle of its metal wheels on the track. The presence of this startlingly modern conveyance at Sedgwick Coal & Coke had surprised him at first, until he'd counted how many men the single car could carry. At only sixteen miners a trip, it would probably take an entire twelve-hour shift to shuttle all the workers to their headings. More likely, the man-trip car was reserved for the foremen and mining engineers, leaving the actual coal miners to trudge their own way in and out as they had always done.

"Who found the body? The outgoing shift?"

"Hell, no." The white glare of Flinn's modern carbide lamp flashed painfully across Kachigan's eyes, making it hard to see the police chief's scowl. "What kind of idiot do you think I am? Would I have gone to the trouble of not mentioning anything about a dead body in my telegram if half of West Tarentum already knew about it? I'm prudent, Kachigan, not paranoid."

"Then who found him?"

"I sent a police sweep through the mine after the last union men left, to make sure they hadn't sabotaged any roof trusses or disconnected any pumps. One of the guards found the body."

It told you all you needed to know about labor relations in the Allegheny coalfields, Kachigan thought wryly, that Bernard Flinn considered those actions prudent rather than paranoid. "Is that why the coal dust is so thick down here? Because the air pumps were turned off?"

Flinn's laugh became a cough before it even had time to echo in the man-trip. The haze of coal dust that hung in the mine had grown noticeably thicker as they descended, turning from a faint prickle at the back of the throat to a choking assault on each breath, as bad as downtown Pittsburgh in the grip of its worst winter smoke. Before the coal policeman could recover his voice, the third shadowy figure in the dark car stirred.

"There's no air pump in this mine, sir," said Riley. "If there was, all the side passages would be blocked with doors or canvas curtains, to keep the good air moving through the active cuts. I think Mr. Flinn was talking about the water pumps that keep it from flooding."

"Thanks, Owen." Kachigan hadn't deliberately picked the Tarentum native to accompany him to the underground murder site, he'd just been the only one willing to come. Nevertheless, it was good to have someone along who knew enough about coal mining to pick up on the anomalies Kachigan might miss. And to show him how to clip on the paraffin lamp that went with his borrowed miner's cap. It still felt like he wore a miniature watering can on his forehead, but at least Kachigan could look around without getting scorched by the flame from the metal spout. The old-fashioned lamp was nowhere near as steady or as focused as Flinn's headlamp, but Pittsburgh Coal apparently had only enough carbide lights for top management to wear.

The man-trip squealed to a stop, the sharp smell of scorched metal curling back in on them until the driver released his brake. A silence descended afterward, but it was not as complete as Kachigan had expected. The empty mine talked to itself constantly, in drips and trickles and splashes of water, in muffled groans of settling timbers and even the occasional clatter of falling stones. Trying not to think about how many hundreds of feet of solid rock sat on top of his head, Kachigan followed Flinn out of the man-trip. When he tried to straighten up, however, his soft padded cap thumped against the low rock ceiling, sliding a shower of loose shale down the back of his collar. Kachigan reached up to rub his smarting head, felt the warning heat of his paraffin lamp, and settled for cursing instead.

Riley slid out beside him, keeping his own head carefully bent. "You all right, sir?"

"Fine." Kachigan glanced around, not easy to do when you were hunched over like a skulking dog with the nape of your neck pressed against cold damp rock. The combined glow of their paraffin lamps illuminated an intersection of two mine passages, each side pocked with hollow shadows where coal had once been dug. A coffin-shaped mining machine occupied one of those empty niches, trailing thick black cables up to the roof's knob-and-nail electric line. Kachigan wondered why, if Sedgwick Coal & Coke had electrified this mine, they hadn't bothered to put in electric light fixtures as well. Then he remembered the coal cars outside, loaded to a flat four and a half feet to match the mine height. That left no room for electric bulbs on the ceilings.

"The body's hidden behind that mining machine?" he asked, studying the massive chunk of industrial machinery. Nothing about it looked out of place, and there was no trickle or trace of blood to be seen in the dust that had settled over its gouged tracks. He glanced back at Bernard Flinn suspiciously. He couldn't see much of the other man's face below the glare of his carbide lamp, but the lazy way he had squatted against the front of the man-trip car suggested that being hundreds of feet underground didn't bother him. "How did your policemen ever find it there?"

"You tell me," Flinn retorted. "You've got ten minutes to figure it out, before we turn on the cutting machine and get that body out of there."

Kachigan gritted his teeth and crossed to the parked mining machine. Thick coils of cloth-wrapped cables connected it to the overhead knob-and-nail electric line, and he reached out to tug on them the way a company policeman would if he was looking for evidence of sabotage. They barely moved in response, their droop weighted down by something more than mere gravity. He peered around the edge of the dust-furred machinery and saw the out-flung arm, its canvas glove caught on the connecting cables by the coal-stained cuff.

"Smart-ass," said Bernard Flinn.

"You haven't moved him at all since you found him?" Kachigan leaned as far as he could into the foot of space that surrounded the mining machine in its rock enclosure. His wavering paraffin flame threw just enough light to show him dark streaks where the layers of greasy dust on the machine's lid had been rubbed away by the passage of a body. All he could see of the crumpled form itself was the gleam of the wickedly thin knife that stuck out from its back.

"How could we? Does it look like any of my guards could get behind that machine?"

Kachigan eyed the foot of space between the cutting machine and the lumpy shale above it. A long metal bolt stuck out of the roof-rock in one place, but it was off-center enough to leave him room. "I think I can," he said. "Riley, come over here. I'm going to need a shove."

The young detective obeyed him without question, although the paraffin light flickering on his forehead revealed a puzzled look. Kachigan didn't bother wasting time with explanations. Instead, he took off his own mining cap and handed it to Riley, then turned his head sideways and squirmed into the space between the machine and the mine roof. More shale fell down the back of his collar from above, and from below he could feel coal dust and grease scraping off on his woolen coat and vest. The Chinese laundry on Corbet Street was going to charge him triple for this.

"All right, Riley." His voice was necessarily muffled, since his cheek was pressed hard against the cold metal lid of the coal-cutter to keep his other ear from tearing off. "Shove."

The tentative push against the soles of his shoes barely added to his forward momentum. Kachigan lifted his head against the cold rock roof long enough to growl, "*Harder!*"

"But I think you're going to hit—" Riley's uncertain voice broke off as Kachigan was shoved ruthlessly across the top of the coffin-shaped machine, scraping his shoulder against the jutting metal spike hard enough to add a mending bill to his laundry charges. He didn't complain, since that shove had also freed him at last from the clinging embrace of metal and rock. He grabbed hold of a four-foot cutting blade edged with blunt chain links and pulled himself carefully sideways, so he could stretch a leg down to solid ground and slide off without stepping on the body he'd come to examine.

"You all right?" That was Flinn's voice, not Riley's, accompanied by a beam of carbide-bright light refracting through the narrow opening.

"My suit coat's missing a sleeve, but I've still got the arm that goes in it." Kachigan reached out to retrieve his cap with its wavering paraffin flame. "I don't suppose you'd lend me your carbide light?"

"Why don't you just pull the guy off the blade, so we can move the coal-cutter without splattering him across the mine? Then you can have all our lights."

"All right." The empty echoes of Flinn's voice had already told Kachigan the passageway extended far behind him into darkness. He paused a moment before he moved the dead man, eyeing the pool of still wet blood that darkened the scraped steel cutting blade. Although the awkward twist of torso and neck suggested the murder victim had been dead before he'd been stuffed back here, the amount of blood spilled around his body meant death must have occurred shortly before disposal. What hadn't spilled anywhere was wax, although the paraffin lamp on his miner's cap was completely empty. Kachigan wondered if the molten contents had poured out when the man had first been struck down.

"Riley, look around on the floor out there before they start up the coal-cutter," he ordered. "Do you see a pool of hardened wax anywhere?"

The army-brisk sound of quartering footsteps again made Kachigan grateful that the newest detective had elected to come with him. Neither Taggart nor Frick could have performed that highly efficient sweep. "Not here in the main intersection, sir," Riley reported after another moment. "Should I look farther away?"

"As long as you don't get out of sight of our lights. I don't want you getting lost." Kachigan pulled the body free of the coal-cutter's blade, trying to disturb it as little as possible. "All right, Flinn, you can start the cutting machine now."

He'd thought he'd known, from his stint in a Monessen steel mill several years ago, just how loud modern industrial machinery could be. But those immense cranes and conveyors had roared their noise out into the equally immense space around the blast furnaces. The rumble of this coal-cutter's electric motor probably wasn't anywhere near as loud, but when the dust-choked scream of chain links being whirled at high speed around the blade was compressed into an area four feet high and barely any wider, the fierce vibration of sound slammed pain deep into Kachigan's ears and made the shard of metal buried in his cheekbone resonate with an excruciating internal buzz. He covered his ears and turned his back to the noise, but the pain didn't fade until the machine had been wheeled around the corner by their man-trip operator and parked out of sight. Even after the sound of its cutting blade stopped, his cheekbone hummed in sympathetic vibration for a long time.

"So, what do we have?" The beam of Flinn's carbide angled downward as he stooped to enter the vacated passage. He joined Kachigan beside the body, squatting down close enough for him to hear the hiss of the gas being generated by the contact of carbide with water in his lamp. The reflected glow of the flame swept across the coal-stained miner's overalls to fasten on the dead man's face. "Hunky, eh?"

"Slovak or Croatian," Kachigan said, although he wasn't sure why he bothered to correct the police chief. No matter how clearly he could read ethnic identity in the slant of facial bones, the curvature of a nose, or the particular crinkle of an eye, to a man like Bernard Flinn all Eastern Europeans were still "Hunkies." "Do you recognize him?"

Flinn snorted. "I told you, Kachigan, I don't know all the men who work for me by sight. Just the troublemakers."

"So this man wasn't a troublemaker?"

"No." Flinn prodded the dead man with a toe, turning his face more clearly into the light of his carbide. The brown hair, pale staring eyes, and big blunt nose were unfamiliar to Kachigan too, although he had no difficulty recognizing the type. There were a lot of Slovakians mining coal along this stretch of the Allegheny Valley. "Looks like he was one of the longtime veterans, though. You see the black marks on his forehead?"

Kachigan frowned and bent over the dead man. The brighter light of Flinn's headlamp showed him a thin spiderweb of lines, even blacker than the man's coal-smudged skin. "What are they?"

"Coal creases. The dust works its way into your skin after you've been mining for a while, and it just won't come out. It's especially bad for the machine men." Flinn waved at the thicker haze of the dust that had been thrown up by the spinning chain-link blades. "They've got the dirtiest job in the mine."

"Do you think that's what this man was? One of your cutting-machine operators?" That would narrow his possible identity down to one among a handful of skilled workers, rather than the hundreds of ordinary miners.

"Could have been." The coal policeman pulled one limp arm up into the light to scrutinize the type of glove the dead man wore. It was his intent curiosity, rather than his previous disavowals, that convinced Kachigan he truly didn't know the identity of their murder victim. "But they usually make enough money to wear padded leather gloves, not this cheap canvas. I'd say this guy was just an ordinary miner."

Kachigan nodded and leaned over the corpse, sliding a hand down into the nearest pocket of his overalls. Flinn swung his carbide light down to see what he was doing, then grunted in amusement. "Looks like Big Roge McGara finally taught you what to look for on a murder victim, Kachigan. You're not going to get any walking-around money off this guy, though. Our miners usually keep their wallets back in their changing room baskets, along with their day clothes."

"I know." He'd left Art Taggart and J.P. Frick fighting over who would get to guard the prisoner and who would have to lower down those hundreds of baskets, hung on ropes from the rafters of the cold changing shed, to see if any still contained day clothes instead of dirty overalls. "I'm looking for the coal checks miners use to tag the cars they load. We should be able to use the number to identify him, provided he didn't use them all up during his shift."

"Or trade them away to other miners for favors," Flinn said in annoyance. "I'll load a car for you while you spread some union bullshit, you load a car for me while I take a nap.''

''What are you complaining about? You get your coal either way.'' Both back pockets of the dead man's overalls were empty, except for lint and flakes of shale. Kachigan withdrew his hand and gently turned the corpse over, careful not to disturb the stiletto still embedded in the blood-stained back.

''I'd get more coal if they would quit wasting time with their damned union politics.'' Flinn's big voice bounced frustrated echoes off the mine walls. ''I never thought I'd say a good word about the steel workers' union, but at least they didn't split into twenty factions and fight with each other worse than they fought with management—''

He broke off, just as Kachigan's fingers touched a scatter of thin metal disks and what felt like a soft wad of crumpled paper in the dead man's hip pocket. He pulled both out to examine, but the brighter carbide glow of Flinn's headlamp had swung away. From out in the main mine passage, a young voice was shouting in muffled excitement.

''—found something, sir, I think it tells us who he was. Detective Kachigan, can you hear me? I think I know who the dead man was!''

''I'd better go see what—'' Flinn stood up too abruptly and banged his own padded cap against the mine roof. The resulting spate of Irish curses made Kachigan feel a little better, but it wasn't until his eyes adjusted to the weaker glow of his own paraffin headlamp that he felt a satisfying jolt of vindication.

''Detective Kachigan!'' Owen Riley's voice lost its cloud of echoes as the younger man skidded into view. ''I found the lump of wax you said to look for, and this was lying in the dust right beside it.'' He lifted an unlit lantern, cylindrical and punctured at numerous intervals along its polished brass walls. It had a glass casing at the bottom, but looked like it wouldn't throw much light.

''What is it, Riley?''

''A gas-detecting lantern, sir.'' Riley looked as proud as if he'd invented the device instead of just finding it. ''It brightens up whenever coal gas is present in the mine air, but it doesn't make it explode. The fire-boss of the mine is usually the only one who carries it.''

Kachigan whistled softly, pleased to have more pieces falling into place. "Do you know who your fire-boss is, Flinn?"

"There's a different one for each shift. The payroll clerk can tell you who would have been down here today." Flinn was scowling at the gas-detection lantern as if it had made matters worse instead of better. Perhaps for him it had, Kachigan reflected. Just because the coal police chief didn't know a particular murder victim didn't mean he wasn't neck-deep in the whole mess. "But the fire-boss usually goes in to check for gas an hour before the work-shift starts and then leaves an hour before it ends. Why would this one have stayed late enough to catch that scab coming into the mine?"

"Because someone made it worth his while." Kachigan held up the lump of soft paper he'd found along with the coal checks in the fire-boss's back pocket. The brighter gleam of the carbide lamp turned his way and brightened it to the unmistakable grayish-green of money. "I haven't counted it yet, but it looks like about two hundred dollars."

"It was a meet," J.P. Frick said stubbornly. "The dead guy owed the Black Hand a payoff and the dago here was the pick-up man." He prodded the shoulder of the young man he was guarding and got a resigned look of incomprehension in return. "They argued over the amount of the payment and the dago won, because he had a knife. What's wrong with that?"

Kachigan scrubbed a hand across his cheekbone, trying to scrub away the pain. The long bumpy ride back out of Bull Creek's mine had strengthened the headache the coal-cutting machine had started, and Frick's loud voice wasn't helping it go away. He couldn't decide if the older detective was being deliberately obtuse to annoy him or if he honestly couldn't see the holes in his theory.

"The main problem, Jape, is that the victim wasn't Italian," Taggart said from the dark backseat of the trolley, where Kachigan had thought he was sleeping. "I don't know about where you come from, but back in the East Pittsburgh Valley the Black Hand never picked on anyone but their own."

"Kachigan *says* he wasn't Italian," Frick said, his voice somehow managing to express good-humored tolerance and complete disbelief at the same time. "I guess he thinks he's an expert because he's got a dago girlfriend—"

Kachigan felt his face tighten. "That's not—"

"I saw the body, when they brought him out of the mine," Taggart said. "He sure looked Slovenian to me."

"Slovak," Riley corrected.

The elderly trolley driver cleared his throat and glanced back at them. "You boys said the dead man was a fire-boss here at Bull Creek, didn't you?"

"Yes, sir," Riley said.

"Well, then, you're exactly right. As far as I know, all Bull Creek's fire-bosses are Slovak."

Kachigan straightened in his seat. "You know all of them personally?"

"Nah. I got twenty different men in this car every day, the number of trolleys we run when the mine's working full-shift." A faint glimmer of lights was starting to show through the fog and darkness, as Bull Creek's narrow valley opened out toward the Allegheny River. "But Slovaks are the biggest gang working that particular mine, so of course that's who they pick the fire-bosses from."

"Why?" Taggart asked.

"The men have to trust 'em with their lives, that's why. It's the fire-bosses that tell them there's no white damp, or black damp, or gas, in the place where they're going to mine. Who do you think they'd rather believe, some pie-smacker like me or one of their own?"

"Pie-smacker," Frick repeated. "What the hell is that?"

"Johnny Bull," the old man said dryly. "English."

Through the fog-beaded window, the highest hillside houses of Tarentum were coming into view. Some of the windows glowed gold with gaslight, while others burned a brighter electric hue. This was the town's richest section, at the very top of the east side where the merchants and mine-managers lived. The coal barons themselves had moved down the river to more elegant resort towns like Oakmont and Aspinwall.

"Too bad we don't have a Polk Directory," Kachigan said, almost to himself. "We could get out right here and have a talk with Sedgwick's paymaster. We know the dead man's coal check number was fifty-three—"

Frick groaned. "Kachigan, it's after ten! Can't we leave the poor man alone until tomorrow morning? He's probably got a wife and children."

"And the dead coal miner probably does too!" Kachigan snapped. Helen Sorby had managed to instill the rudiments of social conscience in him over these last few months. "I'd like to find them before the rumors of a murdered fire-boss travel through town."

"No one will hear it from me," the trolley driver assured him. "I live over in New Ken."

"Thanks, but you're not who I'm worried about." Kachigan tried to give Frick a meaningful look, but the older detective had busied himself unlocking the prisoner's handcuffs from the seat-rail and relocking them behind his back. The mute Italian boy barely seemed to notice the difference. His thin face, shiny with bruises and darkening fast, was turned resolutely toward the window. Kachigan wondered if he was hoping to see a fellow Italian who could intercede for him, or if he was just trying to ignore his captors.

The Bull Creek trolley clattered down the last of the hillside track, then bumped over connecting rails to join the main line. A flat strip of floodplain stretched ahead and behind them now, seamed with company tenements and Tarentum's modest sprawl of steel and glass factories. The reflections from their fire-bright chimneys turned the Allegheny into a glowing ribbon, one that stretched from the saltworks up at Natrona down to the aluminum-plating mills of New Kensington.

"What the hell is going on?" The trolley seat creaked

under Art Taggart's considerable weight, pulling Kachigan's attention back from the river to Tarentum's business district. The streetcar line began to parallel the railroad here, both of them fitting easily into the unusually wide street that marked the site of the former Pennsylvania Canal. Usually, there was more than enough room left beside the tracks for carts and carriages to pass, but despite the late hour, Kachigan could see that horse traffic was backed up almost to the bridge over Bull Creek. After a moment, their trolley also braked to a halt, far short of the town hall and lockup that was their destination.

"Men on the line," their driver said succinctly. "Miners."

"A lot of them?" Riley leaned over to peer out the window, pressing his nose and wine-stained cheek up against the glass as curiously as if he were ten years younger. "Do you think they're celebrating having a night off from work?"

"Afraid not, Owen," Kachigan said. Even from here, he could hear the irregular thunder of men chanting and shouting, and it didn't sound like a religious revival. He made a mental note to kick a certain annoying union activist in the pants. "I'd say they're having a rally for the coal strike."

Riley gave him a startled look. "Right here in town? Are they allowed to do that?"

"Not unless the town magistrate gave them permission after we left for Bull Creek."

Taggart turned around from the trolley's back window. "It looks like Saturday at the pay-window all the way from here to the town hall. If we want to get our boy into the lockup before tomorrow morning, we'll have to walk."

Frick hauled the prisoner upright. "Good thing you listened to me and brought the shotguns."

Kachigan gritted his teeth against the pain that irritation jabbed into his cheekbone. "You can't have yours," he said flatly. "You're going to need both hands to hang on to the prisoner."

"No, I'm not." Frick shoved the baffled-looking Italian

boy across the trolley aisle instead of down it. "From now on, that's Riley's job."

Kachigan didn't bother fighting with him. He reached out for Riley's shotgun and handed it to the trolley driver. "This should help you get back to the car garage," he said. "Bring it back to our detectives' office tomorrow, and we'll have your tip waiting for you."

"Sure," the older man said, not sounding as if he really believed it. Or perhaps it was their ability to get through the union rally in one piece that he doubted. Still, he took the shotgun gratefully enough, and waited until all the detectives were clear of the steps before backing the car down the tracks.

The hole the trolley had left in the crowd vanished in minutes, the smell of sweat and coal dust closing as thick around them as the milling mine workers. Kachigan had been in crowds of strikers before, but these staring eyes seemed to belong to the night rather than to individual people. The miners wore their day clothes, not their overalls, but the combination of coal-smudged faces and beer-breath told Kachigan they had come straight from work to the downtown bars. He could almost believe this unscheduled rally was just the result of closing time, except that in industrial Tarentum most bars stayed open until at least one or two in the morning.

"We're not here to break up the rally," he told the circle of men tightening around his wary detectives. "All we want to do is escort this prisoner to the lockup."

That sparked a chorus of derisive voices.

"Can't you find enough criminals in town? You have to import them on the trolley?"

"You think he's beat-up enough, or do you want us to pound on him a little more?"

"What are you arresting him for? Working overtime?"

"Takes four of you yellow dogs to handle one miner, huh?"

Kachigan gritted his teeth again. "We're not coal police," he said, bracing his feet against the jostling crowd. "And he's not a coal miner."

"Oh, no?" This voice was more belligerent. "I guess he's wearing a padded cap just to keep his head warm, eh?"

"No." Kachigan took a deep breath, not seeing any way around the truth. "He's a scab."

The barely seen mass of bodies clenched tight around them, just as he'd expected them to. Kachigan found himself with his back slammed up against their prisoner and only the gleaming barrier of his shotgun barrel between himself and the mob. Riley and Taggart managed to close ranks with him, pressed elbow to elbow in a triangle around the Italian boy, while Frick cursed and tried to struggle against the crowd that was pushing him farther away.

"Smart move, Milo," Taggart said beneath his breath. "I can't wait to see what you're going to do next."

Kachigan reached for the full-throated shout he'd used to cut through the hubbub of ethnic social clubs and the chaos of snarled horse traffic back when he was a police patrolmen. "*Quit shoving!* We're not bringing him in to work, we're arresting him for crossing union lines!" That wasn't strictly true, since Bull Creek wasn't actually being picketed by the coal miners' union yet, but Kachigan didn't think Flinn would mind if he stretched the truth. "Do you want us to lock him up and make an example of him? Or would you rather get locked up yourselves?"

That drew an explosion of laughter, but no lessening of pressure. "How you going to arrest us, you damned cossack?" called back one reckless voice. "You don't even know us."

Someone shoved at Kachigan's left elbow, slewing him sideways around the prisoner. "*He* may not know you, Nicky Kozubal, but I do!" The scorn in Owen Riley's voice more than made up for his less-powerful shout. "And if you're not smart enough to know the difference between the state police and the County Detectives' Bureau, maybe you'd better go back and finish fourth grade after all!"

"*Spaghetti-face?*" One of the miners shoved his way forward, peering up at the younger detective. His light-colored eyes looked particularly disembodied in his coal-dusted face. "When the hell did they let you out of the army?"

"About a month ago, you dumb Polack." If the reference to his reddish birthmark bothered Riley, his voice didn't show it. "If you bothered to do anything outside the pit except drink beer and board the wife—" He broke off, sliding an embarrassed look across at Kachigan. "Sorry about that, sir."

"That's all right." The exchange of hometown pleasantries had done more to vent the pressure and cool off the mob than any of Kachigan's logical arguments. He tested the unspoken truce with a single forward step. The grudging wedge of space that opened in front of him wasn't much, but it gave him room to haul the prisoner forward to face the crowd. "I'd like you to look at this man and tell me if you recognize him. He doesn't seem to speak English. Is he from around here?"

The miners fell silent more abruptly than he'd expected, so silent that he could hear a distant female voice singing the praises of the Industrial Workers of the World. Kachigan couldn't read enough expression in their carbon-dark faces to decide if what they were feeling was surprise, bewilderment, or fear. Before he could ask, the answer to his question dropped out of the sky behind his back.

"No one from around here would work as a coal mine scab, Detective Kachigan. They'd never get a shot and a beer in this town again."

Kachigan swung around, scowling at the sound of that annoyingly familiar voice. Atop the high stone wall that rimmed Canal Street's upper side, a lithe figure sat like a leprechaun, kicking one heel restlessly against the stones. He wore the same collarless flannel work-shirt and cheap trousers as the rest of the crowd, but his clean, freckled face—and the gleam of a real gold crucifix around his bare throat—showed just how far in the past his mining days were.

"As if you'd know, Danny Boy," Taggart retorted, before Kachigan could reply. "When we arrested you for vandalism last week, you told us you had just come in from Chicago.''

''Only my latest trip of many.'' The union organizer vaulted down from the wall in one easy leap, the crowd parting to let him through as respectfully as if he were a younger version of Moses. Kachigan had patrolled enough labor rallies in the South Side to have seen that kind of charisma before, in men like John Mitchell and Frank Feehan. But only Leon Daniels combined that confidence with the annoying charm of a prep-school graduate. He swore he'd worked in an Illinois coal mine in his youth, but Kachigan suspected Daniels had still managed to get considerably more than a fourth-grade education. ''And I wasn't committing vandalism. I was using the sidewalk to call attention to the kind of living conditions the coal companies around here consider fit for their workers.''

''With a can of paint and lot of expletives,'' Kachigan reminded him. ''Both of which violate town ordinances.''

''Then why wasn't it the town constables who arrested me?'' Daniels inquired. His eyes sparkled with amusement at their silence. ''Could it be because the County Detectives' Bureau doesn't want a coal strike to mess up their lovely payoffs?''

''No,'' Kachigan said sharply. ''It's because you picked the sidewalk in front of the county lockup to vandalize first!''

The labor organizer gave him a mischievous leprechaun's smile. ''I always like to know what I'm up against when there are new policemen in town.'' He glanced at the silent Italian boy in their custody, and his exasperating smile widened. ''Although I guess I don't need to worry too much, if you don't know any better than to start arresting scabs.''

Taggart and Kachigan exchanged puzzled looks. ''You *don't* think we should arrest strikebreakers?'' the big detective asked at last. ''Why not?''

''Because you're going to need a jail as big as a skyscraper to put them in, if you arrest them all,'' Daniels retorted. ''The mine operators will be shipping Greeks and

Negroes up here by the trainload, as soon as they realize we're serious about this strike.''

Kachigan glanced back at the curly-haired prisoner, who'd made no attempt to struggle out of Riley's vigilant grip. "No Italians?"

That brought a snort not just from Daniels but also from the men around him. "Not a lot of Italian boys work underground, Detective Kachigan. They'll shovel coal at the tipple or load barges until their backs break, but they don't like being out of the sun." He glanced at the young Italian again. "Are you sure this kid's really a scab? Maybe he was a tipple-worker just off the boat and didn't realize the strike was starting tonight."

"Maybe," Kachigan said. "But whoever he is, I've still got to hold him as the witness to a crime." He glanced out at the watchful circle of coal miners, debating how much information to release and how much to allow out into this crowd of potential informants. Bernard Flinn might want to keep tonight's murder a secret, but that was because his first loyalty was to the coal company that paid him, not to the service of justice. But when he picked Kachigan to be his scapegoat, the coal police chief had lost control of the information whether he liked it or not.

"Someone killed the fire-boss up at Bull Creek Mine tonight," Kachigan said. "This boy may be the only one who saw the murder."

The announcement made Daniels whistle in surprise, but elicited only a puzzled mutter from the miners around them.

"The fire-boss, you say?" Riley's friend Kozubal pushed forward again to stare at him. "You mean Mikal Sterchek?"

Kachigan wished he could reach for his evidence book, but he couldn't hold it and write while he was still hanging on to his shotgun. "Was he the fire-boss who worked the last shift up at Bull Creek today?"

"Yeah, I'm pretty sure . . . here, wait a minute." Kozubal ducked back into the crowd, making it stir and mutter around him. He emerged a few moments later hauling with him a stocky older man whose shoulders were hunched in a permanent coal miner's crouch. Even through the usual coating of coal dust, Kachigan could see the thick black lines ingrained into the furrows of this miner's good-natured face. "Yeah, he says he was."

"And this man is . . ." Kachigan glanced over his shoulder at Taggart, knowing his indolent partner was more than equal to the task of remembering several complex ethnic names provided he was actually paying attention.

"Sterchek," the younger miner said impatiently.

"I know that's the fire-boss, but . . ." Kachigan's voice faded as he realized why the miners looked so puzzled and Taggart so surprised. He turned back to stare at the older miner. "You're Mikal Sterchek," he said, not making it a question.

"Sure am. And I been fire-boss for the day-shift up at Bull Creek, going on eight years now." He slanted a good-natured grin at Kachigan, neck stretching awkwardly to meet his gaze. "I had lots of rocks drop on my head and got kicked by mules more times than I can count. But so far as I know, I never yet been murdered."

FOUR

Helen Sorby normally liked Oakmont. Free of smoke and far upstream from Pittsburgh's typhoid-laden rivers but still a convenient trolley ride out of the city, the little resort town had managed to attract a growing number of middle- and upper-class families without ever quite becoming stylish. Its summer homes sat along the main line of the Allegheny Valley Railroad, which carried carloads of coal, glass, and aluminum right through the middle of town day and night. The scatter of shops built to cater to the summer trade shared the Allegheny River floodplain with a boiler works and an old apple orchard, relics of the town's industrial and rural past. Even College Avenue, around the corner from Aunt Pat's modest yellow-brick cottage on Isabella Street, led to a tool works rather than an institute of higher learning.

But no matter how much it pleased Helen's socialist sensibilities to see a middle-class resort sprouting between the working-class tenements of Verona and Point Breeze, on the morning of April first she would have preferred Oakmont to be part of Pittsburgh's exclusive East End. Every road in and out of town was choked with wagons carrying furniture; every seat on the train was so loaded with bundled belongings that all the passengers had to stand. Even the ubiquitous streetcars were stuffed full of people, not to mention yipping dogs on strings, squawking birds in paper-bagged cages, cats and babies wrapped alike in ragged blankets, yowling in indignation. April first was moving day, when every tenement landlord in Pittsburgh released renters from their yearly leases and allowed them to move elsewhere. Despite one ranting editorial after another in the city papers, no landlord ever changed the date on that release for fear their lodgings would be the only ones left uninhabited.

Thomas had warned Helen it would take her hours just to get through the city and even more time to travel north to Oakmont, especially since the chipboard suitcase she was taking for her stay made her look just like one of the dispossessed. "Try not to yell at anyone with luggage," he'd advised her, when she'd insisted on heading out into the Tuesday morning drizzle. "They can't help it that they only have one day to move."

"I know that," Helen said indignantly. "I wrote an editorial about it last year in *The Masses*."

"Yes, but just wait until you're stuck on a trolley with a *studa bubba* and all her chickens," her twin said ominously. "Or with an old *paesan*' and a barrel of dago red that keeps rolling on your toes."

"Thomas, you shouldn't call people by ethnic labels."

"Tell me that again on the telephone tonight," was all he said before handing her a battered umbrella. "If you have enough voice left to talk with, that is."

Helen had managed not to yell at any of the dispossessed or make any ethnic slurs in the three hours she'd been traveling. She had not managed to keep her temper, however. Both her throat and her head ached from the vehement argument she'd had with a trolley driver over his refusal to allow an old Hungarian lady to bring along her pots of peppers, started with seeds she'd carried from the old country. It had taken the full ringing strength of Helen's voice—and all the money she had in her pocketbook—to get the herbage aboard.

The roof of Hulton Station came into view a block farther down the trolley tracks. Helen rang the wire bell several times so the driver could hear it through the hubbub
of the crowded car, but she still ended up getting off at the
corner of G Street, a block beyond her destination. Fortunately, the drizzle had tapered to gray April clouds by then
and the brisk walk back to the Oakmont branch of the Carnegie Free Library, lugging her suitcase all the way, drove
away the early spring chill. Despite the hours it had taken
Helen to get here from the South Side, it still was techni-
cally morning, and she knew better than to show up at her
aunt's cottage. Pat McGregor had only one firm rule in
life—she refused to bestir herself from her cat-festooned
bed until luncheon was steaming on the table. In the meantime, guests were relegated to the company of either her
taciturn Irish serving maid or her annoyingly friendly cats.
Helen preferred to spend her time a little more productively.

"Oh, dear." A librarian whose deep auburn hair looked
as if it had come from a henna bottle glanced up from the
library desk when Helen entered. Her shirtwaist was elab-
orately frilled in elegant tones of mint-green and gray, and
it pinched her into painfully perfect proportions. Helen
wondered how she ever managed to shelve books. "You
can't come in here, miss."

Helen paused on the threshold, frowning. She knew her
brown wool skirts and russet coat weren't up to Oakmont's
fashionable middle-class standard, but she didn't think a
free public library, created by a millionaire steel magnate
for the betterment of his workers, should have a dress code.
"Why not?" she asked. "Is the library closed for moving
day?"

"You want to *use* the library?" The librarian screwed
up her face, not in scorn but to focus more clearly on the
new arrival. She should have worn glasses if her eyes were
that weak, Helen decided, but they probably wouldn't have
looked elegant enough. "I'm sorry, dear, I saw your suitcase and thought you came in to rest while you waited for
the train. If we let one person do that, you know, we'd
have a whole crowd in here."

"And that would be terrible," Helen agreed. The quiet buzz of electric lights in the silence told her just how deserted the building was. When he'd funded his plethora of free libraries, Andrew Carnegie hadn't taken into account the fact that most industrial workers still put in over seventy hours of work a week, leaving them precious little time to sleep, much less read. "Someone might pick up a book and read it while they waited."

Her sarcasm seemed to evaporate right off the fashionable librarian, still peering at her with nearsighted intensity. "You're Mrs. McGregor's niece, aren't you? Helen Sorby, the lady who writes for *McClure's Magazine* and *Collier's*?"

"Yes." Helen was a little surprised by that recognition. She had only visited Oakmont a few times since Pat McGregor had bought her cottage back in February, and she'd never stopped in the library before. Of course, for all she knew her doting aunt carried around her latest article on women in the electric trades and showed her published photograph to everyone she met. "My aunt's invited me to stay in Oakmont with her for a few days. I'd like to do some research in the library while I'm here."

"Oh, dear," the librarian said again. She sounded more worried this time, as if she was afraid she might inspire a muckraking article on the deficiencies of branch libraries. "I'm afraid we don't have very extensive back-holdings— we just opened our doors a year ago, you know. But our subscription list is very solid, and we have all the new bestsellers from the *Book Digest*. Including four copies of Nellie Bingham Van Slingerland's novel, *Toshimytsu Mayeda*," she added, brightening. "Such a wonderful depiction of life in another land. I don't suppose you'd like to look at that?"

"I was actually more interested in Jack London's new book, *The War of the Classes*. Do you have that in your collection?"

"Oh, I think so. People always like his nature books." The librarian rustled out from behind her counter with measured, breathless steps and led Helen back to the half-empty shelves. By the time they reached the "L's", Helen could see one unworn volume standing out among the well-thumbed copies of *White Fang* and *Call of the Wild*. The red-haired librarian pulled it out and handed it to her. "It's odd, but for some reason this one doesn't seem to circulate much."

"Really?" Hoping she looked only casually interested, Helen turned over the book's front cover. As she had suspected, the Oakmont library had adopted the modern system of tucking a cardboard slip into each book to record its travels, rather than keeping their lending list in a bound ledger. The card told her Jack London's socialist polemic had not been borrowed since a Miss Mary Alice Gorman took it out back in September of 1905. "Perhaps people don't care to read about this particular aspect of nature." She tucked the book beneath her arm to disguise the fact she was done with it. Emmy Murchison must have bought her own copy. "What about Helen Winslow's new book, *The Woman of Tomorrow*? I believe that was a *Book Digest* best-seller."

"I don't think we bought any copies," the Oakmont librarian said dubiously. "Isn't it one of those suffragette books?"

"More of a futurist essay." Helen drummed her fingers against Jack London's cheap leather binding and considered what else she might try. If Nellie Bingham Van Slingerland's syrupy romances were indicative of Oakmont's middle-class reading tastes, perhaps the brilliant idea she'd woken up with this morning wouldn't turn out to be quite so brilliant after all. "What about Olive Harper? Do you have any of her novels in the collection?"

"Perhaps." She rustled her way back down the line of shelves to the "H's," then bent stiffly at the waist and came up breathless but triumphant. The small book she was holding looked as if it had been dunked in a bucket of water and then baked dry on a coal stove, with the cardboard beneath its cheap cloth cover swollen in some places and charred in others. "*A Slave of the Mill*," the librarian read, squinting at the disfigured spine. "By Olive Harper. Is this the one you were interested in?"

"Yes." Helen took the lumpy volume with interest. She knew this searing socialist novel had not been out on the market for more than six months, so its condition couldn't represent the accumulated wear and tear of normal library lending. "It looks like someone didn't take such good care of this."

The elegant librarian let out a tiny puff of indignation, probably all the exhalation her imprisoned lungs could make. "That's the price we pay for being a free lending library, I'm afraid. Not everyone respects what they are given the privilege to borrow."

"Really?" Helen flipped the front cover open, hoping the book's lending card hadn't been lost during its travails. Three signatures, water-smeared and barely readable, were attached to due dates within the month of March, the last one as recent as the 27th. And the middle one was the one she was looking for. "Good heavens," she said, keeping her eyes fixed on the card so she wouldn't have to meet the librarian's gaze as she lied. "I wouldn't have expected Miss Murchison to take such bad care of a book. I've always found her to be such a responsible girl."

"Oh, indeed, she is," the red-haired librarian said warmly. "I don't think she's ever brought a book back so much as a day late in her life. No, it was that friend of hers who abused our lending privileges." She tapped a polished fingernail on the lowest signature. "She said she left it out in the rain, but who would do such a thing in March? No one reads out-of-doors in all that sleet and drizzle."

"Not usually." Helen scrutinized the final signature on the card, but could make out only a first name that began with a "B". She tried fishing with another casual question. "Did you ask the young lady to repay the cost of the book, when she brought it back in this condition?"

"Yes, and do you know what she told me? She said she would have been willing to pay for mistreating Mr. Carnegie's books if he had ever been willing to pay compensation to his mistreated workers. Can you imagine that?"

Helen could, although she thought it better not to say why. Those very words had formed the caption of a political cartoon in the *Progressive Worker's Weekly* last month, beneath the sketch of a dumbfounded Carnegie being handed back a battered book by an equally battered steelworker. It looked as if the Murchisons were right in their suspicions about Emmy's socialist friends. "You couldn't send her parents a bill for the damage?"

The elegant librarian let out an elegant little sniff. "Believe me, I would, if I had any idea who they were. Or where they lived. Tell me, Miss Sorby, can you read that signature?"

"No," Helen admitted.

"Well, neither can anyone else here, and I don't think it's an accident. I think that young lady knew exactly what she was doing when she asked Miss Murchison to show her around the library. Just as I expect she knew exactly what she was doing when she left that book out in the rain." The librarian shook her tinted head. "That's the problem with so many strangers coming through town, you just don't know who you can trust. Are there any other books you need, Miss Sorby?"

"No." Stymied, Helen followed her back to the main desk with two books she had no intention of reading and fading hopes of finding out who Emmy Murchison's militantly socialist friend might be. It wasn't until she dipped the desk pen in its ink-filled base and began signing her own name on the two library cards that it occurred to her to look at the name above Emmy Murchison's as well as the one below. The book might have been recommended to Emmy in much the same way that Emmy recommended it to her unknown friend. The name Helen saw there was so startlingly familiar she could have kicked herself for not having seen it before.

"It's the coal strike, isn't it?" she asked the librarian, who was carefully filling in the date beside her signature. She got back an inquisitive, nearsighted frown.

"What is, dear?"

"All the strangers in town that you were talking about.

They're here because of the coal strike.'' Labor confrontations always tended to attract a little out-of-town attention, usually from roving union organizers. A potentially crippling national strike like this one would attract not only labor organizers but also newspaper reporters, Pinkerton agents, industrial spies, and maybe even Federal troops. ''Is there a tent city or a poor coal patch town around here somewhere?''

The librarian blinked at her. ''Why, yes—Harwick's right across the river, up behind the bluffs. How did you know that, Miss Sorby?''

It was her turn to tap at the lending cards. The flowing signature was now upsidedown but still distinctly recognizable. ''Because Jackson Ecklar never visits anyplace unless there's enough human misery, squalor, and destitution to make a prizewinning photographic essay out of it. And somehow, I don't think Oakmont quite fits the bill.''

She didn't have to worry about convincing Aunt Pat they needed to visit the pit of misery, squalor, and destitution that had drawn Jackson Ecklar's attention. Her wealthy relative was never happier than when she was discovering a new charity to which she could devote her time and her money. She was also an ardent admirer of the New York photographer's visual essays, published in all the major magazines along with his own unsmiling but undeniably handsome portrait. All Helen had to do was mention the possibility of his presence over the luncheon table and Pat McGregor flew into decisive action, dislodging cats and disgruntling her maid with the sudden change of schedule. Within an hour, the afternoon's planned tea had been canceled and they were sitting inside a hired carriage with the livery owner himself at the reins, waiting to disembark from the Hulton ferry.

''I can't imagine why no one in Oakmont ever told me how close we were to Harwick.'' Pittypat peered up at the bluffs that rimmed this side of the Allegheny River as if she expected to see a cataract of human misery pouring down the rocks. "I could have asked all the members of my new clubs to start collecting clothes and food a month ago."

"The coal strike is only one day old," Helen reminded her aunt. "And except for the Pittsburgh local district, there's no settlement anywhere in sight. Unless Teddy Roosevelt sends in Federal troops like he did in 1902, you're going to have plenty of time to organize relief efforts for the miners." She held on tight to avoid sliding across the carriage seat as they rattled down the ferry ramp and then bounced up the graveled road over the riverbank. Her aunt, supported by a strong whalebone corset and the small army of flounces that covered her skirt, barely swayed in her own seat. "We don't even know for sure that the miners at Harwick are out."

Pat McGregor gave her a puzzled look. "Out where, dearest?"

"Out on strike." Helen sighed, but it was at her own stupidity, not her aunt's. One of the hazards of becoming a professional reporter, she'd discovered, was a tendency to pick up all the slang and shortcuts your fellow writers used and then forget that no one else knew them. "I don't know whether Harwick Coal Company is unionized or not, but my impression is that most of the mines along the Allegheny aren't. That's why union organizers call it Black Valley."

"Very true, Miss Sorby." Jake Bailey's booming voice came through the screened panel by his knees, as comfortably as if he sat beside them instead of on the driver's seat overhead. The livery stable owner had been chiming into the conversation ever since they rolled out onto West Railroad Avenue, at times so enthusiastically that Helen suspected him of being a closet socialist. Either that, or a would-be suitor for Patricia McGregor's affections. "Only the big Pittsburgh coal operators and a few progressive owners like Sedgwick let their workers organize. But I wouldn't be surprised if the Harwick miners have walked out, union or no union. They've been on the militant side ever since the disaster."

"Disaster?" Helen and Pittypat asked in unison.

"The Harwick mine disaster." Bailey's voice held the same tone of wonderment that a native of Johnstown might have used if asked about the flood. "Don't tell me you Pittsburgh ladies never heard about it? One hundred and eighty men lost in the worst mine explosion in Pennsylvania history? And then the poor fire-boss and the mining engineer who went in to see who could be saved got killed themselves by the white damp."

"White damp?" Pat McGregor said blankly.

"Carbon monoxide, Aunt Pat. It's the gas that poisons you after a fire." Helen racked her memory for some shred of familiarity with this horrible event. She found none. "Mr. Bailey, when did this disaster happen?" He was a gentleman advanced enough in years that he might be recalling an event from before her birth, or at least before she began reading more than the funny pages of the newspapers.

"Nineteen-aught-four," said the livery stable owner.

There was a pause, then Pat McGregor delicately cleared her throat. "I think you were out of town then, Helen. And by the time you came back from your—er—your trip to Chicago—"

"My honeymoon," Helen said grimly, when her aunt faltered to a stop. Her short-lived marriage to James Foster Barton had ended a few months after it began, when the union organizer she thought she had married turned out to be a confidence man and a bigamist, but there was no point in denying it had ever happened. "I didn't pay much attention to the newspapers for a while after that. I know."

She glanced out the window to avoid her aunt's sympathetic gaze, watching the familiar bluffs retreat back from the river's edge as they traveled farther north. A green mist of newly budded leaves had hazed over the wild brambles along the river, hiding the long narrow island she remembered seeing from her previous trolley trips up the Allegheny. The extent of the change startled Helen. It had only been ten days since she'd stopped coming up to Tarentum—could spring really have arrived in the meantime?

"Did the disaster make the remaining miners want to unionize, Mr. Bailey?" she asked.

"Not right away." He brought the carriage to a stop, waiting for an overloaded trolley with luggage strapped to its roof to lurch into motion ahead of them. They were passing through the tiny scatter of houses Helen knew as the trolley stop of Red Raven, although she had never been sure if that was the name of the town or just the adjacent coal pit. "But after some of the IWW and UMW organizers got to talking to them about safety and work rules and such, it did. They been agitating for a local ever since."

Helen mulled that over, while they rattled down the road in the trolley's wake, eventually passing it when it became bogged down in the traffic-clogged main street of another small river town. Unlike Oakmont, Cheswick was an entirely working-class settlement that had coalesced around glass and metal-plating factories, and it was full of duplexes and rental houses. Every block they passed had at least one wagon parked on a strip of front lawn, with boards sloping down from one end and furniture in various stages of loading or off-loading.

"Is Harwick a company-owned town?"

"You could say so, but I wouldn't go so far as to call it a coal patch." The carriage turned left onto a street that began flat but soon rose to scale the bluffs behind the river. The houses of Cheswick, clinging like moss to the river's edge, fell behind them as they climbed. "It's not like Rural Ridge or Russellton, out in the middle of nowhere with mountains of red-dog piled right up to the back porches. Harwick's close enough to Cheswick that they're even talking about getting a trolley line put in."

"That would put a crimp in the sales of the company store, wouldn't it?"

"Already does. You think people don't walk up and down this hill to the stores in Cheswick, if they can cut their grocery bill in half by doing it?" Bailey slapped the reins on his horses' rumps as they neared the top of the grade, and the clatter of the carriage wheels softened as they passed from river gravel to rain-damp mud. The springs began to creak instead, as the carriage bounced and rocked across the corduroy ridges that western Pennsylvania's red-brown clay made after a winter of freezing and thawing. From her increasingly mud-splattered window, Helen could see long rows of dingy look-alike houses in the distance, the hallmark of a town built cheap and quick by a coal company to keep its workers close to their work. Farther up the slope, a coal tipple lifted its incongruous little shed high into the air above a railroad spur, but no thunder of pouring coal echoed down the long ramp and no railroad cars waited at the base. It looked like the livery stable owner was right in his assessment of Harwick's miners.

"Helen, dearest, look." Aunt Pat leaned across the carriage to point. "Doesn't it seem a little early for a county fair?"

Helen glanced across at the large muddy field that separated the rows of houses from the dark hulking piles of tailings that were heaped along the edge of the hilltop. A flutter of white cloth caught her attention, rising in an unsteady motion around a lifted pole.

"Aunt Pat, those aren't fair tents. Those are where the miners are going to live until the strike is over."

"Why would they want to do that? It may be spring, but it's still so cold out—"

Helen took a deep breath, but Jake Bailey's rumbling voice answered before she could. "They don't have a choice, Missus McGregor. The company owns the houses they rent. If they don't work, they get evicted. And they don't have enough money to stay anywhere else."

Pat McGregor's soft face furrowed with real dismay beneath its dusting of rice powder. "Do the companies fire all their workers then, and hire new ones?"

"No, ma'am." Bailey swung the horses toward that field, then pulled them up as the carriage wheels sank into the rain-soaked ground with an ominous sucking sound. "They'll hire 'em all back, soon as the strike's settled. They just don't see why they should be comfortable in the meantime." He slid down from the driver's seat with a wet thud, then opened the door and peered in at them dubiously. "It's pretty much a swamp out here, ma'am. Do you want to wait while I see if I can find your photographic gentleman for you?"

"That would be very kind, Mr. Bailey—"

"—but unnecessary," Helen finished for her aunt. She gathered her skirts and climbed out of the carriage into the sharp hilltop wind, startled at how much colder it was up here than down in the sheltered river valley. "Why don't you keep my aunt company instead, and tell her what kind of supplies the miners and their families will be needing over the next few weeks. You seem to have an excellent grasp of the situation, Mr. Bailey."

As she'd expected, that suggestion made the weather-beaten livery stable owner look modestly gratified. "I'd be happy to do that, Miss Sorby, so long as you're sure—"

Helen buttoned her coat and tucked her fingers into her sleeves, wishing she had thought to bring gloves. "I'm sure."

"But, dearest, how can you be certain you'll be safe out there?" Pittypat leaned out of the carriage door, looking anxious. Helen steeled herself for a lecture on the dangers of a woman walking unescorted among unruly strikers, since her aunt's social activism never seemed to interfere in the slightest with her middle-class sense of propriety. But Aunt Pat had a more practical danger in mind this time. "After all the rain we got these past few days, that field must be a sea of mud."

"It is." Helen could already feel the cold and damp seeping through the seams of her high-laced shoes. "Don't worry, Aunt Pat, I'll do my best not to slip and fall on my backside. I wouldn't want to get Mr. Bailey's best carriage all dirty."

She left the pair of them protesting that dirt was the least of their concerns, and picked her way across the barely vegetated field toward the distant flutter of tents. The wet ground beneath her feet wasn't soil at all, Helen realized as she heard the odd crunching and sucking noises it made as she stepped through it. It was a flattened pile of burnt-out mine tailings, the loose, hard cinders that Pittsburghers called red-dog. A haze of smoke hung over the uppermost part of the field, where newer heaps of cinders still smoldered despite the dampness. The striking miners were pitching their tents as far from that noxious smoke as they could, but the reek of wet sulfur and burnt rock followed Helen all the way into the milling crowd.

It was an oddly quiet group, for all its disorganization and chaos, with only a few scattered shouts of warning given when one of the tent poles began to rise. Helen watched grim-faced women in shawls and babushkas carry huge blanket-wrapped bundles on their backs through the mud. They were followed by mute groups of ragged children, lugging baskets filled with pots and pans, boxes of tinned food, burlap sacks of flour or beans. Many of the children went barefoot in the cold, and wore coats that were nothing more than folded layers of the same burlap as the sacks they carried. Helen frowned, pausing to watch them. This poverty wasn't the result of a single day's walkout by coal miners. This was the result of years of sporadic work, underpaid wages, and enslavement to the company store.

"Hey, lady—catch!" The warning shout came just a few seconds before the arrival of a mud-splashed bundle of rope. Helen grabbed it more by defensive reflex than thought, then turned around to follow the raveled line back to its source. A young miner on a stepladder was nailing the other end of the rope into his main tent support pole. "Pull on that as hard as you can, will you? This upright needs to be straightened out before it's braced."

Helen obediently pulled up the slack, heedless of the scratchy coating of ash and mud the rope left on her palms. As far as she could see, it had no effect whatsoever on the tilted support pole. "Harder!" the young man ordered, adding his own push to the pole despite the perilous tilt that gave his ladder.

Helen dug her heels into the ground and braced all her weight against the rope, praying the tent pole wouldn't give way beneath their mutual attack. The upright groaned and shifted a little, and the man on the ladder smacked it several times with a sledge to set it deep into the ground, then looped the rope around it as efficiently as a sailor anchoring a ship. Helen watched in surprise. Even her former Boy Scout brother had never had the knack of twisting a rope quite like that.

"That's a pretty fancy knot."

"Thanks." The young man clambered down the ladder with surprising grace, then turned to show her a chiseled face darkened by exposure to sun rather than coal dust. "I learned it out in the Indies, from a Chinese sea captain. He claimed you could only do it if you'd smoked some opium beforehand, but I managed to pick up the knack all the same."

"From studying your photographs of the process, no doubt." Helen wiped her muddy hand off on her coat sleeve, then held it out to him. "Helen Sorby, *New York Herald*."

His handsome face cracked into a much less handsome crookedness when he smiled, but the good-humored warmth in his dark eyes made it a change Helen liked. "Jackson Ecklar, currently with *Scribner's*," he said and muddied her hand again with his firm shake. "You recognized me from my photograph."

He said it without either surprise or pleasure, as if it were simply a fact of life he'd learned to live with. Helen tossed him the bundle of rope, then scrubbed her hands clean again on her coat sleeves. Fortunately, the brownish red clay almost matched the color of the faded russet wool.

"Actually, no," she said. "I came here looking for you, Mr. Ecklar."

That made the photographer's thickly feathered dark eyebrows lift into his wind-ruffled hair. "Why? I would have assumed the strike was what attracted you."

"No," Helen admitted. "Although I'll admit I used it to entice my aunt to come with me. She's planning some relief efforts for the miners."

"Ah. It's about time someone did." A handful of gilt-haired children had paused to watch them, wriggling their bare toes down into the mud to keep them warm. They gave her a few shy, sidelong glances, but trained most of their hopeful attention on Jackson Ecklar. He sighed and shook his head at them over the canvas he was unfolding. "No candy bars left today, fellows. Sorry."

"There's a very nice lady in the carriage over there who's making a list of things to bring with her tomorrow," Helen told them. "You could go and tell her what you'd like."

That sparked an excited scramble of pounding feet, shoving arms, and spattered mud, although not the outcry of whoops and squeals she'd expected. Helen watched a dozen other children join the dash to Aunt Pittypat's carriage as the news spread, but still heard nothing but the hammering of tent pegs and the snap of canvas in the wind. Harwick's survivors all seemed locked into silence, as if a voice raised too loud might bring another disaster down on their heads.

"You can tell they survived a tragedy here, can't you?"

"Yes." Ecklar tested the sturdiness of his rope and pole construction with one harsh shake before he climbed back on his ladder and began draping canvas over it. "Not that anyone seems to have paid much attention to that for the past year and a half." He glanced down at Helen, his face hardening back into the severe lines that made him look like his published photograph. "Why is it that you newspaper reporters always wait until some moment of high drama to notice how miserable these peoples' lives are? The calluses on those children's feet didn't form since the coal strike was called yesterday, you know."

"And they haven't gone away during the two weeks you've been here, either," Helen retorted. She was in no mood to be lectured at by someone who did his social work through the lens of a camera, no matter how well he put up tents. "You could have notified some of the local churches and women's clubs about the poverty you found here, if you hadn't been so busy turning it into fine art!"

Ecklar's ladder jerked, as if he'd taken an unbalanced step on its crest. "How do you know how long I've been here?" He sounded as if he was rapidly revising his opinion of Helen, although she couldn't be sure in what direction it was going.

"I saw the date on a book you borrowed from the Oakmont Library." She took a deep breath, glad his attention was on the canvas he was draping rather than her face. She always found it hard to look someone in the eyes while she lied to him. "Right next to the name of my good friend Emmy Murchison."

"Emmy who?"

She frowned, trying to decide if that had been honest bewilderment in his voice or just a polished New York facsimile. "Emmy Murchison. You must remember her, she told me you had recommended Olive Harper's book to her."

"*A Slave of the Mill?*" Ecklar made a rude noise. "Your friend was being polite. I never read one of Olive's books that I liked less."

"But you do remember mentioning it to her?"

The photographer threw a last fold of canvas across the rope, then came down the ladder, scowling. "Excuse me, Miss Sorby, but exactly what are you asking me about? My opinion of Olive's writing or my acquaintance with your friend?"

Helen gave up trying to be subtle. "I'm trying to find out when you last spoke to Emmy Murchison, Mr. Ecklar. She vanished from her home four days ago, and right now, you're my only lead in the case."

His face chilled back into its formal portrait handsomeness. "Because we both happened to read the same library book?"

"No, because you both happen to be socialists!"

There was a long silence filled only with the bluster of wind. Then another voice slid between them, a voice as cool and polished as steel. "We're all socialists here, Miss Sorby. But as a favorite journalist of mine is fond of saying, that doesn't necessarily make us all criminals."

Helen swung around to see a tall, strong-boned girl with unevenly cropped black hair eyeing her across the shadow of the newborn tent. There seemed to be an ironic glint in her eyes, but they were so dark it was hard to tell for sure. She wore a mannish jacket over her sensible skirts and the kind of expensive steel-rimmed glasses that no miner's wife could afford. A labor organizer, Helen guessed, and one who already seemed to know her.

"Have we met?"

"No." The dark-haired young woman threw a laughing glance at Jackson Ecklar. This time the irony was plain to see. "I recognized you from your photograph a few months ago in the *Progressive Worker's Weekly*. My name is Larkin, Bryde Larkin. I'm with the Industrial Workers of the World."

Helen shook her wet outstretched hand, resigning herself to muddy fingers for the duration of her visit. "I thought you might be a Wobbly. Out of Chicago?"

"Yes. We've been up here in Black Valley for several weeks, laying the groundwork for this strike." Larkin's eyes narrowed behind her spectacles. "Now, what were you asking Jack about Emmy Murchison?"

"I wanted to know when he last spoke to her. And I'm sorry if I gave you the impression that being a socialist made you a crime suspect," Helen added over her shoulder to the silent photographer. "As Miss Larkin knows, I'm the last person in the world who would think that."

"*Has* a crime been committed, Miss Sorby?" Ecklar asked.

"I don't know. All I know is that Miss Murchison disappeared last Saturday night and hasn't been in touch with her family since then. They've asked me to look into it."

Bryde Larkin fell silent, although it seemed to Helen that she and Ecklar exchanged meaningful glances. "I haven't seen Emmy Murchison since she was here on Friday with that boyfriend of hers," Ecklar said abruptly. "And Bryde talked to her more than I did then. If you have any other questions, Miss Sorby, you can find me putting up more tents."

He folded the stepladder and strode away before a startled Helen could ask him to elaborate. She frowned after him, then heard Bryde Larkin chuckle.

"Don't be too mad at him, Miss Sorby. Jack doesn't like listening to gossip, much less repeating it."

"And you do?" Helen asked skeptically.

The union organizer shook her head, making her cropped hair fall sideways into her eyes. "There's a lot of things I don't enjoy doing, but they still need to be done," she said, pushing it back again. "Was Emmy Murchison really a friend of yours?"

"No."

"I didn't think so." Larkin's smile was small but genuine. "Both Jack and I thought she seemed awfully shallow, even for a coal baron's daughter. She only visited here a couple of times. At first I thought she was just playing at being a socialist to spite her parents. But the last time she came, she was with one of those so-called labor organizers from up the valley, and I realized she wasn't playing at being a socialist at all. She was playing with him."

Helen frowned at her. "What do you mean, 'so-called labor organizer'?"

Bryde Larkin shrugged. "You've been through strikes before, Miss Sorby. You know the kind of men who hang around the fringes and say they're with the union when they're not. Some of them are just college boys trying out radical politics, some of them are troublemakers, and some of them—"

"—are confidence men," Helen finished grimly. "And Emmy Murchison seemed to be particularly friendly with this one?"

"Friendly," said the union organizer dryly, "is not the word I would have used. Captivated, enamored, enthralled—"

"Seduced?" Helen asked.

"Oh, yes," said Bryde Larkin. "Definitely seduced."

FIVE

"You're sure it's not because you asked her to marry you?"

Kachigan scowled down at the evidence book he was trying to write in. His annoyance wasn't directed at the completely illegible scrawl that the bumpy country road was turning his hand-writing into, or the frustrating lack of information he had to write down in the first place. He'd left Tarentum that morning determined not to have this particular conversation with his partner, but long hours cooped up in a small buggy had exhausted just about every other topic. He should have known that sooner or later, Taggart would manage to bring up the subject of Helen Sorby's recent absence.

"I'm sure," was all he said.

He attributed the deep snort that followed that remark to his detective partner, although it could just as easily have come from one of the tired livery horses. A day spent climbing the stream-carved hills of northern Allegheny County had slowed their pace from a brisk trot to a plod, one maintained more by their desire to get back to their stable in Tarentum than any particular effort from their driver. Although Kachigan knew he could have gotten more speed out of the horses if he'd taken the reins himself, that would have required waiting at every stop until he had finished writing down the responses of the mine foremen and coal pit managers they'd questioned.

"But that *was* the last time you had dinner with Helen, wasn't it?" Taggart persisted. "The night you told me you were going to propose?"

"Yes. And she said no." Kachigan put his evidence book away and shaded his eyes against the painful slant of sunset. The fickle April sky had cleared just in time to make their last hour of daylight an annoyance rather than a help. "Just like she did all the other times I asked her. It never stopped her from coming back to Tarentum before."

That got him the amused look he'd resigned himself to. "You've asked her to marry you before?"

"A couple of times," Kachigan admitted ruefully. "The first time she said, 'No.' The second time, she said, 'No, thank you.' The third time, she said, 'No, and where are we going tonight for dinner?' "

"How polite." Taggart's thin smile flashed beneath his mustache. "She never got mad at you?"

Kachigan rubbed a hand across one ear, wincing reminiscently. "Trust me, Art. When Helen Sorby is mad at you, she doesn't waste any time letting you know it. And I've rung her up at least five times on the telephone since then. She's perfectly happy to talk to me, she just doesn't want to come up and visit."

"Huh." Taggart considered that for a while, letting the horses straggle by themselves up the next hill. "Maybe she's so busy covering this coal strike that she just hasn't had the time."

"I seem to remember saying that five minutes ago, when you first brought it up." Kachigan pulled out the hand-drawn map Riley had made for him over breakfast. "Now shut up and let me see where we've got to go next."

"Why do we have to go anywhere?" Taggart asked, but there wasn't any real irritation in his voice. Irritation took effort and the big man was just too indolent to bother with it. He pulled the horses up as they arrived at the muddy crossroads at Millerstown to wait for Kachigan's instructions. Bull Creek's winding floodplain had widened enough here to hold yet another row of tar-papered company duplexes, but the darkened windows and pervasive silence told Milo the local mines weren't currently active. "Why can't we just go home?"

"Because we've got another hour of daylight left."

Taggart groaned. "How do you define daylight, Milo? Enough light to see your pencil?"

"Enough light to see the road." Kachigan made slow checks beside all the pits they'd already stopped at. He'd started tracking his unknown fire-boss before dawn that morning, resigned to the fact that he'd have to do all the work himself. He didn't trust J.P. Frick any farther than he could watch him, and he'd left Riley guarding their mute Italian prisoner. The earliest part of the morning had been spent on the trolley, visiting the coal mines around Tarentum: McKean, Creighton, Bessemer, and the big one that ran almost two miles along the river, Cornell Number One. Not a single one reported a missing fire-boss.

After he'd hired a buggy and dragged a grumbling Taggart out of bed at ten—for him, the equivalent of predawn darkness—they'd followed the Allegheny River south to Harwick and Red Raven. When those mines reported no fire-bosses missing, they'd worked their way up Little Deer Creek to the isolated hill towns of Rural Ridge, Russellton, Culmerville, and Red Hot. With the exception of Harwick, the tipples in all those nonunion patches were still pouring out coal, although Kachigan heard a lot of talk about men spilling their water if the mine owners didn't raise the scale. He'd written a note in his evidence book to ask Riley what that meant. He'd also written, over and over again, that all the mines' fire-bosses had reported to work on time, that no miners using coal checks numbered "fifty-three" were missing, and that not a single gas-detection lamp was gone.

"If we hurry, we can probably hit the Birdville and Campton mines on our way back to Tarentum. Turn right here."

Taggart wheeled the horses around obediently, while Kachigan folded up the map and watched the sun sink through the trees. The branches were still bare up here in the cold hills, far from the misty Allegheny. "Why don't we just keep going north up the river after that?" the big detective asked sarcastically. "The mines work double shifts around here—we could ask questions all night long."

Kachigan gave him a quizzical glance. "What's your hurry to go home? You miss talking to J.P. today?"

This time the snort he got was far too caustic to belong to anyone but Taggart. "No, what I miss is my dinner! Just because you stop eating when you've got a murder to investigate doesn't mean I have to."

"I don't stop eating," Kachigan said. Taggart wasn't the first one to make that accusation—both his father and Helen Sorby had nagged him about missing meals, back in the days when he still lived in the little house on the South Side, just around the corner from the police station. But his unwanted transfer north to the Tarentum branch of the County Detectives' Bureau had meant putting his house up for rent and sending his father back to Monessen to live with his sister for a while. Of course, until this last week he had still had Helen around to nag him into taking her to dinner, or buying her roast chestnuts on the evening walks back to the trolley station—

"See, you're hungry too," Taggart said. Kachigan scowled and rubbed at his noisy, traitorous stomach. "Tell you what, let's head down to Natrona instead of Birdville. They have a bunch of coal mines there, and I know a great Polish bar that keeps a pot of kielbasa cooking on the coal stove all day long."

Kachigan unfolded the map again, measuring mines and distances. The pits around Natrona were on the trolley line, almost as close to Tarentum as the mines he'd visited that morning. He'd planned to check them out tomorrow, but tonight would do just as well. "All right, we can get kielbasa. But if you drink more than two beers, I'm driving home."

"It's a deal." Taggart slapped the reins against the horses' rumps, startling them into an actual trot. They managed to keep up that quickened pace for most of the three miles back to Tarentum, aided by the descending grade of the road as it followed the iron-stained trickle of Bull Creek. Even so, by the time they passed under the tipple of Bull Creek Coal Mine and saw the necklace of gaslights that was the shoreline of the Allegheny appear through the stream-carved bluffs, the sky had darkened to a deep, star-sprinkled blue.

"Natrona," he reminded Taggart, when the buggy seemed about to turn right, toward their small boarding-house by the river. "Or do you want to walk home from here and let me drive myself?"

"And miss my kielbasa?" Taggart wheeled the horses left on North Canal Street, past the elegant brick edifice of the new Y.M.C.A. A cluster of serious-faced young men stood on the stoop in their shirtsleeves, smoking cigarillos and talking more ardently than the athletic club's guests usually did. Kachigan reached out to tug at the reins, slow-ing the buggy down as they passed. The freckled face of Leon Daniels promptly lifted from the huddle to grin at him.

"Strategy meeting, Detectives," the labor organizer called out cheekily, disregarding his companions' scowls. "You want to stop and listen in?"

"Just don't hold any miners' rallies tonight," Kachigan called back, releasing his hold on the reins. "I wouldn't want to miss the fun."

Daniels's appreciative roar of laughter followed them up the street, until the clatter of evening traffic drowned it out. The rush-hour congestion seemed worse than usual, making Kachigan frown again until a wagon rattling past with fur-niture piled in an ungainly heap reminded him it was April first. It was easy to forget about moving day when you had spent the afternoon in towns whose only landlord was the coal company.

"I don't suppose you've thought about the possibility that our dead man wasn't a fire-boss after all," Taggart said over the noise of the traffic. "Considering that we haven't found a single one missing yet."

Kachigan grunted reluctant acknowledgment. "I've thought about it. But we also haven't found a single gas-detecting lamp missing. Those lamps aren't cheap, and a lot of the older mines probably don't even have them. If one had been stolen, somebody would have noticed."

"Why are you assuming the dead guy had to steal it? It could have been given to him by the same nice philanthropist who gave him the two hundred dollars. And for all we know," Taggart added cynically, "that was Bernard K. Flinn."

"No. I saw how curious he was when we examined the body. Whoever the dead man was, he wasn't one of Flinn's informers."

"Then who the hell was he?"

Kachigan frowned, sorting through the various hypotheses he'd accumulated over the course of the day. "If I had to guess, I'd say he was a worker from some nonunion mine who had come to coordinate strike plans with the nearest union local. The two hundred dollars could have been a contribution toward a strike fund, to encourage his men to join the walkout."

"Then the motive for the killing would have been to keep the strike from spreading?"

"Or to keep the miners' union from getting more of a foothold in the valley." Kachigan sighed. "Which, strange as it seems, probably eliminates Bernard Flinn as a suspect. He's working for a union company now."

"A company that's been shut down by a union strike," Taggart reminded him. "That never makes the owners— or the company police—very happy with their unions. If the dead guy was a Pittsburgh organizer bringing that two hundred dollars as a donation to the Bull Run miners' strike fund rather than vicey-versey—"

"—Flinn might have had a reason to want him dead." Kachigan frowned and scrubbed at his cheek, annoyed at having to defend the man who had gotten him exiled to the County Detectives' Bureau in the first place. "But you didn't see him down in that mine, Art. I'm telling you, he had no idea who that dead man—"

He broke off, startled by the muffled rumble of voices that surged out to meet them as soon as they turned off River Avenue onto Sycamore Street. The hoarse echoes of shouting sounded ominously familiar.

"I don't suppose they're having a parade to celebrate Fools' Day," Taggart said, pulling the buggy to a halt. "Moving day riot?"

Kachigan shook his head. Despite the many duplexes and flats that had jammed themselves into Natrona, the streets were completely empty of traffic, moving wagons and people alike. It looked as if trouble had been brewing here all day. "Miners' rally," he said. "Probably another illegal one."

"Sounds like it's up on Center Street." Taggart slapped the reins against the horses' sweaty rumps and sent them in that direction without waiting to be told. It was one of the things Kachigan liked about his partner—he might be incurably lazy, but he was never reluctant to wade into trouble. "That's where all the offices are."

"For the local coal mine companies?"

"Yeah. Pennsylvania Salt, Murchison Brothers, and Hill Coal."

Kachigan lifted his eyebrows at that casual spill of information. "Since when do you know so much about Natrona?"

"Well, I haven't found a Chinese restaurant yet in the Allegheny Valley. So I settled for a bar with good kielbasa and a pretty barmaid." Taggart's smile gleamed again beneath his sandy mustache. "Hey, I had to do something on the weekends while you were off romancing Helen Sorby."

Kachigan wasn't sure why he opened his mouth, since he couldn't very well deny his partner's statement. Fortunately they turned the corner onto Center Street before he could speak, and the rumble of the mob became a full-fledged roar.

"Uh-oh." Taggart pulled the horses up with a clatter they could barely hear. "This looks more like a riot than a rally."

Men filled the narrow business district to overflowing,

shouting not in response to a speaker on a platform but in unsynchronized mass fury. Their blackened overalls, and the acrid smell of sweat and blasting powder that rode on the cold night wind, told Kachigan they must have come straight out of the mines. Taggart was right—this was not the same kind of union demonstration Leon Daniels had organized yesterday for the strikers in Tarentum. Not if these men had been digging coal after the strike deadline had passed.

"Those are nonunion miners," he said. "Which of the mines in Natrona is nonunion?"

"All of them, I think."

From their vantage point in the buggy, Kachigan could see the crowd coalescing in front of a tall, red-brick office building farther down the street. He squinted, trying to read the gilt lettering on the front window, but it splintered to bright shards and then fell into darkness before he could make it out. He could barely hear the sound of glass shattering over the accompanying shouts of approval. "Must be the office of the company they work for."

"Brilliant deduction, Milo." Taggart watched another brick sail toward an upper window and crash it to splinters too. Glass shards rained down on the miners' heads, but didn't seem to damp their fury. "Here's another brilliant deduction—they're mad as hell about something. I wish we'd brought the shotguns."

Kachigan grimaced. Somehow, even armed with shotguns, he didn't think two county detectives were going to make much impact on this mob. "I wonder where the Natrona city police are."

"If I know him, sleeping under his lockup desk. Tuesday night isn't normally too busy." The crowd of miners was boosting a pair of soot-stained boys up toward the broken second-story window now. The windows on the first floor must have had bars behind the glass. "What are we going to do?"

"Make sure no one in that building gets lynched." Kachigan stashed his bowler hat under the buggy seat, then stripped off the coat, vest, and starched collar that marked him as a professional man. "Let's see how close we can get before they notice us."

Taggart gave him a dubious glance. "You really think anyone's going to believe that I'm a coal miner? Hell, I wouldn't even fit down a shaft."

"True." Kachigan swung down from the buggy and grunted in satisfaction. As he'd hoped, their travels had left more than enough coal-dark mud clinging to the wheels to blacken his face and make his shirt look like it had spent a day underground, at least to a cursory glance. "Why don't you go wake the Natrona police department up from its nap and bring back a couple of guns? In a pinch, a blast might startle them into running—"

The slam of doors bursting open and the responsive roar of the mob cut across his instructions. Without waiting to hear Taggart's response, Kachigan leaped into the mill of shouting miners, letting its momentum carry him with it as it surged toward the conquered territory. His running steps and dark face let him blend into the assault without so much as a second glance being cast at his clothes. He probably could have worn a priest's smock and not been noticed, he thought as he added his own elbowing shove to the crush of men going through the doors. It wasn't for verisimilitude as much as for survival—the fierce pressure of shoulders jostling around him shouted out the miners' rage as clearly as their hoarse voices did.

"Up here, they're up here—" one of the black-faced boys called down from an upper landing, his pure soprano cutting through the curses and shouts below like a church bell. Despite his age, the bitter note of anger in his voice could never have belonged to a schoolboy. "They've barricaded themselves behind a door!"

"Lemme through, lemme through—" A grizzled older miner tried to shove past the crowd packed onto the groaning stairs, one coal-black hand waving the unmistakable shape of a dynamite stick. Kachigan felt his stomach clench in dismay, but by then he was locked inside a vise of angry men, no more able to move than the old man with the explosive. Unfortunately, it wouldn't take the miners long to realize that dynamite could be passed from hand to hand. "Lemme through, dammit! I've got the key to get that bastard Murchison out from there—"

Someone leaned down from the upper landing. "Throw that here to me," a stocky man ordered. "I know what to do with it!"

His Slavic-accented voice was no louder than the other men shouting around him, but it had an edge of pure conviction that made it carry. The older miner peered up at him with some effort, then hooted with laughter and tossed him the dynamite stick. His hunched shoulders might be unable to straighten after so many years underground, but his aim was strong and true.

"Stand back, boys," he crowed. "Let the new fire boss burn out all that bad gas up there! Fire in the hole!" A chorus of voices took up the chant, shaking the office building as they built it to a roar. "Fire in the hole! Fire in the hole! Fire in the hole!"

Kachigan cursed and began to worm his way sideways through the crowd clogging the hall, heading for the open door of a side office whose overturned files and spilled papers showed it had already been ransacked. It might be desperation, but he thought he saw the shadow of an iron fire escape blocking the gaslight that spilled down a narrow side alley. If he could make his way up it, perhaps he could find an escape route for the people trapped on the second floor.

He swung the door closed behind him, pausing to make sure none of the other miners came through. As far as he could tell, however, they were all too busy roaring approval of the activity overhead to notice the motion of one extraneous door. Kachigan exhaled in relief and turned to stride toward the window.

"Stop." The words were accompanied by the cold smack of a pistol barrel being laid along his neck. "Lock that door."

Kachigan paused, but only long enough for his dark-adjusted eyes to catch the tremulous flutter of a dress behind the shadowy figure with the gun. He reached out then and clicked the lock over without a word. Whoever was barricaded behind that door upstairs, it wasn't the coal company's office staff. The open door of a supply closet showed where they must have hidden during the ransacking.

The gun pressed deeper into his skin. "Now, walk over to that window and open it. And don't even think about wrestling me for this gun. I've shot a hell of a lot more coal miners than you've shot company guards."

Kachigan thought about trying to explain who he was, but his detective's badge was back in the pocket of his coat and the sound of dynamite being wedged beneath the upstairs door told him he didn't have time to waste. Instead, he strode toward the window, the man with the gun taking each step along with him, then flung the sash up regardless of the noise. The booming of feet down the stairwell as the dynamite-savvy miners evacuated the building easily covered it.

"Look outside, quick. Anyone in sight?"

Kachigan stuck his head out, although he wasn't sure what difference his answer would make. Fortunately, the shadowed alley between this building and the next was empty, although a thick roil of miners was pouring back out into the main street.

"It's clear." He pulled his head in and swung away from the window, not caring that the motion brought the muzzle of the gun around to point directly at his throat. "Send the women out first."

The man facing him grunted in surprise, although the gun's aim never wavered. In the reflected gaslight, all Kachigan could see of his face was a lantern jaw and thick handlebar mustache, with a square gleam of Teddy Roosevelt spectacles above it. "Henry, get the girls out. *Now.*"

The military snap of command in that voice confirmed what Kachigan already suspected—this was not just a company guard but the head of this company's industrial police force. He made no attempt to step away as a younger man hustled two breathless stenographers past them and out onto the fire escape. The girls floundered and sobbed as their heavy skirts caught on the frame, but their escort pushed both of them through, then scrambled out to guide them down the single flight of stairs.

"And now you—" Whatever else the coal police chief was going to say was lost in the flat crack that exploded through the building. Kachigan saw the gas ceiling lamps burst into a spectral blue curtain of flame and threw himself recklessly toward the open window. He wouldn't have been surprised to be shot just to clear the way, but instead he was slammed from behind with enough force to send him flying through the window and halfway down the fire escape. A broad-shouldered figure pushed ruthlessly past him while he was still hauling himself to his feet, leaving Kachigan alone on the fire escape. He leaped the rail just seconds before the building caught on fire, then scrambled to his feet and followed the sound of running footsteps down the suddenly bright alley. Behind him, a second explosion of cheering and applause out in Center Street momentarily drowned out the roar of the flames.

"Goddamned miners—" The spectacled man swung around as Kachigan emerged from the alley, pistol swinging with swift accuracy to center on his chest. "Don't you make a goddamned sound, or you're going to be the first man killed in this strike!"

Kachigan slewed to a stop, lifting both hands to show his good intentions. Except for the sobbing stenographers and the two coal policemen, this street was as eerily deserted as the rest of Natrona, although he could hear the urgent echoes of voices and hoofbeats coming from the direction of the train station. He wondered if that was Taggart summoning help from the city police lockup, or the town's fire department responding to the sound of the explosion.

"I'm not a miner," he said in a voice he hoped sounded professional through his panting. "I'm an Allegheny County detective. Look at my shoes."

The request was just bizarre enough to make the coal police chief clap his mouth shut on whatever he'd been going to say. He scowled down at the unmistakable gleam of polished leather on Kachigan's feet in the firelight, then back up at his face.

"If you really are a county boy, what the hell are you doing in the middle of a miners' riot without a shotgun?"

"Infiltrating."

The other man grunted and let his gun drop. "You must be the new Turk they sent up to the Tarentum office," he said, his voice so matter-of-fact that Kachigan wasn't sure whether he was supposed to take offense or not. "Take my advice, and either wash that dirt off your face or find somewhere to hide. All hell is just about ready to break loose in this town." The coal policeman turned away, taking the arm of each stenographer in a grip more absentminded than gallant. "Come on, Henry, we've got to get the girls stashed somewhere safe. The Atlantic & Pacific Tea Company ought to still be open down on Garfield Avenue."

He moved off down the street without waiting for agreement, herding the office workers along with him like sheep. Kachigan paused to scrub some of the flaking mud off his face, then strode after them. By the time he caught up, he had to raise his voice to be heard over the shrieking fire whistles.

"Were those the offices of Murchison Coal back there?"

"Until about five minutes ago, they were," the company police chief said grimly.

"What were your miners so upset about?"

That got him only an irritable snort in reply. "How the hell should I know? Go back and finish infiltrating, then maybe you can tell me."

"So you weren't expecting a riot?"

"Hell, no! Don't you think I'd have had more men guarding the office tonight if I'd been expecting trouble?"

"But when the miners started gathering—" Kachigan broke off, hearing a crescendo of hooves roll down the next cross-street. They sounded far too thunderous and rapid to belong to the single draft team that pulled a fire-wagon. "Did you use the office telephone to call your other guards in from the mine?"

The coal policeman glanced over his shoulder, deep-set

eyes glittering behind the angular glasses. "Almost right, Turk. I telegraphed Troop B in Greensburg for help."

"You called in the Pennsylvania State Police?" Kachigan asked incredulously. The rolling thunder of a disciplined cavalry charge answered before the other man could, crossing the street behind them in an ominous billow of black overcoats and shine of spiked metal helmets. "How in God's name did they get here so fast?"

"Special train. It left Greensburg at four-thirty this afternoon, according to the telegram I got back from their lieutenant." They turned the corner into the welcoming electric glow of a modern grocery store, its display windows stacked with colorful boxes of cereal and crackers. The company police chief swung open the door with its distinctive "A & P" lettering, then thrust the two secretaries inside to join the salesclerks and butchers watching apprehensively through the glass. "I was waiting for them to arrive and chase away the mob when you happened to stumble through the door. Good thing I decided to gamble on you instead, eh, Turk?"

"My name is Kachigan." He caught the other man by the arm when he would have turned away. "If you're feeling grateful to me for saving your life, why don't you try calling me by it?"

They stared at each other for a minute in measuring silence. The industrial police chief was the same height and age as Kachigan but far more sturdily built, and the glitter of glasses on his face didn't make him look like any more of a weakling than it did Teddy Roosevelt. From his broad shoulders and stocky torso—and the fancy insignia ring he wore—Kachigan took him for a former college football player. He wondered how he had ended up working as a company policeman for a small-town coal operator.

"Kachigan." The police chief said the name as if he was tasting it to see if it was good or bad, his intent gaze never wavering from Kachigan's face. "What the hell kind of Turkish name is that?"

"The Armenian kind." That wasn't strictly true, since the immigration officers had Anglicized the spelling at Ellis

Island, but Kachigan didn't see any need to tack that explanation on now. "If you can't say it, you can just call
me 'detective.' ''

That got him a scornful grunt, but the tension eased between them nonetheless. "Franklin Truxall," the other man
said brusquely. "That's an American name. And if you
can't say it, you can just call me 'boss,' because Murchison
Brothers pays more than enough money to the County Detectives' Bureau every year to cover your salary. You got
that, Kachigan?"

"Yeah, I got it." Putting up with companies who bribed
his corrupt boss to leave their industrial police forces un-
checked was something Kachigan had gotten used to over
the past few months. He'd also gotten used to maneuvering
around it. "You can leave your guard here to see the secretaries home—I'll watch your back on the way to the fire.
My partner's supposed to meet me there."

Truxall gave him an amused look. "I'd wash more of
that coal off my face before I went to meet the state police,
if I was you."

"I'll take my chances," Kachigan said, unwilling to let
the coal policeman leave without him. He got another grunt
in response, but Truxall didn't try to dissuade him from
accompanying him back to site of the fire.

Thuds of hooves and truncheons striking flesh, and the
resulting howls of pain, met them as soon as they turned
the corner onto Center Street. The troop of mounted men
were charging back and forth through the dispersing miners, striking at anyone who swerved within their reach. The
state police force, created specifically to quell labor distur-
bances in Pennsylvania's immigrant-packed coalfields and
steel towns, might be less than a year old, but the one thing
everyone agreed on so far was that they were good at what
they did.

"Looks like they sent the full troop in," Truxall said in
satisfaction. "Good. If they stick around awhile, those
damn miners won't be using dynamite on anything but
coal."

Kachigan frowned, watching the last few miners try to

drag their fallen comrades out from under the nervous, dancing hooves of the police horses. A rain of truncheon blows drove most of them away, and the stubborn few who remained were promptly caught and manacled. "What makes you think they'll stay here? There must be a hundred other strike-bound coal mines around here."

"Yeah," said Truxall. "But none of those hundred other strikes are hitting the mine that supplies the contract coal for the Pennsylvania Railroad." He stopped outside the fierce halo of firelight, watching the last miners being chased away by a moving wall of horses and bloody truncheons. The fire department's wagon rolled into the space they vacated, the firemen shaking out their hoses and connecting them to the nearest city hydrant. Water began to spray over the burning office building, far too late to do it any good but in time to save the rest of the block. "That's why I think we can count on our trooper friends sticking around for a while. *Lieutenant! Over here!*"

One of the horses spun around in the firelit street, its head bowed deep beneath the powerful pull of its rider's reins. The crisp officer's hat he wore told Kachigan this was the troop's leader, even before he waved a hand in reply. He paused to say something to the fire chief, then cantered down the street to meet them.

"Mr. Truxall, I presume?" The state policeman had a pleasant enough Irish tenor, but its military cadence was so brisk that the question came out sounding like a butler's inquiry. "Lieutenant John Brennan, Pennsylvania State Police. Sorry we didn't arrive in time to save your company office. There was a lot of traffic on the tracks this afternoon."

Truxall grunted. "At least you got here in time to make a couple goddamned coal miners regret what they did." Now that mounted troops had swept the mob away, Kachigan could see the crumpled, unmoving forms they'd left behind them in the street. He frowned, wondering if the state police would leave them there or—like the military force they almost were—would take the time to sort the

living from the dead. "They'll think twice before they decide to storm a company office again."

"I hope you got all the office workers out safely?" Lieutenant Brennan inquired, as politely as if he were asking
about the weather.

"All except the office boy. I had to send him upstairs as
a decoy, while the rest of us hid in a supply closet." Truxall
seemed not to notice Kachigan's deepening frown, but it
must have been disgusted enough to catch Brennan's attention. The state police lieutenant dropped a hand to his hol-
stered pistol and kneed his horse a step closer, as if to move
between them. "Don't worry, he's not a miner," the coal
police chief said, seeing the direction of that wary gaze.
"He's one of Big Roge McGara's county detectives."

"I see." This time the military crispness managed to
convey emotion perfectly—the undiluted contempt of an
upright state official faced with the corrupt ranks of county
government. Kachigan hoped the last traces of mud he wore
hid the annoyed jerk of muscles along his jaw. "Aiding in
the investigation of the missing fire-boss, no doubt?"

The jerk of surprise Kachigan felt couldn't have been
hidden no matter how much mud he had left on his face.
"*What* missing fire-boss?" he demanded, turning to stare
at Truxall with narrowed eyes.

"It's not important," the company policeman said curtly.
"One of our senior employees never showed up for his
shift today. He could be out sick, or avoiding work because
of the strike—"

"That's not what Mr. Murchison told us in *his* telegram," Lieutenant Brennan said, politely inflexible. "He
said he feared foul play by the unions, because the missing
man would never have agreed to go on strike. He also said
your police forces were going to question the workers today
about his disappearance. And about some missing money."

Kachigan blew out a disgusted breath. Knowing exactly
how company police tended to "question" the men in their
charge, he no longer wondered what the Murchison Brothers Coal Company had done to inspire tonight's rampage.
"This fire-boss of yours, Truxall—was he a man about six

inches shorter than me, with light brown hair going bald down the part? Blue eyes, mustache, probably Slovak?''

It was the coal police chief's turn to scowl. ''How did you—I mean, yeah, that sounds like Harry Tamasy. What did you do, arrest him at the miners' rally in Tarentum last night?''

''No,'' Kachigan said. ''I arrested the man accused of murdering him.''

SIX

It was not a door many people knocked on, this blank slab of pine with its peeling gray paint and rusty latch. Helen could tell that from the frantic flight of pigeons that erupted out of the attic windows at the sound of her rap, and from the way the Negro women sitting on the porch next door stopped wrapping bright cloths around their hair and eyed her with equally bright interest. The rotten porch boards groaned and sagged beneath her feet while she waited for someone to answer that summons.

Helen's nervousness had nothing to do with the neighborhood. Her settlement work had taken her to parts of the South Side and East Pittsburgh that were every bit as poor and grimy as this block of Millvale. But she knew this particular tenement, with its long uncut grass and newspaper-covered windows, happened to be the headquarters for some of the most radical socialists and anarchists in the city. She wasn't sure exactly how they would respond to an unexpected knock on the door, but she suspected they'd be a lot surlier than the average Pittsburgher.

"It's Helen Sorby," she called out, when the silence after her knock lengthened. She was sure someone inside knew her name, and also knew she was the one who'd turned Aunt Pittypat's South Side Temperance League from a polite ladies' society to a socialist working group. "I'm alone."

More silence. Then, with reluctant slowness, the rusty latch lifted from the inside and the door swung open a grudging crack. From the curious murmurs and craned heads of the women next door, Helen guessed this was not a common occurrence.

"What do you want?" The darkness inside didn't let her see much more than the suggestion of a man's gaunt figure, but she knew that harsh German-Polish accent. Helen took a deep breath, knowing the hardest part was still to come.

"I'm looking for a missing girl," she said bluntly. With this man, there was no use engaging in social pleasantries or beating around the bush. "Her name is Emmy Murchison."

"Never heard of her."

The door began to close again, but Helen had expected that and had already wedged her sturdy leather shoe into the crack. "Can I come in and tell you about her? I think you'll want to know."

"Why?" he demanded bluntly.

"Because if I'm right, her disappearance might sabotage the coal strike up in Black Valley."

The silence inside the crumbling tenement grew more intense, as if several people had stopped what they were doing to pay attention to her. There was a grating sigh in the shadows, as if her listener knew he was going to regret this but had to do it anyway. Then the door swung completely open, releasing a smell of old wood and new ink. "All right, come in," said Karl Zawisza.

Helen stepped inside before he could change his mind, pausing to let her eyes adjust to the newspaper-shrouded light before she tried to pick her way any deeper into the room. It was a wise decision. This front room might have held sofas and chairs back when a normal family lived here, but it was now a cramped blend of printer's stockroom and dormitory. Several blanket-covered pallets shared the unswept floor with flats of blank paper, glass carboys of ink, and stacks of bundled flyers. Past a narrow set of stairs, in what used to be the dining room, Helen could see the dark bulk of a printing press, surrounded by several more untidy mattresses. The press was silent now, and in both rooms, yawning men and women were propped on their elbows to blink at her or scratching the sleep from their eyes. Helen bit her lip, realizing the delay in answering her knock might have stemmed from a much more prosaic reason than she'd imagined. It seemed radical social action required late hours and—from the unmistakable smell that lingered in both rooms—a great deal of tobacco, beer, and sexual congress. Helen felt heat splash into her cheeks, and was glad the shuttered light hid their color.

"This way." Zawisza led her through both rooms and across a crooked back porch to an outside kitchen shed that shared the weedy backyard with a fetid outhouse. The morning sunlight glinted off his pale hair, still the glacial blond most fair-haired children lost when they grew up. And he still wore a priest's collar beneath his torn, stained work-shirt. But in the months since Helen had last seen him, Zawisza's gaunt face had gotten even more hollow, and the bony wrists that protruded from his sleeves wore bracelets of dark bruises, the kind left by iron manacles. He must have been arrested recently for some march or protest action.

Helen followed him across the lawn in silence, knowing from past experience that he was not a man inclined to conversation. It didn't help that the last time they had seen each other, she had accused him of murder and he had accused her of blackmail. The fact that neither of them had been right didn't make light chatter any easier to summon up now.

The little kitchen shed was already firelit and warm, with a battered teakettle hissing on the coal-fired stove. It was also surprisingly clean, given the anarchic chaos that ruled elsewhere in this house. A moment later, Helen knew the reason why. The blue eyes that glanced up from reading *Mother Earth* might not be quite as piercing as Emma

Goldman's, but the unwavering dedication in them had always reminded Helen of her socialist magazine editor.

"Good morning, Fanny," she said.

"Good morning, Helen." Fanny Sellins had a strange grimace of a smile, one designed not so much to hide her rotting teeth as to keep the ache of fresh air away from them. As long as Helen had known her, the union activist had worn those marks of her malnourished childhood like a badge of honor, refusing the dental services and false teeth that wealthier socialists had offered her. "I'm surprised to see you here. And don't tell me you've decided to overthrow the government, because I saw you voting in the mayoral election last month."

"Which helped elect a progressive mayor for the first time in history," Helen retorted. Unlike many socialists, she was never offended by the tart political jabs that were Fanny's idea of polite conversation. "You can thank me when half the children in Pittsburgh don't die of typhoid this summer."

Sellins snorted. "George Guthrie might have promised water filtration in the election, but it'll take him years to deliver it, if he ever does. He's more interested in annexing Allegheny City than cleaning out the sewage it dumps in the river."

Fortunately—since Helen couldn't think of a good retort to that—Zawisza interrupted. "If you came here to debate city politics with Fanny, I'm going back to bed," he said in his harsh, impatient voice.

"Have some tea, Karl." Sellins poured hot water over loose grounds in a cracked china cup, then thrust it into his hands before he could refuse. "And stop being rude to Helen just because she's female."

"That's not—" Zawisza clamped his thin lips shut on whatever else he was going to say. Instead, he turned his glower on his fellow radical. "You're the one who's always warning us about letting in possible spies. Did you know your friend Helen here sleeps with a county detective?"

"I do not," Helen said. "And even if I did—I mean, would—it wouldn't cause me to inform on every socialist

I know. Any more than I would inform on every priest I knew something about," she added meaningfully.

That made Sellins crow with laughter and Zawisza's gaunt face crawl with streaks of guilty red. His fingers rose to touch the ecclesiastical collar around his neck as if to reassure himself he still wore it, but his response was typically bitter. "That's nice of you, Miss Sorby, but hardly necessary. I've been replaced at Saint Witold's and I'm not going to be sent to a new parish anytime soon."

"And whose fault was that?" Sellins asked unsympathetically. "The bishop told you the diocese wasn't going to tolerate another arrest." She measured out tea and poured hot water into another cup, this one missing a chip as big as a tooth along the rim, and handed the steaming mess to Helen. "Now, we're all going to sit down and behave like the enlightened socialists we are. Right?"

"Right," Helen agreed and looked around for a place to sit. All she found was a set of stained pickle barrels arrayed around the kitchen table. Resigning herself to wearing rings of salt on the backside of her blue wool skirts for the rest of the morning, she settled herself on the nearest one, then gave Zawisza a challenging look. He scowled, but followed Fanny Sellins across the small kitchen shed to join her.

"So." Sellins sipped at her own tea, wincing as it hit her decayed teeth. "What did you come here to see us about?"

"The coal miners' strike." Helen swirled her tea in a vain attempt to settle the cheap, finely ground leaves. "Something's happening up in Black Valley that could wreck any chance of it succeeding."

She glanced up to see Zawisza still scowling, but Sellins looking thoughtful. "Black Valley?" she repeated. "Then you're not talking about the bribe Pat Dolan took from the railroad to derail the union settlement in Pittsburgh?"

"You know about that?" Helen's investigative reporter's instincts suddenly leaped to the fore. "Do you have any proof?"

Sellins shook her head, looking amused. "None that your New York newspaper editor would be willing to publish.

Don't worry, we got the rumors spread about the payoff in time to get Paddy Dolan tossed right out of the district meeting.''

"I know. I was there." Helen took a sip of tea, absently wiping the tea leaves from her upper lip when she was done. "At least, *that* only made the miners look disorganized. What I'm afraid of might turn public opinion so hard against them that the union will never recover."

"That sounds like newspaper melodrama," Zawisza said coldly. "If all you want is to concoct a scandal for your middle-class readers to eat with breakfast, I'm not helping."

Helen scowled at him. "Newspaper melodramas got Big Bill Hayward put in jail and Emma Goldman exiled for years! They also broke up Standard Oil. You can sneer at the power of the press all you like, but you're stupid to ignore it."

"Which I'm not," Fanny Sellins said. "Stop interrupting, Karl. If you don't want to listen to Helen, just go away."

The radical priest scowled, but made no move toward the door of the kitchen shed. "I'm listening."

Helen took a deep breath. "The daughter of an Allegheny River coal baron went missing last week. One of the Wobblies working up in Harwick says she was seduced by a rogue labor organizer. If she turns up later abandoned and pregnant, or held hostage and raped, or even murdered—"

"There'll be bloody hell to pay," Sellins finished. "And the union will spend the next fifty years living down the infamy. I assume the father's mines are nonunion?"

"I think so," Helen said. "The girl's name is Emmy Murchison. Her father owns Murchison Brothers Coal." She saw the somber looks the two radical socialists exchanged. "What's the matter?"

Fanny Sellins shook her head. "Murchison isn't just another nonunion operator, Helen. He's the main supplier of contract coal to the Pennsylvania Railroad and the richest coal baron in Black Valley." She paused, glancing over at

Zawisza. "Which makes your little melodrama a lot more plausible."

Fortunately, since Helen was still grappling with the unpleasant news that she was working for a railroad minion, Zawisza made a sound of harsh disagreement. "No, it doesn't. Murchison's the last man any labor organizer would tangle with, whether they were working for the union or not. He's got the worst yellow dogs in the valley, not to mention the cossacks in his pocket, a slew of Pinks skulking around his mines, and the county boys paid to look the other way."

Helen frowned and shoved down the instinctive protest that rose to her lips. However clean she knew Milo Kachigan to be, there was no denying the rest of the Allegheny County Detectives' Bureau was rotten with corruption. "Murchison has the state police and Pinkerton agents watching his men, in addition to his company police force?" she demanded, translating Zawisza's slang with an ease she might not have had in her pre-newspaper days. "Why?"

"To keep the least hint of union organizing out of his mines, of course." Zawisza emptied his mug, then spat a mouthful of tea leaves onto the dirt floor. "And to keep the other coal companies from undercutting him with the railroads. Murchison Brothers' mines are good, but they're not the most productive ones up in Black Valley. That cosy little contract of his only lasts as long as his company police force can convince the other mines it's not worth their while to compete."

"Coal's a cutthroat business, top to bottom," Fanny Sellins remarked. "There's too many mines for the market, and too many miners for the mines. Only big companies and bastards like Murchison survive."

Helen dug her teeth into her lower lip, fighting an indignant socialist urge to find Charles Murchison and throw his "deal" back in his teeth. She reminded herself that no matter how reprehensible the coal baron was, his daughter might still be the innocent victim of coalfield politics. "So if it wasn't a labor organizer who seduced Emmy Murchison, then who did? A rival mine operator?''

Zawisza and Sellins exchanged another thoughtful glance. "Not one of the coal barons themselves," Fanny said at last. "Those pie-smackers all go to same churches and the same fancy parties. They might hire a Pink to do it for them, but there's a lot of other riffraff that floats around a coal strike too. I wasn't here for the pressed car strike at McKees Rocks back in 1904, but I've heard—'' Sellins bit the sentence off abruptly, as if her glance at Helen had stirred a belated memory.

"—that a confidence man showed up pretending to be an American Federation of Labor organizer," Helen finished steadily. "And seduced a female socialist for her money. Yes, I know. Why do you think I'm so worried about finding Emmy Murchison, Fanny?''

Sellins cleared the gruffness from her throat. "But if your missing girl has run away with a fortune hunter, Helen, isn't it more likely she'll turn up married than murdered?''

"I suspect Miss Sorby considers those to be equally grisly fates," Zawisza said dryly. "If she didn't, that county detective of hers would have put a ring on her finger by now.''

Helen felt her cheeks grow warm, but ignored the color she knew must have risen in her face. "Right now, I'm more worried about the coal strike than Emmy Murchison's marital status," she snapped back. "I'd rather not give her father a chance to sabotage it by splashing stories about the heartless seduction of his daughter across the front pages. Which he could very easily do, whether the man who seduced her did it to steal her money or blackmail her father into giving up his railroad contracts.''

"True," said Fanny Sellins. "It just so happens that we have a few undercover agents of our own up in Black Valley, Helen. I'll put the word out for them to help you look for Emmy Murchison." She smiled, this time broadly enough to show the brown ruin of her teeth. "With any luck, she'll turn out to have been seduced by one of her father's own Pinkerton agents.''

''Or by one of his company police,'' Helen agreed. ''In which case, I'll splash the story across the front pages myself.''

By teatime, much to her niece's relief, Pat McGregor had finally run out of space to pile the spare blankets, old clothing, and cast-off shoes her urgent telephone appeals had conjured up from the middle-class matrons of Oakmont. Helen hadn't objected to spending the bulk of her day collecting and sorting charitable donations for the evicted miners in Harwick, since she was the one who'd told her aunt about their suffering. But ever since Jake Bailey had dropped off a tray of fresh bread and three newspaper-wrapped hams donated by the merchants along East Railroad Avenue, her empty stomach had been reminding her how long it had been since lunchtime. The chime of the grandfather clock out in the hall wasn't loud, but it felt like a factory quitting whistle to Helen.

''Four o'clock. Time for tea, Aunt Pat,'' she said briskly.

''Tea?'' Pittypat blinked at her across the chaos of what had once been a handsome but very formal sitting room. It now looked much more like the McGregor mansion back in the South Side, stacked with bundles and boxes and a disorganized drift of notepapers on which her aunt wrote lists and telephone exchanges and various messages to herself. The decor was completed by two newly adopted cats, a cross-eyed brown and white tom whose many battle scars belied his daytime indolence and a scrawny black kitten whose paws looked as if she had stepped in white paint. Both were currently circling the side table like buzzards, eyeing the ham and bread Jake Bailey had left there for lack of any other space. ''Dearest, how on earth can you be hungry? We had so much food left over from luncheon—''

''That's because I wasn't here for luncheon,'' Helen reminded her aunt patiently. ''And all I had was a sack of roasted chestnuts, coming back on the Hulton ferry.'' She shooed away the kitten, but the cross-eyed tomcat glued himself to the floor and ignored her, his tail thrashing ambitiously as he eyed the ham. Helen sighed and bent to pick him up. She wasn't sure if it was the jacket of her fuzzy wool dress or the nearness of the ham that inspired him, but he promptly began to purr and drool on her shoulder. ''Anyway, we don't have space to put any more donations even if we went out and got them.''

Pat McGregor eyed the assembled alms with equal parts of satisfaction and surprise. ''I must admit, I didn't expect quite so much to pour in so soon. The ladies in Pittsburgh always take a few days to get around to gathering up their donations.'' She intercepted the black kitten in mid-leap from the sofa to the side table by the simple expedient of throwing her pencil at it. A long widowhood shared with dozens of cats had made Pittypat's aim almost as sharp as a twelve-year-old's. Distracted by the clatter—or perhaps in retribution—the kitten chased the pencil deep under the sofa. ''The problem is, dearest, that we can't go out and leave the food alone with the cats. I was going to have Tilly put it in the pantry as soon as she came back from the hairdressers—''

''Something I can do as easily as she can.'' Helen proved her point by dropping the purring tomcat and swinging a ham up in her arms instead. It weighed about the same, and was a lot less messy. ''You guard the rest while I stash it, Aunt Pat. And see if you can arrange for us to meet Lillian Murchison for tea. Tell her I have some information about her stepdaughter.''

''Oh, dear.'' The glance Pat McGregor cast around her sitting room was one of purest panic. ''I know I have her telephone exchange number written down here somewhere, I've been meaning to call her all day—''

Helen made four trips to the pantry in the time it took her aunt to find that particular strip of paper, but by the time she returned from the fifth, Pittypat had already exchanged her work apron for a velvet-trimmed coat and was reaching for the bouquet of watered-silk irises and translucent chiffon daffodils that she considered her best spring hat. Her niece blinked at her.

"Weren't you going to call Mrs. Murchison?"

"I already did," Pat McGregor said briskly. "She said she has an important dinner to attend tonight and wouldn't have time to meet us at a restaurant, but would be glad to serve us tea if we could get to her house before five. And since she sounded quite urgent to know what you'd discovered about her stepdaughter, I accepted the invitation. Don't forget to put on your good fur coat, Helen."

"I didn't bring it with me." She gathered up her old russet wool coat instead, then glanced at the telephone box on the wall. "Have you also called Mr. Bailey down at the livery stable?"

"There's no need to bother him," her aunt assured her. "The Murchisons live just up the hill from here. It will make a nice brisk walk before tea."

"Of course," Helen said. Her legs already ached from the many times she'd gone up and down Oakmont's steep river-cut slopes collecting donations, but it would take longer to remind her aunt of that than it would to follow her. "Lead on."

Pat McGregor did, at the brisk pace of a woman who'd spent her childhood walking the equally steep slopes of the South Side. The lowest parts of town had already settled into a clear, cold twilight, with the sun hidden behind the bluffs on the other side of the Allegheny River. It reappeared when they were halfway up the hill, throwing reddish light across the slate sidewalks and stretching their shadows out far in front of them. They climbed past modest summer cottages and more sturdy brick duplexes, then past larger and larger Victorian homes until they finally emerged—breathless but no longer cold—onto a block that seemed to consist entirely of high-clipped hedges and iron gates. Helen could see an elegant handful of gabled roofs and chimneys rising beyond the hedge walls. From far below, a church bell rang out the hour.

"Just on time," Pat McGregor said in satisfaction, and led Helen toward the third gate on the left. It opened as they approached it, as silently and smoothly as if turned by a machine. It took Helen a minute to see the dark-skinned boy who'd been stationed there to speed them through.

"Thank you very much," her aunt said to him, the same cordial words and tone she probably would have used if the gate had been opened by Mr. Murchison himself. The boy ducked his head in embarrassment, and led them through a garden full of blooming aconites and early crocuses to an elegant leaded-glass front door. It also opened at their approach, making Helen think in amusement of the invisible servants in the Red Fairy Book. She was less amused when she stepped through and saw yet another Negro servant, bowing her head silently when they thanked her for taking their coats in what seemed like a household code of self-effacement.

"Ah, there you are." Lillian Murchison swept into the foyer in an afternoon dress of tasteful dark green, smiling and holding her hands out to them. It was only when she came closer that Helen could see the intricate green-on-green embroidery that turned a seemingly plain dress into a work of art that had probably taken ten women a week to sew. "I'm so glad you chose to walk—it means I can send my donations for Harwick home with you in my carriage."

Pittypat clasped the hand held out to her with automatic politeness, but peered out from under her spring bouquet hat with puzzled eyes. "That's odd, I could have sworn I had your name on my list of people I still needed to ring up. Did I already talk to you today, Mrs. Murchison?"

"No, Mrs. McGregor, you didn't." The millionaire's wife turned and caught Helen's hand too, then led them both to a side drawing room where a tastefully modest silver tea set sat in front of a real fire. "But I heard about your charity drive when I lunched at the Women's Club today, and I wanted to contribute." She sat down behind the teapot with a sigh. "My husband never allows me to help the miners in our own company towns, of course. But since Harwick Coal is a rival company, he's perfectly happy to support the strike effort there."

Helen accepted her wafer-thin porcelain teacup. "He's not afraid the strike will spread to his own mines if it succeeds in Harwick?"

"It already has," Lillian Murchison admitted, pouring out more of the aromatic oolong tea for Pat McGregor. "A troop of state police had to be called to Natrona last night to break up a riot at one of our payroll offices. Unfortunately it was burnt to the ground before they ever got there. But now that they're patrolling the valley, my husband hopes his other miners will think twice before deciding to join the strike."

"I'm sure they will." Although Helen tried to keep the disgust from showing in her voice, her aunt's frown and her hostess's startled look told her she hadn't quite succeeded. She still wasn't sure how comfortable she felt working for this family, whose wealth was not only connected to the exploitation of immigrants but also to the ruthless power of the railroads. Fortunately, the arrival of silver platters full of tea sandwiches, fern cakes, and chess tarts interrupted before she could express her opinion of any mine owner who would call in a police force known for its violent suppression of labor unrest.

"There you go, Miss Sorby." Lillian Murchison surprised Helen by handing her a generously portioned plate. Ladies invited to afternoon teas generally consumed no more than a morsel of each offering, although Helen had never been sure if that was a rule of etiquette or simply an effect of tightly laced corsets. "When your aunt rang up, she said you were so busy looking for our Emmy today that you entirely missed your lunch. I hope you were able to find some trace of her?"

"Nothing specific yet." Helen made a cucumber and watercress sandwich disappear in two bites, then picked out a slightly more substantial one of smoked salmon on rye. "I was able to find some socialist labor organizers up in Harwick who had met Emmy, but they couldn't tell me where she was now. I got the impression from them that your daughter wasn't really a very dedicated socialist."

"But then why would she run away from home?"

"According to my informants, because she was seduced into doing it," Helen said bluntly.

"*Emmy?*" Lillian Murchison shook her head until the elegant strands of freshwater pearls at her ears chimed in soft dismay. "No, Miss Sorby, that's not possible. I told you, my daughter has a—well, almost a distaste for being in the company of eligible young men. Are you sure these people aren't lying?"

"One of them might have been." Helen's impression of Bryde Larkin's steely character could easily stretch to that. "But I don't think Jackson Ecklar would stoop to lying about anything, much less a missing girl. Do you, Aunt Pat?"

"Good heavens, no!" Pat McGregor set down her teacup with unusual decisiveness. "No one who could document the suffering of consumptive children as sympathetically as he did would ever connive at such a thing! You did see that marvelous photographic essay of his in *Collier's* last year, didn't you, Mrs. Murchison?"

"Indeed, yes." Lillian Murchison looked from one to another of them in dawning surprise. "You mean to say that Jackson Ecklar is here in western Pennsylvania, right now? In Harwick? And that he saw my daughter there, along with this young man you think—"

"—seduced her," Helen finished, when the millionaire's wife faltered on that embarrassing word. "Yes. And everyone up there knew Miss Murchison was a coal baron's daughter."

Pat McGregor was the first one to catch that implication. "You think Miss Murchison's er—new friend is after her money, dearest?"

"Or worse," Lillian Murchison said, leaping to the very conclusion Helen had been trying to avoid, with a speed and bleakness she found surprising. "Perhaps he seduced Emmy not for her money but to hold her as a hostage, or to punish her father by—by mistreating her."

"Dear heavens," said Pat McGregor. The dismayed clatter of her teacup on its saucer showed she'd understood

Lillian Murchison despite her carefully evasive phrasing. "Do you really think that could be so?"

"Unfortunately, I do." The millionaire's wife set down her own cup as if she'd lost the taste for tea. "And if you knew the situation my husband's company is in, you'd understand why."

Helen took a deep breath, not sure what annoyed her more: the time it had taken these oblivious wealthy parents to realize the danger their daughter might be in, or the unwarranted damage these wild accusations would do to the miners' union if they turned out to be wrong. "There's no reason to think your husband's workers would—"

"It's not the coal miners I'm worried about, Miss Sorby." Lillian Murchison startled her by rising from behind her tea table and crossing the room with strides energetic enough to make her embroidered skirt billow. At first, Helen thought she'd somehow managed to offend or distress her beyond forgiveness, but then the swish of skirts was replaced by the soft rumble of a pocket door. Their hostess made sure it had latched, then came back not to her formal seat but to a stool closer to their chairs, where she perched with flighty Gibson Girl grace.

"Please don't think badly of me, Mrs. McGregor," she said, glancing up at Helen's aunt first. "What I am about to say may seem disloyal to my husband, but I truly believe it will be in his best interests for you to know. And in my stepdaughter's interests, as well." Her gaze swung back toward Helen. "Miss Sorby, are you aware of the existence of a group called the Black Hand among immigrants of Italian ancestry?"

Helen wasn't sure what she'd expected the millionaire's wife to say in the hushed quarters of this elegant sitting room, but that was certainly not it. She blinked, cleared her throat, and eventually managed to say, "Yes, I am." She fervently hoped her color hadn't changed while she said it.

"Then you know they are criminals who get most of their money through extortion and blackmail?"

"Primarily by preying on their fellow Italian immigrants."

"But there have been cases, have there not, when non-Italian businessmen got Black Hand letters? Letters threatening their homes or stores or families if they didn't pay some exorbitant amount of protection money?"

"Yes." There was no point denying it. Helen had read several of those stories herself over the past year, and wondered which ambitious clan of western Pennsylvania's *Mano Negro* had decided to expand their scope. Given that, it wasn't difficult to see where her hostess was going. "You think Emmy's disappearance may be connected to a Black Hand threat?"

Lillian Murchison took a deep breath, as if putting her dreadful thoughts into words was hard for her to do. In the end, all she could do was nod and say, "Yes. Yes, I do."

Helen frowned and pushed away her forgotten plate. "Has your husband actually received a threatening letter from the Black Hand?"

That got her a glance sharp with both indignation and regret. "Do you think he would have told me about it if he had?" Lillian asked, then answered her own question before Helen could. "No, of course not. He would have considered it far too frightening for me and Emmy to know anything about."

"Despite the fact that leaving you in blissful ignorance also left you unguarded against a Black Hand attack?"

"Yes. Precisely." Lillian Murchison rose with a snap of her embroidered green skirts, as if she couldn't bear to sit any longer, and began to pace the room again with graceful strides. "All I know for sure, Miss Sorby, is that my husband got some kind of threatening letter in the mail last week. He wouldn't tell me anything about it, but he spent hours afterward closeted with his personal lawyer and accountant. And a few days later, our banker's wife began treating me as if someone in the family had died."

"Oh, dear," said Pittypat gravely.

Helen frowned across at her aunt. "What does that mean?"

"Probably that Mr. Murchison had to sell out some closely-held stocks to raise cash in a hurry." Helen knew she could trust her aunt, the former banker's wife, to interpret those kinds of social signals correctly. "The market's not as bad now as it was in 1904, but it's not the kind any banker would want to sell his customer's best investments in."

"Exactly." The millionaire's wife stopped pacing and sank back on her stool with a sigh, as if the confession of money loss had been almost as hard for her as the initial decision to tell them about this. "How would you interpret all of that, Miss Sorby?"

"I would take it to mean that *someone* is threatening your husband," Helen agreed. "But I don't see how it points specifically to the Black Hand."

"By itself, maybe it doesn't," Lillian Murchison admitted. "But when you consider that an Italian boy was arrested two days ago in Tarentum for a Black Hand murder that happened in a coal mine just down the river from ours . . ."

"*What*?" Helen felt her forehead rumple with a scowl. "I haven't read anything about that in the Pittsburgh papers. Where did you find out about it?"

"At the Women's Club, of course," said the millionaire's wife. "Apparently it was only reported in the *Valley Daily News*. Mrs. Lucas Moore told me that was because Bernard Flinn's name carries so much weight with the big city papers—"

"—that they think twice before publishing anything negative about him. I know." It was Helen's turn to leap to her feet and begin pacing, although her angry strides bore little resemblance to her hostess's graceful glide. "Is Flinn the chief of police for the coal mine where this murder happened?"

"He is now, although he wasn't a few months ago." Lillian Murchison looked almost embarrassed by her ability to answer that question, as if a working knowledge of the coal business was something improper in a coal baron's wife. "Sedgwick Coal & Coke is our main rival in the valley and my husband talks about them incessantly at the dinner table," she added, as if to excuse her lapse. "He says Sedgwick hired Bernard Flinn just for the duration of the miners' strike. Apparently he's much too expensive for any company to hire permanently.''

"I know that, too." Helen swung around to scowl at Lillian Murchison. "So just because Bernard Flinn pinned the blame for a murder in his mine on an Italian immigrant, you think the Black Hand may be behind your husband's problems, too?"

"Yes." The older woman's elegant voice sounded almost hushed coming after hers, although Helen had no trouble hearing it. It was only then she realized she'd been shouting. "Don't you, Miss Sorby?"

"No," she said and began pulling on her gloves. "I think the most likely source of all your trouble, Mrs. Murchison, is Bernard K. Flinn."

SEVEN

By the end of Thursday morning, Milo Kachigan was desperate. He had asked politely at the barbershop, he had begged down at the bakery, he had even offered to pay one of the glassworkers at Tarentum Glass for their missed work and cleared it through their foreman. But the news about the young man he had arrested on Tuesday had spread through every nook and cranny of Tarentum's immigrant neighborhoods. Not a single Italian citizen would agree to translate the questions he had for his prisoner, or even meet his eyes as they refused.

"Which answers one of your questions already," Taggart said, folding his paper as the trolley rattled its way down Canal Street from the riverside glass factories to Tarentum's downtown business district. "The kid must be one of the local Black Hand members or they wouldn't all be so afraid to talk to him."

Kachigan grunted, but it wasn't in satisfaction. He'd guessed that much when the old Sicilian barber had made the sign against the evil eye, one thumb pushed through the middle of his clenched fist. But he'd been optimistic enough to think maybe some other Italian in town was tired of paying the enforced "membership dues" to their secret

society, or perhaps was willing to curry favor with the *capo*
of the clan by passing along a message to the prisoner while
they translated. Neither seemed to be the case. He was left
wishing he'd given this useless job to Owen Riley instead
of sending him to find out more about the dead fire-boss
up in Natrona.

"We'll just have to bring someone in from another town
to do it," he said. "Someone who doesn't know anything
about the local Black Hand."

"Might have to go to Cleveland for that," Taggart said
dryly, and thudded down the trolley steps when it braked
to a stop on Corbet Street. Kachigan sighed and followed
him out into the breezy embrace of April's first warm afternoon. Both shop-lined sides of Canal Street were bus-
tling in the sunshine, with a noontime flurry of well-dressed
and well-corseted women, maids in kerchiefs carrying
shopping baskets and businessmen meeting for luncheons.
A handful of school-boys playing hookey raced through the
crowd in an energetic game of tag, exchanging insults in a
cheerful mix of languages. Kachigan watched them for a
moment to be sure the greengrocers weren't losing any ap-
ples or bananas as part of the game. But the boys seemed
far more interested in seeing how close they could come to
killing each other, each one taking a turn at being pushed
and shoved toward the high wall that separated the uphill
part of Canal Street from the railroad tracks.

"You know, I remember doing that down in Monessen,"
he said, still watching them. "But for the life of me I can't
remember why we thought it was any fun."

"That's because it's not fun," said a voice in his ear,
too charming and too well-educated to belong to his partner. "It's practice for when they grow up to be coal miners
and state policemen."

Kachigan swung around in surprise, realizing the man
strolling companionably at his shoulder wasn't Taggart but
Leon Daniels. He glanced down the block and saw that his
partner had stopped at the fruit market near the train station
to dicker over a basket of grapes. With a sigh, Kachigan
paused at the corner of Lock Alley to wait for him.

"Did you play that game when you were in school?" he asked the labor organizer, who had paused with him.

"That game and a lot of others," Daniels agreed. "You can't learn to win if you never play."

"You also can't lose," Kachigan retorted. Seen in broad daylight, with his brown hair neatly trimmed and a clean coat thrown over his collarless shirt, Leon Daniels looked even more like a slumming college boy than an ex-coal miner. Kachigan wasn't sure why that should make the labor organizer more annoying, but it did. "That was the mistake I made the day I arrested you. I just shouldn't have played that game."

"You're learning," Daniels approved. "Although not very fast. Did you really think you'd find an Italian anywhere in Tarentum who would translate for that scab you arrested the other night?"

Kachigan lifted an eyebrow at him. "I thought that's why you were here. Didn't you take Italian lessons in college?"

The verbal jab got him an admiring whistle rather than the start he'd been hoping for. "Sorry, no," Leon Daniels admitted lightly. "My specialties at Haverford were formal debate and lacrosse. I was the best ball handler in school before they kicked me out."

"I should have known." Kachigan let the labor organizer decide for himself what part of his history that comment referred to. "So if you're not here to translate for me, what do you want?"

"A uniform coalfield walkout, a return to the 1902 pay scale and a night with Evelyn Nesbit," the younger man retorted. "But I'll settle for a miners' rally that doesn't include any surprise visits from the Cossacks. You weren't planning to call them down from Natrona tonight, were you?"

Kachigan sighed. "I should say 'yes' just to keep the streets clear and the trolleys running. But since I don't supply coal to the Pennsylvania Railroad, the state police probably wouldn't come even if I did call. As long as you don't burn down any coal company offices, you should be safe."

The labor organizer gave him a glinting leprechaun smile. "What if we burned down the county lockup?"

"Lieutenant Brennan would probably give you a medal for that."

"But Big Roge McGara would string you up by the thumbs, Danny Boy." Taggart's heavy steps echoed off the sidewalk behind them, punctuated by the occasional spit of grape seeds. "And so would the Black Hand, if you burned it down with their boy still inside."

Kachigan scowled at his overly informative partner. "We don't know for sure he's part of the Black Hand—"

"Say no more." Daniels took a step back, lifting both hands in what seemed to be only a half-laughing protest. "I'll take the yellow dogs any day, even the cossacks and Pinks if I have to, over those damned Italian hoodlums. Your lockup's safe from me tonight."

Taggart grunted in satisfaction, watching the wiry young man disappear into the crowd. "There, wasn't that easy? Now we can sleep through the miners' rally."

"No, *you* can sleep through the miners' rally." Kachigan turned off South Canal Street, heading for the Tarentum town hall and the old basement lockup Roger McGara had rented as their branch office. "I've still got to go out and find us a translator." He paused beside the doorway to let the big man finish spitting out his grape seeds. "Maybe I could get someone to come in after dark. Or in a closed carriage."

A thin slice of smile showed under Taggart's sandy mustache. "Or from the South Side? Where you've gone to fetch her?"

Kachigan sighed. "I don't think so," he said over his shoulder as he opened the lockup door. "Helen Sorby might not be mad at me right now, but the surest way in the world to make her furious is to—"

"—arrest an innocent man?"

Kachigan's head swung around in disbelief, but there was no mistaking the familiar rumpled frown that had fastened on him as soon as he stepped into the lockup office. "Helen! What are you doing here?"

"Annoying me with questions." J.P. Frick looked up from the girly magazine he was reading at his desk. "How long does it take you to find a dago in this town, Kachigan? It wouldn't take me five minutes, Little Europe is so lousy with them."

Kachigan gritted his teeth and went past the balding detective without a word, knowing the question was meant only to irritate him and Helen Sorby both. He opened his mouth to apologize for Frick's language, but as usual when she was annoyed about something Helen didn't waste any time letting him know.

"Milo, which side of this coal strike are you on?"

"What?" He stopped a few feet away, more startled than offended by that question. "What's that supposed to mean?"

She gave him a smoldering look. "It means that four coal miners were killed up in Natrona last night and twenty more were injured! And I just found out you were there, helping the state police break up their rally."

Kachigan threw an aggravated look back at Frick, knowing where her information had to have come from. None of the stories Taggart had read out to him from the morning papers had made any mention of county detectives. "It wasn't a rally, Helen, it was a riot that killed a young office boy—"

"That's funny, because the afternoon paper said the office boy escaped out a window after Murchison's police chief left him to die," she retorted. "With the aid of some of the pit boys from your so-called riot!"

"There, you see, Milo," said his partner placidly. "All that fulminating you did about Truxall on the way home last night was for nothing."

"No, it wasn't," Kachigan said curtly. "He still left the boy up there. And for your information, Helen, I'm not on *any* side of this strike, miners or mine owners."

"Then why are you doing Bernard Flinn's dirty work for him?"

"Who told you *that*?" He swung back to scowl at Frick,

who was now squirming under the heavy hand Taggart had dropped on his shoulder. "Jape?"

"No. Lillian Murchison."

It was the familiar last name that dragged Kachigan's attention back to her, but it was the determined set of her chin that kept it there. He'd gotten to know Helen very well over these last months. That particular tilt of her strong-boned face usually meant some issue of social injustice had come to her attention, and she was hell-bent on correcting it. And there was only one thing he'd done recently that could be taken as an act of oppression against the working class.

"Murchison's wife told you about the Italian boy we arrested up at Bull Creek Mine?"

"Yes." Helen's scowl deepened. "Milo, you know Bernard Flinn can't be trusted! He's the most ruthless and corrupt company police chief in Pittsburgh. How could you arrest someone just on his say-so?"

"I didn't do it on his say-so," Kachigan said, frowning. "I did it because there was a dead body and no other witnesses."

"And because Flinn was trying to teach the kid how to speak English with the barrel of a gun," Art Taggart added, from where he now sat at Frick's desk. There was no sign of the balding detective, although his magazine still lay where he'd dropped it. Ordinarily Kachigan would have ascribed his sudden departure to the fact that the town clock was ringing the start of the noon lunch hour, but in this case he suspected Taggart's hard grip and hard-toed shoe had also had a say in the matter. "Those are Flinn's handprints on the kid's neck, Miss Sorby, not ours."

"I don't doubt that, Mr. Taggart," Helen said dryly. "I wasn't accusing you of torturing him."

"Then what *are* you accusing us of?" Kachigan asked.

"Of letting Bernard Flinn use you like—like stooges," she said indignantly. "To help him carry out whatever scheme he's using to crush the miners' union in this valley."

"Flinn's not cooking up any schemes to crush the

union," Kachigan retorted. "He's working for a union company, one that's probably going to settle for the higher scale in a few days."

"Of course he is," Helen said, sounding exasperated. "Where else would the coal operators put him, if they didn't want anyone to know what underhanded deals he was cutting?"

"Do you have any evidence of that?"

"I know someone bribed the union's ex-president to convince coal miners to take the old pay scale," she said. "And when that didn't work, he encouraged them to strike instead of taking the new higher pay scale."

"But that was in Pittsburgh," Kachigan pointed out. "If Flinn's behind all that, why has he been working up here in Tarentum, almost an hour away from the city by train or trolley?"

"*Exactly!* This is Bernard K. Flinn we're talking about, a man who makes as much in a year as some of the steel barons. Why in the world would he take a job working at a single mine like Bull Creek? I looked up Sedgwick Coal & Coke in the newspaper stock listings last night and they're so small they're not even there. I refuse to believe they're paying Flinn's usual wages just to see them through this strike. Especially when they're already unionized!"

Kachigan had opened his mouth to argue with her when he realized he already agreed with most of what she had said. He stared at her in exasperated silence instead, not sure whether he was feeling annoyance or relief at having her socialist diatribes delivered in person again, instead of over a scratchy telephone line.

"I told Milo that Flinn was just using us for scapegoats," Taggart said, his voice coming muffled through the pages of the girly magazine he was now unrepentantly reading. "But since he'd fooled us into coming up there with a telegram sent through the local operator, we couldn't very well turn around and go home."

"And we couldn't leave the murder witness up there with him," Kachigan added. "If Flinn didn't have a convenient county detective to dump him on, I suspect he would have killed him and hidden his body in some abandoned part of the mine.''

"Just to get revenge for his murdered miner?''

"A man who wasn't even one of his employees?'' Kachigan shook his head emphatically. "No, Helen. He would have done it to keep from having trouble with the Black Hand.''

That made her eyes widen in unexpected dismay. "That's not just a rumor? Flinn really is having trouble with the Black Hand?''

"I don't know whether he had any trouble with them in the past,'' Kachigan said wryly. "But if they had seen the way he'd slammed one of their boys around, he would certainly have had trouble with them in the future.''

"And you're sure the boy you arrested really is— '' Helen bit down on something she would have said, then cleared her throat, and finished, "—one of theirs?''

Kachigan turned away, reaching for the ring of keys that hung on the wall beside them. When he turned back, Helen Sorby was giving him the look he'd missed most over the last ten days—half annoyed and half amused, but willing to tolerate his fits and starts because she trusted him. It was a look she used to bestow only on her beloved twin brother, but sometime during this last month of fierce political arguments and shared dinners, Kachigan had realized he'd become the recipient of it too. Seeing it now, after her unexplained days of absence, made a little knot he didn't even know he'd been carrying around in his chest melt away.

"All we know right now is that he's wearing a Black Hand tattoo,'' he said, clearing his throat to cover his delay in speaking. "That's because I haven't found anyone in town willing to translate my questions into Italian for him, so he can tell us who he really is. What do you say about doing it, Helen?''

"What do I say?'' Her chin lifted resolutely. "*Andiamo!*''

• • •

The young Italian boy's bruises had faded to purplish marks with yellow edges, and the gunshot wound across his ear now sported a neat cap of bandage, courtesy of Owen Riley and his army field-dressing skills. But the mute incomprehension in his eyes when he turned to look at them through the bars was as solid as ever. Around him, the rest of the lockup's cells were silent and empty.

"*Quando mi scaricavate?*" the Italian boy asked softly. It was the only thing he ever said. He said it in response to every question or comment they put to him, he said it first thing in the morning and last thing at night, and for all Kachigan knew, all it meant was, "What time is it?"

He lifted an eyebrow at Helen, who was staring fixedly at the boy through the bars, then returned his own gaze to the prisoner. He wanted to see whether the expression on his face would become joyful or wary when he realized Helen could translate for him.

"What is he asking?"

"When you're going to get rid of him," she replied. Not a flicker of awareness disturbed the resigned look on the boy's face at that exchange, and Kachigan relinquished any remaining suspicion he had about the young man's lack of English. "I think he means when you're going to let him out of here, but I'm not sure. What do you want me to say?"

Kachigan had had two days to think about that. "Tell him we're not going to kill him. Tell him that if he can explain what happened down in Bull Creek Coal Mine, I might let him go."

That got him a flashing upward look. "And you might not?"

"Not if what he saw puts him in danger from the real murderer." Kachigan looked down at her steadily. Helen always judged the truth by the straightness of your gaze, since she could never keep her own gaze from dropping when she lied. "But we'll eventually let him go once we've caught the man who did it. You can tell him that too."

She nodded and translated it all into a smooth torrent of Italian. The imprisoned boy cursed and jumped to his feet, then came across the cell toward her almost helplessly, like a fish being reeled toward a fisherman. The only expression Kachigan could see on his face was the uninformative one of complete surprise. Perhaps he didn't think that ladies who wore pretty pleated shirtwaists with high lace collars should know how to speak Italian. He said something in return when she was done, but even Kachigan could tell it was just a simple interrogative.

"He wants to know who I am," Helen said, confirming his guess. "What should I tell him?"

Kachigan paused, sorting through possible responses. He discarded "my fiancée" because he knew it would start a fight; threw out "a newspaper reporter" because it might frighten the boy back into silence; and reluctantly decided that "a social worker" would be too confusing for a recent immigrant to handle. "Do you know the word for 'secretary' in Italian?" he asked at last.

That got him another flashing look, but no argument. *"Helena Sorby. Sono segretaria di polizia di contea."*

That got a quick reaction, although it didn't look like the one that Kachigan was hoping for. The young Italian immigrant stepped back, gazing at her suspiciously through the bars. *"Polizia di stato?"*

"Niente affatto!" Helen said vehemently. *"Il polizia di Alleghenia contea."* She glanced back at Kachigan, looking a little guilty. "I'm sorry, I tried to explain that I worked for the County Detectives' Bureau, but he thought I meant the state police."

"Is that right?"

She scowled, as if she'd guessed what he was thinking. "That doesn't mean he's a criminal, Milo! Anyone from around here could be afraid of the state police."

"Anyone who's been in the country long enough to know about them," he agreed. "See if he'll tell you his name."

"Come si chiama?" Helen asked.

The boy frowned at her for a long minute, then shook his head so emphatically that coal dust flew out from his uncombed hair. He said something long and liquid in Italian, something that sounded nothing like a name. Then he went back across the cell and sat down on the metal cot that was its only furniture, folding his arms across his chest in a resigned gesture that could have belonged to a grizzled peasant half-a-century older. Helen frowned after him, looking frustrated and annoyed.

"Well?" Kachigan asked.

"He says he was told on the boat never to give his name or information about himself to any policeman in America. He says he was told they were all corrupt and would only try to get money from his relatives to release him."

Kachigan's mouth twisted in wry amusement. "I suppose that's one way to describe the bail system. That's all he said?"

"That's all."

They stood in silence for a moment, staring at the bruised boy. He continued to sit stolidly in his cell, clearly not rattled by either their presence or their gaze. Was that the patient incomprehension of an immigrant used to the failures and abuses of government in his own country, Kachigan wondered. Or was it the stubborn code of silence the Black Hand exacted from its members? It was frustrating to realize that even with his questions translated into Italian, he was no closer to an answer for that question than he had been two days ago.

"*Io sono anche di Mano Negro,*" Helen said softly. "*Monte Albano.*"

The words were meaningless to Kachigan, but their effect on his prisoner was both immediate and electric. He vaulted off his cot, metamorphosing in an instant from a grizzled peasant to a dangerous young man. Before either of them could back away, his hands were reaching out for Helen through the bars as if he wanted to pull her close enough to damage. Kachigan cursed and shoved between them, managing to get an arm and a shoulder in front of Helen before she was dragged up against the cold steel. He was left with his back toward the prisoner, fervently hoping he didn't have a stiletto hidden in the sole of a shoe. Helen was pressed so close to him that he could feel the rapid rise

and fall of her breathing through both their coats. The grip
the young man had on her neck and hair to keep her that
close must have hurt, although she never made a sound.
Kachigan cursed again, in soft but fierce Armenian, and
lifted a hand to chop at the prisoner's outstretched arm.

"Milo, no." Helen's hand clamped on his wrist with
surprising strength, but it was the way she brushed her lips
upward across his throat that really stopped him. "Don't
call for help," she said, when her mouth finally arrived at
his ear. The words were carried on a gossamer breath,
nearly voiceless. Kachigan might once have assumed that
meant she was frightened, but he knew her well enough
now to know it was just the only way Helen Sorby could
soften her ringing voice into a whisper. "He's going to talk
to us."

Kachigan frowned, barely able to believe what that whisper had to mean. He ducked his own head down into the
jasmine-scented darkness of her hair and hissed, "In
English?"

"I think so." She straightened up and banged her fist
imperiously against his blocking shoulder. With a grunt,
Kachigan slid out from between the two Italians, although
he was careful to keep his arm curved around Helen's
waist, stepping behind her protectively. From here, he could
tear off the young man's grip and haul his translator out of
reach at the first sign of danger.

"*Dite mi chi conoscete!*" the Italian boy commanded.

Kachigan could feel Helen gather herself up with one
decisive breath. "*Il Merlo,*" she said firmly. "*Niccolo Santangelo. Lui è mio cugino.*"

"*Ahh.*" He glanced up over her shoulder at Kachigan,
assessing him in silence for a moment. The blank mask of
his face had cracked open like the door to a coal stove,
allowing a glimpse of the fiery intelligence burning beneath
it. "*Chi è?*"

"*Cosa pensa?*" Helen startled Kachigan by sliding a
hand down the arm he'd wrapped protectively around her
waist, not to pull it free but to press it tighter against her.

"*Il mio fidanzato. E il soltanto onesto poliziotto di questa contea.*"

That made the young man laugh bitterly and release his hold on her, turning away with what Kachigan recognized from his street-patrolling days as a dismissive Italian gesture, the outward flip of fingers from beneath the chin.

"What did you just say to him?" he demanded, frowning.

"That you were the only honest policeman in the county."

Kachigan cursed and stepped back, pulling Helen with him. It wasn't the shock of hearing perfectly unaccented English, coming out of a mouth that for so many days had spoken only Italian. It was the bare edge of polished steel that glinted in the young man's voice, the controlled sound of someone who commanded men and made decisions. It was getting harder and harder to think of this curly-haired youngster as a boy.

"Is it true?" the prisoner inquired.

Kachigan frowned at him. "True that I'm honest, or that I'm the only one who is?"

"The answer is yes, either way," Helen said impatiently.

"Then I still shouldn't talk to you, whether you're engaged to marry *Il Merlo*'s cousin or not." The young Italian's mouth curved in what was not quite a smile. "You may release me for the murder now, but you'll remember me for the other business later. Eh?"

Without meaning to, Kachigan tightened the grip he still had on his translator. He was starting to guess how she'd convinced their prisoner to talk, although he still wasn't sure exactly what lever she'd used to crack through his perfect shell of peasant stupidity. "I'll remember you for that anyway," he said. "No innocent coal miner would hide the fact he knew English this long, even from the County Detectives' Bureau."

"True," the young man admitted, with the charming honesty Kachigan had seen before in this kind of ethnic criminal. For the initiates of these ancient secret societies, disregard of the law often became more of a social obligation than a personal act of hostility. "All right, then, let's make that deal you wanted. I'll tell you about that dead man in the mine, and you let me out of here."

"Maybe." Kachigan refused to be rushed into a promise he'd regret. "Did you kill him?"

"No."

It wasn't a swift denial or a furious one, just a cool and simple statement of fact. The trouble was, now that he knew how good an actor this young man was, Kachigan wasn't sure how much trust to place in anything he said or any way he said it. He glanced down at Helen, still standing watchfully inside the curve of his arm.

"Is there a way we can make him swear he's telling the truth?" he asked.

She glanced up at him over her shoulder, and he could tell from the way her teeth were digging into her lower lip that she wasn't sure how much to tell him. It occurred to Kachigan that although he'd heard about and met several members of the Irish side of her family, Helen had never said much at all about the Italian side. He was starting to guess why.

"The only one he has to tell the truth to is his *capo*," she said eventually. "He's not allowed to tell anyone else anything. So if you're asking me if he's lying to you, I'd have to say—"

"That's only true if it's our business," the young man interjected smoothly. "If it's not our business, I can tell you as much about it as I want."

Kachigan gave him a measuring glance. "You expect me to believe that a man stabbed in the back with a stiletto wasn't any of your business? How stupid do you think I am?"

"Pretty stupid." The Italian boy grinned at him, then winced as the expression stretched the bruises splattered across his face. "After all, you're the only honest policeman in the County Detectives' Bureau."

"Whether or not the murder was any of your business," Helen said firmly, "working in a coal mine certainly isn't. What were you doing down there in the first place?"

"Ah, *la rompiballe scrittrice*!" the young man said, sighing. "For the answer to that, you're going to have to ask *Il Merlo*."

Helen scowled and shook herself free of Kachigan's grip with sudden violence. He wondered if the prisoner had called her something vulgar in Italian, but the way her fingers locked around his wrist was urgent, not embarrassed. "I'm leaving," she said, before Kachigan could disagree. "You don't need me to talk to him anymore, now that you know he speaks English. See me out."

Kachigan bit down on the protest he was about to make, knowing Helen Sorby was the last woman in the world who would demand an escort to the door for the sake of politeness.

"Very well." He turned his arm inside her grip to the intimate hold a fiancé would use. Helen not only didn't protest, she curled her fingers around his arm with what looked like equal affection. From the cell behind them, Kachigan heard the sound of undeceived laughter.

"All right," said the young man. "Go talk to your cousin, then, if you need to do that before you'll believe what I saw. And while you're there, tell him Sandrino Racca never got the goods, because some damn yellow dog grabbed me and beat me up before I could even look for them."

"Don't worry," Helen said fiercely. "I will."

She dragged Kachigan out of the row of quiet cells with more speed than grace, but the sound of Racca's quiet laughter still followed them all the way through the door to the front hall. Taggart looked up from doodling with a pencil on the pages of J.P. Frick's girly magazine, then discreetly opened the desk's top drawer and slid it out of sight.

"Sounds like you managed to amuse our boy in there." He lifted an eyebrow at Helen's glower. "But he sure didn't amuse you. What did you find out?"

"That he knows I'm a newspaper writer. Which means my Black Hand cousin Niccolo has told him all about me." She dropped Kachigan's arm without even looking at him.

He would have put her diffidence down to embarrassment at owning up to such a disreputable relative, if her mouth hadn't tightened into the resolute line of a coal miner storming the picket lines. "I'll go and talk to him about it right away."

Kachigan cleared his throat. "You mean, *we'll* talk to him about it, don't you?"

Helen Sorby shook her head. "There's only one place I can be sure of finding him, and that's at Cousin Lena's. If I bring a policeman there without warning him, Niccolo will stick a knife into both of us before his mother can finish making tea."

He knew it was probably a mistake even as he said it, but he couldn't help himself. "Even if the policeman was your fiancé?"

"*Especially* if he was my fiancé." Helen buttoned up her coat and pulled her crumpled muff from her coat pocket. "Which he isn't," she added tartly, before she stepped out the door.

There was a long silence, then Kachigan turned and scowled at his detective partner. "Don't say it," he warned.

"I wasn't going to say a thing," Taggart assured him. "Do I look stupid?"

Kachigan snorted. "Stupid enough to be an honest policeman in the County Detectives' Bureau."

The big man grunted. "No, Milo, that's you. I'm just too lazy to bother getting any more corrupt than the job demands. What did you find out from our boy back there?"

"That he really is part of the local Black Hand," Kachigan said. "That he probably saw the murder and possibly committed it. And that we can't trust a thing he says, whether it's in English or in Italian."

"Not exactly an improvement on what we knew before," Taggart commented. "Have you noticed that the more we find out about this case, the less we seem to know?"

The door was flung open before Kachigan could reply and Owen Riley nearly fell through the doorway, keeping himself upright by hanging on to the door for support. Kachigan frowned and leaped toward him, but when he got close he could see the young detective wasn't wounded, just breathless. His face was far redder than his wine-colored birthmark could account for, as if he had come all the way from the train station at a dead run.

"Captain—I mean, sir—" Riley paused to swallow and collect himself, like an army recruit reporting for duty. "Detective Kachigan, you've got to come out to Bull Creek Coal, right away!"

Kachigan frowned. "Another telegram from Bernard Flinn?"

"No, sir—" Riley stopped hanging on to the door and swung it wide enough to show them the afternoon sky outside. A column of black smoke was punching its way up into the clear April sunshine, roiling like a thundercloud. It was coming from too high up the slope of Tarentum to be a cleaning blast from any of the town's factories. "I heard the blast myself, sir, on the train down from Natrona. The mine must have exploded."

EIGHT

For as long as Helen could remember, the little house on Owl Alley in Tarentum had always smelled like anise and vanilla. That was because her mother's cousin Lena always had a fresh stack of *pizelli*, those Italian pressed-wafer cookies, sitting beside her *pizelle* iron. Today, however, the delicate scent was lost in the more earthy aromas of garlic, fried peppers, and dark roasted coffee. The coffee smell alone would have told Helen her cousin Niccolo was back in residence after his well-deserved stint in the Butler County Jail. Lena Santangelo, a widow with two married daughters in Coraopolis and only this single ne'er-do-well son, never drank anything but tea.

"*Cugina* Lena?" Helen had already knocked on the front door, left open so that warm April afternoon air could circulate through the winter-chilled house. She could hear the regular thumping of something from the backyard, but couldn't decide if it was a laundry wringer or a butter churn. No one was in the kitchen to ask, so she set her unneeded muff down on a chair and stepped out through the narrow door to the back pantry. Out in the backyard, beyond a golden fuzz of budding forsythia, she could see what looked like a rippling curtain of dust flying away on the spring wind. Enlightened, she slipped sideways out the door, rounding the laundry line on the upwind side.

"Do you need some help beating the rugs, *Cugina* Lena?" she asked, letting the soft accent that always tinged her Italian deepen. Her mother's cousin had emigrated from Calabria as a grown woman, and retained more of her Catanzaro accent than the other branch of the family.

"No, but I could use some help beating the county police." The voice that answered her in Italian had the same accent, but it rang as deep and sonorous as a cathedral bell. "Isn't that what you came here for, *Cugina* Helena?"

She ducked around the other side of the rugs and scowled at her second cousin. Niccolo Santangelo still had the dark hair that had given him his "Blackbird" nickname, sleek and long as the feathers of a raven's wing, but it was thinning fast on either side of his intelligent forehead. Combined with his winter-pale skin, it made him look more like a medieval monk than the *capo* of a large clan of the *Mano Negro*. He was beating dust from the draped rugs with efficient strokes, wielding an ornate and brand-new tin rug-beater that his mother would never have bought for herself.

"I told you the first time you asked, *no*." Helen shielded her eyes against the treacherous April breeze that was now blowing dust her way. "I'm not giving you anything you can use against the Allegheny County Detectives' Bureau! Not even me."

"I noticed." Niccolo Santangelo paused to let the wind clear itself out, giving her a grin that would have made his thin face look boyish if it hadn't been for the knife scars that riddled his cheeks. One of them was new, a pink raised path that led from one ear to the corner of his mouth. "All I want is for you to ask one little favor from your detective boyfriend, and the next thing I know you've stopped coming to visit Tarentum."

"That's because you didn't want just one favor," Helen snapped. "You wanted to blackmail Milo Kachigan with the fact that he'd done it, over and over, until he'd practically be a member of the *Mano Negro* himself."

"Maybe so, maybe so," Santangelo admitted, looking

more amused than guilty. He was still, in his late thirties, every bit as addicted to deceit and danger as he'd been when Helen first knew him, back when he'd been an alley-cat teenager who drove his family crazy with his truancies and his knife fights. In retrospect, she realized he'd probably been a member of the *Mano Negro* even then, following in his taciturn Sicilian father's shadow. But all she could recall from her childhood memories was how impressed she and Thomas had been by the neat way Niccolo could skin an apple with his knife.

"Helena!" That wheezing voice was her elderly cousin's, made scratchier than usual by the exertion of carrying a basket of laundry up the basement stairs. Helen went to take it from her quickly. During the time she'd been coming up to Tarentum to visit Milo Kachigan, she'd gotten into the habit of helping Cousin Lena with the laundry to ease some of the stress on her worn-out lungs. That was another thing that had stopped as soon as Cousin Niccolo had been released from jail. "What a nice surprise to see you! You'll stay for tea and some *pizelli*?"

Helen opened her mouth to say she couldn't, but the heavy basket of wet curtains was lifted out of her arms before she had a chance. "Of course, she'll stay, she came here to make a deal with me. Mama, I told you to let me carry these. When are you going to listen to me?"

Lena Santangelo snorted, and wiped her damp hands on her apron. Her hair had been silver-mottled even in Helen's infancy, but it was nearly white now, and her once-strong shoulders had started to shrink into a dowager's hump. Her dark eyes still crackled under their white eyebrows, however, full of peppery temper and every bit of her son's intelligence.

"If you want to help me around the house, why don't you go out and get me a daughter-in-law, eh?" she demanded. "It's not a man's job to be washing clothes and beating rugs."

"Or cooking?" Niccolo demanded in turn, his voice rising to the good-natured shout of an Italian discussion. "I

didn't notice you complaining when I made breakfast today!''

''Ah, cooking, anyone can cook! Even Helen's brother
Tommaso, that silly Irishman who cooks with his beer,
knows how to make such a *bagna calda*—'' Lena kissed
the tips of her fingers and then spread them apart to indicate
perfection and astonishment in one economical gesture. Helen listened in reluctant amusement. She had never been
sure why her twin always got labeled with their father's
Irish blood while she herself was treated like a full-blooded
Calabrian. It must have been her darker hair and eyes.

''I don't want to hear about Tommaso's *bagna calda*,''
Niccolo declared. ''I want to hear some coffee perking and
some eggs and hot sausage frying for lunch, eh? It's hard
work beating rugs—''

''But honest, at least,'' his mother snapped, then pushed
through the rugs and disappeared before her son could reply.

Niccolo Santangelo shook his head, admiringly. ''Still
full of piss and vinegar, my mamma,'' he said in English.
''And before you say, 'She's right and you should respect
your mother,' keep in mind you have a deal to make with
me, Hell.''

Helen scowled at him, not sure whether she was more
annoyed by the hated childhood nickname or the fact that
her cousin was right. ''How do you know? I might just
have stopped by to help with the laundry.''

''Except this isn't Mamma's usual laundry day. She's
doing spring cleaning.'' Santangelo began beating dust
from the rugs again with vigorous and practiced strokes.
His mother might berate him for it, but there was no denying that when he was home he worked as hard at keeping
their little house clean as any daughter-in-law would. ''So,
what do you need me to do for that county detective of
yours? And more importantly, what are you going to have
him do for me?''

''Nothing,'' Helen said sharply. ''Except maybe arrest
you someday if you keep trying to corrupt him.''

Without warning, the man she was facing across the rugs

turned from a cousin into the *capo* of the local Black Hand. His face froze into a stiff, scarred mask whose only living spark was the cold blackbird gleam of his eyes. With a shiver, Helen realized this was what he must look like when he conducted the business of the secret Italian society.

"That might not be such a good idea," was all Niccolo Santangelo said.

Helen grimaced. She knew how much hidden, serpentine power her cousin wielded in this valley full of Italian immigrants, whose acceptance of the *Mano Negro* was stamped into them back in the impoverished and ungoverned mountains of central and southern Italy. She also knew just what kind of man Milo Kachigan was.

"This isn't a deal," she said at last, meeting Santangelo's gaze without a quiver. Her words might be carefully selected, but they also had the advantage of being true. "It's just the way things are. Kachigan is holding Sandrino Racca as a material witness to a murder. If you order Racca to cooperate in the investigation, there's a good chance he'll be released."

Santangelo shrugged. "And if I don't order him to cooperate? From what I hear, your boyfriend is too honest to charge a man for a crime he didn't commit."

"True, but he might get curious about what it is you're trying to hide," Helen retorted. "And if he starts looking into the activities of the *Mano Negro* around here ——"

"You don't think I can stop him?"

"Only by killing him," she said flatly. "Or by threatening to kill me."

Santangelo grinned and turned back into her irritating cousin. "Oh, that would make Mamma real happy, me threatening to cut the throat of her favorite cousin's baby girl. I'd never eat a *pizelle* again as long as I lived."

"Because I cut *your* throat before you do it," said a raspy voice on the other side of the rugs. Helen jumped and Niccolo Santangelo cursed, both of them staring at the snowy head that had poked through the overlap of two carpet pieces. Lena Santangelo switched back to her preferred language of Italian. "I told you last time Helen was here, you stop badgering her about that detective of hers. She's going to marry him and he's going to be part of the family and you don't blackmail family. Understand, Niccolino?''

''I understand.''

''I'm not—'' Helen cut her automatic protest off, since it occurred to her that this might not be the best time to proclaim her firm intention of remaining single. Instead, she sighed and brushed the dust off her russet coat, then followed her Italian relatives back to the quiet warmth of the kitchen.

Lena Santangelo waved her to a seat, pouring coffee so thick it looked like mud into her son's cup. Thankfully, Helen saw she'd already been given hot tea. It smelled almost as aromatic as the expensive kind Lillian Murchison served.

''I have a message for you from Sandrino Racca,'' she said to Niccolo's back, while he washed his hands in the sink.

''So you got him to talk in the lockup? I told you that password would come in handy someday.'' Her cousin rinsed his hands and dried them. ''What did he say?''

''That he got arrested and beaten up by a yellow dog before he could even look around for the goods.'' Helen lifted her eyebrows. ''I don't suppose you'd be willing to tell me what that means?''

Niccolo sat and began scooping up his scrambled eggs and sausage with a slice of bread, not bothering with the fork his mother had set beside the plate. Helen would have put his lack of manners down to his recent stay in prison, if she hadn't seen him eat the same way when he was only sixteen years old. ''Yellow dog? Sure, I'll tell you what that means. It's slang for a coal company policeman.''

Helen gritted her teeth. ''I *knew* that. I meant the 'goods.' ''

''Ah.'' Santangelo polished off his eggs with a single-minded efficiency that probably did date from his stay in prison, then began making himself a sandwich from the plate of fried hot peppers on the table. Helen winced when

he added a layer of grape jelly, but didn't look away.
"Well, that's a little harder to explain."

"Try," she suggested. "If you do a good enough job,
maybe Bernard Flinn won't get away with blaming this
murder on the Black Hand."

That got her the full intensity of *Il Merlo*'s blackbird
gaze. "You think the police chief up at Bull Creek Mine
wants to blame us for that? Why?"

"Because it would cover whatever he's doing to break
the miners' union," Helen said. "Flinn's famous down in
Pittsburgh for stopping strikes. He's got to be doing more
up here than just sitting guard on one little Tarentum coal
mine."

"Maybe so, maybe so." Niccolo poured more strong
coffee into his mug, stopping only when the sludge of
grounds at the bottom of the coffeepot began to clog the
spout. "I have to admit, I wondered why he threw Sandrino
to the county boys when he found him up at Bull Creek,
instead of ripping his fingernails off to find out what he
knew. But if Flinn was the one behind the murder—"

"—then all he needed was a scapegoat." Helen finished.
"Tell me the truth, Nicco, on your mother's immortal soul.
Did you send Sandrino Racca up to that mine to kill that
man, whoever he was?"

"No." Santangelo sent a laughing look across the table,
switching to Italian for a moment. "Although my mother's
going to hell anyway, because she spends my blood money
but never gives any of it to the church."

"That's what the new priest said," Lena Santangelo
agreed through a mouthful of *pizelle*. "I told him I'd see
him down there."

"So what *was* Racca doing up in that mine?"

Her cousin switched back to English, although she
wasn't sure why, since his mother could understand him
equally well in either language. Perhaps it was a sort of
filial politeness not to talk about crime in his native tongue.
"He was there to meet a payoff, of course. It just wasn't
one of ours."

Helen frowned at him. "Who did it belong to, then? Another clan of the *Mano Negro*?"

"Holy Mary, Mother of God, no! What do you think, I'm crazy or something? *Niente affatto!*" Niccolo Santangelo drained the last coffee slurry from his cup. "That was the problem, Hell. We weren't sure who the payoff was being made to. All we knew was where it was coming from, because we had an inside man."

"At Murchison Brothers Coal, you mean."

She'd hoped to surprise him with that educated guess, but had to settle for a gleaming look of admiration. "You always were the smartest one in the family, little cousin. After me, of course. Yes, we have a friend in Murchison's front office."

"Someone who owes you a gambling debt," Helen translated. "They told you Charles Murchison was cashing out a lot of his stocks to pay some kind of extortion threat?"

"Right again." Niccolo leaned across the table, his face once again chilling into that stiff, scarred mask. It made his mother glance at him worriedly. "And it wasn't just *some* kind of threat, Hell. It was a Black Hand threat. I saw the letter."

"A fake," Helen guessed.

"Of course. We don't do stupid things like blackmail the heads of companies for fifty thousand dollars."

"*Fifty thousand—*" Enlightenment blazed inside Helen, lifting her voice almost to a shout. "In return for the missing securities!"

That did get her a surprised look. "Yes—but how did you know about that? My informant swore only a few people in the company were told."

Helen weighed her options, torn between paying back the favor her cousin had done her and giving him information that could make him even more dangerous. After a moment, the look of kindling suspicion in his blackbird eyes made the decision for her. "The Murchisons told me about the securities themselves, when they hired me to look for their daughter Emmy. She ran away from home, the same day the securities disappeared. They were afraid she was the one who had stolen them.''

''And was using them to get her inheritance a little early?'' Niccolo Santangelo sat back, frowning and then rubbing a hand across his newest scar, as if the expression made it ache. ''Maybe so, maybe so . . . but can you see a millionaire's daughter pretending to be the Black Hand and setting up a payoff inside a coal mine?''

''No,'' Helen said flatly. ''I can see Bernard Flinn doing it, though. Especially since it was his coal mine.''

Her cousin nodded. ''And especially since the man who came to deliver the payoff is the one who was killed in it.''

She took a deep breath, staring at him. ''Then what happened to the payoff?''

''That,'' said Niccolo Santangelo, ''is what I was hoping Sandrino Racca could tell me.''

''Then let's go pay him a visit and talk to him!''

Her cousin lifted an eyebrow. ''In the town lockup? I don't go there unless I'm in handcuffs, little cousin. It sets a bad precedent. And even if I did, you think I'm going to be stupid enough to let Sandrino tell me where that payoff money is while your boyfriend's listening?''

Helen made a face, silently conceding that, and consoled herself with a *pizelle*. ''What if I could get Kachigan to bring Racca here, so he could talk to you in private about the payoff money? Would you let him tell us what he knows about the murder?''

''If it implicates Flinn, sure.'' Her cousin gave her a smiling but unfriendly look. ''If it implicates someone I'd rather blackmail, all bets are off.''

Helen frowned. ''I don't know if I can get Milo to agree to that.''

''Then just don't tell him. Because if we're betting on who actually committed this murder, *my* money's on Bernard Flinn.''

''Mine too.'' Helen thought about it for a moment, then sighed. ''All right. I can't promise anything, but I'll see what I can do.'' She drank the last of her tea, then glanced at the watch pinned to her shirtwaist and gathered up her coat. "I'll get back to you after supper, if you're going to be here."

"For a chance at fifty thousand dollars, I think I can manage to stay home one night." Niccolo stood up and handed over her muff. "I'll walk you down to the trolley stop."

Lena Santangelo accepted the kiss Helen pressed onto her wrinkled cheek. "That means he wants to talk to you in private, probably about that Armenian boyfriend of yours," she said in Italian. "Don't let him try to tell you an Italian boy would be better, Helena. Look what I got by marrying his father!"

Helen hugged her elderly relative, feeling the fragile give of once-sturdy bones. "Don't worry, *Cugina* Lena. I won't."

Her cousin lifted a quizzical eyebrow at that, but followed her outside before he spoke. The streets of West Tarentum were surprisingly quiet despite the coal strike, with only a few housewives taking advantage of the warm weather to hang out their laundry. Helen hoped the miners here were sleeping in, and not off rioting at the picket lines.

"You're really going to get married to a county detective?"

"Maybe," she said, making herself able to meet Niccolo's gaze only by adding a mental "not" to that sentence. Right now, it was more important to keep Milo Kachigan free of the dirtier side of her family than to stand up for the rights of unmarried women. "Why?"

Her cousin's eyes gleamed wickedly. "It's never too early to start thinking about a wedding present. How does getting rid of your ex-husband sound to you?"

That brought Helen spinning around to stare up at him, heedless of the startled looks this confrontation was getting from the housewives across the street. "What are you talking about?"

"Your ex-husband," Santangelo repeated patiently. "What was the name he used when he married you? James Foster Barton?"

"What about him?"

Her cousin shrugged. "Oh, nothing much. It's just that I thought it might be easier to take a new husband if the old one wasn't still hanging around, embarrassing you with his confidence tricks. Would you like me to kill him for you?"

Helen stared up at him, shaken completely wordless. When she finally regained her voice, it was a measure of her shock that she didn't respond to that outrageous final question but the assumption buried inside it.

"You've *seen* him?" she demanded.

"Not personally," Santangelo said. "I've been in prison for the last six months, remember?"

"But you know for sure he's back in the area?"

"I'm the head of the family now, Hell," Niccolo Santangelo reminded her. "And I take my responsibility more seriously than my father did. I cut Barton's picture out of the paper when he ran out on you, and put him on our watch list. Pittsburgh is the richest city in America, after all. I figured he'd show up here again sometime."

"And you wanted to know when he did, so you could kill him?"

"Oh, no," said her reprobate cousin. "Originally, all I was going to do was send him a Black Hand letter and get back as much of your stolen dowry as I could. But once I heard you were marrying again, I thought it would make a nice little wedding present—"

Helen opened her mouth, although she wasn't sure whether she was going to deny her impending nuptials or condemn her cousin's idea of an appropriate way to celebrate them. A burst of Italian commentary from their fascinated audience of housewives made her snap her mouth shut again instead and start hastily down the street. Niccolo Santangelo followed her, looking amused.

"Don't worry, they're all Calabrian and Sicilian up here," he assured Helen. "They'd never inform on me."

"No, but I will, if James Barton's body ever shows up with a stiletto in the back!" she said. "Where did your men see him?"

"Verona, Cheswick, Tarentum—all up and down the Allegheny Valley. I guess he figured that with you on the South Side, he'd be safe up here.''

"Maybe." Helen was thinking so hard she would have walked right over the trolley tracks if her cousin hadn't pulled her to a stop. "Or maybe he saw the possibility of making so much money that it was worth the risk of exposure."

Santangelo saw her expression and whistled softly. "You don't think it's a coincidence, Hell?''

"That when my ex-husband shows up in the area, securities go missing, an heiress disappears, and people start getting murdered in coal mines?" Helen shook her head. "No, Nicco, I don't.''

"I'm not sure this is such a good idea.''

Helen heaved a tired sigh, watching through the carriage window as one gas lamp after another brightened and then dwindled back into the thin evening mist. After a day in which she'd exposed a member of the Black Hand, confronted her daunting cousin Niccolo, and then found out that her swindler of an ex-husband had returned to western Pennsylvania, the last thing she could bother to be worried about was her aunt's social qualms.

"All I'm going to do is drop in and ask for a photograph of Emmy Murchison, Aunt Pat," she said for the fifth time since they'd left Isabella Street. "It will only take a moment."

"But it's dinnertime, dearest, and the Murchisons are probably entertaining." They passed a long row of parked carriages, whose carved wooden panels and feathered coach horses wore a golden sheen of mist and reflected lamplight. The open gates of the coal baron's household proved he was the one hosting this particular social gathering, making Pat McGregor wince as they turned onto the gravel drive. "It's so rude to drop in uninvited during a party. You really should have come by earlier in the afternoon."

"Earlier in the afternoon, Aunt Pat, I was kicking up my feet in the detectives' office at Tarentum, waiting to see if

Milo Kachigan was ever coming back.'' Helen felt her fore-head rumple at that irritating memory. "All that idiot De-tective Frick would tell me was that he'd been called away to an emergency. It wasn't until I went out for tea that I found out there'd been an explosion up at Bull Creek Coal Mine. And I couldn't even report on it by then, because the last trolleys had already run!''

"Oh, dear.'' Her aunt pushed back the drooping silk lil-ies on her hat to give Helen a worried look. "Were very many miners hurt?''

"Shouldn't have been, Missus Pat.'' That was Jake Bai-ley's rumble coming through the roof, still respectful but sounding much more comfortable with his new client than he had the day before. The long hours spent delivering do-nated food and blankets to the impoverished miners at Har-wick seemed to have cemented their friendship. "All those Bull Creek boys are out on strike right now.''

Pat McGregor grabbed at the carriage strap to steady her-self as they drew to a stop in front of the Murchisons' handsome stone portico. "How fortunate for them.''

"I don't think fortune had anything to do with it, Aunt Pat,'' Helen said dryly. "Not when the only unionized coal mine in Tarentum blows up on the third day of a strike, without anyone working inside it.''

"Can't blame that on the miners hitting a pocket of coal gas,'' Bailey agreed as he opened the carriage door for her. He gave her a curious look. "You think the union did it, Miss Sorby?''

"No,'' she said and gathered up her skirts. "I think the owner of some nonunion coal mine did, in revenge for what Bernard Flinn did to him.''

"*Helen!*'' Pittypat turned her name into a disapproving wail, making the carriage jerk so hard it nearly knocked Helen back into her seat. The horses had apparently mis-taken her aunt for a banshee, or possibly a teamster. "Swear to me you're not going to throw that accusation at poor Mr. Murchison! His wife donated fifteen turkeys to my Harwick relief effort!''

Helen wisely vaulted out of the carriage before she answered, and Bailey scrambled back up to grab his reins with equal foresight. "I can't promise not to say what I think if someone asks, Aunt Pat," she said as she shut the door on her aunt's worried face. "But I promise not to hunt Mr. Murchison down at his dinner party if I don't have to."

She left her aunt loudly prophesying disaster and the livery stable owner soothing his nervous horses. Fortunately, the sound of a three-piece orchestra mechanically sawing their way through the classical sonatas considered appropriate for an elegant dinner drowned out whatever noise the visitors might have made. Helen rapped the door-knocker briskly to make sure it carried past the viola and cello drone. A dark-skinned butler opened it with the same self-effacing silence that all the Murchison servants used to greet guests, although he was at least bold enough to throw a puzzled look at Helen's obvious lack of evening skirts beneath her coat. She shook her head at his silent offer to take her coat.

"I have an urgent request for Mrs. Murchison." Helen tried to soften her voice as much as she could, knowing how easily it could carry. She could see the bright glow of the formal dining room just down the hall. "Can you tell her that Helen Sorby is here?"

The butler shook his head. She was puzzled by the almost panicked look he gave her, until she remembered this household's odd code of silence. "Would you rather I wrote her a note for you to deliver instead?"

She took the butler's sigh for agreement, and began looking around the mansion's foyer for a scrap of paper. She didn't need a writing instrument, since her favorite Waterman fountain pen now hung on a matching silver chain around her neck, a Christmas gift from her doting aunt. Helen pulled it out and crossed to the mahogany receiving table, shuffling through the thick stack of cards that filled Lillian Murchison's engraved silver tray. With any luck, Aunt Pittypat's card would be near the top—

"Is this your way of investigating our daughter's disappearance, Miss Sorby? Sneaking into our house to steal our silver?"

Helen yelped and dropped the cards in a startled scatter around the tray, swinging around to see Charles Murchison frowning at her from the hallway. "I'm not—" The wrinkles on his face deepened to harsh furrows and Helen lowered her voice. "I'm not stealing anything," she said between gritted teeth. "I was looking for a piece of paper—"

"—to copy down our guest list?"

"To write a note to your wife!" Helen flung a hand out toward the butler, who had done his best to efface himself against the mahogany sideboard. "I didn't want to interrupt your dinner and unfortunately none of your servants seems to be allowed to speak on their own behalf. Allow me to inform you, Mr. Murchison, that sneak thieves don't usually drive up to the front door in a carriage and announce themselves with a loud rap on the front door!"

"Charles, hush. Everyone can hear you brangling down here." Lillian Murchison appeared beside her husband, dressed in an amber evening gown so richly bronzed with metallic embroidery that it threw off a thousand glitters with each graceful step. "Miss Sorby, what on earth is the matter?"

"As I told your butler," Helen said, "I have an urgent request for you, Mrs. Murchison."

Murchison glanced at his dark-skinned servant and got back a confirming nod. "Well, Lillian's here now," he said, and although irritation still crackled in his voice, Helen took the words as a retraction of his previous accusations. "What do you need to ask her?"

"For a photograph of your daughter," Helen said without hesitation. "I have reason to believe she was seduced into stealing your missing securities by a well-known confidence man, who is also a well-known bigamist. I want to start tracking them both, tonight."

"*What?*" There was no hushing that affronted roar. Charles Murchison came across the foyer toward her, moving with enough unnecessary force that for one startled moment Helen thought the coal baron was going to pick her up and pitch her out the door. Instead, he halted a foot away and gave her a glare that probably made accountants tremble and secretaries cry. Helen scowled right back at him. "What the hell makes you think you can throw dirt on my daughter like that? Just because you're a damned debauched socialist yourself—"

"Charles, Charles—" Lillian hurried after him and leaned heavily on his arm, as if she was more afraid he would strike Helen than evict her. "Miss Sorby is trying to save Emmy's reputation, not ruin it!"

"Then tell her to stop spreading rumors like that!"

Helen took a deep breath, making her voice as neutral as she could. "I only found this out five hours ago, Mr. Murchison. If you heard rumors about Emmy before that, it probably means they're true."

He looked as if she'd slapped him. "They can't be!"

"Then give me a photograph of Emmy and let me prove it."

An uneasy silence followed that demand, broken at length by a small guilty sigh from Lillian. "I'm afraid there *are* no photographs, Miss Sorby," she said at last. "At least, none that date from this century. Emmy always hated to have her likeness taken, and after the age of eleven she simply refused to have it done anymore. She wouldn't sit for paintings or sketches either, not even if we promised her the most flattering of artists."

Helen gnawed on her lower lip, unexpectedly stymied. She had never thought it would be easy to wrest the missing heiress away from James Foster Barton, but if she couldn't even track her through the valley with a picture, her task was going to be nearly impossible. She knew from bitter experience that her former husband had a swindler's ability to shift his looks to match whatever part he was currently playing. Even if she hadn't burned their wedding photograph over a year ago, the elegant gentleman with the swooped hair and debonair mustaches might not be who she was looking for.

"I could try drawing a picture of your daughter, if you described her," she said at last. "I've helped the police that way in the past—"

"No doubt, Miss Sorby," Lillian Murchison said gently.

"But perhaps we can do that tomorrow? I don't think the middle of a dinner party is quite the best time—"

"Mrs. Murchison?" The voice was familiar enough to catch Helen's attention, but it took her more than a moment to recognize the handsome young man in the evening suit as the mud-soaked photographer she'd met in Harwick two days before. Jackson Ecklar lifted his feathered dark eyebrows high when he saw her, but it seemed to be more in amusement than surprise. Helen wondered if he found her voice as recognizable as she found his. "Forgive me, I couldn't help but notice that something had disturbed you and your husband. May I perhaps be of some assistance?"

"No," Murchison said flatly. "The only assistance this distraught young woman needed was directions, so she could find her way back to the relatives she's visiting."

Helen glowered at her employer, but didn't bother informing him that his dinner guest already knew who she was. "Thank you so much," she said to Lillian Murchison pointedly. "I'll try to follow your suggestion."

Conspiratorial laughter glinted in her eyes. "Please do. I think you'll find that route much more effective."

"No doubt," Helen said, and let the butler show her out.

"Well?" Pat McGregor gave her a shrewd Irish glance as she clambered back into the hired carriage. "Don't tell me it went well, I could hear the shouting from here. Did you manage to offend Mr. Murchison after all?"

"Yes," Helen said, "But not nearly enough."

NINE

From his childhood days in Monessen, Milo Kachigan knew what a mine explosion looked like: a knot of anxious wives and children watching from the hillsides while grim-faced men hurried in and out of a portal that seemed no different from any other mine opening in the area. Perhaps an occasional trickle of dark smoke or dust would drift out from the mine as the rescuers shifted rock to uncover the trapped miners, but most of the long hours passed without a single sound or sight to mark the ruin that had taken place deep underground.

Bull Creek Coal Mine looked nothing like that.

"Holy hell," said Art Taggart and Owen Riley in unison, the moment their trolley clattered through the greening locust trees to meet the iron-stained ravine of Bull Creek. Kachigan remained silent, but he felt his stomach lurch with the same disbelief he heard in their voices. They were still a mile away from the mine's portal, but the damage was already obvious. All along the high wooden scaffold of the coal tipple, the metal chute that carried the mine's coal down to the railroad spur was twisted and shattered and wrecked. In some places it looked as if it had been pierced through with shrapnel, leaving long gouges through which

Kachigan could see the pale blue of the April sky. In other places, it had been blasted completely apart at its riveted seams and lay in enormous curled shards on the ground, black smoke still rising from its charred supports.

"That was no mine explosion," their trolley driver said, slowing their car to survey the damage. It was the same elderly man who'd taken them up to the mine on the first night of the strike and then delivered them back to the chaos of the miners' rally. Kachigan wasn't sure if he'd volunteered for this special run because he'd liked the generous tip they'd given him when he returned their shotgun, or if he was just the company's spare driver. "If it wasn't such a clear day, I'd have said it was a lightning strike that done it."

"An anarchist strike is more like it," said Taggart. "That looks like bomb damage to me."

"No, it looks like war damage." Riley's grim expression made his wine-stained face look older than it was. "A single bomb couldn't have ripped that metal apart all along its length. It looks just like the way we used to rip up the Spanish train tracks down in Cuba—"

"Owen's right." Kachigan had been counting the spacing between completely charred trestles as they continued to parallel the wrecked tipple up the slope toward the mine. "Someone climbed up there and planted dynamite at every fourth support."

"Dynamite in metal canisters," Riley corrected him. "That way, they not only knocked it down, they ripped it apart too."

Taggart whistled softly. "A real *guerrillero* operation, huh? And where the hell were Bernard Flinn and his coal police while all this was getting set up?"

The trolley driver shook his head. "Not patrolling the way they were supposed to, that's for sure!"

"No," Kachigan agreed, standing up for the door as the trolley rolled into its siding by the mine. "And knowing Bernard Flinn, I can only think of one reason for that."

He dropped off the trolley while it was still moving, his imagination already seeing the sprawled shapes of ambushed company policemen in the heaps of coal and silent mine cars that littered the yard. A closer look showed him nothing but shadows cast by the bright April sun, but that didn't ease the ominous feeling in his chest. In broad daylight, the stairs up to the mine's headquarters building were easy to see, with a neatly painted sign whose pointing finger showed the way to "Bull Crick HQ." Kachigan took the trembling wooden steps two at a time, with Owen Riley once again right on his heels. He could hear Taggart pounding after them, slow but determined.

"Wish we'd brought the shotguns this time, sir," the former army policeman said as they ran.

"Me too." Kachigan threw out a hand to halt Riley at the top of the stairs, waiting for Taggart and listening to the fitful spring breeze stir the budding trees. He wasn't sure if the silence he heard was a good sign or the worst. And in the unrelenting light of the sun, there was no way to sneak across the scruffy lawn to the side window he and Riley had used for reconnaissance before. "Let me go in the building first," he said, as Taggart arrived huffing at the top. "If you hear shots, then head back down the steps and go for help."

"Why the hell didn't you decide that down at the mine?" Taggart demanded, his face red and shining with sweat in the warm afternoon. "I could have stayed at the bottom of the steps and heard you get yourself shot from there."

Kachigan gave his partner an amused glance. "I know, but I figured you could use the exercise."

That earned him a scowl and a stubborn look. "Well, as long as you dragged me up here, you're stuck with me. Riley can run a hell of a lot faster than I can, and if they've got two targets to shoot at, they're less likely to hit either of us. Let's go."

Kachigan frowned, opening his mouth to argue that one of them was a lot more likely to get hit than the other. But Taggart was already heading for the silent company headquarters, and he knew from experience that the big man was impossible to deflect once he'd set a course. "*You* follow orders," he told Riley sharply. "If you don't hear shots, stay here and keep a watch out for anyone else who shows up. I don't want to get surprised the way Flinn's police must have been."

"Yes, *sir*," Riley said and saluted automatically before he could stop himself. Kachigan sighed, but didn't yell at him. Old habits were the hardest ones to break.

He caught up to Taggart without difficulty, since the big man was still half out of breath from the long climb. The door to Bull Creek's mine office stood ajar, he saw as they mounted the steps of the former hunting cabin. It might have been left that way to let in the warm afternoon air, but the smell that drifted out of the dim interior wasn't the mustiness of a long winter. It was the unmistakable odor of recent death, the faint metallic smell of blood overlain with the stronger fetor of excrement and urine. Kachigan pushed the door wide open, already knowing what he'd see.

Five crumpled bodies lay in front of what used to be the fireplace, fallen across each other as if they'd been lined up and shot in turn. Each wore the dark blue uniform of Sedgwick Coal & Coke's company police force, and each of them had been shot several times in the chest with firing squad efficiency. And each of their pistol holsters was empty.

Taggart paused in the door, surveying the damage with his eyes narrowed down to emotionless slits, while Kachigan crossed to kneel beside the victims. The nearest one was a fair-skinned German boy, even younger than Owen Riley. In death, his wide blue eyes still looked amazed, as if he couldn't believe what had happened to him.

"This wasn't a gunfight, Milo," Taggart said from behind him. "This was a goddamned execution."

"I know." Kachigan rolled over the two men who lay facedown, but their wiry bodies had already confirmed his suspicions. "And Bernard Flinn's not one of the victims."

That made his partner whistle. "Then there's going to be hell to pay for the miners' union."

"Is there?" Kachigan closed the young German's astonished eyes, then vaulted back to his feet, wiping his hands more times on his coat than he really needed to. The smell of death made him feel as if his skin was still dirty even when his eyes told him it was clean. "Does this look like the result of a miners' riot to you?"

Taggart stepped back, glancing around the neat office with its undisturbed files and desks. "Not really. But who else could have done it? Hill-bandits would have ransacked the place, looking for the safe."

"But the Black Hand wouldn't have," Kachigan said grimly. "Not if this was done for revenge."

"Just because Flinn beat up one of their boys a little?" Taggart asked incredulously. "Come on, Milo." He glanced down at the fallen bodies. "Even if they did have a reason to shoot these guys, why the hell would they blow up the tipple?"

"Maybe because Flinn wasn't making a payoff they wanted." Kachigan pulled his evidence book from his vest pocket and began slowly writing down a description of the murder scene. "Maybe that was what that murder in the coal mine was all about."

"Huh." Taggart watched him in silence for a long while, only moving to swat an early fly that had come to buzz around the sprawled bodies. "You really think the Black Hand is expanding their extortion schemes from the miners to the mines themselves?" he asked at last. "That would be something new for them."

"I know. But everything about this case tells me that there's something underhanded going on in this valley." Kachigan finished his description of the murder victims and began circling the anomalously neat office, looking for some clue to how the massacre had begun. No stray bullet holes marred the walls, no desk drawers had been ransacked, and although the telephone had been left sitting on a windowsill instead of a desk, its receiver had been hung neatly back on its hook.

"Something more than just the miners' strike?" Taggart asked.

"Yes." Kachigan paused to rifle through the stack of telegraph forms, but saw none out of the ordinary. "And judging from the little bit our prisoner was willing to say today, I think the Black Hand must be involved in it somehow. Maybe they were hired—''

The sound of Owen Riley's urgent voice outside cut across his speculations. "Detective Kachigan, sir—there's a bunch of people coming up the steps, fast."

Kachigan glanced around the coal company office, instinctively looking around for a weapon, then cursed himself for his own stupidity. If there had been any within easy reach, this execution would never have happened. He swung around and met Riley coming in the door. The young detective looked nervous but not rattled. "Could you see who they were?"

"No, sir, but whoever they were, they weren't trying to be sneaky. One of them was shouting out orders the whole way up. He sounded just like a cavalry officer."

Kachigan frowned and listened for a moment. The vagrant spring breeze rewarded him with the familiar sound of a light Irish tenor snapping out a flurry of brisk commands. "That's because he *is* a cavalry officer," he said and went out to meet the Pennsylvania State Police.

They poured up the steps and onto the lawn with their black overcoats billowing and their rifles at the ready, although it wasn't quite as impressive a performance without the thundering horses. Kachigan watched them critically until Taggart poked him in the back, hard enough to make him grunt. "Better put your hands up, before we get shot," his partner suggested.

Kachigan scowled over his shoulder at him. "They saw our trolley driver down there, Art. They must know who we are."

"Yeah, county detectives. That doesn't exactly clear us of suspicion."

He sighed, but joined Taggart and Riley in holding his empty hands up in the air, like a prisoner surrendering on the battlefield. The first line of troopers paused when they rounded the corner of the porch, their rifles swinging automatically in to aim. Then their commanding officer's crisp voice rang out again, and they lifted their rifles and came to take them efficiently into custody.

"We're county detectives," Kachigan said in protest, but he had already resigned himself to having his wrists grabbed and locked behind him in heavy iron cuffs. He just hoped Brennan had brought along the key. "We came up to investigate the explosion. The men inside were dead when we got here."

An officer's cap emerged from the mass of spiked helmets, and Kachigan found himself for once on the receiving end of a skeptical policeman's stare. "So you say," Brennan commented, making no move to unlock his handcuffs. "What was your name again?"

"Milo Kachigan." Considering that the last time the state policeman had seen him, he'd been covered in mud and mingling with a miners' riot, Kachigan didn't hold his suspicions against him. "Go in and see for yourself. They were shot, probably a few hours before the dynamite blast was set off on the tipple. We're not even armed."

Brennan grunted and swept past him, followed by three wary patrolmen with rifles at the ready. They remained inside the coal company's office for a long time, but when they came out, the frown on the state police lieutenant's face had a completely different cast. "Let them go," he told the subordinate holding on to Kachigan's heavy iron cuffs. "Yell down the steps for that office manager," he told another, and then pointed out five more among the group. "Go out in the woods and see what tracks you can find. Whoever did this left a while ago."

The state troopers scattered with military precision. Kachigan watched them go, rubbing at his wrists. "Who called you in?" he asked Brennan curiously. "Or did you see the smoke all the way up in Natrona?"

Brennan compressed his thin, carved lips for a moment, as if he was deciding whether he should set the precedent of answering Kachigan's questions. "The management of Sedgwick Coal & Coke telegraphed our headquarters in Greensburg two hours ago, and they wired the alert on to us. They said a routine business telephone call was in progress when some kind of emergency interrupted. The person on the other end of the line became alarmed when the call was never resumed.''

"Really?" Kachigan turned to go back into the company office, and found a tall young trooper blocking his way. He frowned across his shoulder at Brennan. "You may not like me, *Mr.* Brennan," he said, deliberately addressing the state policeman as the civil servant he supposedly was. "But unless the state legislature has just ruled otherwise, I believe I have equal jurisdiction in this case."

"In general, that would be true, *Mr.* Kachigan," Brennan said crisply. "But during labor disputes like this, the statute governing the state police gives them the authority to conduct an independent investigation."

"We don't know for sure that this is the result of a labor dispute."

That put an expression on the lieutenant's rigid face at last—an expression of genuine surprise. "Five company police guards killed in the middle of a miners' strike—"

"—by a military-style firing squad?" A month spent arguing mayoral politics with Helen Sorby had broken Kachigan of any restraint he might have felt about interrupting his opponent. Or about outshouting him. "You might convince me a mob of miners sabotaged that coal tipple, Brennan, although I don't know why they'd want to, since this coal mine's not hiring scabs or fighting the settlement. But don't ask me to believe they were coordinated enough to line up those guards and shoot them one at a time, because I just don't believe it!"

"I'm sorry to hear that." The stiff politeness of Brennan's face never wavered, although the tips of his ears seemed to be getting a little red. "But since your disbelief wouldn't carry much weight in a court of law—"

"Dear God in heaven!"

That new voice, shocked and quivering and genteel, cut across their argument not with its strength but with its palpable frailty. Kachigan and Brennan swung around, each reaching a hand out to steady the old man who stood swaying on the edge of the porch, staring through the open door of the company office at the slaughter inside. His face looked as white as his long and elegant mustaches, a bloodless contrast to his crimson silk tie, green shirt, and bright lavender collar. The fashionable clash of colors would have told Kachigan this was someone far more important than an office manager, even if the sudden change in the state policeman's manner hadn't.

"Mr. Sedgwick, I asked you not to come up here." Brennan's Irish tenor had softened to a respectful murmur. He jerked his head at the troopers around them, and one of them hastily pulled the door closed. "You were supposed to send your office manager up instead."

The old man tried to straighten his bony shoulders, although there was still not much color in his ashen cheeks. His gaze slid across Kachigan blankly and then focused on the state police lieutenant. The faded blue of his eyes, soft as wilted violets, looked vaguely familiar, but despite having a moment to think about it while Sedgwick gathered himself together, Kachigan couldn't track the resemblance down to a known face or name.

"My apologies, Lieutenant," the old man said at last in a voice that was both gracious and unapologetic. "I know you meant well, but this is still my coal mine. I may not run it from day to day anymore, but as long as my name's Hayden Sedgwick, it's still my responsibility to know what's going on. Now, please tell me exactly what happened up here."

Brennan took a deep breath, meeting Kachigan's gaze in a moment of surprisingly mutual frustration. It was all very well for the public to place implicit trust in their police officials, but the other side of that coin was the public's expectation that all crimes should be solved within fifteen minutes of the police arriving on the scene. "We don't have a clear idea of that yet, sir," the state trooper said politely. "All we know right now is that five men from your company police force have been shot to death, in what seems to be a very organized sort of attack. It may have been a prelude to the sabotage of your coal tipple."

"All uniformed men?"

That curt request seemed to startle Brennan, but Kachigan could guess what inspired it. "Yes," he said, before the state policeman could answer. "I checked all the bodies. Bernard Flinn wasn't there."

"He wasn't?" The old man swung around to face him, his faded eyes no longer blank but gleaming with relief. "Then can I talk to him now?"

"Talk to whom, Mr. Sedgwick?" Brennan asked gently. He was looking at the mine owner as if the old man might be a little more senile than his fashionable clothes and polished manners suggested.

"Bernard Flinn, of course." The coal mine owner's voice had started to shake again, ever so slightly. "The head of my company police force." He swung around to frown at Kachigan. "You said he wasn't dead."

"No, sir," Brennan corrected him. "Detective Kachigan said he wasn't here. There's no one here but me, my troopers, and these three men from the County Detectives' Bureau."

"Then where's Flinn?" Sedgwick began to sway again, as if the fitful April breeze was too strong for him to endure any longer. "He must be here somewhere, I was talking to him on the telephone when he heard the shouting." The pale blue eyes swung back to the closed door of the mine office. "Perhaps he was hurt and ran away to hide?"

"No bloodstains," Kachigan and Brennan said in one voice. Hayden Sedgwick peered at them without comprehension, and this time the state police lieutenant left it to Kachigan to explain. "If Flinn had been wounded, he would have left a trail of blood droplets on the floor as he left the office, Mr. Sedgwick. There wasn't any such trail."

"Does that mean he wasn't wounded when he left?" the old man asked hopefully.

"Maybe." Kachigan glanced back at the office door himself, recalling the brutally efficient way the company policemen had been executed behind it. It seemed unlikely any man, even the equally brutal and efficient Bernard Flinn, could have walked out of a situation like that unharmed. "Or when he was taken away," he added somberly.

Hayden Sedgwick's arm turned inside Kachigan's supportive grip, grabbing on to his wrist with urgent, trembling fingers. "Taken away, you say? You mean abducted? Kidnapped?"

Brennan broke in, reaching out to remove the old man's grip soothingly. "Sir, that's pure speculation. We don't have any evidence that—"

The coal mine owner shook him off with a spasmodic burst of impatience. "He said, 'I think they're here to get me.' That's exactly what he said to me on the telephone line." He turned back toward Kachigan, as if he trusted him more than the state policeman now. "You really think Flinn's been kidnapped?"

"Yes," Kachigan said without hesitation, ignoring Brennan's disapproving frown. There might be no physical evidence of an abduction, but if you knew the iron-willed company police chief, you really didn't need any. "If Bernard Flinn was here when his men were killed, the bodies of the murderers would have been waiting for us when we arrived. Or his own body would have been."

The old man stared at him for a long shaking moment, then he simply closed his eyes and swayed. Kachigan tightened his grip on the frail arm he held, afraid for a moment that Hayden Sedgwick was going to pass out. He could see Brennan scowling at him from behind the mine owner's back, clearly put out by this development. Kachigan wasn't sure if it was his assumption of authority that had annoyed the state policeman or the blow he seemed to have inflicted on a fragile and elderly man.

"All right," Sedgwick said, gathering himself up with greater effort than before. "All right, that's fine, it's always best to know the truth. I just have to think how to break the news to Margaret—"

"Margaret?" The stir of memory tugged at Kachigan again, this time stronger than before. And this time it came with a name attached. He gave the arm he held a gentle shake to catch the old man's attention. "Do you mean Margaret Flinn, sir?"

Hayden Sedgwick sighed and nodded. The wrinkled skin that draped the bones of his aristocratic face had gone bloodless again, and the lines around his faded blue eyes had deepened in what looked like regret, or perhaps remorse. "She didn't want him coming to work here, you know, with that other job in Harrisburg starting so soon. But I asked him to. I knew I didn't have the kind of police force he usually headed up, but with the strike I needed a stronger hand on the reins than old Horace Denny could give me. . . ." He shook his head again, this time looking bitterly angry at himself. "I should have just left Horace in charge. All these men would still be dead and the tipple in ruins, but at least I wouldn't have made my daughter a widow."

Kachigan felt a muscle jerk along his chin. He remembered a night from last November, filled with smoke and anger, a night when Helen Sorby had almost died. And he remembered Margaret Flinn, the fragile woman with eyes like faded violets who graciously let him wait in her elegant brocade drawing room to accuse her husband of attempted murder. No matter how much he might dislike and distrust the coal police chief, he felt nothing but pity for his wife.

"We don't know for sure that your son-in-law is dead, Mr. Sedgwick," he reminded the mine owner, clearing the rustiness from his voice with a cough. "I might be wrong about what happened here."

"That's true." Sedgwick's voice strengthened slightly, although his face was still furrowed with remorse. "I suppose I should wait at least until tonight to tell Margaret her husband is missing. You'll be searching the area around the mine, won't you?"

"We'll be searching all around Tarentum," Lieutenant Brennan assured him, taking back command of the situation. "As well as stationing several troopers to patrol the property here and protect it from further damage. If Mr. Flinn is found anywhere, sir—and in any condition—I can assure you that you'll be the first to be notified."

Sedgwick nodded unhappily. "That's the best we can do for now, I suppose. Later, perhaps a published reward for information would be appropriate—but I'll have to talk to Margaret before I do that. In the meantime, you can reach me at the Hotel Harrison in Tarentum if you need to. I always keep a room reserved there for visiting the mine." He sighed and finally released his hold on Kachigan's arm, but his first step toward the porch edge was so uncertain that the detective had to reach out and steady him again. Brennan frowned and snapped his fingers at two of the troopers still waiting by the door.

"McGee, Mallory—see Mr. Sedgwick back to the trolley car we came up in."

"That won't be necessary," Kachigan said, sliding a hand down to support the old man's shaking elbow. "I'll see Mr. Sedgwick back to Tarentum myself. I have some questions I'd like to ask him, about another investigation I'm pursuing."

Brennan scowled. "And what would that be, Mr. Kachigan?"

"The influence of the Black Hand along this stretch of the Allegheny River," Kachigan retorted, and was pleased by the startled look that appeared on the state policeman's face. "A matter which you do not have the authority to investigate, Mr. Brennan, unless you've been asked to help by the local authorities. And that's me."

It had been a gamble, and Kachigan had lost.

When he'd offered to escort Hayden Sedgwick back to Tarentum, Kachigan had suspected it was going to take a while to get the shaken and fragile mine owner settled in his hotel suite. But he'd wanted the opportunity to delve into the possible link he thought might be forming between the Black Hand and this rash of mine-related violence. When he added in the hope that Helen Sorby might be waiting for him back at the lockup with the information she'd managed to get from her own Black Hand connections, the decision had been easy to make.

At first, it seemed as if he'd struck pay dirt. His experience with his own arthritic father had allowed him to carry Hayden Sedgwick down the long wooden stairs at Bull Creek Coal with a minimum of fuss and embarrassment. The elderly mine owner had been surprisingly grateful for that. He had also, after recovering his composure on the trolley ride home, been surprisingly garrulous. A simple question about the Black Hand had given Kachigan page after page of information—almost all of it based on old newspaper stories and even older gossip. Kachigan had spent an hour and a half trying to sort out wheat from chaff, and left the hotel lobby sure of only one thing: Hayden Sedgwick himself had never received a Black Hand threat and had never heard his son-in-law say anything about getting one either.

His frustration level wasn't improved in the slightest when he returned to the lockup and discovered Helen Sorby had in fact been waiting for him, but had given up at tea-time and returned to her aunt's home in Oakmont. He'd actually tried ringing up her number there, but a taciturn Irish maid had informed him that both Miss Sorby and her aunt were out on a social call, and weren't expected back soon.

He hung the telephone up with a sharp Armenian curse, one that gained him a sympathetic look from Owen Riley and a laugh from J.P. Frick, loitering in the door at the end of his shift. "Hey, I told you a month ago dago women were the worst for holding grudges." The balding detective's voice was warm with spurious fellowship. "If you ask me, you never should have tried to push your luck—"

Kachigan snarled and spun around to grab the older man by the shirtfront, slamming him back into the lockup desk. "You don't know the first damned thing about it! And if I hear you call Helen Sorby a dago one more time—"

"Sir!" Riley was on his feet now and tugging at Kachigan's arm, trying to separate him from the struggling Frick. "Sir, there's someone here to see you."

Kachigan stepped back, feeling the skin over his cheekbones pull tight with embarrassment. He swung around to see Leon Daniels grinning at him from the open door. "Ah, that's just what I like to see," said the union organizer cheerfully. "Law and order at its finest."

Frick cursed and tried in vain to straighten his mangled collar. To Kachigan's surprise, however, the sarcastic blast of retribution he expected never came. "You'd better watch out, Kachigan," was all the older man said. "Because *you* don't know the first damned thing about what's happening in this valley. And it's going to get you killed."

Daniels lifted an eyebrow, skipping nimbly out of the way as the detective shoved past him. "Pleasant fellow, isn't he? Do you have to slam him against desks often to keep him in line?"

Kachigan scowled at the young socialist. "Are you here for a reason, or are you just trying to stir up more trouble?"

"What would you say if I told you I was here for the pleasure of your company?" Daniels grinned again at Kachigan's caustic look. "Never mind. I came to find out if my miners' rally tonight is going to get crushed by the state police, now that they've stationed a detail up at Bull Creek."

"In other words, you want to know if the union's going to get blamed for the damage?"

"Yes." Daniels came over to perch on the nearest desk. "All I've heard is that the coal tipple was sabotaged and a lot of coal policemen are dead. Is that right?"

Kachigan shook his head, astonished at the speed with which rumors spread. It had been less than two hours since their trolley had returned from Bull Creek Coal with the driver who must have been the source of that particular information. "That's right," he said. "Bernard Flinn is missing and presumed kidnapped."

Leon Daniels cocked his head in a deeply quizzical look. If he had been wearing a jester's motley he would have looked just like one of Maxfield Parrish's gelatin advertisements. "Why on earth would anyone kidnap a coal police chief?"

"For extortion," Kachigan said shortly. "Or for revenge."

Daniel's keen gaze darted toward the door that led to the cells, and came back enlightened. "You think the Black Hand is behind it?"

"Yes," Kachigan said.

The union organizer stared at him for a long moment in silence, then the amusement faded from his face like a mask he no longer needed. It left him looking much older than before. "Do you trust that boy sitting behind you?" he asked Kachigan, in a voice at least an octave lower than the one he'd used a moment before. His gaze never wavered from the detective's face.

"Riley? Yes."

Daniels nodded, then reached in his vest pocket. What he pulled out made Kachigan's eyes widen and his jaw drop abruptly. Except for the lettering around the edge, the metal shield looked like a twin to the one in his own coat pocket.

"You're a *policeman*?"

"Not quite." Daniels tossed the badge across to him with a smile. Kachigan read the words around the edge and grunted, then tossed it back to his visitor.

"So," he said. "Who hired the Pinks to infiltrate the local miners' union?"

Daniels clicked his tongue against his teeth reprovingly. "The Pinkerton Detective Agency doesn't only deal with labor disputes, Kachigan. They handle all kinds of problems."

"And what problem are you handling here?"

"I'm looking into the activities of the Black Hand," Daniels said soberly. "At the request of a local coal mine owner who's being blackmailed by them."

The unexpected confirmation of his suspicions should have made Kachigan happy. Instead, it made his stomach churn with something that felt surprisingly like dread. "Which mine owner?"

The Pinkerton detective grinned and shook a finger at him, metamorphosing back into his leprechaun persona. "Now, now, Detective Kachigan. You know I can't tell you that."

"Then what can you tell me?" he demanded in exasperation. "The going rate for a solo Pink? Or whether your name is really Leon Daniels?"

Daniels sighed and put a hand on the desk, vaulting off it with one athletic twist of his wiry body. "Neither of those, I'm afraid. But I will tell you this: the longer you hold on to that boy in there, the more dangerous your job is going to get. And if the Black Hand thinks you've actually convinced him to tell you anything about them—" He clapped one fist into the other palm to make a surprisingly violent sound. "Look out."

And with that, the private detective slid through the door and out into the busy twilight bustle of Tarentum, disappearing almost as magically as the leprechaun he resembled. Kachigan scowled after him, then closed the door with a slam that made Owen Riley jump.

"Sir?"

Kachigan shook his head, scrubbing a hand at the annoying ache of his cheekbone. "Yesterday, Riley, I had one dead man and one suspect in jail. Today I have six dead men and a hundred suspects up and down the Allegheny Valley, none of whom I even know. If this gets any worse, I'm going to have to call in the state police myself."

"Could it get worse, sir?"

He smiled at that naïveté. "Of course it could. Bernard Flinn's dead body could get dumped on our doorstep, another coal mine could be sabotaged, J.P. Frick could sweet-talk Big Roge into promoting him—"

"Over you, sir?" The sound of Riley's honest laughter made the pain in his cheek ease a little. "I don't think so. Even Roger McGara would get tired of—"

The crack of sound that interrupted him wasn't loud, but it was followed by an ominous cry and thump from the lockup cells. Kachigan cursed and leaped for the hall door, but Riley was on the nearer side of the desk and beat him to it. He took the first step into the gaslit interior of the lockup, heading for the crumpled form in the first cell. It was Kachigan, one pace behind him, who saw the flash of a rifle barrel through the barred window. He shouted and grabbed at Riley, yanking him back into the office seconds before the shot thudded into the wall behind them. Plaster chips showered them through the open door.

"Shotguns," Kachigan said between his teeth, and shoved Riley toward their gun cabinet. He didn't wait for the younger detective to unlock it, instead leaping for the front door in the hopes of catching a glimpse of the assassin even at the risk of getting shot at again. But by the time he'd rounded the corner of the alley where the shot had come from, it was as silent and dead as the Italian boy back in the lockup.

TEN

Helen woke up early on Friday morning, although it wasn't by choice or design. After staying up late to wire a story on the Natrona miners' riot to the *New York Herald*, she'd been so tired that she'd forgotten to close her bedroom door. That was always a serious mistake when staying with Aunt Pittypat. The massive white and brown tomcat had been a suitably polite bedroom guest, merely putting her foot to sleep by leaning against it all night long. But the scrawny black kitten had decided dawn was a good time to play hide-and-seek among the covers. By the time Helen finally managed to catch and evict her, hopping on one numb foot the whole time, a gust of wind had blown up off the river and was rattling the shutters outside her window so hard that even the tomcat looked disgruntled. Helen listened to the banging for a moment, then sighed and headed for the indoor bathroom instead of back to bed. Perhaps she could ring up Lillian Murchison and arrange for an early morning visit.

Since she had the time—and thought her reputation with the Murchisons might stand in need of a little repair—Helen spent the better part of the next hour lacing and buttoning herself into the fashionable dove-gray walking suit

Aunt Pat had made her wear at her Oakmont housewarming, and which she'd never bothered to take home to the South Side again. Fortunately, its fashionable skirt of shaggy zibeline wool was long enough to hide the fact that she was wearing highly unfashionable leather walking shoes beneath it. To make up for that lapse in taste, Helen excavated the matching muff from the closet of her guest room, then went downstairs to find out that she needn't have bothered with any of it.

"For you, Miss Helen." In the front foyer, her aunt's Irish maid looked up from placing a large, cheap manila envelope and a smaller folded note on the receiving table, carefully apart from her aunt's overflowing basket of mail. "They both arrived this morning."

"Hand-delivered?" Helen asked, grabbing her skirts up in both hands so they couldn't wrap around her ankles and trip her on the way downstairs. "Or special delivery?"

"Hand-delivered, I expect. There's just your name written on 'em, but they were both in the mail slot when I came out to dust." The maid handed them over to Helen with a little sniff, as if the extra work of picking them up had put her entire schedule out of joint. "And there's no coffee perked yet for breakfast. You'll have to make do with tea."

"That's all right." Helen reached for the small note first from long habit, although as soon as she touched the creamy linen bond and saw how gracefully her name was written on it, she knew it couldn't be from Milo Kachigan. Inside, the same extravagant hand had written, with several flourishes and many unnecessary capital letters, "Miss Sorby, a Very dear Friend in Pittsburgh has lost her Husband and is in great need of Consolation. Please call Tomorrow to make your Drawing. Lillian Lyell Murchison."

Helen dropped the note back on the receiving table with a scowl and watched the elegantly dressed woman in the mirror do likewise. By the time she got herself out of this multilayered walking suit, with its vertical connecting bands of white silk and black velvet that hooked the jacket to the skirt, not to mention the lace-trimmed silk shirtwaist that buttoned into the black velvet vest, she might as well have stayed in bed all morning with the cats, exactly like her aunt. With a sigh and a mental vow to wear her plainest serge skirt and cotton shirtwaist tomorrow, Helen ripped open the remaining manila envelope.

The sheet of paper inside looked blank and meaningless at first, but as soon as she reached in to pull it out, Helen recognized what it was from its stiff resistance and the vinegary smell of chemicals that clung to it. With a quick, indrawn breath, she turned the photographic print over to reveal a background of dripping mist and trees and run-down coal patch houses, the kind of evocative scene that had gained Jackson Ecklar his fame with the New York magazines. In the foreground, a young woman in an expensive plaid wool coat and a small feather-trimmed hat stood watching what looked like the eviction of a mining family from their house. Her face, shadowed by the hat brim and seen only in profile, still startled Helen with its angry jut of chin and deep-set scowling eyes. The resemblance to her father was unmistakable, but even if she hadn't seen it, Helen would have known who the young woman was. Someone who hadn't been afraid to mar an expensive photograph had written ''Emmy Murchison'' across the scene in heavy India ink, and then added the puzzling phrase, ''Red Hot This Week,'' beneath it.

''What on earth—'' Helen tilted the photograph up to the light, trying to see if there was anything else written on it, but its polished surface showed only the indentation of those six words. Before she could even begin to speculate on what they meant, the delicate tap of the front door knocker made her jump. Tilly poked her head out from the kitchen, looking put-upon.

''You know, Miss Sorby, we never had these kinds of interruptions before you got up here to Oakmont.'' The maid went to answer the door before Helen could respond. Jake Bailey stood on the other side, looking both hesitant and conspiratorial. His livery horses stamped and snorted out on Isabella Street, making the heavy wagon they were hitched to creak in the morning cold.

''Mr. Bailey.'' Helen glanced at the grandfather clock

and lifted both eyebrows. Its ornate gold hands told her that her aunt wasn't due to rise from bed for another four hours. "Are you sure this is when my Aunt McGregor—"

"Shh, shh." The livery stable owner slipped inside, much to Tilly's displeasure. Helen suspected it wasn't his unexpected presence so much as the straw and mud flaking off his boots onto her clean floor that annoyed the house-maid. "I know Missus Pat's not expecting me. But my weather knee told me this morning that it was coming on to rain later today. I thought I'd just run the last of the relief supplies up to Harwick before she was up and about. To save her from getting chilled, you know."

Helen bit her lip for a moment, then gave in and smiled at this evidence of middle-aged gallantry. "That's very considerate of you, Mr. Bailey."

"No, it's not." He turned away, reddening a little, to lift a twine-wrapped bundle of blankets. "It's just good business. I have a delivery to make over to Red Raven anyway and as long as I'm halfway there—"

"Red Raven." The name of the little trolley stop across the river sent Helen spinning around to pick up the pho-tograph she had dropped, reading the phrase on it now in a completely different light. "Mr. Bailey, is there a town around here called 'Red Hot'?"

He balanced the blankets on one broad shoulder, looking dubious, and for a moment Helen's spirits sank. "Well, I don't know that I'd say it was around *here*," the livery stable owner said at last. "It's up Little Deer Creek, nearly all the way to the Butler County line—"

"But it is there? And it's a mining town?"

"If you can call a little collection of company shacks like that a town," he said frankly, and disappeared out the door with his burden before she could ask more.

Helen took a deep breath, silently thanking Jackson Eck-lar for whatever good spirit had prompted him to point her way to the missing coal heiress. She glanced around the foyer, grabbing for the plain gray hat that fortuitously matched her suit, and the russet wool coat that didn't. When

Bailey came back for the rest of the blankets, she was waiting for him at the door.

"I'd like you to take me to Red Hot, Mr. Bailey, after we've delivered the relief supplies to Harwick. I have an urgent mission to carry out there."

"In *Red Hot*?" Whatever he read on her face made his disbelief darken to worry. "Miss Sorby, that's a two-hour drive from here, and that far north we might even hit snow when the weather moves in. It wouldn't be a bit comfortable for you in the wagon."

"Then can I hire one of your buggies and drive up there myself?"

His broad face furrowed with remorse. "Normally, yes, you could. But today, every single one of them is bespoke."

Helen frowned, considering her travel options. "There's no trolley that runs that way, I'm sure. Is there passenger train service?"

"Not on that line. The Bessemer trains don't take people, only coal." Jake Bailey paused, then said hesitantly, "Of course, if you know one of their engineers, you can sometimes slip them a couple of bits and hitch a ride in the caboose."

"Can you?" Helen gave him a speculative look. "Do you know one of their engineers, Mr. Bailey?"

"No, but the local mapping lad who surveys coal mines around here travels that way all the time. He says it's the easiest way to get up to the patches along Little Deer Creek."

"Good." Helen turned to pick up the next bundle of supplies herself. "Let's finish loading the wagon, while Tilly makes us some tea. After breakfast, you can take me to his office."

Helen had been hoping the "local mapping lad" would be a Sanborn Map Company employee like her twin brother, or at least someone who knew him. In her experience, surveyors and mapmakers formed a tight-knit fraternity, bonded by their work and their extensive travels. But when she stepped into the modest offices of the Valley Mine Service Company, the only "mapping lad" in sight turned out to be a tall coal geologist named James Hower, whose polite, polished manners marked him as a graduate of an Ivy League college. He cheerfully admitted to riding the Bessemer trains up Little Deer Creek valley himself, but seemed unable to believe Helen could want to do so.

"It's very dirty, Miss Sorby," he said for the third time, as patiently as if he thought she somehow just hadn't heard him before. "You'll come out smelling like coal smoke and grease and cheap cigars."

Helen took a deep breath, striving to keep her voice down to a civilized level. It was getting harder by the minute. "I understand that, Mr. Hower. And I assure you that I can survive a little dirt."

"Can you?" His skeptical look made Helen want to hit him, until she remembered exactly what clothes she had put on that morning. With a sigh, she decided against telling him she was a professional newspaper reporter and instead pulled the rolled photograph of Emmy Murchison out of her muff.

"Mr. Hower, I didn't want to burden you with this—but I'm looking for my half sister, Emmy Murchison. She ran away from home last week, and I'm very much afraid she's in the company of a confidence man."

It was hard to keep her voice from shaking as she lied, but when Helen looked up from the photograph, Hower's grave expression let her hope her faltering had been put down to emotion rather than bad acting. He glanced down at the photograph for a long moment, then nodded. "That does look like she's in Red Hot. And it must be a recent picture—the miners there only went out on strike yesterday, after those rioters were killed in Natrona." He nodded again, this time apparently to himself, then stood up and pushed his chair back. "All right, let's go."

Helen bit her lip to hold back a smile rather than the tears he probably thought her on the verge of, and followed him down to the Oakmont train station. She was less pleased when they made their sub-rosa transfer to a greasy Bessemer caboose in East Oakmont, and she discovered the young geologist intended to accompany her all the way to Red Hot.

"That's not necessary, Mr. Hower," she protested. "I can look for Emmy by myself—"

"But you can't get back onto another train by yourself, Miss Sorby," he said patiently. "Unless you can find your sister in the time it takes this train to fill up with water and put the locomotives on the other end, you're going to need me to talk another engineer into letting you aboard."

Since she couldn't think of a good rebuttal for that, Helen sighed and resigned herself to his company. It was undemanding enough. As soon as the Bessemer train huffed across the high bridge at Acmetonia and into the stream-cut western bluffs of the Allegheny, Hower pulled out a scientific notebook and began making rough sketches of the landscape. Helen watched him in discreet silence for a while, as she thought a preoccupied older sister should, but her curiosity eventually won out over her acting performance.

"What precisely are you trying to draw?"

Hower laughed, and handed her the notebook while the train passed without stopping through the tiny coal patch town of Rural Ridge. "Evidence for the geologic structure that I think runs along Little Deer Creek. And trying is the operative word, Miss Sorby. I'm not much of an artist."

"Well, I am." Helen glanced at the sketches, then back out through the smoke-smeared window at the landscape. She wasn't sure what geologic features Hower saw there, but she took his pencil and made a quick sketch of the surrounding hills, as well as the valley that Little Deer Creek cut through them. For good measure, she added an impression of the shale and sandstone layers she could see exposed along the stream banks. "How's that?"

"Wonderful." Hower leaned over the drawing, tracing the sketched valley with a finger. "You see how those layers are tilting and thickening?"

"Not really," Helen admitted. "What does it mean?"

"That the rocks here were deposited during a geologic revolution," he said promptly. "We're a long way from the folded mountains, but based on the strike and dips of the Upper Freeport in these new mines, I'm almost positive we're crossing a buried syncline."

Helen considered telling him she hadn't understood a word he'd just said, but long years of one-sided conversations with her brother about surveying assured her that it really didn't matter. "Is that right?"

"Yes. And where Little Deer Creek has cut down into the fold, the thicker coal seams are more accessible." They passed through another coal patch, this one a larger sprawl of neat, freshly painted duplexes with a substantial-looking company store near the station. The variation in upkeep told Helen this town must belong to a different coal company than the one at Rural Ridge. "It's why all these mines are here in the first place."

"All the towns along this line are coal mining operations?"

"Every one," Hower agreed. "Rural Ridge and Russellton are sitting right on the axis and mining eight-foot coal. Curtisville and Culmerville are a little farther off, so they're only making seven-foot seams."

"And Red Hot?" Helen asked.

Hower shook his head. "The coal's not much more than three feet thick there. That makes it the poorest patch on the line."

"I see." She absently sketched another rock-cut along the creek as the railroad crossed it again. Now that she was actually on her way to Red Hot, she had time to think about what Emmy Murchison was doing in such a distant and inconvenient place. If James Foster Barton had already seduced her into marrying him, as he'd seduced so many other innocent young socialists with a little money of their own, a company-owned coal town seemed like an odd place to set up household while he depleted her dowry. But if Barton hadn't yet convinced her to marry, just to steal her father's securities and run away, Red Hot would be the perfect place to hide her while he set the rest of his confidence scheme into motion. No one but a few trapped coal mining families and an occasional railroad engineer would ever have seen them together—

Helen lifted her pencil abruptly from her landscape sketch. "Mr. Hower, when was the last time you came up this way?"

"Last Thursday, I think. I had to survey a new main passage at Culmerville."

Helen chewed on her lip thoughtfully. Thursday would have been two days before Emmy disappeared, but that didn't mean James Foster Barton wasn't already setting his plans in motion. "Did you notice a man who looked like this—" She turned the notebook to a fresh page and began to sketch a portrait of her ex-husband. It surprised her to realize, a few strokes into it, that she didn't actually remember his face from life. Only by concentrating on an image of their wedding picture as it looked when she set it aflame a year and a half ago could she manage to reconstruct the firm chin, the straight nose, the smile. All she could actually remember from life were his eyes—so clear and shining when you first thought you knew him, so transparent and shallow when you really did.

"He does look vaguely familiar," Hower admitted, peering down at the sketch as she made it. "But I can't say for sure I've seen him along Little Deer Creek. This is the man you think your half sister may have run off with?"

"Yes," Helen said. "From what I've been able to find out so far, he's a known confidence man and a swindler who goes by the name of James Foster Barton."

The young geologist frowned. "I don't know anyone by that name around here, but then names are easy to change. All you have to do is keep the same initials, so it matches the monogram on your luggage."

"Or be smart enough not to monogram your luggage to begin with," Helen retorted. The train clattered over another stone bridge and into a third coal patch town whose faded train station sign announced it to be Curtisville. She opened her mouth to ask Hower why they weren't stopping to load any coal, but before she could speak, her question was answered by their slowing pace. By following Little Deer Creek, the railroad line had to climb an increasingly steep grade up into the Allegheny hills. On a round trip like this, it would make more sense to go uphill empty, saving time and fuel, and then load the cars with coal on the way back down to the river. And there certainly seemed to be coal to load.

"Aren't any of these other coal patch towns on strike?" she asked, frowning. The black flags of windblown dust that had flown over the coal tipples at Curtisville and Russellton had clearly announced that both those mines were still working. "Or are they all using scab labor?"

Hower gave her a startled look, reminding Helen again that she was dressed like the well-bred lady she had never been. She was starting to think she should write an editorial for Emma Goldman about the different standards of behavior women were expected to conform to when they dressed according to their class.

"They haven't shipped in any replacement workers yet, as far as I know," the geologist said, using the more genteel phrasing. "So far, the only miners who've spilled their water around here are the ones up at Red Hot."

Helen tilted her head, intrigued by a mining phrase her newspaper work hadn't yet acquainted her with. "Spilled their water?"

"You can't mine all day without a full pail of water under your lunch-bucket," he explained. They clattered over a railroad junction, and in the distance Helen saw another coal patch town on a barren hillside, half-hidden by its own dark flag of dust. "If the miners spill their water on the ground before the day's over, it means they're mad about something and are going home."

"And what were the miners at Red Hot mad about?"

"Mining three-foot coal," Hower said dryly. "Living in shanties without running water. Having the cost of dynamite and lamp oil deducted from your husband's back-pay for a week after he dies in a rockfall. The usual problems that come with living in a coal patch town."

Helen frowned at his casual tone. "You don't think those problems should be corrected, Mr. Hower?"

"Miss Sorby, there's no way to correct a three-foot coal seam. And if the company's barely making money on its product, it's got nothing to spare to make life easier for its workers." The train began to slow more than the grade could account for, and Helen wondered if that meant they were finally coming to a stop. The whistle of air brakes cut in a moment later, confirming it. "If you ask me, mines like Red Hot shouldn't have been opened in the first place, but there's no lack of immigrants willing to work them once they are. You just can't improve working conditions so long as there are too many mines for the market—"

"—and too many miners for the mines," Helen finished. She held up the notebook with James Foster's picture in it. "Do you mind if I tear this out, to show people along with the photograph of my sister?"

"Not at all." Hower tore the page out himself, careful not to disturb the other sketches she had made for him. "There you go, Miss Sorby. Good hunting."

"You're not going to insist on coming with me?"

"I would have," the geologist admitted, smiling. "But the only way I could get the Bessemer engineer to come up here with the strike in progress was to claim that the colliery manager wanted me to look over some new mining plans. I'll need to disappear into the office for an hour or so to make that seem right. I'll also need to bribe the local telegraph operator to send a signal down to Culmerville when you're ready to leave, so we can get a train to take us back to Oakmont."

Helen frowned, turning to look at him through the beginning of a chilly drizzle. The weather that Jake Bailey's knee had predicted would hit Oakmont before noon had already arrived in Red Hot. "Will that be very difficult?"

"Not at all." Hower gave her an unexpected wink. "She's young, she's pretty, and she doesn't have a boyfriend here in Red Hot. I'm looking forward to negotiating the bribe."

Helen laughed and left him at the train tracks, turning

toward the small company store. Her search had to start somewhere, and the thickening rain was making her regret not having brought an umbrella. The goodwill she'd engender by buying one here, she thought, could be a great help in tracking down her quarry.

That was before she saw the price tag.

"Six dollars?" Helen's voice was never soft, but inside the cramped confines of the little, dirt-floored shack that was the company store, it echoed like a clap of outraged thunder. "For a cheap little canvas umbrella?"

The scrawny young storekeeper grinned at her, not at all intimidated by her shout. He was probably used to that reaction. "It's not cheap, miss, and it's not little. It'll cover two with ease, three in a pinch—and remember, we had to pay the costs of shipping it all the way up here from Pittsburgh."

"You also have to pay the costs of shipping your coal all the way down to Pittsburgh," she informed him. "So far as I know, that doesn't treble its market price! I'll give you three dollars for it, which is a dollar more than it's worth."

"No haggling!" said the young man, with the snap of someone who really meant it. "Take it or leave it, that's the rule in Red Hot. It's not like you can go across the street."

Helen glared at him. As much as she hated to enrich the coal company that profited from this legal extortion, she suspected from the shopkeeper's shrewd gaze that if he wanted to, he could tell her where Emmy Murchison was at this exact moment. "All right, you can have six dollars for it," she said reluctantly "Provided you answer one question for me. Have you seen this girl around here anywhere?"

The scrawny young man glanced down at the photograph she'd extracted from her muff, and let out a crack of laughter. "Sure, who hasn't?" He pushed the cheap umbrella across the rough wooden counter. "That'll be six dollars, miss."

"Where is she now?"

"That," he said sweetly, "is more than one question."

Helen gritted her teeth, pulling all her pocket change out of her muff and slapping it on the counter beside the umbrella. "And *that* is more than six dollars. Where is she now?"

The shopkeeper counted out the dollar coins and assorted quarters before he answered. "Try the tents, miss," he said at last. "That's where all the socialists are. The only ones left on the company-side of town are us capitalists."

"You robber barons, you mean," Helen retorted and grabbed up her umbrella, barely resisting the urge to hit him over the head with it before she left.

Outside, the rain had faded to drizzle again, but the dark ridge of clouds bunched up against the northern line of hills promised worse to come. It was hard to believe that just yesterday, she'd stood among forsythia and watched her cousin beat rugs in the sunshine. With a sigh, Helen put up her cheap umbrella, gathered her skirts, and started hiking toward the canvas tents and cook-fires she could see across a field of barren bony piles. As she'd expected, the sodden coal waste sucked and splashed at each step, splattering mud and rock debris up over the top of her sturdy lace-up shoes. By the time she made it across to the tent city, Helen could feel a handful of stones crunching painfully beneath her heels and toes.

She'd expected to see a stir of activity in the strikers' camp as she approached, and she wasn't disappointed. Warned by the sound of her footsteps over the hissing rain, one miner after another popped a head—and sometimes a rifle barrel—out from between the flaps of their closed canvas tents. To Helen's surprise and growing frustration, however, each of them threw a quick, derisive look at her and then disappeared again, sealing their tents shut fast behind them. At first she thought that meant there must be a strike organizer present, someone whom the other miners knew would step out into the rain to meet her. But when she finally stood in the middle of the tent city, surrounded by nothing but blank canvas, swirling smoke, and the smell of poorly dug latrines, Helen realized she'd once again been labeled by her clothing and deliberately shut out.

Another woman might have stood there fuming and wondering how to proceed. But Helen had the great advantage of knowing from her brother's Boy Scout days just how easily sound could carry through canvas. She also had a voice that could ring echoes off the hills, when she wanted it to. She took a deep breath.

"My name is Helen Sorby and I'm looking for Emmy Murchison!" Sound traveled through canvas both ways, and Helen could clearly hear the ripple of surprise that washed across the tent city after that shouted announcement. *"If Emmy Murchison is here, send her out. If not, come out and tell me where Emmy Murchison is. Because I'm not going away. And I'm not going to shut up!"* she added, deliberately letting her voice rise to an out-and-out bellow on that last threat.

Someone cursed in an adjacent tent and then shoved their way through flapping wet canvas. Helen swung around to see a glitter of spectacles glowering at her through the drizzle. "Emmy Murchison's not here," snapped Bryde Larkin, her voice sounding more like steel than ever. "And for God's sake, stop shouting, or the yellow dogs are going to come roust us all out into the rain just to see what's going on."

Helen blinked from under her umbrella at the young female labor organizer, initial surprise fading slowly to suspicion. "When did you come up here from Harwick?"

Larkin's dark eyes narrowed behind her glasses. "Two days ago, to support the new walkout."

"And you're *sure* you haven't seen Emmy Murchison?"

"No, of course not. What in God's name makes you think she'd be hiding in a place like Red Hot?"

"This," Helen said simply, and shook Jackson Ecklar's photograph out of her muff, holding it out toward the union organizer. When Bryde Larkin frowned and reached to take it, Helen dropped both it and her umbrella into the mud and grabbed the younger woman's wrist instead, hauling her out of the tent and then ducking through the open space where she'd been.

"Hey!" Larkin's warning cry brought two of the tent's inhabitants to their feet, lunging forward to grab at Helen. But for once her walking suit stood her in good stead. Both coal miners seemed aghast to find themselves holding on to a well-bred lady instead of a company policeman. They dropped their grip and backed away, muttering apologetically in Hungarian.

"It's all right," Helen said, both to them and to Bryde Larkin, who'd come charging in breathless and worried behind her. And oddly enough, it was. Emmy Murchison's wealthy parents might have been horrified to find their daughter dressed in muddy immigrant's clothes and sitting cross-legged in a striker's tent, with a sleepy child nestled on one knee and a copy of Karl Marx open on the other. But to Helen, who knew James Foster Barton would rather die than actually participate in the labor movement he used as a cover, nothing could have looked nicer.

"Thank God." She smiled across the tent at the startled coal heiress. "You haven't fallen into bad company after all."

That comment stopped whatever Larkin was going to say, and made Emmy Murchison's deep-set eyes gleam with laughter. Her stepmother was right—although the mismatched slant of mouth and eyebrows on either side of Emmy's fever-marred face kept her from being pretty, it didn't detract in the slightest from the sharp-edged intelligence that made up her charm.

"Told you, Bry," she said, closing Karl Marx and passing the sleepy child she'd been holding back to its mother. "No one who writes for the *Progressive Worker's Weekly* would ever betray a fellow socialist."

Helen exchanged quizzical glances with the union organizer. "That just shows you haven't been a socialist very long, Em," Bryde Larkin said at last. "But I'll be glad to be proved wrong about Miss Sorby. I *am* wrong, aren't I?"

"In thinking I would run right back to Oakmont and tell Charles Murchison where his daughter is hiding? You're wrong about that." Helen seated herself on the canvas-covered floor of the tent, thankful for the zibeline skirts that insulated her from the cold ground. The two mining families whose tent this seemed to be rearranged themselves to make room for her around the smoldering charcoal brazier, murmuring in Hungarian and redistributing their two thin blankets to cover the handful of squirming children more thoroughly. Helen made a mental note to put Red Hot on the list of places where her aunt's next shipment of relief supplies should go. She watched Bryde Larkin take the empty place beside Emmy, and shook her head in mingled relief and exasperation.

"If you had only told me that Miss Murchison—"

"Emmy," the coal heiress said firmly.

"—that Emmy had joined your union organizing drive, Miss Larkin—"

"Bryde." The dark eyes behind those steel-rimmed spectacles glinted with ironic amusement.

Helen scowled at the labor organizer, not mollified in the slightest. "And you can call me 'Helen' too, but that doesn't make me any less annoyed with you. It would have saved me a lot of trouble if you'd answered my questions honestly the other day. Why did you have to make up a fairy tale about Emmy being seduced by a confidence man?"

Bryde Larkin sighed, taking off her glasses to rub at the red mark they'd left across the bridge of her nose. Her voice held no regret. "Because that was the rumor we were already spreading around Oakmont and Natrona. It was the story we wanted her parents to hear."

"Well, they heard it." Helen winced at the memory of her incursion into the Murchison household the previous night. "They got an earful of it from me, embellished with details you never even imagined. But why did they need to hear that instead of the truth?"

Larkin didn't answer, but her gaze slipped across to Emmy Murchison, whose fingers had clenched tight around the battered copy of Karl Marx. After a moment, the coal heiress looked up at both of them with a little self-deprecating grimace, as if she was aware of the melodrama of what she was about to say.

"The truth, Miss Sorby, is that I didn't just decide to join the union organizing drive. I left home because I was afraid if I stayed, I'd get blamed for a crime I didn't commit."

Helen took a deep breath. "Stealing the securities from your father's coal company, you mean."

"Yes."

"You didn't steal them? Not even to cash in so you could help out the labor movement here in the valley?"

"No," Emmy Murchison said indignantly. "I didn't even know they were worth anything, until I heard my father cursing and screaming that they were gone. At first he was absolutely convinced some rival coal mine operator had stolen them, but I knew sooner or later, he'd start to think about all my new socialist friends." She glanced across at Bryde Larkin with a grimace that accentuated the mismatch of her face. "The last thing we wanted to do was to ruin the coal strike by getting the labor movement accused of theft and blackmail."

Helen couldn't restrain a snort. "And you thought disappearing without an explanation *wouldn't* make you look guilty of theft and blackmail?"

"No, I knew it would," Emmy said candidly. "But we figured if my father heard I'd been seduced by some confidence man, he wouldn't be able to blame the stolen securities on either the socialists or the miners. And while his coal police were busy hunting for someone who didn't exist, the union organizers would have a chance to make some headway in organizing his mines."

"It might have worked," Bryde Larkin said thoughtfully, "if your father hadn't brought in the state police to suppress his miners while his company police were busy looking for you."

"And if the man he sent to pay fifty thousand dollars in ransom for those missing securities hadn't been murdered in Bernard Flinn's coal mine," Helen added. "That started a private little war between their companies—"

"It didn't *start* it." Emmy Murchison's mouth hardened into the angry line Ecklar had captured in his photograph.

"My father's been trying to put Sedgwick Coal & Coke out of business for years, because they're the only unionized mine in Black Valley. It's just gotten a lot worse since Bernard Flinn was hired as their company police chief."

Bryde made a disgusted noise. "And with the state police here to 'investigate' the mayhem, union strikers are probably going to get blamed for everything Murchison and Sedgwick do to each other."

"The state police aren't the only ones investigating this mess," Helen said. "There's a county detective—an honest one—who will help us expose the real blackmailer and clear the strikers. All we have to do is prove it was Bernard Flinn who stole those securities and wrote the Black Hand blackmail note to your father—"

"Bernard Flinn?" Emmy Murchison didn't sound cynical or despairing about the possibility of convicting the coal police chief—she just sounded completely astonished. "You think my father was right and Flinn is really behind all of this?"

Helen's eyes narrowed. "Don't you?"

"Oh, no," said the millionaire's daughter. "I think it was the man who seduced my stepmother last fall, while my father was out west buying coal mines for the railroad."

"What?" Helen stared at her, then yanked her folded sketch out from her muff. She nearly burned her hand on the brazier as she thrust it out to the coal heiress. "Is this him?"

Emmy glanced down at the sketch obediently, but Helen could see she was already shaking her head. "I've never actually seen him," she said regretfully. "Lillian is always careful to keep her love affairs discreet. The only ones who've seen her lovers are her own servants, and she makes sure they never talk. It was years before they trusted me enough to tell me, and no matter how much I tried to reassure them that they'd keep their jobs, I never could get them to tell my father." She passed the drawing to Bryde, who frowned and then handed it back to Helen.

"He looks familiar, but I can't place him," the labor organizer said. "Who is he?"

Helen glanced at the sketch she'd drawn of the confidence man who'd bigamously swindled her and a dozen other women like her out of their small middle-class dowries. It wasn't hard to imagine him renaming and reinventing himself yet again, this time to set his sights on a higher class of victim. And on a much bigger payoff.

"I hate to say it," she said. "But he's my ex-husband."

ELEVEN

After a day of explosions and assassinations and a night of no answers and no sleep, the last thing Milo Kachigan wanted to hear at ten o'clock on Friday morning was that Helen Sorby had disappeared without a word of explanation. Unfortunately, that was exactly what her distraught aunt had rung up to tell him.

"I got up early to talk to her, but she was already gone." The distress in Pat McGregor's voice was undimmed by the crackle and hum of the multiple telephone exchanges the call had been connected through to get from Oakmont to Tarentum. "And all Tilly knows is that she told Mr. Bailey she had an urgent mission to carry out and needed one of his buggies."

Kachigan rubbed at the ache in his cheekbone and shifted the telephone receiver to the other side of his face, even though he knew the pain came from tension rather the touch of cold metal. Outside the lockup, he could see pedestrians and horse traffic alike slow down and stare as if they could see some visible trace on the basement walls of the "bloody Black Hand murder" that Tarentum's morning papers had bannered across their front pages.

"Who's Mr. Bailey?" he asked. When Helen's Aunt Pittypat got into this kind of dither, he knew the best way to get information out of her was one small piece at a time.

"The livery stable owner in Oakmont." Pat McGregor sounded surprised, as if a county detective should know the name of every person living in his jurisdiction. "That's why Helen asked him for a buggy, of course."

Kachigan took a deep breath. "And did he hire one to her?"

"Oh, dear. I didn't think to ask Tilly—" He heard the thump of the telephone speaking bell being dropped, then an exchange of muffled women's voices. After a moment, Pat McGregor came back to the handset, sounding even more upset than before. "No, Mr. Kachigan, he didn't. Tilly thinks he put her in touch with some sort of train hobo instead, who could show her how to ride the rails. She says Helen wanted to go to some place named Red Hot, and there wasn't any other way to get there."

Kachigan tried to envision Helen Sorby hopping a freight to carry out this urgent mission of hers. Unfortunately, it wasn't difficult. "Why did she need to go there, Mrs. McGregor?"

"I don't know, but I'm so very afraid it was because of the note," Pittypat said anxiously. "I might be wrong, of course, but with all this talk about the Black Hand—well, when I heard Helen got a hand-delivered note early this morning and then had to leave at once—"

Kachigan cursed, but in muttered Armenian so as not to alarm Helen's aunt any more than she'd managed to alarm herself. "I don't think your niece is in any danger from the Black Hand, ma'am," he forced himself to say. It came out sounding stiff and uncaring, but that was only because he'd clamped his jaw tight against the alarm he felt himself. "If that note had been a threat, Helen would have come straight here to tell me."

"Would she?" Pat McGregor sounded doubtful. "You know how very stubborn she can be sometimes—"

"I know." He saw the lockup door open to admit Riley and Frick with the tray of sandwiches and coffee he'd sent them out for. Across the room, Taggart lifted the folded newspaper off his face and swung his feet off his desk, yawning. "Don't worry, I'll make sure she's all right. You said she was going to Red Hot?"

"Yes, but I have no idea where that is—"

"I do." Kachigan remembered the little coal patch from the long day he'd spent looking for fire-bosses. Driving straight from Tarentum, with fresh horses and himself instead of Taggart at the reins, it would take a little over an hour to get there. "I'll have Helen back for you by luncheon, ma'am."

That made an earthy Irish snort echo through the crackling lines. "Don't make any rash promises, Mr. Kachigan. Just get her home in time for supper, if you please—and make sure she doesn't bring that hobo home with her!"

He made the drive alone, refusing Taggart's company and ignoring Riley's advice to take a slower, closed carriage in case of rain. With just his weight in the light-wheeled buggy, Kachigan made good time along the iron-stained trickle of Bull Creek, taking only half an hour to get from the ruined coal tipple to the shut-down mines at Millerstown. The horses slowed going across the Allegheny hills after that but picked up their pace again willingly enough once they reached the flat stretch of Little Deer Creek. Kachigan wheeled them north as soon as they crossed the rickety bridge at Culmerville, the cold wet wind whipping at his face.

The first thing he saw at Red Hot was the huddle of canvas tents under the dripping edge of the trees. It surprised him to see that anomalous flare of protest in these subdued, nonunion hills, but it also made the tense grinding in his empty stomach subside a little. He could believe that an unexpected union action had drawn Helen Sorby north much more easily than that she'd been driven here by a threat from the Black Hand. Kachigan was so convinced of that, in fact, that he had already begun to guide the buggy across the tracks and toward the strikers' camp when his attention was snagged by an even more anomalous sight—

an elegantly dressed and attractive couple waiting near the empty railroad siding. It took not just a second look but a third to tell him the lady in the pretty gray walking suit was actually Helen Sorby.

The stab of emotion Kachigan felt was nothing but pure, undiluted jealousy.

By the time he'd maneuvered the buggy over toward them, he'd managed to transmute most of that emotion to impatience and an irritable curiosity about how Helen's overwrought aunt had turned a handsome professional man into a hobo. The gentleman in question annoyed him even further by giving him a friendly glance as he drove up and commenting, "Bad day to be out in a buggy, isn't it?"

"Getting worse all the time," Kachigan said between his teeth. "Good morning, Miss Sorby. Your aunt asked me to make sure you were safe, since she had the impression you were traveling on your own today. Now that I see you're not—"

"*Milo!*" Neither the cold tone of his voice nor his polite use of her last name seemed to diminish in the slightest the flare of relief in Helen Sorby's dark eyes. "How on earth did you know I needed you?"

"You did?" For one angry moment, Kachigan wondered if the polite young man beside her had somehow forced Helen to travel with him against her will. The smiling face she turned toward her companion disproved that hypothesis before he could embarrass himself by putting it into words.

"Mr. Hower, thank you so much for your help with riding the train," Helen said and gave him a grateful farewell handshake. "I'm sorry to have made you wait here all morning for nothing, but I had no idea Milo—I mean, Detective Kachigan—was going to be passing through. He—um—has been helping me investigate the disappearance of my sister. You won't mind if I ride back to town with him?"

Hower gave her a startled look. "In an open buggy, in this weather?"

"I have an umbrella." Helen waved it over her head with an amused look Kachigan didn't quite understand. From the baffled look on his face, neither did Hower. "And I don't melt in the rain. Don't worry, I won't come to any harm."

"Not if you hurry. But the rain's turning to sleet, and the roads will ice over soon. You shouldn't dawdle getting back." Hower gave Kachigan a warning frown. He didn't take offense at it, since it was the same look he would have given the other man if their places had been reversed.

"Miss Sorby's Aunt McGregor asked me to bring her home." He answered the other man's look rather than his words. "You can ring her up and verify it when you get back to Oakmont, if you like. She'll be happy to hear her niece has come to no harm."

"Oakmont nine-four-two hundred," Helen added helpfully. She closed her umbrella and handed it up to Kachigan, then swept her fuzzy gray skirts up well past her ankles and climbed into the buggy without waiting for him to help her. Kachigan's mouth kicked up at the sight of the sturdy mud-splashed walking shoes she wore beneath her finery, and the last of his doubts about finding her with another man in Red Hot quietly washed away. "Tell her I'll try to be home by supper."

"All right." Hower stepped back to avoid getting splashed as Kachigan shook the reins and wheeled the buggy team back toward the road. "And good luck finding your sister, Miss Sorby!"

There was a long silence after that, filled only with the wet slap of the horses' hooves and the patter of sleet as it bounced off Helen's cheap umbrella. Kachigan kept his eyes on the road and his hands firmly on the reins, leaving it to his other senses to appreciate her presence: the warmth where her soft skirts pressed against his leg, the sound of her breathing, the faint drift of rose-scented soap and jasmine powder—

"Go ahead, say it."

He frowned at the glaze of ice he could see on the bridge ahead of them. "Say what?"

"That it would take an awful lot of luck for me to find a sister I never had," Helen said tartly. "Or that you don't appreciate being called away from work just to escort me back to my worried aunt. Or that you didn't like the story I wired to the *New York Herald* about the Natrona miners' riot. Whatever it is you're sitting there glowering about.''

''I'm not glowering.'' Kachigan eased the buggy slowly across the bridge, feeling the iron-rimmed wheels slip sideways beneath them. He didn't speak again until he had guided the horses safely back to the graveled road on the other side. ''I'm trying to decide whether to shake you for scaring me to death or kiss you for still being alive.''

''*What?*''

Her startled upward look made the choice for him, since it put her face at exactly the right angle. By the time he was done, Helen was breathless, her hat had been knocked askew, and her umbrella lay upside down and trampled at their feet. That was all right, though, because by then the sleet had turned into wet, melting flakes of snow.

''What on earth was *that* for?'' Helen demanded, although she sounded more amused than annoyed. ''When we've got the whole mess with Murchison Coal and Bernard Flinn to figure out, and Aunt Pittypat is waiting for us back in Oakmont—''

''I know.'' Kachigan picked up the reins and started the team back into motion, dislodging the layer of slush that had accumulated on their harness and the buggy roof. ''I just wanted to make sure you still liked it. After the way you disappeared the last time I proposed to you—''

''I didn't disappear,'' she said indignantly, but her eyes dropped away from his. ''I got busy down in Pittsburgh, covering the coal strike for the *Herald*—''

''Don't lie to me, Helen.''

She frowned, and looked back up at him. ''All right, maybe I did disappear for a while. But it wasn't because of your silly conviction that if you keep asking me often enough, I'm going to forget I swore not to get married again. I've told you what we can do—''

''No,'' he said hastily, to stop her from finishing that thought. It wasn't the impropriety that worried him as much as the impossibility of them ever getting home if he gave in and stopped the buggy again. "It's all right, I'm willing to wait until you change your mind. Which you will."

"No, I won't," Helen said. "And in the meantime, don't you think we could—"

"No." He captured her hand and put it back into her stylish muff. "I think it's time for you to tell me what you know about this mess with Murchison Coal and Bernard Flinn. No," he corrected himself, wheeling the team left onto Millerstown Road. "It's time for me to tell you how much worse this mess has gotten."

The laughter faded from Helen's eyes. "How much worse *has* it gotten, Milo?"

"Five coal policemen were executed yesterday at Bull Creek Coal and the coal tipple was blown up with dynamite. Bernard Flinn is either dead or missing," he said grimly. "And before I had a chance to talk to him again, our friend Sandrino Racca was shot to death through the bars of his cell last night."

He could feel Helen stiffen against him. "Did you catch the man who did it?"

"No. We turned out every policeman in Tarentum and spent the rest of the night searching the town and questioning men in bars and pool halls. No one saw anything." He glanced down at her through the pelting snow. "Or at least anything they're willing to talk about."

Helen didn't miss that implication. "You think the Black Hand was behind it all?"

"I don't know." He thought about telling her what Leon Daniels had said about his secret Pinkerton assignment, then decided he didn't have the right to expose the other man's cover. To the people she liked and trusted, Helen Sorby was loyal to a fault, but her opinion of Pinkerton agents wasn't much higher than her opinion of the Pennsylvania State Police. "Don't you?"

"No," she said flatly. "Not after I talked to my cousin Niccolo yesterday."

"What did he say?"

"That Murchison Brothers Coal had some important company securities stolen a few days ago, and got what

looked like a Black Hand letter offering to give them back
in exchange for fifty thousand dollars. The payoff was supposed to be made in Bull Creek Mine. The trouble is, the
Mano Negro weren't the ones who issued the threat.''

Kachigan frowned. ''Then who did?''

''Niccolo didn't know. That's why he sent Racca to
watch the exchange, to find out who the extortionist really
was.''

''And you're sure this cousin of yours is telling you the
truth?''

''Pretty sure.'' Helen Sorby looked away, her mouth
tightening to the unhappy line he'd seen yesterday in the
lockup. ''I told you he was in the Black Hand, Milo, but I
didn't tell you the worst of it. He's actually the *capo* of the
local branch of the *Mano Negro*. That means—''

'' —he's the boss.'' Kachigan took his gaze away from
the straight hill-slope ahead of them long enough to give
her an amused look. ''No matter how long I know you,
Helen, you never fail to surprise me.''

''It's not as if I'm proud of him,'' she protested. ''He's
been the troublemaker in the family ever since he was a
boy, with his knife fights and his arrests and his extortion
schemes. I try to only visit his mother when he's in jail,
but we needed to know what Sandrino Racca saw down in
Bull Creek Mine. I knew he would tell Nicco the truth, if
we could just get the two of them together.''

''Well, he can't tell anyone the truth now.'' Kachigan
reined the horses in at the top of the hill to slow their
descent on the other side. Their coats steamed and their
warm breath misted into clouds in the snowy air. ''Someone made sure of that. And if that wasn't your cousin—''

'' —then it was the man who committed the murder in
Bull Creek Coal Mine. He must have been worried that
Racca saw him.''

''Yes.'' He wasn't surprised by the way Helen followed
his thought to its logical conclusion, not after the two previous murder investigations they had worked on together.
He was just surprised by how good it felt to have her doing
it again. ''And no matter what your socialist instincts tell

you, that couldn't have been Bernard Flinn. Even he wouldn't have killed five of his own men and faked his own death just to interfere with the coal miners' strike.''

''No,'' she admitted. ''But then why did he call you in to arrest Racca?''

Kachigan gave her an ironic glance. ''Probably because he didn't want to get his father-in-law's coal company entangled with the Black Hand.''

''What?'' Helen's startled exclamation made a cloud of mist around her face. ''*That's* why Flinn was working for the Sedgwick Coal & Coke Company? You're sure?''

''As sure as you are that your cousin's not the one behind that extortion threat,'' he retorted. ''So neither of them can be our murderer. Now all we have to do is figure out who is.''

''Actually, I think I know that,'' Helen said, reaching out to steady herself against him as one of the horses slid a little on the icy road and made the buggy jolt behind it. ''But you're not going to like the answer.''

''Try me.''

Helen remained silent for a moment, but Kachigan was too busy guiding the nervous team down the last of the icy slope to glance over and see what the reason might be. It wasn't until they had rolled into the vacant, snowy shadows of Millerstown and he pulled the team up to rest for a moment that he noticed how tightly she was still holding on to his arm.

''Helen, what's the matter?'' He turned in the open buggy to block the pelting snow with his back, not liking the tense set of her face. ''Why should it matter to me who the blackmailer is? Unless you're going to tell me it's Art Taggart or your brother or Aunt Pittypat—''

''It's my ex-husband.''

Kachigan stared at her in astonishment for a while, until Helen's face grew even more tense and it occurred to him she was mistaking his silence for anger. He opened his mouth to deny it, but before he could speak, two sets of hands clamped onto his shoulders from behind and yanked him violently backward.

"What the hell—" He caught himself with one hand on the side-rail of the buggy, wrenching his shoulder hard in an effort to keep from slamming headfirst onto the road. He had a single glimpse of Helen's face, eyes startled wide and mouth opening to cry out in alarm, but before he could warn her there was no one to hear, the steel-hard crack of a gun barrel across his arm numbed his hand and knocked him away from her. Kachigan felt the ground slam hard against his back, driving all the air from his lungs. He heard Helen's startled cry lift to a furious shout just as a muddy boot smashed into his chest. Ribs cracked beneath the impact, and the snow-gray sky overhead turned abruptly to streaks of diamond-glittered black.

By the time Kachigan had recovered enough to gasp air past the tearing pain, he'd been hauled to his feet and had both hands tied painfully behind his back. A clatter of hooves made him lift his head, squinting past the mud in his eyes to see if Helen had somehow managed to escape. But even before he'd cleared his vision, a volley of furious Italian curses told him only their horses had been set free. He started to curse himself and gasped instead at the pain that speaking caused him.

"Shut up, or I'll shut you up like I did your boyfriend." The hard voice sounded familiar, but it wasn't until Kachigan saw the square glitter of Teddy Roosevelt spectacles that he recognized Franklin Truxall. The police chief of Murchison Brothers Coal stood in the middle of Millerstown's vacant street as if he owned it, which perhaps his company did. He was scowling at Helen Sorby, who despite her elegant dress was struggling so hard that it was taking two men to tie her hands behind her. "Or I can just shoot you and leave you here, since the Turk's the only one Mr. Murchison asked me to talk to."

"No talking," was all Kachigan managed to croak past the stab of pain down his left side, but it was enough to turn the police chief's cold eyes back toward him. "Not if you touch her."

He regretted the instinctive protest when he heard the satisfaction in Truxall's answering grunt. "Yeah, I thought she might come in handy,'' the Murchison Coal police chief said. "For Chrissake, Wes, just get her tied and let's go.''

One of Helen's captors growled in frustration and gave her a slap that knocked her hat off and left her hair spilling down her neck and face. She fell silent after that, but when Kachigan threw her a worried glance, the expression he saw on her face was one of determination, not fear. His own jaw hardened in response. They weren't dead yet, and between the two of them, they might just be able to outwit Truxall.

That conviction lasted through the pain of being dragged on a long walk through the snow and then shoved down a set of stairs whose crooked treads jarred his side and made sparks sizzle across his dimming vision. It lasted through the slamming of a door and the darkness that descended afterward, through the flares of oil lamps being lit and then the brighter flare of a carbide light. But when one of Truxall's coal policemen threw him into a cold metal car and then slid in beside him, Kachigan squeezed his eyes shut and let despair begin to creep in. It grew stronger as the car rumbled down a slope, the unmistakable smell of coal and rock dust washing over them. When the electric traction motor finally stuttered to a stop at the end of a long descent, all Kachigan's hope for an easy escape died with it.

Truxall had brought them down into the closed Millerstown coal mine to interrogate.

"Let her go," Kachigan said, as soon as he'd recovered his breath after being dragged out of the man-trip car. The roof of this mine was even lower than at Bull Creek, and the way it forced him to bend at the waist made breathing harder than ever. It might have been his imagination, but it seemed to Kachigan he could also hear more creaks and drips and clatters here than he had in the working mine, and smell more sulfur in the air. He wondered if Truxall had bothered to bring along a gas-detecting lamp. "Let her go and I'll tell you whatever Murchison wants to know.''

That got him a considering look from the coal police chief, but only a contemptuous glance from Helen Sorby.

"If he takes me away, it'll just be as far as the nearest mine shaft, Milo," she warned. "He won't let me go free to testify against him. Stop trying to bargain with him."

Kachigan gave her an irritated glance as the police guards led them down the dark passage, shadows bouncing away in front of their paraffin headlamps. "Did you have to mention testifying? He might not have thought about it if you hadn't."

She shook her head, hair sliding down across the shoulders of her elegant suit. "I'm not leaving you down here, hurt like that," she said stubbornly. "I wouldn't go even if he let me."

"Stop that damned chattering." Truxall shoved past them to open a sliding wooden door that blocked off a side-passage of the mine. Inside, his brighter carbide light illuminated what must have been a supply area back when the mine was working. Shelves and tables lined the crumbling rock walls, and the ubiquitous knob-and-nail electric wires that ran along the roof fed in here to an actual light fixture. Truxall flicked it on, although its feeble orange filament barely added to the glow of his modern headlamp.

"Have a seat, Kachigan." The stocky coal police chief kicked a ladder-back chair out from the wall and watched without emotion as one of his company guards yanked Kachigan's arms up and slid them ruthlessly down over the chair back. He cursed and blinked to chase the blackness out of his vision, but it wasn't until he felt something dripping off his chin that he realized the pain had made him bloody his lower lip. "You too, Miss—"

"—Sorby," she said pointedly. "Helen Sorby. You may have heard of me, I was hired by Charles Murchison last week to look for his missing daughter."

"Yeah, I heard." Truxall motioned, and a company policeman thumped Helen down into another chair hard enough to make her stop talking, sliding her arms over the back as well. Once she was settled, Truxall swung a third chair around for himself, easing the strain of constant stooping the low roof imposed on captors and captives alike. "I also heard how little progress you've been making. I don't think Mr. Murchison's going to mind the loss, unless you managed to discover that damned girl between last night and today.''

Helen scowled at him, but for once seemed to have nothing to say. "I thought so," Truxall said, his eyes glittering behind his glasses with something a little too cold to be amusement. He scraped his chair closer to her and reached out to yank at a strand of her loosened hair, hard enough to make Helen gasp and then curse him in Italian. "So now we can use you to make your boyfriend talk."

"Just tell me what you want to know," Kachigan said. "There's no need to torture her."

"Isn't there?" Truxall wound his fingers deeper into Helen's hair, unintimidated by the way she was baring her teeth at him. "Does that mean you're actually going to admit taking the payoff money off Harry Tamasy's body, back when you examined him at Bull Creek Number One? And tell us where you stashed it?"

"The two hundred dollars he was carrying?" Kachigan asked in surprise. "It's in my desk back at the lockup."

"Wrong answer."

He couldn't see what Truxall was doing, because the mine's supply room was suddenly much darker. Something rattled inside a can, something splashed, and then abruptly something hissed. An instant later, the anguished sound of Helen screaming brought Kachigan to his feet, banging his head on the roof and tearing pain through his chest in a vain attempt to drag his roped wrists over the back of the chair.

"That wasn't fun, was it?" Metal screwed back into metal, a match sizzled, and the room was suddenly bright again. Kachigan blinked against the light and saw the streaks of tears down Helen Sorby's face first, before he saw the angry red burn along her neck. "When carbide hits water, it just naturally burns—and with you being so wet from the snow, we've got a lot more places to burn yet." He turned his head, and the upward flare of the carbide lamp he now held in his hands made his eyes nearly invisible behind his glinting lenses. "Now, Turk, let's try this again. Where's the missing money?"

TWELVE

The pain was an annoyance. That's what Helen told herself, over and over again, blinking her eyes against the involuntary tears the fumes of burning gas had sparked, streaming up from the fiery contact of carbide with wet skin. She'd burned herself a dozen times before on the coal stove, the clothes iron, the coffeepot. She knew the exact dimensions of that kind of pain, she knew it would throb and ache and linger but that eventually it would have to go away. It was just an annoyance, just an obstacle she had to get around so she could think and listen and plan—

"The payoff money, you mean." She barely recognized Milo Kachigan's voice, between the strain of talking past his broken ribs and the harsh rasp of outright fear. "Murchison's decided he wants it back after all?"

"Wouldn't you, if you hadn't gotten what you paid for?" Truxall turned the carbide light between his fingers, letting its harsh beam dance across the county detective's face. Helen saw Kachigan wince and narrow his eyes against it, the dark streak on his chin turning blood-colored in the glare. "I told the old man not to trust that damned Slovak fire-boss of his, but he swore he'd deliver the money safely. And what happens? The fire-boss gets himself killed, nothing gets returned, and the Black Hand's still yelling for their money.'' The coal police chief tipped his chair forward with sudden violence and backhanded a slap across Kachigan's face. ''Which *you* must have taken off his body, you damned Turk, since you were the first one to examine it.''

Helen took a deep breath. ''The Black Hand aren't the ones blackmailing your boss,'' she said loudly.

''Helen, shut up.'' Kachigan's face had two streaks of blood on it now, from where Truxall's signet ring had cut him, but he didn't seem to notice. His thin, bony face had stiffened to a mask that almost reminded her of her cousin. ''You kidnapped Bernard Flinn, didn't you?'' he asked Truxall. ''That's how you know I took the payoff money.''

Helen shot the detective a startled glance, wondering if he was playing for time or honestly trying to make Truxall believe he had the missing extortion money. The stocky man tilted his chair back with a little, satisfied smile.

''Starting to see you can't wiggle out of it now, huh? So where's the money?''

''Under my bed, back in Tarentum.'' Kachigan didn't betray himself with any hesitation or awkwardness that Helen could see, but Truxall merely grunted at that reply.

''Wrong answer again,'' he said, and dropped the supply room back into dim paraffin light with one twist of the carbide can. Helen's breath locked and she braced herself against her chair, twining her hands fiercely into the ropes that bound her to it. ''We've already looked there, and in the lockup too. Try again.''

Helen heard Kachigan curse in Armenian, violently enough to make his voice break off with a painful jerk. In the silence that followed, the terrifying rattle of carbide sent her the inspiration that pain alone hadn't been able to provide.

''Tell him the truth,'' she snarled at Kachigan. ''My cousin Nicco can't kill me if I'm already dead! Stop giving in to his damned blackmail.''

There was a long pause, during which Helen fervently prayed that Truxall had taken the bait and Kachigan would know how to reel it in. The twist of metal, the scratch of a match, and the sudden brightness of the supply room answered the first question, but the continuing stiffness on her companion's face left Helen in doubt of the second.

"What cousin?" the coal police chief asked.

"No," Kachigan said suddenly. "No, Helen, he'll kill us both if we tell—"

"Not if he gets killed first." She turned her head, hoping her glare at Truxall didn't show any of the relief she felt. She focused on the disheveled reflection she could see in his spectacles to be sure her gaze didn't waver as she lied. "My cousin is the one who has your missing money, Mr. Truxall. My damned Black Hand cousin Niccolo Santangelo, the *capo* here in Tarentum. You've heard of him?"

Truxall grunted. "But the Black Hand said they never got the payment." He turned the painful beam of his carbide lamp toward her this time. "Don't lie to me, or I'm not going to leave that pretty face of yours alone much longer—"

"*I'm not lying!*" Helen spat the words out at him with enough conviction to ring loud echoes off the rock walls. It was easy to do, since she really was telling the truth now. "I told you before, the Black Hand weren't the ones who made that threat against your boss. And they don't appreciate someone using their name and hiding in their shadow! My cousin sent Sandrino Racca to watch that payoff being made, not to accept it. He wanted to know who it was really going to."

"But Bernard Flinn interrupted before the blackmailer could take our money? Leaving it for your boyfriend here to find?" Truxall looked past her, lifting a skeptical eyebrow at Kachigan. "Kind of convenient that you were right on the spot to deliver that money to the real Black Hand, wasn't it?"

Somehow, the county detective managed a bitter crack of laughter. "Not really. Why do you think I got transferred up here in the first place? Because Roge McGara liked my work?"

"McGara got a little whisper in the ear from the Black

Hand, eh?'' Truxall grunted again, sounding more amused this time. ''I have to admit, that does explain a lot. But before I'm buying this cart of stinking fish, Turk, you better tell me one thing right about the man you gave that money to. What's his Black Hand nickname?''

Helen sucked in a breath, hoping it hadn't been loud enough to betray her. They were going to die and it was all her fault, because she'd let her mortification at having a Black Hand criminal for a cousin keep her from telling Kachigan anything about her Santangelo relations. Now he was going to blow their cover story into smithereens, just because she'd been arrogant enough to think she could keep him innocent of it all—

''*Il Merlo*,'' Kachigan said, and threw a glittering look across at Helen. ''There, are you happy? Now I'll get to die with a knife in my back, even if this yellow dog decides to let us go. You know the Black Hand never forgets a traitor.''

Truxall scraped his chair back. ''You're not going to die for a while, not until I'm sure I got the truth out of you. If I didn't, you'll only live long enough to regret it.'' He reached over to grasp at Helen's hair again, scraping a wet strand of it across the burn on her neck. She gasped and jerked upright in her chair. ''Where can I find this cousin of yours, girl?''

''Five-twenty-one Seventh,'' she said without hesitation. ''In West Tarentum.''

''And how many men will he have there with him?''

''Only a few—'' This time it was his hand that scraped across the burn, the metal of his ring jabbing its dull ache to agony. Helen glared up at him through watering eyes. ''All right, maybe a dozen! Or more, it depends on the time of day.''

''That's better.'' The coal policeman swung away, clipping his lamp back up on his forehead at last. ''I'm going to need all of you with me,'' he said to his company guards. ''Tie their legs to the chairs so they can't walk themselves out of here, and turn the light out so they can't see. They

can entertain themselves by hopping around in the dark
until we get back.''

Helen thought she knew what darkness was: moonless
nights, storm cellars, the blindfolds you wore for blind-
man's bluff. At first, when the orange glow of the lightbulb
overhead had faded into black, she thought the darkness in
the coal mine would be only a little worse. But as the sound
of voices echoed back down the passage and were lost below the hum of the coal car's electric motor, she realized
her eyes had still been depending on the faint reflections of
those distant headlamps to orient themselves to the space
around them. Now that the mine's ominous, creaking silence was all she could hear, sliding silver phantoms of
afterglow were all she could see, no matter whether she
shut her eyes or left them open. The lace-trimmed collar
around her neck suddenly seemed much too tight, the unmoving air around her much too lifeless—

"Helen, stop it," Kachigan said sharply.

"Stop what?" she demanded, but her breathlessness
gave her away. "I'm sorry, I know it's stupid, but it's just
so *dark*—"

"It won't be in a while." The confident way he promised
that seemed every bit as stupid as her own mindless panic,
but for once Helen bit her tongue and kept her opinions to
herself. "Truxall dropped his matches on his chair the last
time he lit his carbide lamp. Do you remember?"

Helen gnawed on her lip, trying to recall anything beyond fear and burning pain. "I think so."

"Can you slide your chair over there and get them?"

Helen flexed her toes experimentally against the rock
floor of the mine, picking her weight up and then throwing
it forward to nudge her chair in that direction. Going backward would have been easier, but she knew Truxall had
been facing her. Trying not to remember the coal policeman's final caustic comment, Helen skidded and hopped
her way to where she thought the chair should be, her arms
aching from the tight ropes, and the burn on her neck flar-

ing each time she moved. From the way her scraping sounds seemed to echo unevenly back at her through the darkness, she guessed Kachigan was doing the same thing. Helen wondered if he was trying to reach the light-switch, just in case the matches weren't really there.

She found Truxall's chair by the simple expedient of bumping into it with her knees. Now all she had to do was get her rapidly numbing fingers within reach of the match-box. Thanking God that the Murchison Coal police hadn't tied her feet as tightly as they had tied her hands, Helen began to turn herself around with little jerks and shoe-scrabbles. She had nearly gotten into position when one jerk skidded her a little too hard on the sloping floor. With a yelp of alarm, she felt herself falling sideways.

"Helen?"

"I'm all right." Her full, gored skirt of shaggy zibeline wool had been worth its annoying weight for once—all her hopping and spinning had wrapped the material so tightly around her chair that it cushioned her fall to a soft thump. And now that she lay sideways, with gravity no longer on the chair's side, Helen found herself able to stretch up in her seat and slide her bound wrists completely free of the chair's narrow back. With her feet tied to the chair legs, she still couldn't get her hands in front of her, but at least now she was able to lurch forward to her knees and hobble, hauling the fallen chair behind her. Except for the irritating way her coat and skirts dragged beneath her, it was a far more efficient mode of travel.

Within minutes, Helen had relocated Truxall's chair, but when she tried to bend sideways to grope with her hands for the matches, she discovered her stiff whalebone corset just wouldn't permit it. She spent five minutes swaying and twisting in the darkness to no avail—not a single brush of fingers found the matchbox she knew had to be there. Finally, in sheer frustration, Helen hauled herself around and bent forward at the waist, not to look with her useless eyes but to feel with her cheek and nose and mouth. Her chin bumped against the lightweight balsa wood box almost immediately. With a sigh of relief, Helen nudged it as far toward the edge of the chair as she dared with her cheek, then twisted around to fold it securely into the palm of her hand.

"Milo, I have the matches."

Only silence answered her, and it occurred to Helen that it had been a while since she'd heard his chair scraping an echo to her own. With the stress of immediate confrontation gone, perhaps Truxall's ruthless assault had finally caught up with him. Had he passed out, or was he just too short of breath to respond? How would she know, if she couldn't even locate him in the darkness?

"Milo?"

"I'm right here." He didn't sound groggy or unable to breathe, just preoccupied. Now that she knew what direction to turn her head, Helen could hear the soft clink and whisper of objects being touched and moved along a wooden board. He was looking for something among the supply shelves, she realized. "Hold still, I'll be there in a minute."

"No, *you* hold still." As much as her knees were complaining about this odd mode of transportation, Helen knew his cracked ribs had to be hurting even more. She hobbled her way toward the sound of his search, praying she still had the matches in her numb fingers. It was becoming harder and harder to tell. "What are you looking for?"

"This." The soft clink of metal was followed by a dusty thud. "Damnation, I dropped it."

"That's all right. I can pick it up." She bumped into the supply shelf first, making it rattle with loose metal and glass jars. Helen paused to listen for the sound of his breathing, close enough now that she could hear the irregular catch each time he inhaled, then shuffled sideways until her arm touched the warmth of his leg. She slid her fingers back along it to find his own bound hands. "There, do you have the matches?"

"Yes." He didn't sound as happy about that as she thought he'd be. "Helen, your fingers are ice-cold. How tightly are your hands tied?"

"I can't wiggle loose, if that's what you're asking," she

said tartly, although she knew quite well it wasn't. It was a little harder to pick up the metal object he'd dropped, with almost no feeling left in her fingertips, but fortunately it had what felt like a spout on one side and a clasp on the other. She used those to balance it between her palms. "Milo, is this an oil lamp?"

"A paraffin lamp," he corrected. "I noticed a bunch of them on this shelf before Truxall turned out the light. They must have been put here to be fixed, most of them had missing wicks, but I found one whose only problem is a cracked handle. There should be enough paraffin left to—" He broke off, sounding startled. "What's so funny?"

Helen bit down on her lower lip, trying to make her giggles subside. Knowing they were half-hysterical didn't make it any easier to quell them. "It's just—this seems like such a ridiculous amount of effort to go to for light—and I keep remembering what Truxall said about us entertaining ourselves."

The man she couldn't see in the dark made an odd sound, half gasp and half choke. "Don't make me laugh, Helen, it hurts. Can you hold the lamp under my hands, so the spout's close to my fingers?"

"I think so." She had to kick her dragging chair around behind his to manage it, but she got the paraffin lamp tilted at the correct angle and managed to hold it there, while Kachigan fumbled out a match and struck it. The burst of yellow sparks lit up the supply room astonishingly well, to eyes that had spent ten minutes trying to adjust themselves to no light at all. Helen frowned over her shoulder, lifting the lamp so the wick touched that fizzing flame. After a tense, shaking moment, the paraffin-soaked string flared into a two-inch flame, so surprisingly high and bright that Helen almost dropped the lamp.

"Well, now that we can see—"

"Don't move!" Kachigan glanced down at her over his own shoulder, his blood-streaked face looking fierce enough to truly belong to a member of the *Mano Negro*. "I want that flame right where it is."

Helen glanced over her shoulder again, biting her lip as

she saw he had moved his rope-knotted hands so the little paraffin lamp sat directly under them. "Milo, it's going to burn—"

"I know, but it won't be bad if I do it in little spurts. Don't try to move the lamp for me, I can feel where the ropes should be—"

"I'm not trying to move it. I'm trying not to drop it!" Helen could barely feel the weight of the little metal pot between her numbing palms. The way she had to twist her arms back to keep the paraffin lamp in place was making her bonds cut even more tightly into her wrists. "Let me push my chair back so I can get closer."

"Never mind," Kachigan said between his teeth. There was a note in his voice that made her crane her head, despite the aching protest of her burned neck, to see what was happening behind both their backs. To her surprise, the sight of her numb hands actually helped her keep them more steady. But it also meant watching the insides of Kachigan's wrists turn first red and then white before the ropes around them finally began to char in the fierce paraffin flame.

"Ah!" He jerked away abruptly, startling Helen into dropping the paraffin lamp. It rolled onto its side, but steadfastly continued to burn, although she could see melted paraffin begin to drip out the edge like an overturned candle. A second light appeared above it, a sullen crimson glow that brought with it the acrid smell of burned hemp and singed hair. Kachigan cursed and something snapped, and then the ropes fell in a smoldering pile to join the miner's lamp on the ground. Helen dragged her trailing skirts away from the flames with a final twist and jerk, then collapsed back against her chair, letting her head bow forward to ease the ache along her neck.

"Hang on, Helen, I saw a saw blade somewhere along this wall—" She heard a muffled thud and a fierce Armenian curse followed by an even fiercer American one. "Damn these four-foot seams! Why can't someone invent a machine to mine this kind of coal?"

"They have," she said, lifting her head again. "It's called unlimited immigration."

Kachigan chuckled, and a moment later she felt the distant tugging in her numb hands as he sawed at the ropes between them. "That's my good, fierce socialist. Keep yelling at me about something, because the next few minutes are going to be hell."

Helen scowled and tugged her hands apart as the ropes finally loosened. She pulled them around in front of her, rubbing at the pale, puffy fingers and red gouges where the ropes had bitten deep. "It can't hurt any worse than my neck, can it?"

"Don't bet on it." Kachigan bent to saw at the ropes around her feet, and this time even through her tough shoe leather Helen could feel the motion better. She continued rubbing grimly at the unfeeling slabs that were her hands. "Come on, keep yelling at me."

"I don't have anything else to yell at you about."

"I doubt that," Kachigan said. "Did you really send Truxall to your cousin's house?"

"Don't be silly, Milo. As much as he might deserve it, he lives with his sixty-year-old mother."

"Then where *did* you send them?"

"To the Slovak Catholic Church in West Tarentum. It was the only place I could think of that couldn't possibly be a Black Hand headquarters." She stood up too fast when the ropes around her feet fell away, and banged her own head on the low rock roof. Her unpinned hair didn't do much to cushion the impact, and Helen was left cursing at herself in Italian and rubbing a numb hand across her scalp. "Don't you dare laugh!"

"Don't worry, I can't." Kachigan leaned down to saw through the ropes at his own feet, but the first awkward movement made him gasp and freeze in pain. "Maybe you'd better start out of the coal mine now," he said between harsh, indrawn breaths. "It's only going to take Truxall about an hour and a half to get back here, and he's going to be damn mad when he does. I want you gone by then."

Helen hadn't thought she'd welcome the first hot twinge of returning circulation in her hands, but the ability it gave her to clench her fingers was worth the pain. She reached up and took the rusty blade away from Kachigan, then knelt beside his chair and began sawing at the ropes around his ankles. "Save your breath for walking out," she said before he could protest. "I told you before, I'm not leaving without you."

"See, I knew you could find something to yell at me about." The words were amused, but the brush of his hand across her spilled hair said something very different. Helen winced as he lifted the tangled mass free of the aching burn on her neck. "I'm going to kill Truxall," Kachigan added quietly, in a tone from which all trace of amusement had vanished.

"Let's concentrate for now on making sure he doesn't kill us." Helen broke through the last tangled strands of rope and scrambled to her feet before he could stand up, although this time she was careful to keep her head ducked down as she did it. "Here, let me help you up. Watch your head."

Kachigan wasn't stupid enough to refuse the offer, although he insisted on picking up the fallen lamp before he let her haul him by his good arm to his feet. But when Helen would have slid an arm around his waist to steady him, the detective scowled and shook her off. "Let me go first," he said holding his left arm tight to his side. "Just in case Truxall left a guard at the mouth of the mine."

For a second time that night, Helen bit down on all the unconstructive things she wanted to say. Instead, she followed the sound of Kachigan's footsteps and the dancing glow of the paraffin lamp out into the colder draft of the mine's main shaft. The metal tracks ended right outside the supply room doors, making it easy to know which way was out. The only hard part was keeping her aching neck bent at the angle that the roof demanded, while still looking out for the rusty metal spikes that seemed to protrude from it with random malice. Fortunately, her hands were screaming with such intense pain by then that she could ignore the milder ache of the real burn beneath her ear.

"Keep talking to me, Helen." Kachigan didn't swing around to look at her, probably because that would have strained his cracked ribs. The breathless urgency in his voice made her suspect this request wasn't just for her sake. "Tell me why you think your ex-husband is the one who has Murchison's missing securities."

"Because he's here," she retorted. "My cousin says he's been seen up and down the Allegheny Valley for the last few weeks."

"And based on nothing more than his presence, you think he's the one behind all of this?" Kachigan tried to chuckle and ended up cursing instead. "If you were Bernard Flinn, Helen, you'd accuse yourself of smearing an innocent man."

"James Foster Barton isn't innocent, and you know it!" Anger was a great painkiller, Helen discovered. She barely noticed the hot throb of her fingers beneath the hotter spike of indignation. "He's a devious, conniving bastard who makes a living out of seducing women and stealing their fortunes! That makes him the *most* likely suspect in this case, Milo. The only difference is that this fortune's being stolen while the man who made it is still alive."

"Murchison, you mean," Kachigan said, following her thought with the ease of long practice. "So who's the woman he seduced into helping him?"

Helen sighed. "All this week, I thought it must be Murchison's daughter Emmy," she admitted. "She ran away from home at the same time as the securities went missing, and friends of hers told me she'd been seen with a man who fit Barton's description. But I found her this morning up in Red Hot—"

"You didn't tell Truxall that."

"I wouldn't have told him if I'd found Lizzie Borden there!" Helen retorted. "Emmy said the one who'd been seduced was actually her stepmother, Murchison's second wife."

"And you believed her?"

"Milo, she's sitting in a cold muddy tent in the snow,

reading Karl Marx and eating weevily biscuits. And the friend who told me she'd run off with a young man admitted she lied to protect her. Neither of them recognized my sketch of Barton.''

''What sketch—'' The county detective broke off, pausing to catch his tearing breath. Helen took advantage of the delay to slip into the innermost circle of light, close enough to see how hard Kachigan was pressing his left arm to his chest, trying to steady his cracked ribs against the strain of this exertion.

''Shouldn't we wrap your chest up with something before you puncture a lung?''

''Not enough time,'' Kachigan said shortly. ''And my ribs aren't broken, just cracked. I've done this before, remember, chasing a burglar across a—''

His words broke off, but this time not because he'd lost his breath. A long low moan had skated out of the darkness, drowning out the normal creak and drip of the mine. It was deep enough and inhuman enough to make Helen think of splintering beams and shifting rock. She caught at Kachigan's arm without thinking, prepared to drag him the rest of the way up the slope to the thin glimmer of daylight she could see at the very end. To her surprise, he resisted her pull despite the grunt of pain it wrenched from him.

''Milo, come on, the mine's falling—''

''No, it's not.'' The fingers of his good hand slipped across her mouth, hushing her protest. ''Listen again.''

Helen frowned, waiting tensely inside the circle of his arm. At first, all she could hear was her own pulse, thundering in alarm at the cold rattle of rocks in the distance. But then the moan washed across them again, so uncannily similar to the first time that its inhuman quality abruptly vanished.

''Someone's down here!''

''Or something.'' Kachigan stepped away from the narrow railway, Helen on his heels. The outward glow of the paraffin lamp sparked glitters off the exposed coal seam all around them except for one place, where a side-passage led off to more darkness. ''I've heard about mules and dogs getting lost in these mines, making men think they were ghosts—''

The moan assaulted them again, sounding more desperate and breathless this time. ''That's not a ghost,'' she said grimly. ''That's a man trying to shout past a gag.''

''Stay here,'' Kachigan said and headed into the yawning darkness. Helen didn't bother arguing, she simply followed him. ''Helen, there might be coal gas back here—''

''—but there's more likely to be an injured man you can't carry by yourself.'' The passage split without warning into four right-angled corridors, and she had to skid to a stop to avoid running into Kachigan's back. ''What's the matter?''

''We're going to get lost if we're not careful. We have to leave some sort of mark—''

Another moan exploded nearly at her feet, startling Helen into a backward jump and wordless yelp of her own. Kachigan swung around, holding his paraffin flame before him like a weapon. The shifting glow threw a massive shadow across the left-hand corridor, cast by something that looked like a blanket-wrapped log. It took a moment for Helen to see the spit sodden rag clenched between the teeth and the furious glitter of eyes above it, looking up at her from a face so mutilated with blisters and burns that she couldn't even recognize it. It wasn't until Kachigan had dropped to one knee, despite his own gasp of pain, and ripped the gag off with a savage jerk that the deep groan of relief jogged her memory.

It was Bernard Flinn.

''Oh, my God.'' Helen scurried over to kneel on his other side, forcing her tingling fingers to help Kachigan unknot the ropes trussing the larger man inside his dirt-encrusted blanket. ''How long have you been here?''

The coal company police chief spat out the remnants of his gag. ''Not as long as Truxall's going to spend regretting he put me here.'' He grimaced at the stretch and weep of the crusted burns on his face. ''Where is he?''

''Helen sent him off on a wild-goose chase to West Tarentum.'' Kachigan dragged the last stubborn loops down the length of Flinn's sprawled body, and Helen pulled off the blanket beneath. To her relief, the only stains she saw on it had the unmistakable tang of human urine rather than the sticky stench of blood. Truxall evidently liked to restrict his torture to the ultramodern mixture of carbide and water. "We should have about an hour before he gets back."

Flinn grunted, not making the mistake of scrambling to his feet and slamming his head against the ceiling. Instead, he rolled up to a crouch and began to stretch the stiffness from his arms and legs, looking like a fire-branded monster preparing to get revenge on the peasants who'd chased him. "Any men left on guard outside?"

"I don't know. We didn't get that far." The icy edge in Kachigan's voice startled Helen. She glanced across the circle of lamplight to see him scowling at their fellow prisoner. "Why don't you go out first and see?"

"Milo!"

Flinn snorted and lifted himself cautiously to his feet. Being so much taller, his stoop was far more pronounced than either of theirs. "Don't waste your breath, Miss Sorby. The minute I heard your voice down that passage, I knew your boyfriend was going to want to kill me. He gave me hell six months ago, when someone almost pushed you in front of a trolley, and I didn't even have anything to do with that."

"You also didn't have anything to do with this."

"Oh, yes, he did," Kachigan said between his teeth. "Remember, he's the one who told Truxall I was the first to examine that dead fire-boss."

"Which happened to be the truth," Flinn retorted.

"Maybe, but that's not why you said it. You just wanted to get me stuck down here with you, on the off chance I might get away and rescue you in the process!"

Helen watched, hovering warily as the two men confronted each other. Kachigan's Armenian temper sounded well and truly lost, a state she'd seen him in once or twice before and had learned to be cautious of. If Bernard Flinn, never a man of very placid composure himself, decided to take offense—

"It worked, didn't it?" Flinn said mildly. "Tell me you wouldn't have done the same thing if the situation had been reversed."

"I wouldn't have dragged in your wife!"

"Well, how the hell was I supposed to know you were back on speaking terms with Miss Sorby? The last report I got was that she hadn't come up to see you in a couple of weeks!"

"You've been watching her?" Kachigan demanded.

"No, idiot, I've been watching you." Flinn shook his head in disgust. "When you're a company police chief, it pays to know the whereabouts of the only honest policeman in town."

Helen glared at him, as angry as Kachigan had been on her behalf. "Why? So you can drag him into your wars with rival coal companies?"

"No, so I can use him when I have a crime that actually needs to be solved, not just swept under the rug. Like this one." Flinn reached out and snagged the paraffin lamp from Kachigan. "Which is not going to get solved if Truxall comes back and finds us still here shouting at each other. Let's go."

The county detective cursed and grabbed at the lamp, but Bernard Flinn was already moving. Kachigan took Helen's throbbing hand instead and pulled her down the corridor after the coal police chief.

"We can't just walk out of this mine and into the woods," he reminded Flinn. "We've got to find transport back to Tarentum. That means taking out Truxall's guards."

"Just make sure I'm headed back to the portal," Flinn said grimly. "You can leave the guards and the transport to me."

Helen followed them back down the mine passage, frowning. She had no problem with the first part of Flinn's statement—she'd seen the way his powerful shoulders had rolled and his hands had knotted into massive fists—but the second part worried her. "I'm not a very good rider," she warned him. "And Milo's got two cracked ribs. If you're planning to steal some mules and take us on a bare-back ride—''

Flinn threw her a smile over his shoulder, despite the pain it must have caused to stretch the seared blisters on his face. "Don't worry, Miss Sorby. I know there's a work-ing telegraph somewhere in this dump, because Truxall sent a telegram back to Tarentum in the middle of questioning me. All I have to do is find it, and twenty minutes later we'll be escorted back to Tarentum by a full troop of Penn-sylvania State Police, in a hospital wagon with a field medic there to bandage us. And I hope we meet that four-eyed bastard along the way," he added viciously. "So I can stop and tell him exactly how I'm going to kill him."

Kachigan cleared his throat. "I thought the Pennsylvania State Police were in Murchison's pocket," he objected. "After all, he supplies contract coal to the Pennsylvania Railroad."

"True," said the company police chief. "But as soon as this coal strike is over, I'm going to Harrisburg to head up the state police. When he gets my wire, John Brennan's going to arrive like the charge of the Light Brigade." Flinn caught Kachigan by the shoulder when he would have walked out through the mine's timber-framed opening, shoving him back toward Helen. "If there are guards out there, you're going to be more of a hindrance than a help. Just stay out of my way, and out of the line of fire. You two will be lying snug in bed before sundown." He glanced from Kachigan's hunched posture and tightly held arm over to Helen and snorted. "For all the good it'll do you, Miss Sorby."

THIRTEEN

Sleep was ragged, cold, and painful but awakening was worse. His bruised and cracked ribs yelled out a protest when he tried to lift up on one elbow, then complained again when he let himself fall back to the mattress. For one disoriented minute, Kachigan thought he was back in the cheap South Side boardinghouse he'd rented as police patrolman, trying to recover from his fall off an icy roof. But then a sleepy protest drifted out of the blankets that had piled up on the other side of his narrow bed, and he felt the unmistakable push and settle of a warm back against his good side.

"Helen?" All he could see beneath the blankets was a tangle of dark hair on the pillow and the curve of a shoulder under a pale chemise. But the slanting light from his dormer window showed an astonishing number of clothes scattered around his Tarentum lodging. Kachigan could barely see his own cheap suit beneath the layers of dove-gray wool, black velvet, and white lace that foamed across his clothespress and chair. "What are you doing here?"

"Trying to sleep," she said, without turning to face him. "Where did you expect me to spend the night? In Taggart's bed? Or Frick's?"

Kachigan growled and levered himself up again, this time using his good elbow. It still hurt, despite the tight pull of bandages bracing his cracked ribs. "I expected you to go back to Oakmont where you'd be safe! This is the first place Truxall's going to come looking for us—"

"Which is why Flinn and Brennan left state policemen stationed all around the property." She rolled over and frowned up at him, freeing one hand from the tangled blankets to sweep her hair out of her face. A clean white bandage hid the burn on her neck, but the dark rings around her wrist were clearly visible. "Stop worrying and go back to sleep."

Kachigan stared at her bruised arm for a moment, then gave in and reached out with his own bandaged hand to bring it close enough to kiss. "I can't," he said against her skin. "You stole all the blankets."

Helen's frown melted first into a startled look, and then into warm amusement. "Actually, you threw them at me," she said, straightening the tangle of bedclothes. "But if you want them back—"

Kachigan groaned and let himself fall back abruptly on his hard pillow, but the resulting smack of pain still wasn't bad enough to erase the impact of Helen reaching over him, the dangling laces of her sleep-tousled chemise brushing across his chest. "Helen, I *can't*—"

"I know. Flinn warned me." Amusement settled deeper in her voice, warming it like sunlit honey. She finished spreading the blankets across him and then lay back at his good side, this time facing him. Before Kachigan could protest, she'd slid her hand across his chest and nestled her head into the curve of his shoulder as comfortably as if they'd been married for a dozen years. "But you will."

"No, I won't," he said, although he wasn't sure his strained voice carried the same conviction hers did.

Her warm breath blew exasperation across the bare skin above his bandages. "Milo, no other sane man in the world would be arguing with me about this. What do you have against—"

"It's what I *don't* have." He lifted his left hand to spread the bare fingers in front of her face. "No ring, no marriage license, no—"

"—*wife*," she finished sharply. The sun-warmed sweetness of her voice vanished abruptly. "And that's the way it's going to stay, whether you like it or not. I've told you a hundred times, I'm not getting married again, Milo. I found out the hard way that Emma Goldman is right when she says our current laws make marriage just another kind of worker oppression!"

Kachigan took a deep breath to yell back at her, then hissed it out again in pain as his ribs protested the incautious motion. Helen cursed herself in a vehement mutter of Italian. "I'm sorry, I'm sorry—"

"It's not your fault," he said between his teeth. "I'm just going to have to add your ex-husband to the list of people I've got to kill."

She lifted her head from his shoulder, staring down at him with such wide and startled eyes that his chest shuddered painfully again, this time with the effort of trying not to laugh. "Milo, you wouldn't—"

A tentative rap on the door interrupted before she could say anything more. For all her enlightened socialist notions about free love outside of marriage, Helen Sorby was still enough of a middle-class Irish girl to yelp and burrow down into the bedclothes beside Kachigan. He pulled the blanket up across her bare shoulders.

"Who is it?"

"Me," Art Taggart said warily. "And—uh—Helen Sorby's brother. You two decent?"

Kachigan exchanged resigned glances with his companion. "No," she said, loud enough for Taggart to hear. "And tell Thomas he'll just have to live with it—"

The door swung open, wide enough for a chipboard suitcase to slide through. It was followed by a knife-scarred face whose only resemblance to Helen lay in the intelligent darkness of his eyes. "I brought your clothes up from Oakmont, Hell," said a voice that was not her twin's. "And told your aunt where you were. I also advised her to go visit your brother on the South Side for the next few days, just in case that yellow dog you sent after me decides to look in Oakmont next.'' He paused, as if waiting for some comment on this early-morning industry, but for once even Helen appeared to be speechless. ''Come downstairs when you're ready, I brought some cold polenta to fry for breakfast. We need to talk.''

The door closed again, leaving silence in the wake of its soft click. ''Oh, *that* brother,'' Kachigan said dryly. ''The one you call a cousin, and Racca called *Il Merlo*.''

''Yes. And if Niccolo Santangelo knows I sent Truxall after him, you're going to wish you'd said 'yes' to me this morning, Milo Kachigan.'' Helen sat up and shook her head, scattering coal dust across the sheets. ''Because that may have been your last chance.''

After the ordeal of getting himself cleaned and dressed with one arm barely able to move—and a bare-shouldered Helen Sorby brushing out her hair a few feet away—Kachigan went down the steps of his quiet lodging house with gritted teeth and the ominous feeling that the day was going to get worse. The smell of maple syrup and the sound of friendly voices drifting out from the coal-fired warmth of the kitchen made him hope for a moment that the deterioration hadn't started yet, but as soon as he stepped through the doorway, he got hit with the full force of a Black Hand *capo*'s knife-sharp gaze.

''Well?'' said Niccolo Santangelo. ''Are you really going to marry my cousin?''

Kachigan's teeth ground together hard enough to make him feel the twinge of buried metal in his cheekbone. ''Yes, I'm going to marry her.'' It was a good thing Helen hadn't finished dressing yet—if she'd overheard that resolute pledge, she might not be quite so willing to spend her free time with him. ''As soon as I can convince her that marriage isn't some sort of worker oppression.''

The Black Hand *capo* grunted and went back to frying up something that looked like sizzling yellow bricks. ''Not any time soon, eh? Then I guess you didn't slap that yellow dog at me just to get rid of an embarrassing in-law.''

Kachigan sat down in the chair Taggart had kicked out for him, moving slowly and carefully so as not to jostle his ribs. ''Helen said she sent him to the Slovak church.''

''Yeah, where he was stupid enough to ask after me. You think Hunkies and dagos don't talk to each other in this town, Kachigan?'' Santangelo put three of his hot yellow bricks onto a plate, poured maple syrup over them from another steaming pan, and handed them to Taggart. The big detective eyed them uncertainly, then passed them along to Kachigan. ''What did you tell him?''

''That you have the missing extortion money his boss is looking for.'' Kachigan took a cautious forkful of steaming yellow mush, and to his surprise found that the flavors of maple syrup and butter blended as nicely with cornmeal as they did with buckwheat. ''It was the only way to convince him that we didn't. I would have blamed Bernard Flinn instead, but Truxall had already questioned him.''

''And Flinn had put the blame on you.'' It was hard to tell if that stiff, scarred face held amusement or exasperation. ''So who does that leave for me to put the blame on?''

''My ex-husband,'' Helen said from the doorway. Kachigan glanced up at her warily, but her voice sounded matter-of-fact rather than prickly. ''He's the one who deserves it, after all.''

Her cousin said something to her in Italian, lifting a sharply angled eyebrow. A sudden wash of color swept up Helen Sorby's strong-boned face, but all she said was, ''None of your business, Nicco. Is there any polenta left for me?''

''As much as you want,'' Santangelo proved he knew her by putting just as many yellow slabs of fried cornmeal onto her plate as he had on Kachigan's. She carried the plate back to the table and sat down in the chair Taggart held out for her.

''You're not having any, Art?'' she asked in surprise. ''Aren't you hungry?''

''I'm not awake,'' retorted the big detective. ''It's only nine-thirty, and I had midnight guard duty.''

Kachigan glanced up at him, frowning. "At the lockup? Why? There's nothing left there to guard."

Taggart snorted. "On the front porch, Milo. Bernard Flinn might trust those damned state troopers of his, but Riley was worried they'd disappear in the dead of night and leave us sitting ducks. He took the evening shift, and Frick's out there shooting the breeze with them now." A thin slice of smile showed beneath his mustache. "Although I think what Jape's actually doing is fishing for a new job."

"That's because he knows he's going to need one," Kachigan said, putting down his fork with his last brick of cornmeal uneaten. "Truxall told me yesterday that he knew the missing payoff money wasn't stashed here or at the lockup. The only way he can know that is if he has a county detective in his pocket."

Taggart gave him an amused look. "And you just made a wild guess it wasn't me or Riley?"

"You were up at Bull Creek Mine with the state police the night Racca was shot," Kachigan said grimly. "And Riley was with me the whole time. Frick was the one off duty."

"So Frick's the one who took my boy out?" Santangelo asked. His voice sounded no different than it had a few moments before, but the scowling glance Helen threw at him made Kachigan realize that working through all his possible murder suspects in front of a man whose notions of justice were limited to dynamite and thin steel was probably not the smartest thing he could do.

"No," he said. "Not if he was working for Truxall and Murchison. They wanted Racca alive for the same reason you did, to tell them who the real blackmailer was. The only one who had a reason to kill Racca is—"

"—the man who murdered the fire-boss up in Bull Creek Mine," Taggart finished. "So why does Jape going off duty that night make him the stool pigeon, Milo?"

"Because that night was the only time someone could have searched our lodging for the payoff money, after Bernard Flinn blamed me for taking it." He glanced across the table at Helen. "And that telegram Flinn said Truxall sent from Millerstown—"

She picked up the thread of his logic easily. "—could have been to Frick, ordering him to go look for the money. But if Truxall was already paying Frick to spy for him, wouldn't he have known you didn't find the payoff money down in Bull Creek Mine in the first place?"

"Jape didn't go down in the mine," Taggart told her, reaching out to borrow Kachigan's fork and taste the polenta cautiously. Niccolo Santangelo was eating his straight from the frying pan, spearing each section with a knife and dipping it in syrup while he listened. "For all he knows, Milo brought back a pocketful of diamonds along with that Italian boy."

"The Italian boy *you* sent down there," Kachigan said to Helen's cousin. "Why?"

Il Merlo shrugged. "To see who was stupid enough to write Black Hand letters in my town. And to find out what Murchison was so afraid of that he was willing to pay fifty thousand dollars to get it back."

Taggart whistled softly, pulling the rest of Milo's breakfast over to his side of the table to polish off. "A bit more than the usual secret society dues, isn't it? Whatever this Murchison guy lost must be something big."

"And according to Truxall, he didn't get it back." Helen finished the last of her own polenta. "He didn't get his money back either."

"So maybe the blackmailer's not so stupid after all," Kachigan said. "Maybe he killed the messenger, took the money, and kept the securities to blackmail Murchison with again."

"Or to sell, if Murchison refuses to pay," Helen agreed. "That's just the kind of double cross James Foster Barton would pull. Now all we have to do is figure out how to catch him." She glanced over her shoulder. "Nicco, hasn't that coffee boiled enough? It's starting to smell burnt."

"Just getting good." Santangelo carried a pot full of coal-colored sludge over to the table and poured some into her cup, laughing at her grimace. "Drink up, it'll make you smarter."

"Why do I need to be smarter?" Helen said suspiciously.

He poured out more sludge for Kachigan and Taggart before he answered. "For one thing, because our friend the blackmailer didn't get that payoff money either. My contact at Murchison Coal told me last night that there'd been another threatening letter sent, one that accused Murchison of sending only two hundred dollars instead of the agreed-upon sum. Why say that if you had kept the securities and the payoff both? Why not just ask for more money?"

"Then what happened to the rest of that first payoff?" Helen asked.

"Maybe Murchison's fire-boss stole it," Santangelo suggested, drinking straight from the pot of boiled coffee grounds. Fortunately, one taste had told Kachigan he wasn't going to want seconds, although the thick, bitter liquid was already starting to jolt him awake. "To cover what he owed to the company store."

Taggart grunted his appreciation of that. "Or maybe to donate to the miners' union for their strike fund."

"If he did that, why would he still have met the blackmailer?" Helen asked. "Why not just take the money and disappear?"

"A fire-boss's job is to be cautious," Kachigan said slowly. "To check and double-check everything. If I were given a lot of money and told to deliver it to an unknown blackmailer, it would sure as hell occur to me that I might get killed after the payoff. But if I hid the money instead, the balance of power would be in my hands. I could force the blackmailer to follow me somewhere safer for me before I gave him directions to the payoff." Kachigan lifted an eyebrow at his partner. "And maybe when I hid that money, I would keep back a few hundred to pay off the company store."

"For my trouble," Taggart agreed. "Sure."

"But the fire-boss's plan didn't work," Helen said. "The blackmailer killed him without getting the rest of the payoff."

"Probably because he never asked to see the color of the

money before he capped off the carrier." Her cousin's quiet voice held the distaste of a professional for an amateur, nothing more. "In which case, the payoff's still hidden where the fire-boss left it."

"And Murchison, not knowing what his fire-boss did to protect himself, figures someone stole the money after the blackmailer left the body in Bull Creek Mine. That's why he has Truxall trying to track it down," Kachigan said.

"So he can pay it off again, without needing to sell off any more stock," Helen agreed. "That makes sense."

"Yeah." Taggart scraped the last syrup from his plate, then pushed it away. "So what are we going to do?"

Kachigan had been thinking about that, but he wasn't sure the plan he'd come up with was going to get the cooperation it needed to succeed. He glanced back at Niccolo Santangelo. "Did your contact at Murchison tell you when and where this next payoff exchange was going to happen, just like the first one?"

"No," the *capo* said calmly. "It hasn't been arranged yet."

"Because Murchison doesn't have the money," Helen said. "But when he does get it, Nicco, do you know how the exchange will be set up? The blackmail letter must have had some instructions."

"It did." He drank off the last of the coffee, then wiped a dusting of grounds from his scarred lip. "Murchison is supposed to write the location and time of the exchange on a sheet of notepaper and leave it lying faceup at the stationery desk of the Commercial Hotel in Tarentum."

There was a long moment of silence after that, broken at length by Helen's frustrated sigh. "The blackmailer *has* to be James Foster Barton," she said in disgust. "That's exactly the kind of devious plan he'd come up with to keep from being found out. In a hotel that busy, a hundred people a day must stop by to use the writing desk."

"Whether they're guests or not," Taggart agreed. "There'd be no way to prove Barton was the blackmailer, even if you stood there and watched him read the note."

"Oh, yes, there is," Kachigan said. "All we need to do

is leave a note with a time and place of our choosing, and let Barton bring himself and the missing securities right to us."

That made his partner look impressed, but Helen Sorby and her Black Hand cousin merely exchanged exasperated Italian glances. "*Capitosto*," she said, and Santangelo agreed with a grunt. "Milo, don't you think Barton's going to notice this new note doesn't look anything like the first one? Not the same paper, or the same handwriting, or the same phrasing of directions?"

"We could pretend it was written by Truxall instead of Murchison—"

"That assumes the first one wasn't!"

He frowned and scrubbed a hand across his face, feeling the remnants of stubble left by one-handed shaving. "That's true, damn it. It was such a good plan—"

"Don't worry, it still is." Niccolo Santangelo slid a hand into his worn flannel shirt and tossed a folded square of paper casually onto the kitchen table, amid the sticky plates and half-full cups of coffee. "This is what I came here to give you."

Helen and Taggart both reached for the folded sheet, but despite broken ribs and burned wrists, Kachigan got it first. With a minimum of fancy scrolling, the words "Commercial Hotel, Tarentum, Pennsylvania," were printed across the top. Beneath that, in an angrily scratched and blotted hand, someone had written, "Bull Creek Number One, main entrance, March 31, 5 p.m. C.M."

He passed it on to Helen when he was done reading, then levered himself painfully to his feet to meet her cousin's dark eyes more directly. "You took that from the hotel's stationery desk?"

"At six-fifteen Monday night," Niccolo Santangelo admitted. "Why not? The cleaning girl would only have thrown it out the next morning."

"And you thought you could use it to blackmail Charles Murchison yourself someday." With a courage he didn't have, or perhaps with a cousin's immunity, Helen had put Kachigan's unspoken thoughts into biting words. "Right?"

Il Merlo smiled at her, a smile that never touched the shrewd glitter of his eyes. "Maybe so, maybe so. But I decided I'd rather give it to you instead, Hell." He glanced back at Kachigan and his smile widened to pure wickedness. "Call it an early wedding present."

Tarentum's Commercial Hotel wasn't located on the toniest part of North Canal Street, with a vacant hillside behind it and the dingy warehouses of the Pennsylvania Railroad across the tracks. But the electric glow of its bar lights were visible from the train station, and the aromas of its backyard ovens traveled almost as far, drawing an enthusiastic crowd of salesmen, drummers, and traveling engineers into its lobby at lunchtime. Kachigan paused on the doorstep, perusing the advertised blue plate special of chicken and dumplings, and trying to look like a man undecided about his lunch.

"What are we waiting for?" Helen demanded, frowning up at him through the April sunshine. Under its fickle warmth, yesterday's snow was already melting to puddles on the slate sidewalk. "Aren't we going to go in and write that note?"

"Yes, we are, just as soon as a bellboy comes to the door—"

Helen disengaged the arm she'd twined through his good one when they left his lodgings on Third Street. "Why, here he is now," she said and hauled the heavy brass-plated door outward with one strong tug. Kachigan scowled, but his aching ribs gave him no choice except to let her hold it for him as he passed through. His companion's smile told him she knew exactly how much he disliked that.

"Now you know how it feels to be treated like you're utterly useless," she said. "I can hold doors for you, help you into carriages, carry all your packages—"

Kachigan gritted his teeth and followed her toward the Commercial Hotel's stationery desk, a small mahogany counter that had been tucked into a corner of the crowded lobby. A single burly drummer stood beside it, scratching out a letter with the cheap dip pen the hotel provided for its guests. He finished and put the pen back into its hard rubber inkwell, then gave an appreciative tip of his bowler hat to Helen as they passed. Kachigan scowled at him to speed his departure. Fortunately, Helen was too busy tapping excess ink from the dip pen's metal nib to notice.

"Do you see James Foster Barton anywhere?" she asked him quietly, pulling an unused sheet of stationery from among the messy piles of postcards, envelopes, and telegram forms that littered the writing surface after a busy morning of use.

"I don't think so." Kachigan leaned his good elbow on the desk and turned to scan the crowd, squinting against the blue drift of cigar smoke from the side bar. "But considering the only time I've ever seen him was in a newspaper clipping from a police file I looked at when I first met you—"

"Why didn't you say so?" Helen's pen splattered and jerked across the paper angrily, but Kachigan didn't take it as a personal response. He'd watched her practice writing like that all morning, until she could achieve a penmanship identical to that of an infuriated coal baron. "I drew a picture of him yesterday for Mr. Hower and Emmy to look at."

"Do you have it with you now?"

"No, it's in my muff." She bit her lip, then gave him the smile he hadn't seen enough of lately, the one that made her serious face glow with laughter. "Which is lying on the ground somewhere back in Millerstown."

"Doing us a lot of good." Kachigan turned back and began sorting idly through the scatter of papers at his elbow. Many were ink-stained and crumpled, drafts of letters ruined by a blot or a misspelled word. "Given how busy this place is, Barton would have to check this desk several times a day to be sure to catch Murchison's reply. Which means he's either staying in this hotel—"

"—or one of the others down the street," Helen finished his thought, in the way they had increasingly fallen into as they worked together. "Wait until I finish writing this note, and I'll draw another quick sketch of him for you to show the desk clerk.''

Kachigan opened his mouth to agree, but a random shift of hotel postcards through his hands made him curse instead, sharply enough that Helen's pen jerked and splattered ink across the paper.

''Milo! I was almost done!''

''Don't bother,'' he said and showed her the sheet of stationery he had just excavated. ''Look at this.''

Her eyes widened. In letters almost identical to the ones now disappearing under wet spreading droplets of ink, someone had written, ''Emmy Number Two, main entrance, April 5, 5 p.m. C.M.''

''*Emmy* Number Two?'' Helen asked.

''Probably the name of one of Murchison's coal mines.'' He tucked the note carefully back among the postcards. ''A lot of pits around here are named for wives or daughters.''

''Then those are instructions for another payoff exchange. Do you think Murchison really wrote them?''

''I doubt there are two forgers as accomplished as you in this town, Helen. And unless your cousin showed that note he took to someone besides us—''

''—no one but Murchison would have phrased it the same way.'' She tapped the cheap hotel pen against her fingers absently, disregarding the freckling of ink she was putting on the cuffs of her shirtwaist. ''What do we do now?''

''Now we draw that picture of James Foster Barton.'' Kachigan started to lift his left arm, then winced and let it drop again. ''Can you reach in my vest pocket for my evidence book?''

For a miracle, Helen managed to do it without even a tart comment, bringing out both his notebook and the pencil stub he used to write in it. She flipped it open to a blank page but paused before she began to draw. ''Do you need the sketch right now, Milo? We know exactly where Barton will be at five tonight, after all.''

''And it's also exactly where Truxall and half of Murchison's company police force will be.'' He watched intently as a penciled face took shape on the page of his evidence book. Either her talents as a police artist were getting more polished with practice, or this was a face Helen had indelibly stamped in her memory. It was a thought he immediately wished he hadn't had. "They're too smart to make the mistake of sending a single messenger in to meet Barton again, and this time the meeting's on their own territory. Unless you'd like to invite Bernard Flinn and the Pennsylvania State Police along to back us up, we're not going to—"

His voice broke off in a hissing intake of breath, harsh enough to make Helen look up from her sketch. "What's the matter?"

"Get rid of his mustache and make his hair a lot shorter," Kachigan said grimly. "And give him freckles."

"*Freckles?*"

"They're easy enough to paint on with henna hair dye."

"If you say so." Despite the doubt in her voice, Helen obediently erased the mustache and wavy center-parted locks she had drawn and replaced them with short hair, then dappled the nose and cheeks with light pencil marks. Even on the page, those cosmetic changes made Barton look startlingly different, giving the suave charm of his smile a mischievous leprechaun twist. "Who is this, Milo?"

"A union organizer named Leon Daniels. I arrested him for vandalism last week."

That elicited a mirthless chuckle from her. "Leon Daniels! And did he tell you he was a member of the Industrial Workers of the World, just like its founder Daniel De-Leon?"

"No," Kachigan said. "He told me he was an undercover Pinkerton agent investigating the Black Hand."

"*What?*" Helen stared down at the picture of her former husband in disbelief, then turned the same look up onto Kachigan. "That can't be right, Milo. Barton would never—"

"I know." He swept the evidence book up and shoved it back in his pocket, disregarding the protest of his ribs. "I also know where he's staying. Come on."

She scowled and tugged at his arm, but only to hold him back so she could hold the hotel door. "When was the last time you saw him?"

"About ten minutes before Racca was shot." Kachigan swung right on North Canal Street, heading toward the brand-new brick building that towered over the street even from three blocks away. "Dammit, I should have known that wasn't a coincidence! That was the second time that day I caught him hanging around the lockup; he was obviously casing it to find the best place to fire from —"

"But, Milo —" Helen followed him across a set of trolley tracks and into the shadow of a majestic brick building. Her startled gaze lifted to the name emblazoned in gilt across the massive transom window. "Barton's staying *here*? The Young Men's Christian Association?"

"All the union organizers are, I think. At least, all the male ones, since they don't admit women." Kachigan gave her a stern glance. "I want you to wait out here while I go in and arrest him."

"By yourself?" Her incredulous voice told him just how much faith she had in him. "Milo, you can't do that! Let's head back to the lockup and get Taggart or Riley—"

"No." It was his own stubbornness driving him rather than the urgency of the situation, he knew, but that didn't lessen Kachigan's determination to confront her ex-husband. He lifted his voice to be heard over the clatter and spark of a trolley going past. "Barton's not stupid enough to do anything to me, not if he knows you can identify him as the blackmailer."

"I said he was devious, Milo, not intelligent!" Helen shot back furiously. "He was stupid enough to murder that fire-boss, wasn't he? What makes you think he won't kill *you*?"

"Whoever you're arguing about, I sure hope he's deaf," said a familiar lazy voice from the curb. "I could hear you a block away, from the trolley."

Kachigan swung around to snap at his detective partner, but to his surprise he saw Taggart wasn't alone. Not only J.P. Frick and Owen Riley but also a couple of black-coated state police troopers had exited the trolley with him and now stood watchfully in front of the big Y.M.C.A. building. Kachigan could see a pair of uniformed Tarentum constables heading up the street from their own lockup at a trot.

"What's going on?"

"I figured you'd heard, since you're already here," Taggart said. "We got a telephone call from the room clerk here just a little while ago. He heard a shot in the dormitory room and found one of his young Christian men had—uh—gone to heaven. No sign of who did it."

Kachigan exchanged a look of shared foreboding with Helen Sorby. "Did he know who the dead man was?"

"He sure did, and we won't miss him." J.P. Frick's laugh somehow managed to be both hearty and completely humorless. "It was that union wiseacre, the one we arrested for painting on our sidewalk. Looks like someone finally got fed up with his shenanigans."

Kachigan and Helen exchanged glances of mute frustration. "Yes," she said at last. "It looks like someone finally did."

FOURTEEN

"They refused to let me in! Can you believe that?" Helen paced down to the corner of the Tarentum Y.M.C.A. and back, her unfashionable skirts kicking out with each angry stride. She glared at a young man in a passing buggy who slowed to gawk, irritated more by his gender than his ankle-directed gaze. "Just because I'm a woman!"

Her audience of one sighed. Sitting on the building's stoop, with a bulky traveling camera on his lap and a solemn expression on his face, Jackson Ecklar looked a lot like a photograph himself. Helen suspected that at least some of the slowing traffic along Canal Street was caused by recognition of his handsome profile.

"Why do you think I'm sitting here with you, Miss Sorby?"

She paused in her pacing to scowl at him. "I assume it's because you came up to Tarentum today to photograph the sabotage at Bull Creek Coal Mine. And when you heard about the shooting, you thought a picture of a murdered socialist martyr would make a nice little addition to your essay on this coal strike."

Ecklar lifted his thick, feathered eyebrows at her, looking impressed. "No wonder the *Herald* employs you," he said, the genuine admiration in his voice taking a little of the sting out of the words. "How on earth did you know I came up to photograph the Bull Creek tipple?"

"Because there's a transfer slip for the Tarentum Traction Company sticking out of your hat band," she retorted. "And because that camera back looks much too wide to be used for portraits or close-up work."

"I know." Ecklar threw a rueful look down at his equipment. "I'm going to have to do a lot of cropping, and I'll probably still have terrible resolution on this negative. Assuming I even get a negative," he added gloomily. "Do I look like a woman in man's clothes to you?"

Helen broke stride, startled out of her irritability by that question. "No, of course not."

"Then why aren't they letting *me* in there either?" His smile cracked the cold handsomeness of his face and made it likeable instead. "Somehow, I suspect it has more to do with our politics than your sex. Policemen distrust socialists even more than the Y.M.C.A. distrusts women."

"Yes, I know." Helen paced back to the corner again, but this time it was more to avoid Ecklar's gaze than to burn off her irritation. There was at least one policeman in that building who didn't entirely distrust socialists, but she hadn't yet shared that information with Ecklar. It seemed like a good time to change the subject. "Why did you send Emmy Murchison's picture to me the other day, Mr. Ecklar?"

"You have a remarkable voice, Miss Sorby." He gave her another crooked smile. "It wasn't hard to overhear you telling her parents that you needed one."

"But if you knew Emmy was in Red Hot, you must have also known why." Helen came to a stop in front of him, frowning. "Bryde Larkin certainly didn't trust me with her whereabouts. Why did you?"

"Ah." The famous photographer tilted his head back to look past her at the sky, in a meditative pose she recognized from some of his seafaring photographs. "Let's just say I have some friends in this area whom Bryde doesn't share,

Miss Sorby. They reassured me about your good intentions.''

She paused to consider that. ''I don't suppose they live in Millvale?''

''I don't suppose they do,'' Ecklar said gravely. ''I also don't suppose they run an underground printing press. Do you?''

Helen couldn't restrain the smile that tugged at her lips. ''No, certainly not. So, is there really going to be a photo-essay on this coal strike in *Scribner's*, Mr. Ecklar?''

''Of course. They let me decide what my assignments are, these days.'' He gave her a smile. ''There may also be some photographs the *New York Herald* will be interested in buying from me, when you file this news story with them, Miss Sorby.''

''I'm not going to file any news story if I can't even get in to gather the facts.'' She took out her frustration at missed deadlines and lost opportunities by glowering at the young state trooper who had been stationed at the door to keep them out. ''Regardless of our politics, we're both bona fide members of the press. In this country that's supposed to give us the freedom to—''

''—get evicted from private property.'' Taggart's lazy voice didn't drown out the grunts and curses of the reporter from the *Valley Daily News*. It was that glib young man's easy entry into the building, under the guise of needing a room for the night, that had sparked Helen's feminist outburst a few minutes ago. Watching him get summarily hoisted out the door by the big detective soothed her indignation a little, but the narrow smile Taggart gave her afterward made her wary instead.

''Miss Sorby,'' he said. ''You'll be glad to know the Allegheny County Detectives' Bureau has overruled the Y.M.C.A.'s prohibition on women. We'd like you to come in and identify the recently deceased since you're his—uh—next-of-kin.''

Helen wasn't sure what annoyed her most—having to admit she'd once been married to James Foster Barton in front of her curious fellow reporters, or being made to wait nearly forty-five minutes in order to do it. "He was not my *kin*," she told Taggart, incensed enough not to care if she was cutting her nose off to spite her face. "If you would like to invite me in as a person who was unfortunately acquainted with the deceased—"

"You can be invited in as his funeral director, I don't care." Taggart reached out and hauled her up the steps with about as much politeness as he'd shown in booting the *Valley News* reporter down them. "Just come in *now*, or Milo's going to add me to the body count. There's only three hours left until that damned deadline—"

Helen threw him a startled look, not even caring that she had just become the first female to pass through the Tarentum Y.M.C.A.'s sacred masculine portals. "What are you talking about?"

"The five o'clock payoff meeting up in Natrona." The big detective took the wide marble stairs at an urgent trot he wouldn't have been able to manage three months ago. Working with Milo Kachigan might not be trimming Taggart's gut, Helen thought, but it was definitely improving his stamina. "At that mine named after Murchison's daughter."

"But there's no reason to go there now." It wasn't her sensible corset and skirts that made Helen breathless by the time she reached the top of the stairs but a sudden horrible thought. "James Foster Barton *is* dead, isn't he?"

"Leon Daniels is dead," Kachigan corrected her. Helen turned to see him crossing the central dormitory hall to meet her. "Right now, that's the only thing we're sure of."

"What do you mean?"

"I mean that a question has been raised about who Leon Daniels really is. Are you ready to look at his body?"

"Of course." She followed him through the door of one dormitory-style room, silent and empty in the mid-afternoon sunlight. Its spartan bunk beds and whitewashed walls reminded her more of a prison than an exclusive male club. Down at the far end, a few red-brown rivulets against the white lime seemed to be all that disturbed the room's sanctity, but as she got closer, Helen could see the limp sag of a body across one narrow bunk. The short hair and freckles didn't startle her, since she'd been expecting them, but the cheap workman's boots and the worn flannel shirt that had darkened with blood around a single gunshot wound made her eyes widen. When she'd known him, James Foster Barton had always worn fine clothes and fitted shoes, even when he'd posed as a labor organizer.

"Take a good look, Miss Sorby." John Brennan, the fair-haired state police lieutenant who'd been such a polite rescuer yesterday, seemed to have lost all his cordiality overnight. He reached down and turned the dead man's slack face into the afternoon sunshine so she could see it better. "Do you really think you know this man?"

"Yes," Helen said without hesitation. Painted-on freckles or not, that particular combination of nose, cheeks, and chin flared such a memory of resentment and rage in her that she had to grit her teeth to keep from shouting. "His name— the name he used when I knew him—was James Foster Barton. He's a confidence man. And a bigamist." She took a deep breath, making sure her gaze did not touch Kachigan's. "If you want to be completely sure, look at his back. He has a brownish-green birthmark between his shoulder blades."

The state policeman looked uncomfortable. "Really, Miss Sorby, I don't think—"

"I do," Kachigan said. "Look for it."

Brennan frowned, but bent to roll the dead man over and tug the tail of his shirt out from between his suspenders. Helen couldn't view Barton's back from where she stood, but the deeper jerk of Brennan's frown let her know what he saw. "Well?"

"Yes," he said stiffly. "He does have that mark."

Kachigan took a step closer to Helen, not to touch but to align himself with her, creating a united front against the state policeman. "Now that you know I was right," he said, "are you finally going to tell me what you know about this man?"

Helen looked from one adamant face to the other, digging her teeth into her lip to keep from blurting out the questions clamoring in her head. But as the silence drew itself out into humming tension, she finally couldn't stand it anymore.

"What could the state police know about James Foster Barton, except for his criminal record?" she demanded. "He was a confidence man and a swindler, and he was probably behind the attempt to blackmail Charles Murchison."

"*No.*"

It was all Brennan said, but it came out with the flat snap of a military order. Helen blinked at him, more startled than intimidated.

"No, he wasn't a criminal?" she asked. "Or—"

"No, he wasn't behind the attempt to blackmail Mr. Charles Murchison." The state policeman's mouth jerked again, as if what he had to say tasted bad. "Mr. Daniels— or Mr. Barton if you prefer—was actually in the employment of Mr. Murchison at the time of his death. Through the aegis of the Pinkerton Detective Agency."

"Did Daniels tell you that himself?" Kachigan asked.

"No. I saw the signed order from the head of the Pinkertons." Brennan paused, then reluctantly added, "We've been coordinating a mutual investigation of Black Hand activity with them for the past several months. Obviously, however, we have no control over the—er—backgrounds of the men they hire."

"*Months?*" Helen exchanged startled looks with Kachigan. "I thought you said Daniels had just arrived here in Tarentum."

"He had. That's because this particular phase of the investigation had just opened." The state policeman gave them a knife-sharp look. "But we've been investigating the Black Hand throughout western Pennsylvania ever since the state police was first formed. The criminal element has been running rampant in isolated communities of uneducated Italians."

"Communities isolated on purpose so that employers can pay low wages and exploit their workers," Helen shot back.

Brennan stiffened. "I am not prepared to debate politics

or economics with you, Miss Sorby. All I can say is that the Black Hand remains a legitimate target of state police and Pinkerton attention in many areas. And it would be a shame if a *premature* news report compromised any of those investigations!"

It wasn't the state policeman's glare but Milo Kachigan's warning clasp on her bruised wrist that kept Helen from responding to that.

"If I guarantee that no such premature reports will be published, Lieutenant," Kachigan said, "will you tell us exactly what you and Leon Daniels found out when you investigated the Black Hand threat against Charles Murchison?"

There was a long pause, then Brennan surprised Helen with an almost human-sounding sigh. "I should say yes to that," the lieutenant said. "But in good conscience, I can't. Mr. Daniels was not particularly punctual about reporting his discoveries, either to his employer or to us. All I know is that a wire was received at Pinkerton offices sometime last night, saying Daniels had gotten a good lead on the missing securities and would be calling for reinforcements soon."

"Not soon enough." Kachigan glanced down at the dead man sprawled on the bed, then back up at Helen. She wasn't sure how to read what looked like an apology in his eyes until his next words. "I'm not going to make the same mistake. Lieutenant Brennan, we've discovered that the missing securities are scheduled to be exchanged for the payoff money at five tonight in Murchison Brothers' Emmy Mine, up in Natrona. Are you willing to coordinate efforts with me to trap the blackmailer?"

For once, the state police officer's stiff military mask cracked to show a surprising glint of boyish eagerness beneath it. "Gladly, Detective Kachigan," he said. It was the first time Helen could remember hearing him actually use Milo's rank when he addressed him. "We'll need to move fast to plan this maneuver, though. The site should be reconnoitered long before any of the guilty parties has had a chance to arrive, and it's already half past two."

"I know." Kachigan's grip tightened around Helen's wrist again. "But if you can give me just a few minutes to see Miss Sorby out—"

Brennan's gaze dipped to that unromantic handclasp and then came politely back to their faces. "I think that would be acceptable," was all he said.

Helen managed to tamp a lid down on her simmering temper, at least for as long as it took them to walk back down the hall and past the discomfitted Y.M.C.A. attendant. She started to speak at the head of the stairs, but the glint of sunlight off J.P. Frick's balding head, from where he stood chatting with a state trooper at the far end of the dormitory hall, tightened her lips even before Kachigan's grip had tightened on her wrist. Instead, she waited until they'd descended two flights of steps and were crossing the dim lobby of the first-floor auditorium before she swung around to confront her escort.

"All right," she said flatly. "I know you're not coming with me to hold the door or kiss me good-bye. What did you want to talk to me about?"

The county detective gave her an unreadable look in the shadowed light. "I wanted to make sure you weren't upset."

"Upset about what?" Helen demanded. "Cooling my heels outside the Y.M.C.A. for three quarters of an hour? Not being consulted before you decided to trust the state police? Or about what I'm sure you're about to tell me, that General Brennan back there won't allow me to be part of this 'maneuver' of his?"

"Upset about seeing your ex-husband murdered!" For once it was Kachigan's voice that was the first to rise above the volume of polite conversation. He winced, as if the shout had sent a twinge through his bandaged ribs. "I thought you might still—"

"Care about him?" she demanded incredulously.

"—be mad at him," Kachigan finished. "Sometimes it's almost as hard to lose an enemy as a friend."

"Milo, the only one I'm mad at right now is *you*." Helen reached out, heedless of his broken ribs and her aching wrists, to wrap her fists in the cheap, harsh cloth of his suit coat and shake him. He grunted at the motion but didn't try to push her away. "You're half-crippled and you're walking into this payoff exchange blind, with allies who are more likely to be enemies! You know J.P. Frick is working for Truxall and Murchison, and the state police could be working for Bernard Flinn or even the railroads. The only ones you'll be able to trust down in that mine are Art Taggart and Owen Riley!"

"Not Taggart," he said wryly. "He wouldn't fit through the portal."

"Then why are you going? Let Murchison pay his fifty thousand dollars and get back his precious securities—"

"And allow a triple murderer to walk away free?" Kachigan shook his head. "I couldn't, Helen, even if I wasn't worried that we'd be the next victims on his list. I just have to hope Truxall's company police and the state troopers will neutralize each other, so I can make my arrest and come home."

Helen heard the familiar ring of determination in his voice and closed her eyes, overwhelmed by the sheer frustration of trying to forge an equal relationship with a man so fiercely grounded in the ethics of protectiveness. She might have been able to convince him that the risk to his own life was tolerable, but she knew she'd never get him to agree that the same thing was true for hers.

"Helen?"

She opened her eyes again to find him peering down at her, and took advantage of his closeness to brush an exasperated kiss across his frown. "Go plan your maneuvers with General Brennan before he decides to leave without you. In the meantime, I'm going to go pull out the one thread in this tangle that we haven't touched yet."

His frown deepened. "What's that? I don't want you traveling alone this afternoon, not before five. Remember, Truxall thinks I stole his boss's first payoff. And he knows he can use you to blackmail me."

"I promise not to go alone," she said, meeting his gaze

steadily. "And I won't be anywhere near Tarentum or Natrona. All right?"

His suspicious look didn't fade. "Then where *will* you
be?"

"In Oakmont," Helen said. "Talking to the person who
helped to steal those missing securities in the first place."

The afternoon sunlight had faded behind soft clouds by the
time Helen drove her rented livery buggy off the Hulton
ferry and through the pink budding haze of Oakmont's old
apple orchard. The humid air promised more rain later in
the day. She spent an irritable moment wondering why she
hadn't brought her new umbrella along, until she remembered she'd lost it along with her muff back on the deserted
road through Millerstown.

"I've got a knife digging into your ribs," the man in the
buggy reminded her. "Try to look a little more scared."

Helen gave him an unimpressed look. "No, you've got
a knife digging into the bones of my corset. It would probably take you an hour to saw through and hit skin."

Niccolo Santangelo's smile tugged at the pink track of
scar tissue on his face. "Well, I wouldn't want you to hit
a bump and get a hole poked in your hide. Mamma would
never forgive me, and that detective boyfriend of yours
would probably give me a bullet hole to match."

Helen shook the reins, sending the horses straight up the
river-facing slope toward the fine houses at the top. "I
don't know why you couldn't just wait until we got to the
Murchisons' driveway to pull out your knife."

"Because then you don't have a nice big hole torn in
your coat for all the servants to see," her cousin said simply.

Helen glanced down toward her waist in surprise. She
hadn't felt so much as a tug while she was driving, but
there was now a gaping rent slashed through the worn, russet wool and frayed silk lining of her old winter coat. She
took in a cautious breath against the pressure of the knife
tip, suddenly aware of just how sharp the thin stiletto must
be.

"There," Santangelo said in satisfaction. "That's a much better scared look."

Helen bit her lip, but didn't argue with him. Instead, she guided the buggy through the gauntlet of high trimmed hedges and iron pickets toward the closed gate of the Murchison mansion. A moment after she pulled up in front of it, there was still no sign of movement. "No one's coming to let us in," she said, frowning. "Maybe no one's at home."

"All the better to look for those missing securities." He clambered out of the buggy, taking his stiletto with him. A moment later, something clicked inside the gate latch and the black wrought iron swung open under its own weight. Helen chirruped the horses through, then drew them up again to wait as Nicco latched the gate behind them.

"Telephone line," she reminded him, before he could climb back in. "We don't want the Oakmont police coming to my rescue. Wouldn't it be better to cut it out here?"

Santangelo glanced up at the droop of wires that spoiled the pretty view of landscaped yard and hedges. "I don't want to warn them inside by cutting off the electric power too," he said. "Give me five minutes, then drive to the front door. I'll meet you there."

He vanished into the garden before she could reply, somehow finding enough shadows to hide in between winter-bare branches and severely pruned topiary. Helen glanced up at the opulent glitter of curved windows in the round turret that anchored one corner of the big house, hoping Lillian Murchison wasn't up there keeping watch on her graveled drive. The inhospitable gates probably meant Charles Murchison had gone to oversee the latest extortion payoff and left her safely mewed up at home, but somehow Helen doubted that his second wife was waiting with bated breath for his return.

She glanced down at the watch pinned to her coat lapel, then shook the reins and urged the horses down the drive. Before she had even rounded the curve that led to the portico, however, the horses shied and whinnied in protest at

the ruthless jerk that tore the reins out of her grasp. Helen
swung on her seat to see who had intercepted her, but all
the movement got her was the slap of heavy cloth across
her face. She gasped and reached up to tear it free, but a
man's hand clamped around both bruised wrists and
dragged her hands away again, then shoved what felt like
a burlap bag over her head. A second later, Helen was
dragged out of the buggy entirely and hauled struggling and
screaming across the graveled drive. Where in God's name
was her cousin when she needed him?

She never heard the ring of a bell or thud of a knocker,
but the press of warm air and the startled gasp of another
person told her someone inside the house had responded to
her cries of alarm. "What are you doing?" The soft Southern voice rose to a shriek as Helen was dragged blindly
across the threshold. "You can't come in here like that!"

"Trina?" That was a more familiar voice, distant but
rapidly approaching. "What's the matter?"

There was no reply, but the bag was abruptly dragged
from Helen's head. At first all she saw was the frozen face
of a Negro housemaid staring at her across the foyer, and
then a sapphire satin shimmer came down the hall and
floated to a clinging halt. "Miss Sorby!" said Lillian Murchison. "Are you all right?"

"No." Helen spit out wet threads of burlap and twisted
her head around to see who had attacked her. Across the
thin glint of a stiletto, pressed dangerously close to her
throat, the stiff scarred mask of Niccolo Santangelo's face
stared at her without the slightest hint of laughter or make-
believe. At that stomach-churning moment, Helen knew
with certainty that her Black Hand cousin had betrayed her.
"No, I'm not."

"Trina, ring up the police." All the dancing Gibson Girl
charm had left Lillian Murchison's voice and left it tight
with fear or perhaps desperation. "Tell them to hurry—"

"I wouldn't, if I were you," Santangelo said softly, but
with enough steel showing in his voice to make the housemaid pause on her way to the mahogany telephone box.

Helen felt the sharp kiss of the knife against her throat and
wondered if she would feel its bite or would only know if
she'd been cut when she felt the wet dribble of blood across
her skin. "If you do, you're going to get bloodstains all
over your carpet."

There was a tense moment of silence, when all Helen
could hear was the sound of strained breathing. Then Lillian Murchison said again, in a voice almost as steel-hard
as Santangelo's, "Trina, go ring up the police."

The frozen tableau exploded into violence. The Negro
housemaid shrieked and flung herself to the ground, but it
wasn't her Santangelo had lunged at. In a flurry of blue
satin and spill of chestnut hair, he grabbed the millionaire's
wife before she could back away and hauled her disrespect-
fully into the circle of his restraining arm, the knife now
pressed against her lace-trimmed throat. Helen stared across
at them from where her cousin had left her standing, un-
damaged and speechless. A wild suspicion was beginning
to soak through her shock.

"That wasn't very nice of you," Niccolo Santangelo said
to his captive reproachfully. "I thought you liked my
cousin."

Lillian Murchison gave him a sharp sidelong look. It was
not at all the kind of expression Helen would have expected
to see on the face of a sheltered society wife confronted
with senseless violence. "What do you want?"

"The money, of course."

"What money? My husband doesn't keep more than—"

Santangelo shook her, not lightly. "Don't be stupid. I
want the money your husband already thinks he lost, the
money you and your lover got by pretending to be me."

"I don't know what—" This time it wasn't a shake but
a thin line of red running down the knife blade that made
her voice break off. Niccolo Santangelo clearly felt no com-
punction about keeping the millionaire's wife as undam-
aged as he had kept his cousin. Helen bit her lip and forced
herself not to speak, despite the growing clamor of suspicion inside her. "I don't even know who you are!"

"But you know who I must be. Even up here on society

hill, you've heard about the Black Hand, haven't you?'' Santangelo bent closer so that his knife-scarred cheek rubbed the powder from hers. "You just didn't hear enough to know that you should never use their name unless you're prepared to pay for the privilege."

"I didn't—" Another ribbon of red joined the first on his stiletto blade. Lillian Murchison spit out a curse no millionaire's wife should know and jerked her neck away from the knife. "All right! All right, I'll pay you what you want—but you'll have to take it in the securities, not in cash. We never found that damn payoff, no matter how we searched!"

"There, you see, Hell?" Laughter crept back into Niccolo Santangelo's blackbird eyes, although he never took the threat of his knife away from his prisoner's neck. "You think we could've got her to admit that if I hadn't tricked you into acting scared?"

Helen blew out a tense and still half-disbelieving breath. "I liked my plan better," she said, and came across the foyer to help the silent housemaid to her feet. "We still don't know where the missing securities are."

"But we got the *puttana* to admit she has them, in front of witnesses." Santangelo's smile chased the stiffness from his face again. "I think her husband will know where to look when he finds out."

"He's not going to find out."

The sharp ring of certainty in Lillian Murchison's voice dragged Helen's gaze back to her. Despite the blood-soaked lace at her neck and the ragged disorder of her hair, despite the continued threat of Santangelo's knife, the millionaire's wife somehow managed to look more in command of herself and the situation than ever. Her intelligent eyes glittered with both triumph and contempt.

"All that fine playacting for nothing, Miss Sorby," she mocked gently. "But I suppose you really couldn't bring that detective boyfriend of yours along as a witness, since it would have ruined your little Black Hand masquerade."

"It's not a masquerade," Helen said, but she could tell by the flare of Lillian's nostrils that the other woman didn't

believe her. And it still didn't explain that exultant certainty
in her voice. She hadn't said that her husband wouldn't
believe the accusations against her, she'd said that he'd
never find out about them. Helen opened her mouth to ask
what she meant, then realized the stupidity of expecting
cooperation from a woman whose crimes she had just exposed. She chose a different strategy. "Not the kind of
masquerade your marriage is. Did you intend to swindle
Charles Murchison out of his fortune when you married
him, Lillian Lyell? Or did you betray him first and then
decide to blackmail him?"

"Fine words, coming from you, Helen Sorby!" Lillian
Murchison retorted. "You must know what the divorce
laws are like in this country. How can you blame me for
wanting more of the fortune I helped my husband make
than any judge would ever give me?"

"I can't," said Helen. "But I can blame you for driving
your stepdaughter out of your house and getting three men
murdered for crimes they had no part in. Not to mention
all the dead miners and company policemen who would
still be alive if you hadn't started a war between Sedgwick
and Murchison Coal—"

It wasn't anything Lillian Murchison said or did, not a
twinge of guilt or jerk of apprehension that gave her away.
It was the way her expressive eyes flared with fierce and
sudden triumph.

"What have you done?" Helen demanded. The quick
dart of the other woman's eyes to the mahogany grandfather clock in one corner of the foyer told her at least part
of the answer. The hands stood at nearly four. "It's got
something to do with the payoff meeting, doesn't it?"

"I don't have to tell you anything—" Lillian gasped as
Niccolo Santangelo's arm clamped tight around her waist
again, squeezing out what little breath her hourglass silhouette left her room for.

"Yes, you do," said the *capo* of Tarentum's Black Hand
in her ear. "If you don't, we'll load you into the buggy
and take you up to Emmy Number Two to see for our-

selves. And you know what bad luck it is for women to go into coal mines—"

"*No!*" The vehemence in Lillian Murchison's voice was surprising, given her lack of breath. "No, don't do that. Bernard Flinn's going to be there."

"Flinn?" Helen's stomach churned with apprehension. "You told him about the payoff meeting?"

"I told his wife over tea this morning, pretending to be worried sick that my husband was meeting the Black Hand. And since all she can talk about is how Flinn is going to be the next head of the Pennsylvania State Police, I'm sure she passed the news along as soon as I was gone."

"Giving Flinn enough time to retaliate for the way he was kidnapped and interrogated," Helen said between her teeth. "You're hoping he'll set a trap that will kill your husband."

"Precisely." Lillian Murchison gave her a savage little smile. "Not to mention those annoying county detectives—"

Helen cursed and threw herself across the foyer, but her cousin swung the millionaire's wife out of her reach, fending her off with his elbow. "The phone line's not really cut," Niccolo Santangelo said. "Ring up Flinn now, and tell him not to spring the trap!"

"Ring him up *where*? He's probably already up at that mine, running wires for the dynamite—"

"Then we'll telegraph the state police in Natrona and tell them about the trap. Since some of their men will get caught in it too—"

"—they might actually believe us." Helen's fierce anger turned to equally fierce urgency. "Come on, let's go. The telegraph office is down on Railroad Avenue."

"What should we do with the *puttana*?"

"Bring her along." Helen shot a fierce glance over her shoulder. "Because if we're not in time to stop Flinn, I'm going to make sure she spends her rich widowhood in prison."

FIFTEEN

This was it, Kachigan thought grimly, as the darkness closed around him except for the flickering halo of his miner's lamp. This was the last coal mine he was ever going to set foot in for the rest of his life.

It wasn't the pall of dust inside Murchison's strikebound Emmy Mine that made him vow that, although his cracked ribs ached with the effort of trying not to cough. And it certainly wasn't the roof, since the seven feet of coal they were mining here left more than enough room for timbers, roof bolts, and even the dark glitters of unlit electric lights. It wasn't the groan and settle of rock or the constant mutter of falling shale. No, what bothered him about Emmy Number Two was the water.

Unlike the other mines Kachigan had been in, the portal for this one was located only a stone's throw from the Allegheny River, and the steep descent of the entrance slope seemed to parallel the shore rather than depart from it. From the start, the floor of the mine passage had been at best muddy and in many places full of standing water, despite the echoing racket of electric-powered pumps. Kachigan could see why they'd been left on, even though Emmy's miners had refused to return to work after their riot. The mine's ceiling dripped and the walls sweated, and occasionally he had to swerve to avoid miniature waterfalls pouring from cracks in the rock. Within minutes of entering, Kachigan's shoes were soaked and his miner's light was sizzling from the water that had fallen into the paraffin. A cold, constant trickle was running down off his cap and dripping down the shoulders of his overcoat.

"If Frick is working for Truxall and Murchison, sir," said Owen Riley from behind him, "I say we bring him down here and leave him."

Kachigan bit down on a spurt of laughter. Thanks to John Brennan's military efficiency, they were entering the mine almost thirty minutes ahead of the prearranged meeting time, but Franklin Truxall might have brought his own policemen down early too. That was why Kachigan had agreed to let two state police troopers, unmistakable with their black overcoats and bright tin badges, lead the way into the mine, with Brennan close on their heels. Two other troopers followed him and Riley, their heavy boots splashing with impunity through the puddles he was trying to avoid.

The rest of their state police detachment, along with Art Taggart and a seemingly relieved J.P. Frick, had been left outside the deserted mine, hidden in an outbuilding in case the payoff participants met and made their exchange without bothering to enter the mine. It had taken Kachigan and Brennan a half-hour to hammer out that arrangement—the state police lieutenant had wanted to simply arrest Frick on charges of corruption to prevent him from ruining their trap, while Kachigan wanted to bring him into the mine and give him enough rope to hang himself with. They'd compromised on leaving the older man outside, where Taggart had strict instructions to watch his every move and intercept him if he tried to follow them into the mine.

"Detective Kachigan?"

"Yes?" Kachigan took an unwary step into a trickle of water and his paraffin flame flickered and hissed in protest. The state policemen had come to a stop in front of him, at a cross-passage whose steady draft made the coal dust swirl and eddy in the glow of their bending lights. Kachigan skirted another oily-looking puddle and went to join them. "You think this is as far as they'll come?"

"I wouldn't call it the main passage after this split," Brennan said, his steady tenor sounding as confident in this dripping darkness as it did in the saddle of a powerful horse. "Mr. Riley, do you agree?"

"Yes," said the Tarentum native. "We should probably go down one of these side-passages a little way and wait there."

"With our lights blown out," Kachigan added. He saw the apprehensive look that two of the state troopers exchanged. "Don't worry, once our eyes have adjusted, we'll be able to see the glow of their lights. And they'll never see us coming."

"Good point," Brennan conceded, and led the way around the corner and into the colder breeze of the cross-passage. To his credit, the state police lieutenant was the first to lift off his paraffin light and blow the wick-fed flame out of its spout. His men gritted their teeth and followed suit, with Riley's light the last to go. The afterglow of ruby wicks kept the darkness at bay for a few seconds longer, and then it closed around them like a clenched fist.

"Don't panic," said Kachigan, as the indrawn rasp of breath from someone in the group reminded him of Helen Sorby's reaction to the utter lack of light. "If you're feeling a little nervous, pull out a match and hold it ready to strike, right next to the wick of your light."

The rustle of pockets being emptied and balsa wood boxes being slid open told him his advice had been followed by more than one member of the group. Kachigan himself merely blew on his paraffin lamp to cool it, then tucked it into a pocket of his water-streaked overcoat. His experience at Bull Creek and Millerstown had taught him that he didn't need a light on his own head as long as someone around him had one. And he didn't want the delay of fumbling with a match to interfere with his assault on the men who would be meeting here.

Time passed, measured in steady drips of water from the

roof and the occasional crunch of coal underfoot as men shifted to relieve their weight. The draft of cold breeze up the passage never paused and never varied, leading Kachigan to eventually lean close to where his memory put Riley's ear and murmur, "Where's the wind coming from, Owen?"

"Other mines," the young detective said in the same muffled voice. "They're mostly all connected down here somewhere. My dad used to walk underground from Tarentum to Brackenridge on bad snow days, so he'd come out closer to home."

Kachigan considered that for a moment. "So Murchison's fire-boss didn't need to sneak into Bull Creek from the trolley line? He could have walked there underground the whole way?"

"Assuming he never hit a pocket of gas or a patch of bad roof in the abandoned parts—"

"*Sssh!*" That was Brennan, of course, but he sounded too urgent and too quiet to just be exerting his military authority. "Listen."

Kachigan shut up and listened. At first, all he heard was the thrum of the pumps and the coal mine talking to itself in watery splatters and gurgles. But then one of those splashing sounds began to separate itself from the rest, to repeat at regular intervals occasionally, then vanish, then repeat again. He realized he was hearing the splashes of footsteps through puddles rather than the drier echoing thuds his brain had stupidly expected.

"That can't be Truxall's police," Riley whispered to him. "It only sounds like one or two men."

"Maybe the blackmailer," Kachigan muttered back, although the clock in his head insisted it was still at least a quarter to five.

"No talking," Brennan hissed at them. "Matches ready, but wait for my command!"

Kachigan twisted his head, staring back toward the passage they had come from. The slender fringe of diffracted light illuminated the straight line of the corner first, then brightened so swiftly and steadily that Kachigan knew the men approaching them must be wearing carbide lamps. There wasn't even a hint of flicker.

"All right, Frank." Kachigan didn't recognize that harsh old man's voice, but the confident power in it rang clearly off the mine walls. "This is far enough. Where are you going to set up to shoot from? Around the corner?"

"No," said Franklin Truxall curtly. "From right here."

"*What?*" Feet scraped and splashed as someone turned abruptly. "What the hell are you doing?"

"Stopping this idiocy before I get any wetter," said the coal police chief irritably. "I told you a week ago, if you'd just given that payoff money to me to deliver, everything would have gone fine. But you insisted on having that damned fire-boss walk through the mines the first time, and then you insisted on coming this time to deliver it in person. It's really all your fault."

"*My* fault?" Charles Murchison's arrogant voice sounded as if he was choking on coal dust, although Kachigan suspected something much more bitter had caught in his throat. "I give you a job after that damned football scandal that nearly disgraced my alma mater, and you have the gall to say this is my fault! What's the matter, Frank, didn't I give you enough money to let you gamble the way you really wanted to?"

"No, and you didn't give your wife enough money to keep her faithful to you either." Truxall sounded matter-of-fact rather than malicious about that, but the irregular splash of footsteps told Kachigan that one of the two men had staggered back from the other. He frowned and glanced through the dim, diffracted light at Brennan, wondering how much longer the state policeman would let this drama play out before he gave the signal to attack. "You're lucky you lived this long, you know. Lillian's wanted to kill you since last November, but I told her to wait for the coal strike, when we could blame the whole mess on your war with Sedgwick Coal & Coke."

"So it was never Bernard Flinn or the Black Hand behind this?" The coal baron's arrogant voice still sounded

248 Karen Rose Cercone

more irate than frightened. "It was you and Lillian, all along?"

"All along," Truxall confirmed. "Now, why don't you hand over the fifty thousand and I'll make this merciful rather than excruciating—"

"*Now*," said Brennan.

Kachigan lunged forward before the matches had even scraped against their lighting strips, ignoring the jab of pain the motion sent through his cracked ribs. The matching splash of someone else's footsteps told him he hadn't been the only one to disregard light in favor of immediate attack. When he turned the corner and threw himself toward the carbide glare of two headlamps, it was John Brennan who slammed him abruptly sideways into the wet wall of the coal mine. A moment later, the echoing thunder of a gunshot told Kachigan why. He'd been so intent on taking out the gun he could see pointed between those two men that it had never occurred to him there might be another aimed at them from further up the mine passage.

"Hold your fire!" Brennan yelled, although Kachigan wasn't sure if the command was for his own troops or the unseen sniper. The state police officer lay sprawled in the mud of the floor, his own pistol pointed unwaveringly at Truxall. "One more shot and Truxall's dead."

The coal police chief's glasses turned toward them, light from Murchison's carbide lamp turning them into solid squares of white. All Kachigan could see of his expression was the scowl beneath his handlebar mustache, but it didn't look like he was panicking. The gun in his hand never wavered from the still, frozen figure of his employer.

"Stop shooting, Frick," he said. "They're not going to do anything while I've got a gun pointed right at the old man."

There was a spurt of mirthless laughter from the darkness. "Just because Murchison's in bed with the Pennsylvania Railroad doesn't mean those damned cossacks are going to let you line them up and shoot them like the idiots up at Bull Creek," said the disembodied voice of J.P. Frick. "At least let me take out that bastard Kachigan. If he hadn't kept me away from a telephone all day, I could have warned you this was a trap.''

"Then it would have been the first useful thing you've done." Truxall sounded more irritated with his hireling than anything else. "Keep your damned finger off that trigger. Nobody needs to get hurt here tonight. Lieutenant, if you let us walk out of here with a little of the railroad's excess profits, I guarantee we'll leave Murchison alive to make some more. Is it a deal?''

"I would prefer not to endanger Mr. Murchison's life,'' Brennan said stiffly. "But I'm not going to let you walk out of here with him just so he can be shot elsewhere. And I'm not going to exchange any of my men's lives for his.''

"That's all right. There's someone else here you probably wouldn't mind sacrificing." Kachigan saw the police chief's glasses flash back his way and stopped his slow soundless crawl through the mud. From the other side of the passage, he could hear a soft muddy slither like a delayed echo, and guessed Brennan was taking advantage of the turn of Truxall's attention to edge his own way into striking distance. "Did the Turk have a gun on him when he came down here, Frick?''

"Kachigan? No. He said he couldn't fire one, with his ribs all busted up like that.''

Truxall grunted, and looked back at Brennan. The slithering sound didn't stop, since Kachigan promptly resumed his own stealthy approach. "All right, I'll trade the Turk for Murchison if he'll give me what's in his vest pocket—''

"No,'' the coal baron said. The gun-barrel shoved ruthlessly into his gut, driving his breath out in an anguished gasp.

"—or else he'll have a lot more to worry about than some missing securities that prove his company is owned by the Pennsylvania Railroad.''

"It's not—that,'' the millionaire said, his breath choking again in the dusty air. "I didn't bring the money with me. You can look, if you don't believe me.''

Truxall's head yanked toward his hostage. "What the hell are you talking about?''

Murchison's raw, jutting face looked ashen in the glare of his police chief's carbide light. "You're the one who said we were going to make sure we got the securities this time before we showed the color of our money," he said bitterly. "So Lillian convinced me it would be a waste of money—"

"*Lillian* did?"

"Well, I told her we were just going to kill the black-mailer after we made the exchange. And she said in that case, there was no need to take a loss on any more of my stocks."

"You goddamned miserly bastard and your goddamned double-crossing *bitch* of a wife—"

"Don't kill him, Truxall," Kachigan warned, hearing the scratch of the drawn-back hammer. "Remember, he's the only thing keeping you alive right now."

One glance at Brennan's steady pistol—and the array of other guns Kachigan assumed were pointed at him by the state troopers behind them—made Truxall grunt and ease the hammer down again unfired. "Now what?"

"I've still got money in the bank," Murchison said hurriedly. "And at least a thousand in cash at the house."

"Both of which are back in Oakmont," Truxall snapped. "A damned lot of good that's going to do me here. You know the minute I walk out that mine portal, the state police are going to gun me down."

"There used to be a company office right here in Natrona," Frick's disembodied voice said from down the passage. "We could have had some money sent up from there. But someone burned a few too many miners with carbide and got last week's payroll roasted. Between that and the payoff Tamasy hid before he died—"

"Shut up, Frick," Truxall warned.

"—you probably lost more money this last week than you ever gambled away in your life," the older detective finished sourly. "For Chrissake, Truxall, can't you tell when you're beating a dead horse? Let's just kill them all and go out through one of the other mine exits—"

For one gut-wrenching moment, Kachigan thought the

thunderous explosion rolling through the mine was the gun-
fire of Truxall's response, echoed and magnified by return
fire from Brennan's state troopers. But then he felt the blast
of air slam across his back and shove him deep into the
mud. By the time he got his face lifted out of it, the light
in the mine passage had dimmed considerably. The only
illumination came from one of the carbide glows, and it
was on the ground several feet up the passage where the
man wearing it had been thrown by the blast.

"Someone blew out the river end of the mine!" Riley's
voice had broken pitch again, as it did under stress.
"There's water coming in, a lot of it!"

"Out, out, everyone out!" Gloved hands grabbed at Kachigan's shoulders and hauled him out of the mud, then
Brennan left him and went to do the same for Murchison.
The shadowy figures of his state troopers splashed past,
their paraffin lamps still unlit. Kachigan bit down hard on
the panic rising like the cold swirl of water around his feet,
and forced himself to stop and light the wick on his own
paraffin lamp before he moved. He paused before he
snapped it back on his cap. "Riley, where are you?"

"Right here, sir." The younger detective skidded to a
stop beside him, and Kachigan held his lamp's spout to the
younger man's head, lighting his dark wick with a quick
brush of leaping flame. The water was lapping at their ankles now and rising fast. "Do you need help getting out?"

"No, but Brennan does." Kachigan could see the state
police lieutenant hooking Murchison's limp arm around his
neck in order to drag him up the passage. He couldn't tell
if the millionaire had been shot or just stunned by the full
force of the blast, but Truxall's equally limp body made
him suspect the latter. "Give him a hand. I'll be right behind you."

"Yes, sir." Riley went to duck under the old man's other
arm, helping Brennan drag him through the rising water.
Kachigan paused before he followed them, frowning over
at the sprawled coal police chief. Truxall lay faceup in the
oily water, his carbide lamp throwing bright ringed reflections all around him. In another few moments, the water

would reach the level of his face and probably wake him, but for now he was unconscious. And as much as he wanted to see the man who'd burned Helen Sorby pay for it, Kachigan just couldn't make himself take the coal policeman's gun and use it on him. Instead, he turned away and left him to the mercy of the flood.

There was an ominous silence spreading through the mine now, as one after another of the electric pumps drowned beneath the rising waters. But the flood itself was eerily soundless except for the splashing of his footsteps. It would have seemed almost peaceful except for the relentless rise of cold water farther and farther up the glittering walls of coal. Kachigan tried to break into a run when it went past his knees, but the effort jarred his ribs into such jagged stabs of pain that he couldn't keep the pace up for more than a few strides. He walked as fast as he could instead, more grateful than ever for the seven-foot-high roof that let him stay upright as he moved. And gave him at least a little breathing space—

Dynamite thundered through the mine again, this time followed by a deep liquid roar of released water. Kachigan threw himself toward the timbers bracing the sidewall, scrabbling for some hold against the next shock wave. When it came, however, it was a wall of water instead of exploded air. Kachigan felt himself lifted by the flooding surge and thrown hard against the mine's ceiling. His desperate fingers flailed sideways, more in a swimming stroke than for any hope of contact. The jerk and pull of rope against his wrist startled him so badly he almost missed grabbing on to it. Another wild swing got him a firm grip with his good hand. He reached the other up despite the ache of his ribs and pulled himself up against the return suck of the flood wave. To his surprise, he felt his head and shoulders rise into dark dry air, although the slap and crash of the roiling water still threw water across his face every few minutes. He must have gotten close enough to the entrance to be at least a little above the level of the river outside.

The rope beneath his hands tugged and quivered, and

Kachigan tightened his grip on it. Panic sizzled through him briefly when he realized it wasn't hemp or twine he was hanging on to in the darkness, but the cloth-wrapped cable of an electric line. But no shocks danced under his fingers and there were no warning sparks leaping out from along its unseen length. Either the first contact with the flood had shorted it out, or someone outside the mine had been smart enough to break the power circuits. It had now become a lifeline—and an unerring guide back through the blackness to the portal of the mine.

Kachigan caught his breath, and began the painful task of putting all his weight on his left arm while he edged the right forward along the electric line. His bruised ribs and chest muscles protested as they took the brunt of his water-sodden weight, and he paused to rest them as soon as his right hand was in place again. He was growing more sure by the minute that the water level had stabilized in the mine, giving him the time he needed to make his way out.

"Goddamn it, Turk," said a panting voice behind him. "How come you're always in my way when I need to get out of someplace fast?"

Kachigan twisted to look over his shoulder, then wished he hadn't. With his weight hung from both hands, the motion made his entire left side spasm in pain. And he didn't need the approaching glow of Frank Truxall's carbide lamp to know the coal police chief wasn't joking. His voice held the frustrated snap of a man who'd gambled too long and lost his patience along with all his money.

"There's no hurry," Kachigan said. "The water's not coming up any higher than this—"

"Good. Then maybe you'll have fun swimming around in it." Another painful glance showed Truxall hauling himself hand over hand up the electric cable, his athletic shoulders rolling easily with the motion. Kachigan only managed two forward lunges of his own before he felt a hand drop onto his shoulder and yank him backward. The cable dipped under the force of that pull and doused him in cold water up to his gritted teeth, but Kachigan hung on grimly. If he let Truxall tear him from this lifeline with his paraffin lamp doused, there was no guarantee he would be able to catch hold of it again.

"I said, get out of my goddamn way—" The pressure on his shoulder increased, and Kachigan managed to catch only a slice of breath before he went all the way under. With a grimace, he uncurled his fingers and let one hand slide off the line—his right hand, the one nearest Truxall. That forced all his weight and all of Truxall's drag onto his bad arm, but it was only for an instant. Sensing victory, the coal policeman released his grip on Kachigan's shoulder and reached out to grab at his straining left wrist.

He got razor-sharp steel instead.

Kachigan resurfaced in time to hear Truxall curse and see him jerk back, almost losing his own grip on the line. The relentless glow of the carbide lamp picked out the bloodred flow swirling off on the dark floodwaters.

"Stay back," Kachigan gasped, reaching his right hand back up to steady himself on the cable without losing his grip on the stiletto. "I've still got the knife."

Truxall cursed again. He tried to use his slashed palm to get a new grip on the electric cable, but Kachigan's upward thrust must have cut too deeply into the ligaments and tendons of his hand. The fingers wouldn't close.

"You god-damned Turkish bastard—"

"Armenian." Kachigan slipped the stiletto back into his jacket pocket and moved out of reach of the coal police chief by sliding first one hand and then the other backward up the cable. It tugged and jerked under his weight but held firm. "I told you, the water's not rising anymore. Just hook your elbow over the wire and wait here. I'll send the state policemen back—"

"To arrest me?" Behind the metal-rimmed spectacles, Kachigan could see the bitter resentment in Truxall's eyes. It was the look of a man who has cheated his entire life and been cheated by life in return. "I don't think so. Arrest Frick when you get out of here—and tell Lillian Murchison I'll see her in hell."

And before Kachigan could argue or even try to reach

out and stop him, the coal police chief released his one-
handed grip on the wet electric cable and let the mine's
floodwaters sweep the glow of his carbide light into darkness.

SIXTEEN

Helen knew something was wrong when she heard a dozen different whistles sending echoes down the river from the direction of Natrona. Only an industrial disaster could wring that level of response from the factories and fire companies of the Black Valley. And her mind told her what the disaster had to be, even if her heart vehemently denied it.

"Our telegram didn't get to the mine in time."

"You don't know that for sure." Santangelo was driving the rented buggy now, not because Helen thought he would be faster, but because she feared she would push the horses so hard she'd overturn them. It was her job to keep an eye on the silent, resentful figure of Lillian Murchison. They'd wedged the millionaire's wife into the buggy's cramped backseat, where her stiffly embroidered skirts kept her from making any move to escape. "They might have gotten everybody out before the mine blew up—"

Helen shook her head, biting so fiercely at her lower lip that it ached and burned beneath her teeth. "No. Either the state police didn't get there in time or Flinn got the message and decided he didn't care enough to change his plans. In which case I'm going to *kill* him too," she added, vehemently enough to make her renegade cousin give her a speculative glance. She ignored him, knowing now exactly what Milo Kachigan felt like when someone made a threat against her.

The mournful wail of the whistles grew louder as they rolled around the curve of River Avenue and into downtown Natrona. Citizens spilled into the streets in the twilight, talking in high, excited voices. Helen looked at them and frowned. No one seemed to be hurrying or crying or wandering around in shock, but she couldn't decide if that was a good sign or not. The mine in which the payoff should have taken place was the one whose miners had rioted earlier that week, so perhaps no one in Natrona had lost a loved one. Except for her.

"Hey, you!" Santangelo shook the reins and pulled the buggy up close to where a fire department's wagon had parked in front of a hardware store. The volunteer firemen were obviously getting ready for a long night of work, coiling extra hoses on every available hook while the horses stamped in their harnesses, but there seemed to be no particular urgency to their movements. "What happened up here?"

"The damnedest thing," said one of the young firemen, coming over to lean a sociable elbow on the buggy step, as if he had all the time in the world. He didn't seem to notice the anomalous shine of Lillian Murchison's satin evening gown in the backseat. "That waterlogged Emmy Mine of Murchison's finally decided to flood itself out. And didn't it go and do it not four hours after all the other mines along the river decided to join the walkout! Not a single miner hurt, thanks to God and the United Mine Workers—"

"No one was hurt?" Helen demanded, for once in no mood to hear praises sung for the miners' union. "No one at all?"

"Well, I hear there was one guy swept away—"

Santangelo kicked the young man's arm off the buggy and shook the horses into a fast trot. "Don't worry, I know where the mine is," he said in answer to Helen's questioning look. "We're only a few minutes away."

"A few minutes aren't going to matter," said Lillian

Murchison bitterly. It was the first thing she'd said since they'd left Oakmont. "Not if my husband is still alive."

Helen wanted to say it mattered to her, but her voice had somehow gotten so clogged in her throat that nothing could come out, not even a sob. She forced herself to keep staring at the dark road ahead of them, clenching her fingers into her coat pockets to keep from slapping the selfishness out of the millionaire's wife. After a few moments, the sound of shouting voices and the heavy thump of electrical machinery dragged her attention down to a glow of spotlights along the river. She pointed to it.

"I see." Santangelo guided the horses down the mine's muddy access road, swerving recklessly around another parked fire wagon and past a heap of tangled hoses. "Looks like they're trying to pump the water out of the mine."

"Why?" Helen had a voice back now, it just didn't sound like hers. "It's got to be too late to save—"

A shout cut across her words, in a voice she thought sounded like Art Taggart's. Helen swung around in the seat to see the unmistakable silhouette of the big detective pointing at her from the door of a mine outbuilding. He lifted his hands and cupped them around his mouth, but the pounding thunder of all the pumps drowned out whatever he was saying. She frowned and gathered up her skirts.

"I'm going to find out what Art knows," she said over her shoulder to her cousin. "In the meantime, see if you can find Bernard Flinn."

"And kill him for you?" Santangelo asked quite seriously.

"No," Helen said. "Not until I'm sure—"

She reached out to swing herself down from the buggy and found her hand caught in a wet, muddy grip instead. "It really wouldn't be nice of you to get Flinn killed," said Milo Kachigan. "After all, he was the one who insisted on coming down into that mine after everyone else got out. I'd probably still be hanging on to an electric line in the dark if it wasn't for him."

"*Milo!*" She stared down at him in disbelief. He wore unfamiliar miner's overalls and someone else's too-big boots, and his brown hair was so wet it looked like sable in the torchlight. But there was enough of a smile in his eyes to tell her he wasn't badly hurt. Helen scrambled down from the buggy in a graceless flurry of skirts, wanting desperately to hug him but knowing his cracked ribs wouldn't appreciate it. She settled for lifting the hand she had gripped and cradling her face into its palm, regardless of the mud. "I was afraid you were dead!"

He grunted in pain but still managed to wrap his other arm around her waist and pull her close enough to kiss, as heedless of her cousin's presence as she'd been of the dirt on his skin. By the time he was done, there was mud on both their faces. "Flinn told me about the telegram you sent to the state police. I would've sent one back, but I knew you'd already be on your way up here. I had Taggart watch out for you instead, so I could catch you as soon as you arrived."

"That was smart." She stepped back to scowl at him. Now that the first exhilarated relief was fading, all her anger at him was surging back. "About the only smart thing you've done today, in fact."

Kachigan surprised her with a rueful wince. "I'm not going to argue with you about that," he said, then glanced past her up at the carriage. His eyes narrowed. "Lillian Murchison?"

"Yes," Helen said, when the other woman didn't answer. "She's the one who let Flinn know about the meeting tonight, hoping he would sabotage the mine with her husband in it."

"And her lover Truxall," Kachigan added somberly. "She didn't even waste any of her inheritance sending another payoff down with them."

That got them a swift, flashing look from those intelligent eyes. "*Is* my husband dead?" Lillian Murchison demanded.

"No," Kachigan said. "But Franklin Truxall is. He said he'd see you in hell."

Her jaw tightened, making her look a lot less handsome and a lot more like her raw-boned husband. "No doubt," she said. "In the meantime, what are you going to do with me?"

"If it was left up to me, arrest you on charges of theft, extortion, and conspiracy to murder." Kachigan pulled Helen away from the buggy, to make room for Santangelo to haul the millionaire's wife out. Her expensive satin dress tore on the buggy's side-rail under his rough handling, but the Black Hand *capo* remained cheerfully impervious to her glare. "So far, however, your husband has been refusing to cooperate. Let's see if some time spent in your charming company can change his mind."

"It won't." Lillian Murchison shook out her crumpled skirts with what looked like her usual Gibson Girl confidence. "Charles already knows I hate and despise him. But he can't even endure the scandal of a divorce, much less that of having his wife imprisoned. The prospect of seeing me won't change that."

"Maybe not." Helen took a step away from Kachigan, gripping the older woman's arm hard enough to make her wince. "But the prospect of seeing your crimes written up in the *New York Herald* might."

Helen had thought Charles Murchison might lose a little of his arrogance after getting trapped in a sabotaged mine and finding out that his wife had betrayed him with his chief coal policeman. But when she and Kachigan escorted Lillian Murchison into the harsh glow of electric lights that now lit up the main office building at Emmy Number Two Mine, the coal baron blasted them both with a look fierce enough to make the state police lieutenant beside him stiffen with reflexive tension.

"What the hell did you bring her here for?" Murchison snarled, his gaze raking Kachigan and then settling inexorably on Helen. Even wrapped in a fireman's coarse blanket and standing barefoot beside the office's gas-fed fire, the millionaire managed to look mortally offended. "All I asked you to do was locate my daughter. You have no right to interfere in the rest of my affairs!"

Helen glared at him. "When your 'affairs' include black-mail, murder, and torture—"

"My coal police chief was the one who did all that, not me." The old man's glare swung back to his silent wife. "He's dead now and as far as I'm concerned, the matter's closed. I'm not pressing charges. I refuse to have my life and my marriage turned into a damned newspaper melo-drama!"

Helen glared back at him, unintimidated. "You should have thought of that before you decided to start a war with Sedgwick Coal! Because whether you press charges against your wife or not, the story of how your coal police kid-napped and tortured us is going to be wired to the *New York Herald* by midnight. And you can't stop me from writing about the role your wife played in blackmailing you."

Red flags leaped up into Murchison's bony cheeks. "There are libel laws in this country—"

"—which can't be used to suppress the documented truth!" Helen shot back. "If you weren't so—"

Kachigan's hand closed around Helen's bruised wrist, just hard enough to make her snap her teeth shut on the rest of that rant about capitalist arrogance. "Your wife was implicated in the extortion plot by the dead man himself, in front of several reliable witnesses," he reminded the mil-lionaire. "Which means Miss Sorby can easily prove her accusations—"

"Not with hearsay," snapped the coal baron.

"It's not hearsay if we find the missing securities in her possession," Helen retorted. "And since she admitted to having them in front of two other witnesses—"

"—we have enough evidence to conduct a search of your house in Oakmont," Kachigan finished.

"*No!*" Murchison slammed a fist against the wall with enough unnecessary force to make Helen wince. "I won't let you do it! And neither will Big Roge McGara, even if he has to kill you to prevent it. God knows I pay him enough every year—"

"But you don't pay the state police," said a deep voice

from the door. Helen glanced over her shoulder to see Bernard Flinn shove the cursing figure of J.P. Frick into the office. Blood smeared the older detective's face from a broken nose and he was cradling what looked like a badly broken arm against his chest. Despite the fact that he was just as waterlogged as Flinn, Brennan, and Kachigan, Helen guessed from the resentful look he cast at the coal police chief that his injuries hadn't been suffered in the mine disaster. "And since we just got a signed confession from this joker directly implicating your wife in Truxall's blackmail scheme, we can press charges no matter what you want."

Kachigan frowned, glancing from one battered fellow detective to the other two who'd followed Flinn into the office. Riley simply looked wet and bruised from the mine flood, but up close Helen could see that Taggart's head was bandaged and his collar soaked with blood. The half-vindictive, half-sullen glance Frick threw at the big detective let Helen guess how that had happened too.

"A confession given under duress doesn't carry much weight in a court of law," Kachigan reminded his colleagues. "If you tortured Frick to get it—"

"No, sir." Surprisingly, it was Riley who answered that, his young voice candid and clear of guilt. "Jape gave us his statement as soon as we caught him outside the mine, with two state police as witnesses. It was only afterwards that he—uh—resisted arrest."

"Yeah." Taggart lifted a hand to his head, wincing as he touched the visible lump beneath his bandage. "For some reason, he didn't want to let me escort him back to the lockup alone. I can't imagine why not."

"Me either," Flinn said dryly. He handed the sullen older detective over to his coworkers, and crossed the mine office to scowl at Charles Murchison. The coal baron's chin jutted in angry response, but Helen noticed that his gaze couldn't quite stay fixed on the carbide-burnt ruin his police chief had made of the other man's face. "So, Charles, what's it going to be?"

"I don't know what—"

"Oh, yes, you do." Flinn reached out and wrapped a big

fist in Murchison's fire blanket and gave him a not quite gentle shake. Helen saw Lieutenant Brennan wince, but the state trooper made no move to intervene. "Between Miss Sorby's newspaper article and the stories my wife can spread, you're going to be the public disgrace of Allegheny County. Unless you do something about it."

Helen opened her mouth to insist there was nothing Murchison could do to stop her, but Kachigan's hand closed around her wrist again and she fell mutinously silent. "A plea bargain instead of a trial for your wife would keep her name out of the papers," the county detective said. "Especially the Pittsburgh papers, if Bernard Flinn signs onto the settlement."

"Fifteen years for extortion and conspiracy," Flinn suggested. "And I'll make sure the judge and district attorney both keep their mouths shut about it."

"Why?" Murchison threw him a suspicious glance. "What's in it for you?"

The coal police chief grinned, despite the pain it must have caused to the crusted burns around his mouth. "A guaranteed five-year coal contract with the Pennsylvania Railroad, sold for one dollar to Sedgwick Coal & Coke."

"*No!*"

"Oh, yes." Flinn's voice dropped to a rumble, so it wouldn't go any farther than the walls of the mine office. "Or else I'm going to inform Congress about all those coal mines you bought last fall in exchange for railroad securities. Then it won't just be your wife spending time in jail—it'll be you and all your cronies at the Pennsylvania Railroad."

Helen took a deep breath, suddenly enlightened. "So that was what you were willing to pay fifty thousand dollars for! You didn't want anyone to know the railroads had illegally invested in your coal business."

The utterly stymied silence that followed her accusation said more clearly than any confession that it was true. After a moment, Kachigan cleared his throat and looked into Charles Murchison's haggard face.

"Is it a deal?"

The millionaire's bitter gaze was still anchored on Helen. "That depends on this damned socialist reporter. If she tells everyone about the railroad securities anyway—"

"I won't," Helen said between her teeth. "I won't even write up the story about how your police chief kidnapped and tortured us." As much as she hated protecting Murchison's illegal dealings with the railroad, it was the only way to make sure his wife would be punished for her crimes. And her regret at losing a chance to expose capitalist misconduct was at least partially assuaged by the astonished looks her cooperation got from every person in the room. "Provided you give me solid proof that it was your railroad cronies who bribed Patrick Dolan to sabotage the union settlement in Pittsburgh."

The coal baron took two angry strides toward Helen, lifting his hand as if to slap her. Kachigan scowled and stepped forward to intercept him, but Helen had already put her own hand out in front of her. It was wrung hard enough to make her bruised wrist ache.

"It's a deal," said Charles Murchison.

SEVENTEEN

"Anyone home?"

Milo Kachigan glanced up in surprise from the mug of tea he'd been warming his fingers around. Despite the late night quiet, filled only with the steady scratching of Helen's fountain pen on a stack of telegraph forms, he hadn't heard the sound of a door opening at his Tarentum boarding-house. Nevertheless, a young man with a sandy beard and quizzical hazel eyes now stood in the kitchen doorway. Kachigan hurriedly took his stocking-clad feet off the chair they'd been sharing with Helen's bare toes, but there was nothing he could do to keep the visitor from noticing her casually unbuttoned shirtwaist, with the lace of her chemise showing beneath it.

"How did you get in here?" he asked Helen Sorby's brother.

"I let him in." Niccolo Santangelo's knife-scarred face glinted in the darkness of the hall. "When I let myself in."

Helen sighed, setting her pen down and stretching what must have been cramped hands. She'd spent every moment since they'd come back from Natrona writing her newspaper scoop on corruption of the miners' union, based on the information Charles Murchison had reluctantly given her. "Now you see why I stay away from the Tarentum side of the family," she said to Kachigan.

"I'd already figured that out," he said dryly. Niccolo Santangelo threw him a sharp look, but that didn't stop him from going to light the gas-flame beneath the teakettle and rummaging through their cupboard as casually as if he owned the place.

Thomas Sorby chuckled. "Don't bad-mouth the *Mano Negro*—if it wasn't for them, your only surviving aunt would have been carried off by an apoplexy two days ago, when you hopped a train and never came back. Couldn't you have spared at least a minute now and then to ring her up and let her know you were still alive? If we hadn't got a telephone call from Lillian Murchison's housemaid to-night, telling us you'd been carried off by the Black Hand, we really would have been worried."

Helen threw her brother a guilty glance. "I'm sorry, I forgot all about Nicco sending Aunt Pat down to stay with you. I'll ring her up right away—"

"You don't have to. We telephoned Cousin Lena and got the whole story from her. Pittypat's probably fast asleep now." Thomas pulled out one of the kitchen chairs for himself and kicked the other one out to his reprobate cousin. Neither of them seemed particularly disturbed to find Helen alone and half-dressed with Kachigan, but perhaps that was because of all the bandages visible beneath his own unbuttoned shirt. "Which is where I'd be too, if Nicco hadn't said something that worried me. You two are okay, aren't you?"

"More or less," Kachigan said. After the fizzing tension had finally faded from his blood, the abuse his cracked ribs had taken down in Emmy Mine had come back to haunt him with a vengeance. He was fairly sure he'd get no sleep that night, which was one reason why he was keeping Helen company as she wrote her overdue news story. "Taggart got a bad knock on the head. I sent Riley off with him to the hospital, but they haven't got back yet. That's why I'm waiting up."

Thomas nodded. "And what about you, Helen?"

His sister looked up from rereading what she'd written so far. "Me? All I got was a little burned the other day—"

"No blow on the head?" Thomas persisted. "No brain-poisoning from inhaling too much coal gas? No hysterical shock from seeing your ex-husband shot to death?"

Helen scowled. "Don't be an idiot. You're starting to sound like Aunt Pittypat."

Thomas gave her a look of such deep concern that Kachigan knew he must be teasing. "But, Helen, there has to be something wrong. Nicco said you found the missing coal heiress, the lost securities, and the identity of the blackmailer—and you're not going to write *any* of it up for the *Herald* or *Collier's*?"

Helen frowned. "No, I'm not. If I hadn't agreed to keep it quiet, Charles Murchison would never have allowed his wife to go to jail."

"Ah." Her twin brother accepted a steaming mug of tea from Santangelo. "And you thought it was more important to punish a poor oppressed married woman for her crimes than to reveal a national conspiracy between the coal mines and the railroads."

A red tinge stained Helen's cheeks. "She almost got Milo killed," was all she said. Kachigan choked over a swallow of his own tea, and spent the next few minutes trying not to cough. His cracked ribs warned him that he wouldn't enjoy it if he did.

"That's why you made that deal with Murchison?" he demanded when he'd finally got his voice back. "For revenge?"

His investigating partner gave him an exasperated look. "Tell me you wouldn't have done the exact same thing if it had been me in that mine and you making the deal—"

"I'm not the one who's spent the past three months trying to expose the corruption of the railroads!"

To his surprise, that retort got Kachigan a smile that lit Helen's face like an unexpected shaft of sunlight. "Oh, don't worry about that. I may have promised not to write the story up, but I never promised not to tell anyone about it. The word will get passed to the people who need to know."

"Just like in the *Mano Negro*," her cousin said approvingly. "*Molto bene, cugina.*"

She gave him a frown across the table. "What are you doing here? You didn't come just to unlock the door for Thomas, did you?"

"Of course not." Santangelo tossed Kachigan an amused look. "I came to see what the county detectives office is going to do with their fifty thousand dollars."

"*What?*" That incautious demand made Kachigan's sore ribs twinge beneath their bandage. He ignored the pain, twisting around to scowl at the Black Hand *capo*. "Don't tell me you think I really took that money off Tamasy's body!"

"No, no." Santangelo lifted three tea bags out of his mug and squeezed out a liquid almost as dark as coffee from between his fingers. "But I told you before, Hunkies and dagos talk to each other in this town, Kachigan. I could go ask Nicky Kozubal about the money, I guess, but I figured I'd ask you instead."

"But we haven't found any money—"

It was the sound of a throat being cleared that brought Kachigan's attention back to the kitchen doorway. Owen Riley's pleasant wine-stained face stared at him worriedly. The bulky shadow of Taggart standing in the hall behind him told Kachigan it wasn't his coworker's health that was worrying the young detective. He frowned back at him, too disturbed even to notice if Helen Sorby had remembered to button up her blouse.

"What's going on, Owen?"

"Well, sir—" Riley's voice cracked and then started again about an octave lower. "Actually, we did find the money. Sort of."

"How?" Helen demanded. She had come to stand behind Kachigan, resting one hand on his shoulder as if she was afraid he'd injure himself by leaping out of his chair. "And where?"

"Somewhere in between Bull Creek Coal Mine and Emmy Number Two," Riley said promptly. Whatever was making him look worried, it didn't seem to be either guilt or shame. "And the way we found it—well, I never had a chance to tell you, sir, because it was the day you disappeared. But I kept asking questions about that missing fire-boss, Harry Tamasy, up in Natrona while you were gone, and I found out something strange about him. His coal check number was seventeen."

Kachigan frowned. "But the coal check we found on his body said fifty-three."

"I know." Intelligence gleamed in Riley's eyes, something it was easy to miss if all you looked at was the sprawling red birthmark on his face. "But when I took that check coin to show my buddy Nicky Kozubal, he said it wasn't even from a Murchison Brothers mine. It came from Kirby Number Three—one of the old, closed mines between Bull Creek and Emmy." The Tarentum native cleared his throat again. "You wouldn't know, sir, not being from here—but coal mines all get mapped out as they're dug, and every passage is assigned a number . . ."

"And the payoff was in Kirby's fifty-third passage?" Helen demanded.

"That's what Nicky said." Another worried shadow crossed Riley's face. "I didn't go to look for it myself, ma'am. You had just gotten back with Detective Kachigan that night, and it seemed to me like the last thing you would want was Mr. Murchison and his coal police to get their money back. So I—uh—let Nicky take it."

This time it was Santangelo who cleared his throat. "You gave all the money to him? You didn't make any arrangement to split it with the rest of your office?"

"No, of course not!" Riley said indignantly. "I knew Detective Kachigan wouldn't take stolen money, and I didn't want Jape to have it either. And Art—" He threw a half-guilty glance over his shoulder.

"—wouldn't mind being rich, but not if he has to work at it," said the big detective sleepily. "So who got all the loot, Owen? Your buddy Kozubal?"

"He said he took a little, just enough to pay off the company store," Riley admitted. "But he gave all the rest of it to the United Mine Workers strike fund, so they could convince Murchison's miners to go on strike today.''

Kachigan felt Helen take a deep, shaking breath behind him. It might have alarmed him, but a moment later he felt her breath puff in his hair and knew she was laughing. ''Oh, Riley, that's perfect! Having Murchison's lost payoff keep his miners out on strike until he has to settle with them. . . .''

Riley gave Kachigan an anxious glance. ''It's all right with you too, sir? Letting Nicky take the money?''

''It kept a couple of hundred men from getting drowned tonight,'' Kachigan reminded him. ''It's fine, Owen. Now why don't you get Taggart up to bed, before he falls asleep on his feet. And be prepared—he may say he doesn't mind now, but he's going to rag you for the next twenty years about not giving him any of that money.''

''That's all right,'' Riley said in relief. ''I can always outrun him if I get tired of it.'' He turned back into the hallway, and a moment later they heard his lighter footsteps follow Taggart's heavy treads up the stairs.

''*Affangole.*'' Santangelo drained the last of his coffee-dark tea and thumped the mug back on the table. ''Being an honest policeman must be contagious. Pretty soon maybe there'll be nothing but honest men in the county detectives' office, and I'll have to move to Chicago.''

''I wouldn't worry about that any time soon,'' Kachigan said dryly. ''In fact, when Big Roge McGara hears how I treated one of his best-paying coal barons, you may not have any honest policemen to worry about even in this office.''

''Well, it wouldn't be a real murder investigation if either you or Helen didn't get fired at the end of it,'' Thomas Sorby reminded him. ''And with Helen's reform mayor in office, maybe you could get your old job back. Guthrie's already looking into corruption in city government . . .''

The sound that rustled through Kachigan's hair this time was a sigh. Helen released his shoulder and went back to her own seat. ''And I'll be reporting on it for the *South Side Weekly* if I don't get this story filed in time for the

Herald's main edition tomorrow. As long as you're here, Thomas, you can run the first part down to the telegraph office while I finish up the rest. And Niccolo can—''

''—go home and take care of all the business that has piled up while I've been keeping an eye on my family responsibilities,'' said Santangelo. His cold blackbird gaze flashed across the table to Helen, then came back to Kachigan again. ''I can't promise to stay out of your way, because I know you won't promise to stay out of mine. But I'm not going to ask my cousin for any favors from you, and you're not going to ask her for any from me either. Right?''

''Right,'' Kachigan said without hesitation. ''Do you want your knife back?''

A smile tugged at that thin, scarred face. ''No, keep it. I told you, most of the time it's better than a gun.'' His eyes flicked toward Helen and back again. ''Except when you want someone else to get blamed for a *Mano Negro* killing, of course. Or for a *dono di sposalizio*. And I have a feeling you're going to need a knife, if you ever want to drag that cousin of mine to an altar.''

He left the house as noiselessly as he had entered it, despite the total silence he left behind at the table. Kachigan hadn't understood the Italian words, but he'd seen the appalled look they'd made Helen exchange with her twin.

''You don't think—'' Thomas began

''No. He couldn't have.'' Helen frowned down at her telegraph forms, but Kachigan didn't think it was her scribbled story that darkened her eyes. ''I told him I'd inform on him myself if Barton ever showed up with a stiletto in his back . . .''

''Helen,'' Kachigan said and the tone of foreboding in his voice brought her attention back to him. ''What your cousin said about not using a knife—what else was that for, besides blaming someone for a Black Hand killing?''

She took a deep breath. ''He was teasing us, Milo. That's the way he's always been, letting people think he's done twice as much as he really has—''

He knew prevarication when he heard it. "Helen, what did he say it was for?"

"A *dono di sposalizio*," she said reluctantly. "A wedding present."

HISTORICAL NOTE

The violent coal mine strike of April 1906 was one of several that tore apart the nation's coalfields in the first half of this century. Despite the many miners killed in western Pennsylvania during this dispute, the miners' union was not yet strongly established in rural immigrant coal patches and the strike ultimately failed. The politics of union corruption and Patrick Dolan's astonishing turnabout on the five-percent pay hike are taken directly from news reports of the day, as is the threatened exposure of illegal railroad ownership of many nonunion coal mines. In historical fact, it was Frank Robbins, the progressive president of the Pittsburgh Coal Company, who threatened to expose those railroad investments to Congress, in order to pressure nonunion mines to sign onto his deal with John Mitchell, the president of the United Mine Workers. The tactic was only partially successful, and many miners eventually returned to work at a lower pay-scale, without a union.

All of the places mentioned in this book actually exist, including the coal patches of Harwick and Red Hot, but the existence and staff of the Tarentum branch of the Allegheny County Detectives' Bureau are fictional, as are Sedgwick Coal & Coke, Murchison Brothers Coal, and the Bull

Creek, Emmy, and Kirby mines. Although no historical documents place Fanny Sellins in the strike of 1906, as an older woman she was deeply involved in the coal strike of 1916, during which she and a fellow union member were murdered on the picket line in Black Valley by coal mine company police. Her killers were charged and tried, but never convicted.

Now available in hardcover

A Sir John Fielding Mystery

JACK, KNAVE AND FOOL

BRUCE ALEXANDER

Putnam